Amy Andrews is a mul bestselling Australian au fifty contemporary roma and digital markets. She great wine and frequent t together. To keep up with her latest releases, news, competitions and giveaways sign up for her newsletter—amyandrews.com.au.

Alison Roberts has been lucky enough to live in the south of France for several years recently but is now back in her home country of New Zealand. She is also lucky enough to write for the Mills & Boon Medical line. A primary school teacher in a former life, she later became a qualified paramedic. She loves to travel and dance, drink champagne and spend time with her daughter and her friends. Alison Roberts is the author of over 100 books!

NURSE'S OUTBACK TEMPTATION

AMY ANDREWS

ONE WEEKEND IN PRAGUE

ALISON ROBERTS

MILLS & BOON

First published in Great Britain 2022
by Mills & Boon, an imprint of HarperCollins*Publishers* Ltd,
1 London Bridge Street, London, SE1 9GF

www.harpercollins.co.uk

HarperCollins*Publishers*
1st Floor, Watermarque Building,
Ringsend Road, Dublin 4, Ireland

Nurse's Outback Temptation © 2022 Amy Andrews

One Weekend in Prague © 2022 Alison Roberts

ISBN: 978-0-263-30134-2

08/22

MIX
Paper from
responsible sources
FSC® C007454

This book is produced from independently certified FSC™ paper
to ensure responsible forest management.
For more information visit www.harpercollins.co.uk/green.

Printed and Bound in Spain using 100% Renewable Electricity
at CPI Black Print, Barcelona

NURSE'S OUTBACK TEMPTATION

AMY ANDREWS

MILLS & BOON

I dedicate this book to Joanne Grant and Ally Blake.

I will be forever grateful for the hand-holding
and cheerleading.

CHAPTER ONE

CHELSEA TANNER WAS a puddle of sweat. Already. After three steps. The sun scorched like a blast furnace overhead and the heat danced in visible waves from the black tar of the runway. Of course, she knew that Australia was hot in November—Outback Australia even more so. And, yes, she'd checked the temperature this morning and knew it was going to be forty-one degrees when she landed in Balanora.

But knowing it and being plunged into the scalding reality of it were clearly two very different things. Because this was ridiculously hot.

Welcome to hell, hot.

Her pale skin already crackling beneath the UV, she scurried across to the modest terminal, a familiar mantra playing on repeat through her head. *It's for the best. It's for the best.* Because Christmas in England would be worse. Blessedly cool, sure, but ninth circle of hell worse, and Outback Australia was the furthest point she could travel—physically and metaphorically—from home.

So, there was no turning back and, as she stepped through the sliding doors into the frigid blast of air-conditioning, she was grateful for the lifeline, no matter the temperature.

She just needed to…acclimatise.

Expecting to find as per the email, someone waiting for her after she'd grabbed her luggage from the carousel, Chelsea glanced around. People milled and greeted, hugging and laughing as pick-ups were made, but no one appeared to be there for her.

Maybe they were just running late.

She checked her phone—no messages. Finding a set of chairs nearby, she situated herself in view of the entrance to wait. No way in hell was she doing it *outside* the terminal. After fifteen minutes had passed, however, Chelsea grabbed her phone to call the number she'd been given.

'Good afternoon, Outback Aeromedical, this is Meg, how may I help you?'

Meg sounded as peppy in real life as she had in her emails. 'Hi, Meg, this is Chelsea Tanner. I'm terribly sorry to be a bother, but I'm at the Balanora airport and I thought someone was picking me up? I can get a taxi. I just don't want to jump in one and maybe miss my lift if they're just running late.'

'*What?* But…you're not supposed to be here until Thursday.'

Chelsea frowned. 'The plane ticket you sent was for Tuesday. So…here I am.'

'Oh dear, I have it marked on the calendar as Thursday.' There was the tapping of computer keys and a clicking of a mouse in Chelsea's ear. 'I am *so* terribly sorry. I must have got my "T" days mixed up when I was inputting it to the calendar. It's absolutely no excuse, but it can get super-busy here some days and I must have been distracted. Also that whole "pregnancy brain fog" thing turns out to be very real.'

The usual tangle of emotions around pregnancy rose up but Chelsea quashed them. She was thousands of miles away from the convoluted complications of her past and Meg had already moved on.

'Gosh, this is terribly unforgiveable of me, especially after all the flight hassles you've already been through.'

Hassles was an understatement. Between the UK snap freeze, mechanical issues forcing an unscheduled landing and then, of all things, a volcanic eruption in Asia, Chelsea could have been forgiven for thinking this venture was cursed before it had even begun. And, some time during her fortieth travel hour, spent *not* in the air but in a crowded airport terminal, she had pondered whether the universe was trying to tell her something.

'You must be exhausted.'

Actually she hadn't felt too bad when she'd landed in Brisbane thirty-six hours after she was supposed to, despite not having had much sleep. Two further nights of jet-lag-interrupted sleep later, however, had not been kind. And then, with her time in Brisbane cut short thanks to her travel debacle, she'd hopped her flight to Balanora, arriving into the oven of the Outback.

As if, by just mentioning the word exhausted, Meg had made it so, Chelsea's last spark of life leached away. She certainly felt every one of her thirty-two years. 'I could sleep for a week,' Chelsea admitted.

'I bet you could!' There was more key tapping. 'Okay, stay there. I'll be right out to pick you up. Unfortunately, there's a small issue with your house. Aaron is currently staying there due to the air con in his breaking down.'

That would be Dr Aaron Vincent, Chelsea presumed, one of the senior flight doctors on the staff.

'Which is fine, it'll be fixed tomorrow, but Aaron has gone camping with some mates and won't be back until this evening. And, as he's out of mobile range, I can't call him to come and get his stuff out of your house. I mean, it's not much, but still, we like to have our houses spic and span before we hand them over, so we'll put you up in the OA room at the pub. It's permanently reserved for us in case we ever need it for stranded staff or visiting head honchos.'

Chelsea was fading fast. She didn't mind where she slept. As long as there was air-conditioning. 'Oh, thank you. That sounds great.' Once again, not the most auspicious start to her new life, but she was far too tired to care right now.

'Well, it's not the Ritz, but it's clean, safe, friendly, the water pressure is great, they serve good, hearty meals and it's air-conditioned.'

Chelsea sighed. 'You just said the magic words.'

Meg laughed. 'Hold tight, I'll be ten minutes.'

Twenty-five minutes later, Chelsea was saying goodbye to Meg as she followed a guy called Ray, who'd been serving behind the bar at the Crown hotel, up the internal stairs to the first floor. He carried her bag to the door then handed over her key.

A proper, old-fashioned key. That *slid into* a lock.

'Thank you,' she said.

He nodded and Chelsea opened the door to the massive room. Not that she noticed any of the detail. All she noticed was the general stuffiness and the giant air-conditioning unit on the wall above the bed.

Leaving her bag at the door, she crossed to the remote sitting on top of one of the bedside tables. With desperate, shaking hands, she pointed it at the unit and pressed the button labelled 'on'. For a terrible few seconds, it stuttered, whined and didn't do anything, and Chelsea thought, *Dear God, what fresh hell is this?* Then it powered to life, delivering a wave of cool air across her shoulders.

She almost collapsed on the bed in joy and relief. But not yet. Chelsea knew if she got horizontal it'd be all over, and she needed a shower. A nice, cool shower. Then she could crawl onto the bed—no, she didn't care that it was only three in the afternoon—and sleep for the next twenty-four hours.

There was nowhere to be until this time tomorrow, when Meg was picking her up to take her to her new place, so *hibernating* until then seemed like a good plan.

Adjusting the temperature on the control to the lowest possible, Chelsea snapped the heavy curtains closed over a set of French doors that opened out onto a veranda, immediately plunging the room into semi-darkness. Dragging her suitcase to the end of her bed, she grabbed clean underwear and a tank top, along with some toiletries, and headed for the shower, lingering under the spray and hoping the room would be a thousand degrees cooler when she was done.

It was, and Chelsea almost cried as she lay on the crisp, white sheet that smelled of sunshine. Her skin was cool from the shower, her hair was damp and she knew it would be ten kinds of fluff ball in the morning, but she didn't care. Right now this bed felt better than any other surface she'd ever lain on and she shut her eyes, falling head-first into the deep slumber of a person who has finally found her way through the double whammy of world time zones and militant body clocks to the deep, dark relief of unconsciousness.

Aaron Vincent was getting way too old to be drinking several nights in a row and roughing it in a swag on the hard tray of his ute, even if he'd been in the company of guys he'd known since he was a kid. Their annual camping trip out by the river that ran through Curran Downs, his family's sheep station, had been a tradition ever since they'd left school. It had survived, despite three out of the six of them not living in the area any more, and five out of the six of them being married with children.

He being the odd one out.

Luckily their wives, all women of the Outback, were understanding about this sacred time every year. Kath, Dammo's wife, who was five-and-a-half months' pregnant with their third child, called it their *knitting circle*, which they all delighted in giving him shit about.

Aaron found her affectionate description hysterical. In an area known for blokey blokes, all six of them easily fit the mould, although him probably the least. Dammo and the others were still working on the land in one form or another, whereas he'd left over a decade ago to become a doctor before finally returning, three years ago, to work with the OA.

They loved taking the piss about *soft hands* and

Aaron laughed along at the jokes, but he—and they—knew he could still shear a sheep, mend a fence and gets his hands dirty as well as he ever could. And did, whenever his sister, who had largely taken over the running of the property from their father now, needed some extra help.

But he'd be lying if he didn't admit to relief as he passed the *Welcome to Balanora* sign on the way back in to town. He was looking forward to an actual mattress to cushion the twinge in his lower back. Except he stopped into the pub on his way through for a bite to eat, because he couldn't be bothered to cook anything, and Tuesdays were always roast night.

Then he got talking to three women—nurses from Adelaide—who were passing through town on an Outback road trip. They were interested in the OA, and they chatted and laughed, and it felt good to feel thirty-five instead of the seventy-five his lumbar spine currently felt. Not a bad way to spend an evening. Better than five other blokes, who hadn't showered in three days, *and* Dammo's farting dog, Kenny.

Aaron left soon after the nurses departed, only to discover his ute had a flat tyre. Too tired to do something about it or even call a cab, he turned back to the pub to enquire if the OA room was empty. When Lyle, the publican, handed over the key, Aaron decided it was a definite sign from the universe to go to bed and fix the damn tyre in the morning.

Heading up the stairs, he let himself into number seven, the blessed cool of the room only registering at the same time he yanked his shirt over his head. Frowning, he flipped on the light switch to discover he was not alone. There was a barely covered woman he didn't know in the middle of the bed, staring at him wild-eyed.

And then she screamed.

Aaron winced as she sat bolt-upright, her sandy-blonde hair in complete disarray, and dragged the sheet up to cover herself. '*Get out!* Get out *right now*!' she screeched, blinking against the flood of light. 'You come *any* closer and I will scream blue murder.'

If he hadn't been distracted by her cut-glass English accent, he'd be keen to know what colour it was she *had* screamed. 'I'm sorry, I'm sorry!' he apologised, holding out both of his hands, his T-shirt still clutched in his left hand as he backed up until his shoulder-blades hit the door.

'I didn't know anyone was in here,' he continued, keeping his voice even and low and, he hoped, reassuring. 'Lyle gave me the key. See?' He held it up. 'It's just been a terrible misunderstanding.'

She didn't say anything as she sucked in air noisily through her flared nostrils and glared. Someone pounded on the door behind him.

'What the hell is going on in there, doc? Open up or I'll kick the bloody thing in.'

Reaching behind him slowly so as not to panic the woman with any sudden moves, he turned the door handle, stepping aside to admit Lyle. Aaron greeted the publican with a *what the hell?* expression on his face. 'You said the room was empty.'

The older man scowled at him. 'What? There's nobody in the book.'

He glanced across the room at Exhibit A, who was on her feet now and watching them both warily, the sheet wrapped tight around her, one hand clutching it close to her breast.

'Oh.' Lyle stared at her as if she'd arrived from a spaceship…because how else would anyone have got past the high-tech, triple-encrypted reservation system known as 'the book'.

Cursing under his breath, something about *bloody Ray and his testicles*, Lyle addressed her. 'I'm so sorry, m…miss.' He advanced into the room, his hands extended in some kind of apology, but her eyes grew bigger and she took a step back. Lyle halted. 'I didn't know you were here.' He looked at Aaron. 'Somebody hasn't put her in the book.'

Aaron bugged his eyes. 'Clearly.'

Lyle returned his attention to the woman who somehow managed to look haughty despite her obvious discomfort and electric-socket hair. 'Ray shouldn't have rented out this room. It's for Outback Aeromedical use only.'

'I know.' She glared, taking the haughtiness up another notch. 'I'm starting there on Friday.'

'Oh.' Aaron smiled. Now it made sense. 'You're the new nurse? Chelsea Tanner?'

'Yes.'

The team had been looking forward to her arrival this past couple of months. Having someone permanent—even if just for the year of her contract—would give some certainty and stability to the team.

If this very English miss didn't baulk at the first spider and head for home, of course.

Aaron almost walked forward to introduce himself but quashed the impulse. *Not the right time, dude. Not the right place.* She looked as if she'd been roused from a very heavy sleep, and she was a lone female, in not many clothes, confronting two strange men.

'I'm Aaron,' he said, keeping his feet firmly planted on the floor and his eyes firmly trained on her face. 'Vincent. One of the flight doctors. We…ah…weren't expecting you until Thursday?'

She huffed out an impatient breath, neither acknowledging his introduction nor answering his query. 'Yes, I know, there was a mix up with Meg, but do you think we could possibly do this introduction at a later date? Perhaps when we're both more…' She glanced pointedly at the shirt in his hand. *'Clothed.'*

Damn it! He'd forgotten he'd taken it off. Hastily, Aaron threw it back over his head. 'Of course,' he said, emerging from the neck hole and pulling the hem down. 'We'll leave you to get back to sleep.' He started to back out, elbowing Lyle, who looked as if he was still trying to fathom how his system had failed. 'Apologies again.'

'Yes,' Lyle agreed, jumping in quickly, in response to the elbow. 'Huge apologies. I'll be talking to Ray in the morning.'

She just eyed them warily as they backed out, her hand still clutching the sheet tight to her front. Easing the door gently closed, Aaron glanced at Lyle.

'I'm going to kill Ray,' he said.

Aaron might just help. 'You got another room?'

'Nope.'

Aaron sighed. Of course not. Resigned, he went and changed his tyre.

* * *

After the night's interruption had dragged Chelsea out of the deepest darkest sleep of her life she feared she wouldn't be able to get back to that place again but her fears were unfounded. It took less than a minute to slide back into that cool oblivion, ably aided by the vision of a shirtless Aaron Vincent, all six-foot-odd of broad, smooth chest, solid abs and delightfully scruffy hair.

He'd oozed *male* right across the room at her but, despite the potential threat in the situation, she hadn't felt frightened. Sure, she'd been taken by surprise and had reacted as any woman would have at finding a shirtless stranger in her room in the middle of the night, but she hadn't felt he'd had any ill intent.

On the contrary, she'd felt…*attraction*.

Maybe it was just some weird jet-lag or body clock thing. Maybe her foggy brain had been in a highly suggestible state. But, for the first time since her husband's death three years ago, things actually *stirred*. She'd been aware of him as a *man*. Not an intruder, not a threat.

A man.

And that hadn't happened for the longest time.

To make things worse, he was also the first thing she thought about when she finally awoke at two in the afternoon, which was exceedingly disconcerting. She hadn't come to Australia to meet someone, to get involved or put her heart on the line again. She'd come to start anew—*by herself.* To escape the cloying clutches of family.

Stand on her own two feet.

She'd been stuck in a rut, her wheels spinning, and it was time—past time—to start moving forward again. But to do that she'd had to leave London because to stay would have meant continuing to live a lie. Minding her words and grinding her teeth, holding back the torrent of fury that bubbled beneath the surface, until her heart had become a locked box of resentment surrounded by the brittle shell of the woman everyone wanted her to be.

The woman she used to be.

Okay, maybe flying to the other side of the world was extreme, but she knew if she was too close to call on she'd keep being sucked back.

She needed to be out of reach.

She *needed* to be herself again, not just Dom's poor widow. *Poor Chelsea.* And she wasn't going to achieve that by mooning over some other guy. No matter how good he looked with his shirt off.

Rolling out of bed, she picked up her phone as she walked to the doors and drew back the curtains, a blast of light assaulting her eyeballs. Turning back, she grabbed a pair of shorts to go with her tank and stepped into them before scooping up her phone and heading out the glass doors.

Heat enveloped her as she stepped out onto the decking, the floorboards aged and worn beneath her feet. Placing her phone on the small round table situated not far from the doors, she continued several more feet to the gorgeous wrought-iron lace work of the railing, pleased at the full protection of the roof overhead. Squinting against the sun reflecting off metallic awnings and car roofs, she looked up and down the main street of Balanora.

It was wide, two lanes each side, with a generous section of central parking between. The cars were mostly shaded by the huge trees planted at regular intervals down the middle. Shops lined the street on both sides, cars pulling in regularly to angle-park at the kerbs. It seemed busy, with plenty of people coming and going, and more traffic than she'd imagined.

It didn't take long for the beat of the sun to drive her back and she sat at the table, the only occupant on the long veranda as she checked her texts and emails. There were several from friends, checking she'd arrived okay, and several more had come in overnight from her mother-in-law. Chelsea had texted Francesca when she'd landed in Brisbane to let her know she'd arrived safely but hadn't responded to any of the others.

The older woman hadn't wanted her to go, had fretted that she'd be too far away from the people who loved her, but she'd eventually understood Chelsea's need to get away. Still, she wasn't above turning the screws, as the video she'd sent two hours ago of three-year-old Alfie—Dom's son—testified.

Chelsea's finger hovered over the play button. That familiar chin cleft and expression was so like his father's. She wanted to listen to that sweet voice but was tired of the emotional wrench the mere existence of Alfie always caused. Through no fault of his own, Alfie was a living embodiment of her husband's infidelity, and she was tired of pretending she was okay.

Thankfully, a text popped up on the screen, putting off the dilemma.

Hi, Chelsea, it's Charmaine.

Charmaine White was the OA director. She had interviewed Chelsea via Zoom two months ago.

Sorry about the mix-up yesterday. Meg feels awful. I'll be in the bar in an hour if you're awake. If not just call on this number when you are and I can take you over to your new place.

New place. Sounded like heaven. Chelsea hit delete on the video and walked inside.

An hour later, Chelsea was ensconced in Charmaine's Outback Aeromedical badged SUV, driving around the airport perimeter. Charmaine had suggested a tour of the base first, to which Chelsea had enthusiastically agreed. Several aged hangar buildings, languishing in the sunlight, passed by. The largest of them loomed just ahead, gleaming white, with Outback Aeromedical painted on the side along with the logo of a red plane in the middle of a giant yellow sun.

Charmaine parked in a small car park and ushered Chelsea in the front door with a swipe card. Several offices and storage rooms occupied this area and Charmaine whisked Chelsea through, introducing her to anyone she came across, before opening a door that led out to the cavernous space of the hangar proper. Chelsea looked up. The exposed internal roof struts spanned the curve of the roof almost to the ground on both sides, giving the impression of ribs caging them inside the belly of a giant beast.

Two planes sat idle, one larger than the other, both somehow managing to look small in the great yawning space.

'That's the King Air,' Charmaine said, pointing to the smaller one. 'It's a twin turbo prop. We have two in our fleet here. This one did an immunisation clinic at one of the remote communities this morning.'

Chelsea knew from the interview with Charmaine that, as well as assistance in emergency situations, the OA also offered primary care in the form of remote clinics, dealing with things such as women's health, mental health and preventative medicine, as well as routine blood tests and screening.

'The other King Air is out on a job right now but should be touching down soon. They have a range of two thousand seven hundred kilometres. They take two stretchers and three seats.'

Charmaine walked towards the larger one and Chelsea followed. 'This is the Pilatus PC-24.' The door was closed but Charmaine stroked its gleaming white flank as if it was a favoured pet. 'Isn't she beautiful?'

'She is.'

'It's only been with us for six months but already saved five lives in three separate road accidents. It can fly faster and longer, and can use a runway as short as eight hundred metres, which is a godsend out here. It takes three stretchered patients and up to two medical teams. It's like an intensive care in the air.'

Chelsea smiled at Charmaine still petting the plane. 'I imagine these are few and far between?'

'They are,' she confirmed. 'I had to lobby hard for it to be based here. But, because we're situated ideally as far as distance goes between Darwin, Adelaide and Brisbane, and we have a proportionally large amount of accidents, both car and farm, it was a no-brainer.' She sighed. 'Flies like a dream.'

'Well, in that case, I can't wait to go up in it.'

Just then an ambulance pulled into the area in front of the hangar which was now in shadow. Several people whom she'd met earlier came out from the door behind.

'ETA?' Charmaine asked a guy in maintenance overalls—Brett, maybe?—who was heading for a tractor parked just to the left on the inside wall of the hangar.

'Five.'

'C'mon, I'll introduce you to the ambos.'

Charmaine introduced her to Kaylee and Robbo, who were friendly and personable, as they discussed the details of the traumatic amputation of several fingers and partial degloving of the hand that was currently on board the King Air. The plane came into sight and a tiny trill of excitement rumbled through Chelsea's chest. Soon that would be her, flying all over the Outback, bringing help and hope to people who might otherwise find themselves in some dire situations where distance could make outcomes bleak.

This was what she'd come here for and she couldn't freaking wait.

Chelsea watched the plane grow larger and larger, the wheels unfolding from the undercarriage as it descended and landed smoothly on the shimmering tarmac with barely a screeching of the tyres.

'Perfect,' Charmaine murmured.

The plane taxied toward the hangar as Robbo got the stretcher out of the back of the ambulance. The moment the plane's props stopped spinning, the paramedics started towards it. 'C'mon,' Charmaine said with a grin. 'I'll introduce you to the crew.'

The heat was still intense but Chelsea followed her eagerly across the hot bitumen, squinting as the sun dazzled off the metallic fuselage of the plane. She made a note to hit the town tomorrow and buy the best damn pair of sunglasses Balanora had to offer.

It was that or end up with crow's feet ten-feet deep by the end of her year.

The door opened, lowering as they approached to form stairs. A woman, who looked about forty, in navy trousers and a navy polo shirt with the OA logo on the collar and *pilot* stamped in large red letters across the front, greeted them. 'Hey,' she said. 'Looks like we got us a welcoming party.'

'Hey, Hattie,' Charmaine greeted her. 'Textbook landing as per usual.'

'That's why you pay me the big bucks,' Hattie quipped as she descended the stairs and moved out of the way for the paramedics to move the stretcher in for the patient transfer.

'Hattie, meet Chelsea. She starts officially on Friday but I'm giving her the quickie tour today.'

The older woman held out her hand, saying, 'Pleased to meet you.'

Chelsea shook the offered hand and said, 'Likewise.'

'Ready to go?'

Glancing back to the plane at the familiar voice, Chelsea's eyes met Aaron's. Standing on the top step, framed by the door of the plane behind, in navy trousers and shirt with *Flight Doctor* emblazoned on the front in block letters, a stethoscope slung casually around his neck, he looked calm and confident. His hair ruffled in the slight hot breeze as a surge of...*something* flooded her system.

Desire, she supposed. But there was something else too. A tug that didn't feel sexual, an attraction that *wasn't* sexual.

A feeling of...yearning?

'Ready when you are,' Kaylee said.

His eyes broke contact then and a pent-up breath escaped Chelsea's lungs in a rush, her body practically sagging. Holy *freaking* moly. She hoped this was just the jet-lag because this *whatever it was* was seriously inconvenient.

Maybe it was just that she went for a particular sort of man and Aaron had pinged her radar after three years of not noticing *any* man. Dom had been a combat medic, after all. Good-looking, though in a very different way from Aaron. More pretty-boy beautiful—high cheekbones, amazing eyebrows and long eyelashes that had been his mamma's pride and joy. He hadn't been as tall or as broad, and his hair had been jet-black and shiny, his skin bronzed, hinting at his Sicilian heritage.

Hattie excused herself, breaking into Chelsea's thoughts, and she forced herself to concentrate on the activity at the plane door as they unloaded the patient. It took a few minutes, the team all working as one, but the patient was soon out and on the stretcher.

He appeared to be in his fifties, one arm heavily bandaged and elevated in a sling hanging from a pole off the stretcher, the other arm sporting two IV sites. A bag of fluid was running through the cubital fossa site in the crook of his elbow and an infusion of what she assumed to be some kind of narcotic, given he didn't appear to be in any overt pain, was hooked up to the one in the back of his hand.

He was shirtless with three cardiac dots stuck to his chest and his jeans and work boots were well-worn and dust-streaked with some darker patches of blood. A woman about the same age—his wife?—her face creased with worry, stood at the head of the stretcher, her clothes and sturdy work boots also streaked in caked-on dirt, dust and some blood.

Chelsea listened with half an ear as Aaron ran through the details for the paramedics, focused more on the deep resonance of his voice, his accent, than the content of the verbal hand over. Words such as 'mangled', 'traumatic amputation' and 'morphine' registered only on a superficial level until she heard, 'Two fingers on ice in the Esky.'

Esky? Glancing across, she saw a male flight nurse hand over a small Styrofoam container she assumed was a cool box.

The report ended and Kaylee and Robbo departed with the stretcher, the patient's wife following close behind. Aaron turned back for the plane and Chelsea wondered if he was avoiding her after what had happened last night.

'Chelsea,' Charmaine said. 'This is Trent Connor, he's one of our lifers.'

Dragging her attention off Aaron, Chelsea smiled at the statuesque indigenous man in the flight-nurse shirt. He had salt-and-pepper hair, salt-and-pepper whiskers and an easy grin. Trent's level of experience had been evident from his pertinent additions to the hand over process, his quick efficiency with the equipment and procedures and his rapport with the patient and his wife. Then there'd been the synergy between him, Aaron and the paramedics which spoke of a well-oiled team and mutual respect.

'Born and raised right here on Iningai country,' he said, offering his hand. 'Thirteen years with the service next month.'

'Hi, it's lovely to meet you.' They shook hands. 'I'll be counting on you to show me the ropes.'

'Most important thing to remember is not to eat anything in the fridge labelled "Brett" if you want to live.'

'I heard that.' A voice drifted round to them from the other side of the plane.

Trent grinned. 'He puts triple chilli on everything.'

'He does.' Charmaine shuddered. 'God alone knows what the inside of his gut must look like.'

'Still hearing you.'

Chelsea laughed. 'Duly noted.' Although she liked her food spicy too.

'When you get settled in, you should come round for dinner one night. The missus makes a deadly risotto.'

Chelsea assumed that *deadly* in this instance was a compliment and not meant in the literal sense. 'I'd love to.'

'How come I never get an invite to dinner?'

Every sense going on high alert, Chelsea glanced behind Trent to find Aaron striding across to their group, his mop of dark-brown hair blowing all around in the light breeze, the sun picking out bronzed highlights.

His strong legs ate up the distance, his gait oozing self-possession.

'Because you flirt with my wife.'

'Ha,' Aaron said as he halted opposite Trent and next to Charmaine, his hand pushing his hair back off his forehead, where it had settled in haphazard disarray. 'Your wife flirts with me, buddy.'

Trent rolled his eyes. 'My wife is Irish. She flirts with *everyone.*'

Aaron laughed and Chelsea's insides gave a funny kind of clench at the deep, rich tone. 'True. Very true.'

'And of course,' Charmaine said as Trent excused himself and headed back to the plane, 'you've already met Aaron Vincent, one of our four flight doctors on staff.'

Steeling herself to address him directly, Chelsea schooled her features. 'Yeah, we did.'

He grimaced but a smile played on a mouth that dipped on the right. Up this close, and not in a fog of panic and jet-lag, she could see more detail than last night. Such as his eyes, that were a calm kind of grey but nevertheless seemed to penetrate right to her soul.

Thrusting his hand out, he said, 'Nice to meet you properly, Chelsea, and apologies again about last night.'

Keeping her smile fixed, Chelsea pushed the awkwardness from last night aside and took his hand. 'It's fine,' she said dismissively as a pulse of awareness flashed up her arm and their gazes locked. Those grey eyes were no longer laughing but intense, as if he could feel it too. 'These things happen.'

Aaron's features were more…spare than Dom's, she realised. Up this close, it was impossible not to compare him with the only other man who'd ever caused such a visceral reaction. Dom's face had been all smooth and perfectly proportioned, where Aaron's was kind of… battered. Like a thin piece of sheet metal that had been hammered over a mould, the indents still visible as it pleated sharply over the blade of his jaw and curved over the somewhat crooked line of his nose.

There was a slight asymmetry to his face too, the right cheekbone a little lower than the left, making his right eyebrow and eye slightly out of line with their left-sided counterparts, and causing a crookedness to the right side of his mouth, giving him that lopsided smile. A tiny white vertical scar bisected his chin at the jawline.

Once again, she was overwhelmed by the pure masculine aura of him. By a tug that was almost feral in its insistence that she move closer. Panicked that she might actually act on the impulse, she dropped her hand from his grasp, only just quelling the urge to wipe her palm on her shorts to rid it of the strange pulsing sensation.

'Will the patient be transferred to a primary health-care facility soon?' Chelsea asked him, grabbing desperately for normality.

Just two professionals talking shop. *Nothing to see here.*

'Yeah,' Aaron confirmed. 'Balanora hospital isn't equipped for major micro-surgery but he'll get X-rays and have his condition assessed properly here first. Brisbane already knows about him. They'll be sending out a retrieval team, probably in the next couple of hours. His injury is stable but the viability of the fingers makes his transfer time critical.'

'He was lucky,' she said.

'Yep. There was a fencing accident out on one of the properties around here about five years ago that severed an arm and resulted in a fatality when the guy bled out.' He shook his head. 'It was awful. Trent was on the flight and it was an old friend of his. Rocked the community.'

'Does that happen often? Treating people you know?'

'Reasonably often, yes. Balanora might only have a population of three thousand but we're the major centre for the surrounding districts. People from all around shop here or see a doctor here or send their kids to school here. People with kidney disease come to the hospital for dialysis, babies are born here. There are a few restaurants and a couple of churches, and popular social events are run at the town hall every month. Not to mention the OA's regular district clinics. So, yeah, pretty much everyone knows everyone.'

Chelsea nodded slowly. Aaron's voice was rich with pride and empathy, as if he understood all too well the double-edged sword of living *in* and serving the health needs *of* a small community. That wasn't something Chelsea had ever had to worry about when she'd been flying all over the UK for the last decade on medical retrievals, mostly via chopper. The area was a similar size to the one she would be covering out here but the population differential had made the possibility of actually treating someone she knew remote.

Unlike Aaron, obviously. His steady grey gaze communicated both the privilege and the burden of such situations and, for a ridiculous second, Chelsea wanted to reach over, slide a hand onto his arm and give it a squeeze.

She didn't. But it was a close call.

After what felt like a very long pause, during which no one said anything, Charmaine broke the silence. 'You ready to check out your new digs? Your boxes arrived this morning and are in the garage. Or do you want to explore some more around here?'

Chelsea jumped at the lifeline, finally breaking the sudden intensity between her and Aaron Vincent. She did *not* want to explore more—she didn't want to be anywhere near this man and his curious ability to stir her in ways she hadn't been prepared for. She was obviously going to have to deal with this soon, but for now she was happy to pretend it was a combination of jet-lag, unresolved emotional baggage and stepping outside her comfort zone. And would pray that it was a temporary aberration.

'New digs would be good. Might as well get a start on unpacking.'

'Right.' Charmaine nodded. 'Let's go.'

CHAPTER TWO

ALMOST THREE HOURS LATER, Chelsea had made some decent headway on the unpacking in her new house, situated in a modern development on the edge of town. The shady, tree-lined street with row after row of cookie-cutter houses drowsing in the Outback heat—low-set brick with neat lawns, concrete driveways and double garages—had made her smile and excitement stir in her belly as Charmaine had pulled into the drive.

It was as different from Dom's parents' detached Georgian behemoth in Hackney as was possible and she'd felt instantly lighter.

The fact she had subsidised accommodation *and* a car included in the contract—a standard OA offering to attract experienced medical professionals to the middle of nowhere—had sweetened the deal. Looking around her now, she realised the fully furnished house was a true godsend.

Chelsea hadn't packed much to bring with her—just a dozen boxes of her most precious things, a lot of them books. She'd down-sized significantly when she'd sold the martial home a few months after Dom had died. Moving in with his parents had seemed like the right thing at the time, united as they'd all been in their grief. And Francesca and Roberto had needed her in those months that had followed, clinging to her as their one last connection to their beloved son.

Hell, *she'd* needed *them*.

But it had grown increasingly hard since Alfie. Well, since before him, really, but that sweet little three-year-old had been the proverbial last straw.

Chelsea pushed the last of the six remaining boxes full of her books against the far wall in the living room. She was going to need to buy a couple of book cases because, although there were a couple of wall shelves affixed above the boxes, they weren't enough.

Francesca hadn't seen the point in Chelsea taking all her books to Australia when her contract was only for a year but Chelsea had been adamant. An obsessive reader and a voracious re-reader, books had been her comfort all her life. The few memories she had of her mother were of being read to by her and, in those dark days after Dom's death, she'd buried herself in fictional worlds.

Leaving them behind would have felt like a betrayal. Plus Chelsea knew that, if this job was all she hoped it would be, she wouldn't be returning to the UK.

She just hadn't the heart to tell Francesca.

But the truth was there was nothing keeping her back home. Her mother had died in a car accident when Chelsea had been four, and her father had remarried to a woman not much older than Chelsea when she'd gone off to uni in London, and they now lived in Spain. She loved her father, and she was happy for him and had visited him in Spain, but his grief had made him emotionally distant when she'd been growing up and they weren't particularly close.

There were some aunts, uncles and cousins, and of course good friends she'd made over the years, both through work and a couple of friends through Dom, but there were so many ways to correspond these days. Chelsea knew she'd be able to keep in touch. And they could come and visit, just as she would return to the UK in a few years to catch up with everyone.

Including Dom's extended English-Italian family that was big and raucous, with so many cousins and second cousins always in each other's business, Chelsea had lost count. And, of course, Alfie. But by then she'd have had time, distance and perspective, and hopefully seeing Dom's son wouldn't be such a wrench.

Francesca wouldn't like it, she knew, but hopefully over time she'd come to realise that it had been too hard for Chelsea to stay and play the role of dutiful widow when her husband hadn't been the man she'd thought he was.

Or the one his grieving mother tried to paint him as.

She understood Francesca wanting to downplay the inconvenient truth—that her son had not been a faithful husband. He was dead. A war hero. Killed in Afghanistan. But even heroes could be flawed, and Chelsea couldn't keep being a part of the cult of Saint Dom.

Her tummy rumbled. She was hungry but also tired. *Again.* How was that even possible after sleeping for twenty-three hours?

Damn you, jet-lag.

She could eat—that would help. It would give her something active to do and the sugar would perk up her system. Because she was damned if she was going to bed this early after such a long sleep. She'd be awake at three o'clock in the morning.

Of course, she didn't have any food in her fridge, so that was a problem. Charmaine had said the small local supermarket stayed open to nine, so she could go and do some shopping, even though the mere thought made her tired. Nor did leaving the air-con appeal. But it would be something to do. And if she cooked something when she got back it would help to keep her going to a more reasonable hour.

Her phone dinged. A text from Francesca.

Missing us yet?

Chelsea grimaced. She loved her mother-in-law but it was hard to miss her when she texted every five damned minutes. Putting the phone in her pocket, she went to the kitchen to grab the car keys. Her pocket buzzed and she sighed as she removed her phone and read the text.

You must be lonely all by yourself in a strange town where no one knows you.

She almost laughed out loud as she scooped the keys off the white granite top of the island bench. The fact no one knew her in Balanora made it feel as if a boulder had been lifted off her shoulders. The phone buzzed again.

You know you can always come home again if you made a mistake.

'Damn it, Francesca,' Chelsea muttered, scowling at the screen. 'Turn the record over.' Her mother-in-law had been fretting for two months over this move.

Chelsea headed for the sliding door at the end of the kitchen that lead directly into the garage and slid it back just as a knock sounded on her front door.

Who could *that* be?

She didn't know anybody. Not many people, anyway. Maybe it was a neighbour popping by with a welcome casserole, which would save her a trip to the supermarket...

Turning round, she made her way to the front door and opened it, the warmth of the evening instantly invading the screen door that was still shut. Not that she really registered the temperature or the orange streak of the sunset sky behind the head of...*not* a neighbour.

Aaron Vincent.

Looking cool and relaxed in shorts, with a T-shirt stretched across his chest, he smiled his crooked smile and everything south of Chelsea's belly button melted into a puddle.

'I haven't eaten yet, and I took a punt that you haven't either, and thought I'd introduce you to the delights of our very good Chinese restaurant as a formal apology for last night.' He held up a loaded plastic bag.

The outline of takeaway containers confirmed the contents of the bag, as did the aroma of dim sums and honey chicken wafting in through the screen.

'I even brought you a menu for your fridge.' He held up it up in his other hand. 'Because, trust me, you're going to want one.'

Chelsea's stomach growled in response and her

mouth watered like a damned sprinkler. 'You really don't have to apologise again.'

'I know but… I am *really* sorry.'

Chelsea had never known a genuinely contrite man—especially one who looked like Aaron Vincent—could be such an aphrodisiac. Bloody hell. She could *feel* her pulse surging through her veins, beating hard at her temple and neck, and throbbing between her legs.

Gah!

A little voice in her head demanded she send him away. Tell him she was too tired. Because him just standing on her doorstep had put her body in a complete tangle. Spending time with him, just the two of them? God alone knew how she might embarrass herself and there'd been enough embarrassment between them already.

And she was hardly dressed for company. She wore frayed denim cuts-off that probably sat a bit too high on her thighs and a snug tank that moulded her chest. Although, he had seen her in just her tank and undies last night.

Her inertia must have clued him in to her indecision. 'If you're not up for company, that's fine. I'll just leave the food with you and catch up with you tomorrow.'

Tell him you're not up to company. Send him away.

'Umm…'

The phone buzzed in her hand and Chelsea was actually grateful for Francesca's timing, for once. It gave her something to do while she thought about how she could politely decline, even though her stomach was

now growling loudly enough for the entire neighbour-
hood to hear it.

Dom would want me to look out for you. You were the
love of his life.

It was precisely the worst thing Francesca could have
texted in this moment. A spike of rage lanced right
through Chelsea's middle as she read the text several
times. The love of Dom's life… Francesca kept saying
that, but *had she been*? How much had he *really* loved
her? Not enough to be faithful. Not enough to honour
their marriage vows. Not enough to honour *her.*

Just…not enough.

Goaded by the hypocrisy of the text, Chelsea quashed
every impulse to keep Aaron Vincent at a distance and
reached for the handle of the screen door. 'Sounds great,
thank you. C'mon in.'

Chelsea didn't wait for him to enter, just turned and
headed down the hall that led from the front door into
the living area. Entering the kitchen, she placed her
phone and keys on the counter and opened the cupboard
above and to the right of the worktop, grabbing two
plates. She wasn't thinking about what she was doing,
she was just operating on autopilot, the need to lash out
mixing with the irrationality of jet-lag.

When she turned around he was there, on the other
side of the island, big and solid, reaching inside the
bag, pulling out the containers, busying himself with
lining them up next to each other and removing the
lids.

'Chopsticks?' he asked, glancing at her as he brandished a pair encased in their paper wrapper, his eyes drifting to the spot where a chunk of hair had just fallen from her up-do.

Chelsea's belly did a funny shimmy and she sincerely hoped it would stop doing that some time soon. They had to work together and feeling this…caught up every time he looked at her…would not be conducive to that. But his eyes were calm and steady, his *presence* was calm and steady, and that felt like the anchor she needed right now when these unexpected feelings had her all at sea.

'I'm afraid I never quite mastered the art.' She quickly scooped the errant slice of hair up, poking it back into the mess on top before opening the draw beside her and reaching for some cutlery. 'Fork?'

'Nah.' He took the sticks out of the wrapper and separated them, drumming them against the counter top. 'I have mad chopstick skills,' he said, then promptly dropped one.

Much to her surprise, Chelsea laughed. These past three years, laughter had felt like some terrible breach of grieving protocols in a house where the laughter had died along with Dom. But, with the constraints of home thousands of miles away, it was actually liberating.

'So I see.'

She blinked, her words taking her even more by surprise. They sounded…*normal*. As if they were just two people having a normal conversation. Normal felt weird after the tension from last night and the awkwardness on the tarmac earlier. It felt weird, too, being alone with a man in her home like this, something of which she was now excruciatingly aware as they faced each other across the island.

She hadn't even known this man twenty-four hours ago.

He grinned, picking up the stick. 'I hope you don't mind, I just picked up my standard order.'

Chelsea blinked at the six containers on the island and the bag holding two dim sums and two spring rolls. 'You eat *all* this?'

'I usually make it do two nights.'

'Does this mean I'm depriving you of dinner tomorrow?'

'I'm sure I'll survive,' he said derisively. 'Now.' He held out his hand for a plate. 'What's your poison?'

Chelsea glanced at the containers, all heavily meat-based—beef and black bean, chicken and cashew, sweet-and-sour pork and crispy duck. 'Is this a bad time to tell you I'm vegan?'

The battered plains of his face took on a startled expression. 'Oh, crap… Are you?'

For the second time tonight, she laughed. The impulse to tease him had come out of nowhere, but God, it felt *so* good to laugh…*really* laugh. 'Sorry, no, just couldn't resist.'

Placing his hand on his chest, he huffed out a laugh. 'Thank God for that! I grew up on a sheep station. I might have had to reassess our friendship.'

Friendship.

Was that why he'd come? Not just to apologise again but to establish their boundaries? Which was probably a very good thing.

There was nothing but appreciative noises and food

commentary for a few minutes as they tucked into their meals, sitting on the stools on Aaron's side of the island. He was right, the food was delicious, and Chelsea knew she'd be using the Happy Sun's takeaway menu regularly.

'Want water?' she asked as she slid off her stool. 'I'm sorry I can't offer you anything else until I pick up some groceries.'

'Water is fine, thank you.'

Locating the cupboard with glasses, she grabbed two off the shelf. 'You mentioned a sheep station?' Chelsea flipped on the tap and filled a glass. 'Is that Australian for farm?'

He nodded. 'Very, very big farms, yes. Tens of thousands of square kilometres.'

Chelsea blinked. 'That *is* big.'

'Yup. Curran Downs is small comparatively. Almost four thousand square kilometres.'

Small? That was the size of an entire *county* in the UK. She knew Australia was immense but she couldn't imagine being out in the middle of all that vastness. 'Curran Downs?' Chelsea slid a glass across to him as she took her stool again. 'That's its name?'

'Yep. It's about a hundred K north of here. Dad's still out there and my sister helps him run it.'

'You have a sister?'

'Yeah. Tracey. She's two years older than me and a born farmer. Never wanted to do anything else.'

'But not you?'

'It was expected but…' He shrugged, picking up his glass of water. 'When I was fourteen, there was a bad car accident just outside our property. A tourist had had a heart attack at the wheel and ran into about the only tree within a fifty-kilometre radius. He was trapped inside and needed the Flying Doctors to get him out, and I felt so damned useless.'

He shook his head and there was a distant look in those grey eyes, as though he was back there in that day. 'They landed on the road and managed to get him out. He arrested twice after they extracted him and they had to give him CPR before they could put him in the plane. It was very…dramatic. But they saved his life that day right in front of my eyes and it was…'

His gaze came back into focus, resting on Chelsea, and she could see how much the incident had impacted him. 'Inspiring. I knew that day I wanted to do *that*.'

'And what did your dad say?'

Laughing, he said, 'My father looked at me and said, you'd better knuckle down at school, then.'

Chelsea smiled. 'You weren't a good student?'

'I did okay but I just didn't really see the point in busting my gut studying Shakespeare and advanced algebra when I was going to be running sheep all my life.'

'And what did your mum say?'

'My mother was thrilled. She never could understand why anyone wanted to live out in the middle of nowhere. She left when I was thirteen.'

'Oh… I'm sorry.'

'It's fine.' He shrugged. 'She was a city girl. My father met her when he was on a trip to Canberra in his early twenties. She was a translator working for the French consulate. They had a whirlwind courtship resulting in an unplanned pregnancy, followed by a quickie wedding at Curran Downs. Before she knew it, she had two babies under three and… It's hard out here. Isolating. If you're not born to it, if it isn't in your blood—sometimes even if it is—it can be stifling.'

Chelsea could see that. Flying in, over endless kilometres of earth so barren it could have been another planet, the remoteness had left a stark impression. It would be very lonely, Chelsea imagined, for someone who might be used to a very different kind of life.

'Not a lot of interpreter jobs going around out here,' Aaron continued. 'Particularly in the days before the Internet. She stuck it out for as long as she could before high-tailing it to Sydney but, to be honest, I don't know if she was ever that happy. Even as a kid I could sense that about her. She loved us, of course, but Mum also loves art galleries and restaurants and live theatre. She likes to throw dinner parties. She wasn't cut out for the life out here. It…*we*…weren't *enough*, you know?'

Chelsea nodded, feeling that sentiment right down to her bones. She'd never been enough for her father. Or her husband.

A wave of empathy swamped her chest and for a moment she almost reached out and touched his arm as she'd wanted to do earlier today.

Just as earlier, she didn't. 'Could she not have lived in town?'

'She did, to start with, seeing if they could make that work, but it was in the middle of a drought, and Dad couldn't leave for date nights and conjugal visits when he was hand-feeding the stock. Running a sheep station just isn't a nine-to-five job. And the closest thing to theatre in Balanora is the annual end-of-year school concert.'

Chelsea nodded. 'Was it amicable?'

'Sure, as much as these things can be.'

'Is she still in Sydney?'

He picked up a dim sum before answering, 'Melbourne now.'

'Do you see her often?'

'I saw her quite a bit when I was studying and working in Sydney, but only a couple of times since moving back home three years ago.'

'You and your sister didn't go with her?'

'We could have done, but Tracey was adamant she wasn't going anywhere.'

'And what about you?'

'A part of me wanted to go but it also felt incredibly... disloyal to leave, particularly when things were so dire with the drought. It was all hands on deck all the time.'

Chelsea nodded as she took a mouthful of crispy duck, the skin crunching to perfection. She supressed a moan as the sweetness of plumand the tang of ginger exploded across her tongue. 'But you did leave to go to uni, right?'

'Yes, four years later. To Brisbane. The drought had broken a couple of years prior and the station was in good shape. Plus, Tracey was full-time on the farm by then. I went home and helped out in holidays and, now I'm back, I usually head out there once a week on a day off.' He smiled 'Tracey always has a job for me.'

Although she'd seen him earlier in the doorway of an OA plane with a stethoscope around his neck, it wasn't that hard to imagine him in dusty jeans, a checked shirt and cowboy hat. His face had a weathered, outdoorsy quality about it and his body had a hardness and physicality to it that hinted at manual work.

Same as his hands. Currently wielding chopsticks as if he'd been born out the back of a restaurant in China town, they weren't soft or smooth. There was a toughness to them, a thickness, a couple of tiny scars over the knuckles. Like his face, they were a little banged up. Definitely not soft or smooth.

Rough.

A tiny shiver wormed its way right up Chelsea's centre thinking how those big, capable hands might feel on her belly. On her breasts. On her inner thighs.

Oh, God.

Clearly her body had no plans to stop with whatever this was any time soon. But she could hardly kick him out mid-dinner—which *he* had bought for her—because her libido was on the blink.

That was the problem, she decided—after three years in a deep freeze, her libido had decided to roar back to life. It was probably perfectly natural and normal but right now it was inconvenient. Ignoring it as best she could, she said, 'It was always your plan? To come back home?'

'Yeah, since seeing that accident. Just because I wanted something other than the station didn't mean I wanted to move to the city and forget my roots. I just wanted to serve my community in a different way.'

'I get that.'

'Except to work in any kind of Outback Flying Doctor situation I needed emergency medicine experience, so I was away from home for over a decade, working in both Sydney and Melbourne hospitals, building that experience so I could come back to Balanora.'

She detected a streak of guilt in his voice, something

which Chelsea understood acutely right now. Just because something was for the best didn't make it easy to bear.

'I came home and helped when I could, usually during shearing, but it's great to be finally home for good and only a phone call away.'

For good. It sounded very final. 'You're planning on staying with the OA?'

'Absolutely.' He took a drink of water. 'I might need to occasionally go and do a few months here and there in the city to keep my skills up to date or attend a course, that kind of thing. But I *love* this place and I *love* this job. There's such variety, and yet there's a familiarity too that speaks to that fourteen-year-old, you know?'

'Yeah.' Chelsea nodded. 'I know.' She *really* did. She'd left familiarity behind and that had been scary.

But vital.

He drained his glass and set it on the counter top. 'What about you? You're a long way from home. In my experience, people come all the way out here for three reasons. They're from the area, like me.' He held up one finger. 'They're hiding.' He held up a second. 'Or they're running away.' The third finger joined the others. 'Which one are you?'

The frankness in his steady grey gaze was unnerving. This conversation had taken a sudden probing turn. 'What about adventure?' she obfuscated.

'That why you're here?'

'Sure.' She shrugged. 'Why not?' She was *totally* running away but she wasn't going to tell him that.

'A woman after an adventure won't find much in Balanora to satisfy.'

Oh, *Lordy*… Had he chosen *satisfy* deliberately? 'Are you kidding? I'm from cold, rainy England where a lot of people consider an hour's flight and half-board in Lisbon the height of adventurous. Coming to the Antipodes is like the equivalent of climbing Mount Kilimanjaro.'

He laughed. 'Maybe. But you wait until summer reaches its zenith. It'll feel more like a wrong turn than adventure.'

Chelsea paused, a spring roll halfway to her mouth. 'It gets worse than *this*?'

He laughed, and dear God… It was deep and sonorous, settling into her marrow like a sigh. 'It does. Not too late to change your mind.'

She shook her head. 'I have a year's contract which I plan to honour.'

'And after?'

It was obvious that Aaron was trying to ascertain Chelsea's intentions. She supposed that he'd probably seen a lot of people coming and going in his time when they realised all this isolation and vastness wasn't for them. *Including his mother.* So she understood. But she wasn't about to commit to what happened after her year was up—she'd be stupid to do that when she hadn't started the damn job yet.

'I don't like to plan that far ahead any more.'

'Any more?'

Chelsea shut her eyes. Damn it…that had been a slip. Before Dom had died she'd planned everything, because so much of their lives hadn't been in their control due to his military service so she'd tried to control what she could. From meal planning to holiday itineraries to the cat worming schedule—all had been noted on both her phone calendar and a big paper one on the wall.

Now, she lived from one roster to the next and tried to be more spontaneous. Dom had teased her about how rigid she was, and even three years later she wondered if that was what he'd gone looking for in other woman—spontaneity.

When she didn't answer, Aaron said, 'Charmaine mentioned you were widowed a few years ago. I'm sorry.'

His condolences were gentle and Chelsea opened her eyes to find him watching her carefully, his grey eyes soft, radiating the kind of empathy she'd felt earlier. She looked at her hands in her lap, at the white mark on her bare ring finger, the thumb of her other hand stroking over it lightly. Chelsea had taken off her wedding band on the flight to Australia. She'd thought it would be a wrench—it hadn't been.

It had been freeing.

As freeing as it had been reverting to her maiden name from Rossi. She hadn't realised how much she'd resented them both until they were gone.

'Yes.' She glanced up to find those eyes watching the action of her thumb before they were raised to hers again. 'Thank you.'

Holding her gaze, Aaron asked, 'Do you mind me asking what happened? You don't have to answer if you'd rather not.'

'He was collateral damage,' Chelsea said. 'His unit had been engaging the enemy and one of them had been hit. He—Dom…his name was Dom—was a combat medic. It was on his fifth tour of Afghanistan. He was rendering assistance and got caught in some crossfire when the fighting changed direction. He got hit in the neck…his carotid.'

They were the facts as dispassionately as she could tell them, because thinking about him dying in the dirt of a foreign land, his life ebbing away, was always too much. She might be angry with him, his infidelities might have irrevocably damaged how she felt about him, but it didn't reduce the senseless wrench of his death.

Aaron nodded slowly. 'Nothing anyone could have done about that.'

'No.' Obviously, Aaron was used to dealing with sudden death and the people left behind, but his calm statement of fact was worth a thousand trite inanities.

'I'm truly very sorry.'

A hot spike of stupid tears pricked at the backs of Chelsea's eyes and she blinked them back hard. There was *no way* she was going to cry in front of a guy she barely knew over something she'd already shed a million tears about.

'Thank you.' Clearing her suddenly wobbly voice, she wrenched her gaze from his and stood, picking up his empty glass of water and her half-full one. 'I'll get us some more water.'

He didn't try to stop her, for which she was grateful, and by the time she resumed her seat her emotions had been put firmly back in place. 'So, tell me about sheep,' she said as she picked up her fork to resume eating.

'Sheep?'

'Yeah. I assume you know a bit about them?'

He chuckled. 'You could say that. Yeah.'

They continued eating and he entertained her for the next fifteen minutes about sheep facts and his own personal observations about the animal in question. It didn't require a lot of input from Chelsea, and made her laugh, which helped kick any lingering emotion to the kerb. He moved onto shearing anecdotes. Somehow it wasn't a stretch to believe that Aaron could shear a sheep. He exuded the calm capability of a man who could do anything.

Who could do *everything*. And *that* was sexy.

'I bet you're the only doctor who's actively shearing sheep in the country.'

'I don't reckon I'd be the only one, but there wouldn't be many.' He placed the chopsticks on his empty plate. 'I should also stress that, while I am a dab hand with an electric shear, I am nowhere near as fast or as accurate as the pros.'

'How long does it take them to shear a sheep?'

'About one to two minutes usually.'

Chelsea blinked. 'Holy sheep.'

He laughed. 'Elite shearers can do it in under a minute. It takes me about five minutes.'

'Wow, I'd like to see that.' Realising what she'd said, Chelsea hastened to clarify, 'I mean, the pros. Under a minute. That's gobsmacking.'

'We have a team hitting up our place at the end of the month. There are a couple of elite guys in the crew, if you want to come out and spend some time in the shearing shed?'

'Really?'

'Sure.' He picked up his plate and hers and carried them to the sink.

A tiny trill of excitement put a smile on Chelsea's face as she watched him. 'See?' she crowed. 'I've been here for a day and I'm already lining up my adventures.'

He laughed out loud, his head titled back, exposing the light brush of stubble at this throat. 'I don't know what you think happens in a shearing shed, but it's hot and dusty and full of sweaty, uncouth blokes. Nothing very exciting, and probably a bit too Australian for a genteel English woman with a posh accent.'

It was the first time Aaron had mentioned her accent. Dom had always teased her about her *hoity toity* Reading accent. But then, anything had sounded cultured next to his snappy East End accent. Raising an eyebrow, she said, 'Genteel?' Chelsea would admit to sounding posh but she was hardly a *lady.*

'The guys will think you've just stepped out of Buckingham Palace.'

Chelsea's nose wrinkled. Her accent might sound upper-class but it was far cry from plum-in-the-mouth royalty.

'I'm just saying,' he clarified. 'Look at it as a chance to experience some Aussie farm culture, *not* an adventure.'

'I see what you're doing.' She narrowed her eyes. 'You're lowering my expectations.'

He hooted out a laugh as he re-joined her on the other side of the bench. 'Absolutely. Take your expectations, divide them by two then halve them again.'

'I'm sure it'll be great.'

Shaking his head, Aaron leaned his butt against the edge of the island, not resuming his seat. It gave Chelsea a great view of his profile—the crooked line of his nose, the smooth bulge of his bicep, the flatness of his abs. 'I should get you to sign a waiver in case they damage those cute English ears with their filthy language.'

Chelsea lifted a hand to an ear reflexively, feeling the softness of another wisp of hair that had escaped her updo. Nobody had ever complimented her *ears* before. 'If you think a nurse who's worked in emergency departments hasn't heard worse on any given Friday or Saturday night shift, then you haven't been paying attention.'

'That's true,' he conceded.

'I've been sworn at, drunkenly propositioned, *lewdly* propositioned, bled, vomited and cried on by the best of British hooligans, and I would pit them against shearers any day.'

He laughed. 'I'm sure my lot would disagree, but I've been on the receiving end of some very colourful insults from a couple of drunk Barmy Army guys a few years back, so I'm prepared to concede.'

Turning his head, he grinned at her, and Chelsea grinned back. As an emergency doctor, he'd have no doubt seen it all too, and a tiny flare of solidarity lit her chest. Their look went on a little too long, however, their smiles slowly fading. His eyes shifted to where strands of her hair kissed the side of her neck. His hands moved and she held her breath for a loaded second or two, her skin tingling beneath the heat and heaviness of his gaze.

Her pulse thudded as time slowed. Oh, God. He was going to touch her. Worse than that, she wanted him to…

CHAPTER THREE

HE DID NOT touch her. He folded his arms instead and looked away, and Chelsea released her breath, 'Not done unpacking yet, I see.' He tipped his chin at the boxes against the far wall.

Chelsea quashed the stupid tingle running up and down the side of her neck. 'Not yet. Just my books to go.'

'Books?' He glanced at her. 'You must be a serious reader if you had to bring your books with you for a year?'

Chelsea wasn't sure if he was fishing again for her future plans, so she steered clear of that pitfall. 'I am. Always have been.'

They'd been an escape from a home life where she'd often felt like an intruder on the silence and intensity of her father's grief. Inside the pages of a book, however, she could be loud, she could be adventurous. She could be free. Free to feel things she hadn't felt able to express to someone who mostly seemed to look straight through her.

He wandered over to the handful of books she'd placed on the shelves above, giving Chelsea an unfettered view of broad shoulders, firm glutes and muscular calves. Picking up her copy of *Animal Farm*, he said, 'You like the classics?'

'I like pretty much everything. Are you a reader?'

'I am. Usually non-fiction, though. Biographies and books about the history of stuff. You know, empires or buildings or political systems. Mostly on audio.'

'That's wise. They're cheaper to lug around the world and don't require bookcases. Speaking of, is there a furniture store in town where I could purchase one?'

'There's Murphy's. In the main street. They're not exactly cheap, though. Might be better to order something online and get it delivered or check out the local buy-swap-sell pages. Lots of bargains and you could get it straight away. I have a ute, if the seller can't deliver, and can give you a hand to put it together if it's a flatpack.'

She didn't know if his offer to help came from ingrained manners, Outback hospitality or something else, but she felt sure inviting Aaron into her house again wouldn't be a good idea. Not until this…jet-lag-induced crush had passed, anyway. 'Thanks. I'll check it out.'

As if to support her jet-lag theory, a feeling of overwhelming weariness hit her out of the blue and she yawned. Aaron turned in time to see it. 'God, I'm sorry. You've had a few big days, you must be exhausted.'

'It's fine,' she dismissed. Then yawned again. He quirked an eyebrow and she gave a half-laugh. 'I'm sorry. I spend the first couple of days not being able to sleep at all and now it appears I can barely stay awake.'

'Jet-lag's like that.'

Yeah. Didn't make it any easier to tolerate, though. 'It doesn't bode well for Friday.' She had a full orientation schedule the day after tomorrow and Chelsea hoped she'd be over the worst of it by then.

'That's still two sleeps away.' Aaron checked his watch. 'It's almost eight, that's not too bad. And you'll be up later tomorrow night because of the welcome dinner at the pub.'

Chelsea's heart sank at the reminder. The thought of going out and socialising, if she felt like this again tomorrow night, made her feel even wearier. But Aaron was right, being forced to stay awake and sync her clock with Aussie time was a good strategy.

He crossed back to the kitchen, the well-developed muscles of his quads far too distracting in her foggy brain. 'I'll go so you can hit the sack. A good night's sleep tonight and you'll wake up a new woman.'

She wanted to tell him she already felt like a new woman. Moving thousands of miles away from the lush green of England to the dusty dry of the Outback, far removed from the things that had defined her since Dom's death, had seen to that. But coherency of thought was getting harder and harder, plus she didn't want to invite closer scrutiny. She'd already told him far too much about herself.

'Let me help you with the leftovers first.'

Chelsea watched dumbly, her head full of cotton wool as he went round the other side of the island, opened the draw and grabbed a fork. Picking up one half-empty rice container, he forked the contents into the other half-empty rice container. 'Oh,' she said automatically. 'You don't have to do that, I can manage.'

'It's no problem.'

Working in tandem, it took a couple of minutes to rationalise the containers to three and fridge them. Aaron flicked on the tap as Chelsea shut the fridge. 'What are you doing?'

'Just going to wash up the empties.'

Chelsea shook her head. 'No need.'

'It's not a bother,' he said dismissively. 'It'll only take me a jiffy.'

'Nope.' Chelsea crossed to the sink and took the washing-up liquid out of his hand. 'Absolutely not.' She shut off the tap. 'You've done far too much already.'

'Okay, okay.' He held up his hands in surrender. 'I know when I'm not wanted.'

Chelsea rolled her eyes even as her breath caught in her throat. If only she *didn't* want him. 'No one told me the Outback Australian male was this domesticated.'

'Sure we are,' he said with a grin. 'I can even darn a sock.'

His grey eyes sparkled and, as their arms brushed together, Chelsea became aware of their closeness. Of his laughing face, the way his fringe swept sideways across his forehead and his lopsided smile. The scar on his chin.

'Where'd you get that?' she asked, turning slightly towards him as she gave in to the impulse to touch.

Her finger pressed lightly against the raised white pucker at the centre before stroking gently, absently noticing the fine prickle of whiskers. Vaguely, Chelsea was aware of the crinkle lines around his eyes receding and the husky change to his breathing as his smile faded.

'Would you believe me if I told you a knife fight?'

Chelsea laughed, glancing into the steady grey intensity of his eyes. The space around them shrunk and her breathing roughened to mimic his, her pulse a slow throb through her temples. 'Is it true?'

'Sadly, no. I tripped over a sheep when I was a kid and conked my chin on the ground.'

'Not quite as dramatic,' she admitted with a smile, her gaze roaming over his features, wondering about every deed and mishap that had resulted in the fascinating mix of imperfections that made up his face.

He smiled too, his mouth curving up, and she itched to run her finger over the crooked line of his top lip. 'Apparently, I was an exceptionally clumsy child.'

She laughed, but it didn't last long, as their gazes locked and the air between them thickened. The heat of his body, the scent of him—honey, ginger and an undernote of something sweeter—infused the air, drawing her closer. Her heart thumped almost painfully behind her rib cage.

What was happening? *How* was this happening?

Becoming aware that her finger was still toying with the scar on his chin, Chelsea let it slide away. What on earth was she doing? She needed to step back.

Step. Back.

But her finger sliding away had parted his mouth slightly and she couldn't look away, she couldn't step back. No more than she could check the impulse to rise on her tip-toes and press her mouth to his.

Aaron's mouth was a strange mix of soft and hard, and she moaned, clutching at the front of his shirt as her pulse swelled in her head. It had been over three years since she'd kissed a man and it felt strange and unfamiliar. Because it wasn't Dom. But it also felt *good* because it wasn't Dom, and she leaned into it, wanting... She didn't know what.

More? Deeper? Closer?

Whatever it was, it was a moot point, as Aaron broke away, taking a half-step backwards. Her brain saturated in a thick fog of lust, her mouth tingling wildly, it took a second for Chelsea to register the sudden loss of sensation. But awareness came back *fast* and, with it, swift recrimination.

'Oh, God.' Her eyes flew to his face, horrified at what she'd just done. At what she'd instigated. 'I am so, *so* sorry.' She shoved a hand in her hair as she took two full steps back, heat flushing up her chest and her neck. 'I...' She shook her head. 'I don't know what came over me. This isn't me. I'm not after...*this*. It must be the jet-lag.'

Why not? People had murdered other people whilst sleep-walking. Surely a random, unsolicited kiss whilst sleep deprived wasn't that much of a stretch?

He didn't say anything, just stood there staring at her, or her mouth anyway, his eyes not quite focused, his lips still parted, a thumb pressed absently against the mid-point of his bottom lip as if he was trying to commit the moment to memory or maybe...savour it? Whatever the reason, his continued silence made it worse.

'Aaron...' she said, her voice low as she twisted her non-existent wedding band. 'Please say something.' God...she was going to have to resign before she'd even started.

Francesca would be delighted.

His hand dropped from his mouth as he snapped out of his trance. 'Its fine,' he assured her with a smile.

Oh, God, *what*? It was so far from fine it was laughable. 'No.' Chelsea shook her head vigorously. 'It is *not* fine. It was…inappropriate and I've gone and buggered up our professional relationship before it's even begun. It'll feel…weird and awkward now.' She folded her arms, feeling nine kinds of idiot. 'I'm so sorry. I can see Charmaine tomorrow about backing out of my contract. I can cover until they get someone else.'

'Whoa.' Aaron gave a half-laugh as he held up both his hands in a stopping motion. 'Hold your horses. There is no need to resign. It won't feel weird or awkward. We're two adults—two professionals. I'm sure we can work together without this being a thing.'

He might not feel weird and awkward, but she sure as hell would, and she wasn't sure she'd get over it in a hurry either. Maybe he had women he'd just met try and kiss him out of the blue every other day but it was not something Chelsea did.

She cringed again, thinking about what she'd done. 'God…' She cradled her hot cheeks in her palms. 'I'm so embarrassed.'

'Have you forgotten I crashed your hotel room last night? Consider us even in the embarrassment stakes.'

The thought cheered Chelsea for about three seconds. Until she realised it wasn't the same at all. *This* hadn't been an accident. It wasn't as if she'd tripped and her mouth had fallen onto his. It had been deliberate, if not very well thought out.

'But it…' Aaron ran a hand along the sink edge. 'Shouldn't happen again.'

Chelsea dropped her hands. Was he mad? *Of course* not. 'Oh, God, *absolutely*. That will *never* happen again. I'm not after anything like this.'

A curious, fleeting expression crossed his face that looked a lot like regret. 'It's just that… I have a—'

'Oh, no,' Chelsea interrupted, a flush of dread hitting her veins. 'You already have a girlfriend, don't you? Or a boyfriend,' she hastened to add, not wanting to presume, because *of course* there was someone out there. The man was seriously good-looking *and* a doctor.

Just then an even worse thought slunk into her brain. 'Dear God…please tell me you're not married.' He didn't wear a wedding ring but then neither had Dom.

He chuckled, and it was deep, warm and low but somehow not reassuring. 'Chelsea, relax.' He reached out a placatory hand. 'I'm single. I just have this rule… Well, not a rule, really, that sounds very formal. More like a preference, I guess, to not get involved with a woman who's not from around here—'

'Right, yes, of course,' Chelsea said, interrupting again as relief flooded her chest. 'You absolutely don't have to say any more. I totally get that.'

She imagined that being with someone—he'd definitely clarified it would be a woman—who knew intimately what it was like to live way out here so far away from anything made relationships easier. He'd lived through the consequences of how badly it could go wrong with his mother leaving.

For a moment it looked as though he *was* going to say more but he didn't. He just nodded and said, 'It really is fine, Chelsea.'

His gaze sought hers but she couldn't quite meet his. 'Okay, thank you.'

'Well.' He lightly bopped his fist on the edge of the sink. 'I'll head off now but I'll see you tomorrow night.'

Tomorrow night. God…her welcome dinner. She was going to have to sit and socialise with a bunch of new work colleagues *and* Aaron and pretend that she hadn't taken total leave of her senses and impulsively kissed him.

Damn you, jet-lag.

'Yep,' she said, her smile strained. 'I'll be there.'

'Goodnight, Chelsea,' he murmured, then turned and walked away, disappearing round the corner into the hallway.

Chelsea didn't move for a bit, listening to the sounds of his retreating footsteps then the closing of the door. Her hands shaking, she took two steps to the sink, flicking on the tap and splashing cold water on her still hot face. That kiss and the excruciatingly awkward conversation afterwards were nothing compared to the realisation that jet-lag had little to do with what had happened and that she, in actual fact, did have a *crush* on Aaron.

Whom she would be working with and whom had made clear that, even if she decided to ditch all her reasons for coming here—none of which involved hooking up with a guy—and wanted to get into some kind of *something* with him, outsiders were not his preference.

God…how pathetically clichéd was she? Apparently starving-for-affection, widowed nurse sleazing on to sexy doctor. *Ugh.* Chelsea lowered her head, pressing her forehead against the cool edge of the stainless-steel sink.

How was she ever going to look him in the eye again?

* * *

Aaron wasn't sure what to expect from Chelsea on Thursday night. He wouldn't have been surprised if she'd made some jet-lag-related excuse and cancelled. But she hadn't. She was here with a dozen OA staff, mostly medical, although Meg, Hattie and Carl, one of the other pilots, along with Brett, had joined them too.

Not only was she here but she was having a great time, chatting away, asking and answering questions as well as laughing at Brett's terrible dad jokes. She seemed to have slotted in easily, quickly adopting the banter that the team had always enjoyed.

Probably nobody had noticed that she'd barely acknowledged him when he'd arrived and had spoken and looked at him only when necessary. But Aaron had noticed. She was obviously still feeling mortified about the kiss despite his assurances that it was fine.

That he was fine.

The truth was it had been *more* than fine. *He* had been more than fine. He'd been attracted to her from the moment he'd switched on the light in her hotel room and she'd screamed and yelled at him to get out. The gut clench he'd felt in that moment had been *visceral* and it had nothing to do with her being in her underwear. It had been the magnificence of her fire-breathing indignation and how primed she'd been to go on the attack, her eyes spitting chips of brown ice, her messy hair flying around her head with each vigorous shake.

The reaction had been the same when he'd spied her from the door of the plane yesterday, her hair in a slim pony tail flicking from side to side as she talked, fine, escaped wisps blowing around her face.

He'd known plenty of attractive women, had even slept with a few, but none of them had made his abdomen cramp tight or his heart drop a beat the second he'd laid eyes on them.

Unfortunately, the pattern had repeated when she'd opened her door to him last night. It was the closest they'd been physically since she'd arrived and, even through the mesh of the screen, he'd felt the impact of her deep in his belly. He really just should have left there and then. Handed over the food and vamoosed.

But he hadn't.

He'd been too distracted by the way her hair kept falling out of her crazy up-do, sliding against her neck, and then her phone had chimed with an incoming message of some kind and her jaw had clenched and she'd opened the door. By the time he'd noticed her frayed denim shorts and just how well her tank-top outlined her breasts, he'd been committed.

Hell, it had taken all his willpower not to straight-out ogle.

And, when she'd started talking about herself, it had been nigh on impossible to leave because he'd wanted to know all about her, this discombobulating woman from the other side of the planet holding a world of hurt in her eyes. But then of course the kiss had happened and the wheels had fallen off the wagon.

He'd been hoping that by tonight he'd be used to seeing her and the strange pitch of his belly would be no more. Apparently not. His gut had performed its now familiar clench as he'd spotted her sitting between Charmaine and Trent in a strappy green dress, her hair all loose and flowing, dangly earrings sparkling through the strands of sandy-blonde.

It was such a stupid way to feel, given she was patently still in love with her husband. She'd tried, but she hadn't been able to hide the raw emotion when she'd talked about him, her voice turning soft and husky. And then there was that very white line on the ring finger of her left hand. The ring might not be there any more but it had obviously been only a recent removal.

Why she'd kissed him was anyone's guess. Maybe he reminded her of him. *Dom.* Maybe it had been the thought of all the adventures making her reckless. Maybe it had been a long time for her and he'd been there and it'd been a weird moment.

Hell, maybe it *had* been jet-lag.

Whatever had precipitated it, reading anything into it was a dumb idea. Even leaving aside her horrified confirmation that it would *never happen again*. Oh, and the fact *she was still in love with her husband*, and she was here for a year.

One year. If she lasted that long. And then she'd be gone and he was *not* up for that.

Aaron had seen too many mates out here devastated by romances that hadn't worked because a lot of women that came from out of town weren't prepared for the *reality* of living in the Outback. They saw *Farmer Wants A Wife* on the TV and thought it was all picnics around a shady dam and bottle-feeding cute, fluffy lambs.

Thanks to his mother's desertion, Aaron had learned early to guard his heart from women who might not stick around. Especially ones who had signed a one-year contract and had been evasive about what came after. Ones who came from the lush green of a faraway country so different from the red dirt of the Outback, it might as well have been another planet.

Sure, he'd dated local women a couple of times since returning, but it was hard when the eyes of the community were watching and far too invested in the outcome and, frankly, there was zero spark. It had been much easier to indulge in occasional discreet liaisons with women who were just *passing through*. They weren't looking for love, they certainly weren't looking to stay. But a fun night of recreational sex with an Outback flight doctor?

Hell, yes.

And, until somebody came along with spark to burn, he saw no reason to change. Unfortunately, his eyes drifted to Chelsea, his belly going into its usual inconvenient tangle.

No—*not* her. *Absolutely not.*

'Trent, perhaps if you've finished pumping Chelsea for the locations of all the best pubs in London, maybe we could ask some questions too?'

Julie Dawson, another flight doctor, spoke good-naturedly and everyone laughed. She was ten years older than Aaron and had been with the OA in Balanora for six years.

'You can always rely on me to ask the important questions, Ju-Ju,' he said with grin.

Julie shook her head and switched her attention to Chelsea. 'I understand you have a lot of critical care experience.'

Chelsea rattled off her impressive CV that spanned

the last twelve years and included midwifery and both neonatal and adult ICU.

'And Charmaine was saying that you did a fair bit of retrieval stuff?' Julie continued.

'Yep. I was on both the NICU and adult ICU teams. Mostly chopper retrievals, due to the shorter distances. But there was a lot of variety, which always kept it interesting.'

'What was the most interesting thing you ever went to?' Trent asked.

'A man who got his arm ripped off by a lion at a small county fair in the wilds of Berkshire.'

There was a round of gasps. 'Was he the lion tamer?' Julie asked.

'No.' Chelsea grinned. 'He was a random local who'd been dared by the lads at the pub over the road to go and pat the lion.'

Winces broke out across faces. 'I bet he was pissed!' Brett said.

'He was roaring drunk,' Chelsea confirmed, deadpan. 'Pardon the pun.'

Everyone laughed and Aaron's lungs got tight. Chelsea was charming them all. Whatever her reasons for coming to Balanora—he was sure she was running away—old Blighty's loss was their gain.

'And what about—?' Julie began.

'Enough, Ju-Ju,' Trent interrupted. 'Enough with the resumé interrogation, it's time to get down to brass tacks.' He turned to Chelsea. 'I just thought you should know that men outnumber women three to one in the district, which means you could have your pick.'

'Trent!' Charmaine said sharply.

Aaron had always admired the way Trent clomped his way through awkward moments with his huge size twelve feet. The thing was, it was surprisingly effective with patients, who magically seemed to open up about stuff, *personal* stuff, they often wouldn't disclose to a doctor.

Ignoring the warning note in Charmaine's voice, Trent continued, '*If* you were in the market for some romance. Maybe you're not ready yet, and that's fine, but I volunteer to play Cupid if you want. You just say the word, okay?'

His delivery was matter-of-fact but also gentle, and it seemed everyone at the table held their breath, waiting for her reply. Aaron certainly was as he vacillated between wanting to thump Trent for putting Chelsea on the spot and wanting to hear her reply.

What if she indicated she *was* in the market for romance?

Chelsea smiled. 'Thanks for the offer, Trent, much appreciated. I will definitely keep that in mind.'

It was as non-committal as her response to his questions about her plans after the contract expired, but it seemed to satisfy Trent.

'How are you finding the heat?' Hattie asked, changing the subject.

Chelsea grimaced. 'Brutal.'

There was general laughter and commiseration. 'I imagine,' Hattie said, 'it's a little different to back home right now.'

'Oh, yeah.' Chelsea took another sip of her wine. 'I mean, I've been to Australia before, so I knew it was hot, but this…'

'When were you in Australia?' Renee, another flight nurse, asked.

'About fourteen years ago. I came with a girlfriend during summer break at uni. Went to Melbourne and Sydney, the reef and Uluru before flying home.'

'That's *your* summer, right?' Brett clarified. 'Our winter?'

'That's right.'

He hooted out a laugh. 'Yeah…it's not so hot here then. None of those places would have prepared you for the Outback in summer.'

'You know what's worse than the heat?' Renee said. 'The flies. Sticky, black flies buzz, buzz, buzz-ing around your face.'

'Shh, don't tell her that,' Charmaine joked. 'She didn't ask me about the flies.'

'It's fine,' Chelsea assured her with a grin. 'I don't scare that easily.'

Trent pulled a five dollar note out of his wallet and placed it on the table. 'I got five bucks that says new girl here lasts two hours on the ground at her first job before she says *bloody flies.*'

Chelsea laughed good-naturedly as five-dollar notes piled up in the centre of the table and everyone claimed a time. Charmaine wrote them all out on a napkin. 'Nine days,' Aaron said as he threw his money down.

His prediction caused a momentary pause in the hilarity. 'Bold,' Trent murmured.

He shrugged. Aaron knew Chelsea had already been through one of the worst things life could throw at a person and that people put up with a lot when they were running from something. She might wilt in the heat, and for damn sure she'd probably not last the week out without getting sunburned, but the flies would probably take a little longer to get to her.

'Looks like you have a champion,' Trent announced gleefully, snatching up Aaron's money.

Aaron cringed internally. The last thing Chelsea probably wanted after last night was for attention to be drawn to them in that way, but she looked at him properly for the first time tonight with only the tiniest trace of reserve and said, 'Thank you.'

He shrugged. 'You know you *will* say it, right?'

Lifting her chin, she looked defiantly around the table and gave a deliberate little sniff. 'We'll see,' she murmured, a smile playing on her mouth, and everyone laughed.

Which was pretty much how the next couple of hours unfolded as they ate, drank, laughed and chatted through three courses in the cool comfort of the Crown Hotel. They swapped war stories about infamous OA cases over the years, while Chelsea regaled them with her stories, ranging from a ninety-one-year-old man who had fallen down a cliff while mountain-climbing to delivering a thirty-weeker in a cow barn in the middle of a snow storm.

In many ways, the two worlds were as different as night and day. Fire and ice. Feast and famine. Desert and green rolling hills. But it was the job that connected them. The people. Whether they were about as isolated as it was possible to be on the planet, or a fifteen-minute chopper ride to the closest major trauma centre, the work was the same, the mission was the same. *Saving lives*. It was what united them all, no matter where they hailed from, and Aaron felt that link—invisible yet somehow tangible—glowing strong around the table tonight.

He felt it in Chelsea too. Here or there, she was one of *them*. Even if she could barely look at him right now.

Aaron didn't see Chelsea the next day until after lunch—in the store room, of all places. He was whistling as he entered, thinking about the great morning he and Renee had spent out at a remote clinic. The sense of community at these pop-up health sites was palpable, from grandmothers with babies on their hips, to barefoot kids kicking a footy around on a spare patch of dirt while they waited for adults to finish their business, to cups of hot tea poured straight from the billy being shared around under shady trees.

It always reaffirmed why he'd wanted to return to Balanora. Why he'd put in all those years in the city. This was home. He knew he didn't have that ancient, spiritual connection that the Iningai had to their country, but he loved the landscape and the people who lived out here in a deep and abiding way that was hard to articulate.

Seeing Chelsea appear from round the end of the main shelf as the door clicked shut behind him dragged him back to the present. She was in the navy trousers and polo shirt of the OA, *Flight Nurse* stamped in fluorescent block print across her chest. Her hair was pulled back into a pony tail, she held a clipboard in one hand and one of the small wire baskets stashed just inside the door in the other.

'Oh...' Aaron pulled up short. 'Hey.'

She stopped in her tracks too, her eyes widening. 'Hey.'

'Sorry. I didn't realise you were in here.'

'Of course not,' she dismissed, but her throat bobbed and her tone was cautious as if maybe she thought he might have tracked her down here or something. Which was utterly ridiculous. He was *restocking*, for God's sake. He was in and out of this store room most days.

'I was just…' She glanced at the clipboard. 'Searching for these items.'

Aaron nodded. Familiarising themselves with the store room was one of the exercises new employees did as part of the induction day. 'Anything you can't find?'

She blinked, as if her brain had been temporarily elsewhere. 'Oh.' She stared blankly at the clipboard. 'The intra-osseous needles.'

'Around the other side, on the right, about half way, second-bottom shelf.'

'Great.' She nodded. 'Thanks.'

But she didn't move for long moments, apparently rooted to the spot, looking at something just over his shoulder. Possibly the door… 'Something else?' he prompted.

'Um…no.' She shook her head, backing up a few steps. 'Thank you,' she murmured before turning and disappearing around the corner, a pen speared through her hair just above the band of the ponytail.

Man…that had been *awkward*. They were clearly going to need to have a talk because whatever it was they were doing now was bound to be noticed. He'd give her a week and if things were still like this then he'd approach her about discussing the issue.

Turning to his hand-written list, he grabbed a basket

and started to fill it with the things he needed. Restocking after using the plane was a shared responsibility and, with Renee doing the clinic paperwork, it was his turn.

It took longer than it would usually, given how excruciatingly conscious he was of every sound Chelsea was making. His body literally *hummed* with awareness.

'Okay,' came her muffled voice from the other side. 'I give in. I can't find them.'

Despite the situation, Aaron smiled to himself. He remembered how long it had taken him to find things in here in the beginning. Placing his basket down, he strode round to the other side to find Chelsea kneeling on the floor in front of the shelf, scowling at the boxes.

Aaron paused for a moment, leaning his shoulder into the edge of the end panel. 'Want me to have a boy look?' he asked, quirking an eyebrow.

She turned her scowl on him and he couldn't help it—he laughed. It was the first time she'd looked at him with no hint of what had happened between them on Wednesday night and it was such a bloody relief.

'They're *not* here.'

Shaking his head, he pushed off the shelf and, as if she realised he was going to be almost on top of her within a few paces, she scrambled to her feet, the wariness back again.

Oh, well…it had been nice while it lasted.

As further proof the unguarded moment was over, she stepped back a couple of paces as Aaron approached. He refused to let it bother him as he stopped in front of the shelf in question, leaned down and reached for where he knew the box was stashed.

After three years, Aaron knew where *everything* lived in this store room. But the box he pulled out was full of ten millilitre syringes. Frowning, he pushed the basket she'd left on the floor aside with his foot and crouched to inspect the other boxes but Chelsea was right. It wasn't there. He checked behind the boxes at the front and the shelf below and above, in case they'd accidentally been put in the wrong place.

'Hmm,' he said, turning to face her.

Clipboard clutched to her chest, she folded her arms. 'I don't like to be the one to say I told you so, but...'

Aaron chuckled. She was looking at him again and, if he wasn't very much mistaken, there was smugness in those big brown eyes. 'I know we recently had some on order but they arrived this week, I thought.'

Intra-osseous needles—special venous-access devices that screwed into the bone, allowing use of the marrow to deliver emergency fluids when no veins could be found—weren't required that often and tended to expire before they were ever used.

'Maybe the box was removed before the replacement came in for some reason,' Aaron mused out loud. Or Tully, who took care of stores, could have been interrupted in the middle of sorting the stock that had arrived on Wednesday and not managed to get back to it yet.

Moving around Chelsea, Aaron headed for a desk area at the end and to the left where the inventory came in and was checked off before being put away. Grabbing the box cutter that lived on the desk top, he sliced several boxes open before he found what he was looking for. 'Found them,' he called, grabbing a smaller box and returning to Chelsea.

She averted her gaze as Aaron strode towards her then crouched to put the box on the shelf where it belonged. Grabbing one, he rose and handed it to Chelsea.

'Thank you,' she murmured, glancing at him briefly as she took it.

Dropping her gaze, she pulled the pen out from her hair and made a tick mark on the form clipped to the board. Rationally, Aaron knew she wasn't doing it as a turn-on but, bloody hell, something about it or about the unselfconscious way she'd done it was super-sexy, and the urge to kiss her throbbed through every cell in his body.

And he really needed to quash that urge right now because, if that was where she always stashed her pen, he was going to see that a lot, and wanting to kiss her every time she did it would be seriously inconvenient.

'Any time,' he said gruffly. 'Anything else?'

She looked at him briefly and opened her mouth, as if she was going to say something then thought better of it, and shook her head, dropping her gaze to the clipboard again.

Aaron sighed. Okay, maybe *the talk* couldn't wait a week. Maybe they should hash it out now. Staring at her downcast head, he said, 'Chelsea... I think we need to talk.'

It took a beat or two, the only sound the low hum of the air-con before there was a definite rough release of breath and her chin lifted, her gaze meeting his. 'Okay.'

'We can't keep doing this...' He waved a finger back and forth between them. 'We have to work together so—'

'I know, God, I know,' she interrupted, her gaze beseeching. 'I'm sorry, I just…can't stop thinking about how much I embarrassed myself on Wednesday night, and you said it wouldn't be weird or awkward, but it is. It really, really is. And that's on me, and I'm just so sorry.'

Aaron shook his head, taking a step towards her because he didn't want her feeling like this, but he didn't know how to convince her. He wanted to grab her arms and squeeze them a little to really get it across but he kept his hands by his sides.

'You *didn't* embarrass yourself. You should try barging into a woman's hotel room in the middle of the night. A woman you don't know and is in nothing but her underwear and you're going to be working with her two days later. *That's* something to be embarrassed about. To be sorry about.'

Her snort was full of derision. '*That* was an accident. *My*…action was deliberate. God.' She shut her eyes briefly and shook her head. When they flashed open again they were full of anguish and she leaned in towards him, as if to implore him. 'You were just being kind and welcoming and I must have come across as the worst kind of sex-starved…' She bugged her eyes at him, leaning in closer. 'Widow. Making a play for the first guy I've been alone with in three years. I totally blew it and I just…' She shook her head. 'I'm so sorry.'

Her impassioned tirade hit Aaron square in the chest, her torment over the incident palpable, and he couldn't take the rawness of it. His heart was beating fast and his breath was as heavy as wet sand in his lungs. She seemed to be under the impression that she'd been the only one feeling something on Wednesday night.

And he just couldn't bear it.

Lifting hands he'd had clenched at his sides, he slid them either side of her face as he swooped in and kissed her—hard—trying to convey that she hadn't been alone in that moment. That her kissing him had not been some kind of unwanted advance.

Her clipboard clattering to the floor broke the spell and Aaron pulled away, his hands dropping to his sides again. For something that hadn't been more than a pressing together of lips, he was breathing rough. So was she.

Bending over, he scooped up the clipboard then handed it back. She took it and they stared at each other for several long beats, not saying anything.

'You and I are going to have to stop apologising to each other all the time,' he said when he found his voice, although it was rough, gravelly. 'I *liked* it...the kiss on Wednesday night.' His eyes burned into hers. 'You weren't the only one who was feeling it, you know?'

Her eyes searched his for what felt like for ever. She swallowed. 'Okay...'

It sounded tentative, but she wasn't rejecting the premise of his statement, which was a relief. 'But, here's the thing,' Aaron continued, his voice a low murmur. 'I think you're still in love with your husband and, as I said on Wednesday night, I don't get involved with out-of-towners, so what say you and I just be friends? Do you think we can do that?'

'Uh-huh.' Her voice was stronger, surer. 'I'd like to.'

Aaron smiled. 'Me too.' Truth was, he'd like a lot more, but there was no way he could see it ending well for him. Why borrow trouble?

Just then the store room door opened and Chelsea's

eyes widened as she looked at him. 'Chelsea?' It was Charmaine. 'Are you still in here?'

'Yes…sorry,' she called, her eyes never leaving Aaron's. 'Just finished. I'm coming now.' She started to back away, shoving her pen back through her hair, and Aaron gave her his friendliest smile because, man… that move would be the death of him, he just knew it.

Finally, breaking eye contact, she turned away from him and Aaron's gaze snagged on the swish of her pony tail and the poke of her pen as she turned right at the end and disappeared from sight.

The door closed and Aaron let out a long, slow breath, confident that Chelsea and him were on the same page with the *friends* thing. And it didn't matter how much that kiss—or the one on Wednesday night—had affected him. Had made him want *things*. They were on track to managing the situation between them so he just wasn't going to think about inconvenient truths. Or those kisses.

Yeah… He was never going to think about *them* again.

CHAPTER FOUR

BY THE TIME Chelsea's beeper went off the following Thursday evening, she was mentally ready to go out with Aaron in the plane for the first time on an emergency retrieval to an Outback property. She'd had enough short bouts of exposure to him the past week to feel confident about their interactions, and the idea of accompanying him into the middle of nowhere to an accidental gunshot wound to a femoral artery didn't fill her with panic.

He'd suggested they be friends and, as the excruciating embarrassment of her bungled kiss had ebbed in the face of their growing familiarity, interacting with him had begun to feel more natural. Maybe there'd never be that level of easy banter she already shared with the rest of the team but she'd challenge any outsider to say their exchanges weren't friendly.

Buckling up in the King Air, the stretcher immediately in front of her, a familiar buzz hummed through Chelsea's veins. She'd been in the air three times already this week, flying with Julie and Trent to community clinics in the region. They'd been fun and interesting, and she'd learned so much about how things

were done within the organisation and the expectations
of the people they served, but this was to her first emergency situation and her pulse kicked up.

That could, of course, have something to do with
Aaron buckling up diagonally opposite, his chair facing
hers, but she refused to give that thought any air time.

'You guys ready for take-off?' Hattie asked via the
cushioned headphone set already snug around Chelsea's ears and doing a very good job of blocking out
the propellor noise.

'Roger that,' Aaron confirmed into the mic sitting
close to his mouth on the end of the angled arm that
protruded from the left cup of his earphones. His voice,
deep and confident, sounded simultaneously close yet
far away. He smiled at Chelsea and shot her the thumbs-
up.

'Roger,' Chelsea also confirmed into her mic as she
returned the thumbs-up.

The plane started to taxi to the airstrip and Chelsea
turned her head, looking out of the window, watching the OA hangar get smaller in the fading light. She
ran through what they knew about their patient, who
was situated four hundred kilometres north-west on an
isolated property. He was a twenty-two-year-old man
who'd been out kangaroo-shooting with his mates. Quite
how he'd come to be shot in the leg was vague, the more
pertinent fact being that, by the time they arrived in
forty-five minutes, the wound would be two hours old.

Of course, it was still way faster than it would have
been for the patient to get to a hospital. A lot could go
wrong in two hours where blood loss was involved,
and the young guy had apparently bled a lot initially

until someone had thought to apply a tourniquet using a belt. The bleeding had reportedly slowed dramatically, but if a large vessel had been compromised in his thigh then blood loss could be significant. The guy involved already had an elevated pulse and was clammy to the touch.

Having a tourniquet on for a long period of time was not ideal either. It could be life-saving in the face of catastrophic bleeding, but it could also compromise circulation to the entire limb, and cause a build-up of toxins which could have a detrimental effect when it was eventually released.

His friends had loaded him on the back of a ute and had driven him to the airstrip. Most large properties in the Outback had an airstrip for things like deliveries of supplies and mail, and of course for emergencies, and Hattie had been given the co-ordinates. The strip was dirt, and had apparently been graded last month, but the guys on the ground had been instructed to inspect the surface, make sure it was clear of any debris and check for any kangaroos in the vicinity.

They were also going to place lit kerosene lamps from the shed situated off to the side of the parking apron, ninety metres apart down either side of the strip. Compared to what Chelsea was used to in the UK, it all seemed a bit like the Wild West. Farms didn't have their own airstrips and no one had ever been instructed to check for kangaroos—but it added to the adrenaline.

A few minutes later, they lifted into the dying golden light of evening, the sky streaked with gilded clouds. The ground, the hangar and the lights of Balanora quickly fell away as the King Air climbed towards the first stars just blinking through the veil of night.

'ETA forty minutes,' Hattie's voice informed them as the plane levelled out shortly after.

'Roger,' Aaron murmured into his mic. Glancing over at her, he fiddled with the dial on the right ear cup of the headset, obviously changing channels to a private one for just the two of them. 'You ready for this?' he asked. His words, his voice, flowed directly into her ear, causing a tiny shiver.

She nodded. 'Pumped.'

'Might be a bit of a bumpy landing.'

Chelsea shrugged. She'd been landing on dirt strips all week. 'I think I'm getting used to it.'

'Trust me, this will be worse,' he said with a laugh. 'The strips at the communities where you've been the last few days are well-used and well-maintained. A lot of the remote strips on properties are pretty rough and ready.'

It was odd for him to be so close, his mouth moving, his eyes fixed on hers, and yet for him to sound so far away, as if he were in the middle of a vacuum. She was used to the phenomenon but it always felt a little disjointed.

'Hattie doesn't seem too concerned.'

He chuckled. 'Hattie could land one of these blindfolded in the middle of a dust storm on a dry creek bed with one hand tied behind her back.'

His laughter unfurled delicious tendrils through her body, and the shiver became a trail of goose bumps along the top of her scalp and across her nape. 'Good to know,' she said with a grin, ignoring the goose bumps and the unfurling.

'Don't worry,' he assured her, his gaze earnest. 'She'll get us down safely. And, if she thinks it's not safe, she just won't land. It's always safety first. She won't risk any of our lives or damaging a precious, expensive resource such as this plane.'

Chelsea nodded. She knew that pilots always put the safety of people on board and that of the aircraft first but it was still comforting to have that reiterated. Comforting too that Aaron knew Hattie so well, and there was an obvious bond of trust between them that came from years of flying together. During her time in the UK Chelsea had got to know a few of the chopper pilots she'd flown with, but there were so many of them in a busy twenty-four-hour city medivac hub, it was rare to go up more than two or three times with the same pilot.

It was another thing she was looking forward to— getting to know the team the way Aaron did. Becoming part of this well-oiled machine she'd witnessed all week.

Aaron switched them back to the combined channel and turned his attention to the paperwork he had on his lap. Chelsea gazed out of the window, darkness encroaching on the vast red swathes of earth broken occasionally by narrow veins of green that followed river banks, or the more circular patterns of grass formed around the edges of a dam or billabong.

She watched until the day had completely leached from the landscape and nothing more could be seen apart from an occasional light or small cluster of lights on the ground.

With Aaron still busy, she switched on her overhead light and pulled her current read—a saga set in Sydney—out of her bag. Occasional chatter in her earphones between Hattie and comms broke the cushioned silence created by the noise-cancelling ability of her earphones, but it didn't rouse Chelsea from the story until Hattie announced some time later, 'There she blows.'

Chelsea glanced out the window as Aaron capped his pen. Down below, two straight lines of lights lit up the runway.

'Comms have confirmation from the guys on the ground that the strip is safe to land,' Hattie said.

Aaron, who had pushed the angled mouthpiece up and away from his mouth earlier, pulled it down again. 'Thanks, Hattie. Comms, any update on the patient condition?'

'No worse. Patient's pain level, eight out of ten, GCS fifteen,' a male voice informed them.

'Roger that. Thank you.' The plane banked to the left as Aaron looked across at her. 'You got all that?'

Chelsea nodded. 'Yes.'

'We should be on the ground in a couple of minutes,' he said.

She shot him the thumbs-up as a tiny hit of adrenaline sparked at her middle. Nerves over not being fully familiar with the plane and where things were kept tap danced in her belly, but Aaron had assured her earlier that the job should be a scoop and run, so they shouldn't need anything too complicated. Getting the patient back to Balanora and hospital for surgical intervention ASAP was their priority.

Chelsea's ears popped as the plane descended.

'Okay,' Hattie said, her voice steely, 'Going in to land. Hold tight you two, might be a bit bumpy.'

Keeping her eyes on the window, Chelsea saw the first few ground lights flash by then the wheels touched down with a jolt and she braced her feet on the floor as she was jostled about. Glancing over at Aaron, she found him braced too, but grinning, and he let out a loud, *'Whoop!'* She laughed.

'You're a legend, Hattie,' he said into his mouthpiece.

'I know,' Hattie replied, and they both laughed.

Within two minutes the plane had taxied into the parking apron and Chelsea unbuckled herself when it pulled to a halt. So did Aaron. The engines cut out and they both took off their headphones simultaneously. 'How was your first Outback property landing?' he asked.

'Amazing!' Because it had been, and she was totally pumped to get out there.

It took another minute for the props to come to a full halt, during which they both donned gloves. As soon as Hattie opened the door, it was action stations. Chelsea exited the plane first into the warmth of the night, a large bag full of supplies slung over her shoulder and Aaron hot on her heels.

The ute was being parked about three metres away towards the rear of the plane as her feet hit the ground. Their patient was on the back tray along with two other guys, and two more sprang from the ute as soon as the engine cut out, pointing torches at Chelsea and Aaron's feet to light the way.

'Hi,' she said as she approached, the fluorescent letters of her shirt reflecting brightly. 'I'm Chelsea.' She smiled at the faces both on and around the ute, harried expressions telling more than words what they'd been through. 'And who do we have here?'

'You hear that, Gazza?' one of the guys joked. 'They sent the bloody Queen of England herself to rescue you.'

Chelsea laughed, as did the patient, albeit it somewhat weak. 'Lucky me.'

'Hey, Brando,' Aaron said. 'I always knew you'd shoot someone with that bloody gun one day.'

'Aaron, man,' the guy called Brando said. 'Sure glad to see you.' He sounded it too. Every one of the grimy, night-shrouded faces was looking at them as if they were the cavalry.

'All good.' Aaron nodded. 'We'll take over from here.'

And take over they did, two guys helping Chelsea up onto the tray, then moving out of her way while Aaron sprang up unaided like a freaking gazelle, as if he'd been leaping on and jumping off ute trays his entire life.

'Hey, Gazza,' Chelsea said as she got her first look at the patient's face, the torch beams flooding the area. 'How are you feeling?'

He shut his eyes against the light. 'I've had better days.'

It was encouraging to hear him able to joke, but there was a definite pallor to his skin, and his arm was cool to touch despite the heavy coat that had been placed over his torso.

'You kept him warm, that's good,' Chelsea murmured to the guys as she reached for the new oxygen mask she'd hooked up to a cylinder in the emergency bag before they'd taken off. Keeping a shocked patient warm was basic first aid.

'Derek said we should do that,' one of them said.

'Absolutely, you did everything right,' she assured him as she applied the mask to Gazza's face and turned the oxygen up high. All the guys had blood stains on their clothes, so it had obviously been a team effort. 'You put on a tourniquet, you kept him warm, you got help. You did good.'

All the while she talked, Chelsea worked by the torch light, putting on a finger probe to measure oxygen saturation, applying a blood-pressure cuff and slapping electrical dots on Gazza's chest so they could monitor his heart rhythm. The portable monitor bleeped to life with a green squiggle that indicated a normal rhythm but was definitely too fast at a hundred and twenty beats.

Aaron worked too, doing a quick inspection of the wound. The fabric of Gazza's jeans had already been cut away, exposing the location of the injury a few inches above the knee. A cloth soaked in dark red was covering the site and around it another cloth—a T-shirt, maybe, given one of the guys was shirtless—had been tied to secure the makeshift dressing. It was bloodied too but not soaked, which was encouraging. Chelsea knew Aaron wouldn't remove it, wouldn't risk disturbing whatever haemostasis had been achieved.

'Looks like blood loss has been staunched,' Aaron said as he inspected the belt that sat several inches above the entry wound. He wouldn't remove it either.

'BP one hundred systolic,' Chelsea said. Not too bad, considering.

'Okay.' Aaron nodded. 'Let's get in two large bore IVs.'

Under the torchlight, and with Chelsea assisting, both were placed in the large veins in the crook of each elbow within five minutes. She used Brando and Waz, the other guy in the back of the ute, as IV poles, tasking them with holding up the bags of IV fluids.

'Let's run them wide open,' Aaron said.

Chelsea didn't need the instruction, already opening the clamp all the way on her side as Aaron did the same on his. Hopefully the replacement fluid would rally Gazza's system until he could get a transfusion.

'Could someone please take off his right shoe?' Chelsea asked as she plucked the pen from her ponytail and noted his obs in a quick scribble on the glove she was wearing.

The boot was off quick-smart and Aaron sprang off the ute to feel for foot pulses. 'Nothing,' he said when Chelsea raised an eyebrow at him several beats later.

'Okay.'

She made a note of that and the time on her glove as Aaron said, 'He's ready to go. I'll grab the stretcher.' And he strode towards the King Air.

'Is that bad?' the guy who took the boot off asked.

Chelsea smiled at him. 'It means the tourniquet has been very effective.'

She wasn't about to reel off all the potentially damaging side effects of applying a tourniquet for long periods of time and how controversial tourniquets in first aid were, going in and out of fashion over the years, and the plethora of conflicting advice about duration. The bottom line was, without it Gazza would probably be dead. They could do something about any potential circulation compromise when he got to hospital.

Nothing could be done about death.

'Okay, guys.' Aaron approached with the stretcher. 'We're going to need your help to get Gazza loaded.'

'Where do you need us?' Brando said.

CHAPTER FIVE

Two HOURS LATER, they were back in Balanora. Gazza had been taken away by the ambulance and was currently undergoing an emergency operation performed by the visiting flying surgeon to stabilise him enough for aerial transfer to Brisbane for further treatment and management. Hattie had gone home half an hour ago and Chelsea had just finished restocking the plane.

It had been Aaron's turn but Chelsea had wanted to do it so she could keep familiarising herself with where things were, both in the store room and on board. Once she was done, she bade Brett, who was doing checks on the King Air, a goodnight before making her way to the office to find Aaron.

'Hey,' he said, looking up from the keyboard as she opened the door.

The main office was usually brightly lit but at this hour the only light on was the one directly above the desk Aaron occupied.

'Hi.'

It was the first time they'd been alone together at work since the store room and she felt weirdly shy. But it *was* ten o'clock, and kind of dark, with a hush that was the complete opposite of the daytime bustle.

It made her very aware of him, of her attraction to him.

'How do you think it went tonight?' Aaron asked, leaning casually back in his chair.

Chelsea forced her legs to move closer until she was on the other side of his desk. 'I think it went well.' Unless…he didn't think so? 'Why, did I do something wrong?'

'What?' He chuckled. '*No*. You were great. It was just your first emergency call out, so I wanted to check you were okay with how everything went. Ask if you had any questions or observations.'

'Oh.' Chelsea shot him a rueful smile. 'Right. I think it all went smoothly and that Gazza was lucky to have mates who kept their cool. You know them?'

'Not really. Just Brando. I played footy with a couple of his brothers.'

She nodded. 'You think the tourniquet being on for that long will affect the viability of his leg?' His foot had been alarmingly cold and dusky during the flight.

He shrugged. 'It could do. It'll have probably been on for about four hours by the time they take it off. There wasn't another choice, though.'

'Yeah.' Truer words had never been spoken. It had been the ultimate 'rock and a hard place' scenario. 'It'll be interesting to know how he fares.'

'Charmaine will follow up over the coming days and let us know.'

'Excellent.' In her previous jobs there'd been *so* many incidents attended, it had sometimes been hard to keep track. But Chelsea guessed it was different in such a small, tight-knit community.

'Question.' Aaron sat forward in his chair and sifted through some paperwork. Finding what he was looking for, he handed it across to her, pointing with his pen at a numeral. 'Is this a four or a seven? It looks like a seven but that would be odd.'

Chelsea leaned in, taking the patient observation chart from him and inspecting the notation she'd made on the plane. 'It's a four,' she confirmed, passing it back.

His eyebrows drew together as he looked at it again. 'Note to self,' he murmured. 'Chelsea's fours look like sevens.'

She laughed. 'No way. That is clearly a four.'

Letting the piece of paper slide from his fingers, he shook his head. 'And they say doctors have terrible hand writing.'

'They do,' Chelsea said. Except Aaron's, of course, which, despite its bold strokes and slashes, was entirely legible. 'Yours is an exception.'

'What's that you say?' He put a hand to his ear as if he was trying to hear better. 'I'm exceptional?'

He grinned and Chelsea's breath caught in her throat. An outsider might have concluded that he was flirting but, after a week of observing the team and him working together, she knew this was just Aaron being Aaron, bantering as he would with anyone else on the team.

Which was a good thing.

Due to their rocky start, they hadn't got into that groove yet, so maybe this was his attempt to get there. Chelsea was more than willing to pick up what he was putting down because, as soon as their friendship felt more natural, the better for everyone.

'Ha! Good try. Not quite the same thing there, buddy.'

An expression of surprise flickered over his face—whether at her returning his banter or her use of the word 'buddy', she didn't know—but it was gone as quickly as it came as he clutched at his chest. 'Careful, you'll dent my giant doctor ego.'

Her first instinct was to deny he had any such thing. She had worked with some super egos in her past and Aaron's didn't come close. But she went for banter instead. 'Then my work here is done.'

He chuckled and, yes, Chelsea *did* feel the deep resonance of it brushing seductively against her skin. But, hey, Rome wasn't built in a day, right? 'You done with restocking?' he asked.

Grateful for the subject change, Chelsea grabbed it with both hands. 'Yep. All ready for the next take-off.'

'Good-oh.' He nodded. 'You might as well go, then.'

Chelsea shook her head. 'What about you?'

'No, no.' He sighed dramatically. 'I'll be here for hours yet deciphering your writing, but you go on home and get your beauty sleep.'

'Hey,' she protested with a laugh, even though she could see by the twinkle in those grey eyes he was joking. 'Serve yourself right if you are,' she quipped.

Okay, this was *good*. This was feeling really good now. Friends. Banter. *Natural*.

He grinned. 'I'll see you tomorrow.'

'Unless I see you tonight.' An awkward moment passed between them and Chelsea hastened to clarify. 'You know…if we get called out again.'

'Yeah.' He smiled. 'I know.'

'Right, then.' She tapped the desk. 'Goodnight.'

'Night.'

She was halfway to the door when he called her name and she turned to find him looking at her, the spill of light overhead bathing his hair in a golden aura. Something tugged hard down deep and low.

'You did good out there.'

Chelsea didn't need his praise. She knew she'd done a good job because she was confident in her experience and ability, no matter how new and unfamiliar the environment. But she *liked* it nonetheless.

'Thank you,' she said, before turning and continuing on her way.

Sunday afternoon, Chelsea found herself knocking on Trent's door. He'd called that morning to invite her to an impromptu barbecue in her honour—a get-to-know-the-new-girl thing. Stupidly, she'd assumed it was just going to be Trent and his wife, Siobhan, but when she arrived a fashionable fifteen minutes late, with the requested folding chair and a bottle of wine to share, a party was in full swing.

Music met them as Trent ushered her into a back yard playing host to clusters of laughing, chatting people. Some she recognised from work—hell, she'd recognised Aaron immediately, her eyes drawn to him and a pretty blonde in a midriff top—but a lot she didn't know.

'Oh.' She pulled up short. 'You haven't gone to all this trouble for me, I hope?'

'Of course,' he said cheerily, slinging an arm around her shoulder and giving her upper arm a brisk squeeze.

'You're the guest of honour and we're welcoming you, Balanora style. Suck it up, sweetheart.'

'Trent Connor.' A tall, curvy redhead with an Irish accent approached. 'I told you not to spring it on her,' she chastised, but the lilt in her accent softened it dramatically. She shook her head at Chelsea. 'What's he like?' She stuck out her hand. 'I'm Siobhan.'

'It's lovely to meet you, Siobhan,' Chelsea said absently as they shook hands.

'Come on, then.' Siobhan took the chair and the wine off Chelsea and passed them to Trent. 'I'm going to introduce Chelsea around to some people. Be a darling and get her some of that to drink. She looks like she can do with it.'

'Yes, my little Irish clover,' Trent said with an adoring smile.

Chelsea was whisked away then, meeting person after person until her head spun. There were partners and children of OA staff she'd already met and those she hadn't. Also, several more doctors and nursing staff from the Balanora hospital. There were teaching colleagues of Siobhan's from the primary school, as well as about a dozen young local professionals working for places such as the council, the railway, Department of Parks and Wildlife, estate agents, tourism bodies and various other businesses around town.

It seemed Trent and Siobhan knew everyone and, despite the surprise nature of the party, Chelsea enjoyed herself immensely. Between meeting so many new people and getting to know Siobhan—who was an absolute hoot—the very pleasant afternoon under the shady backyard gums flew into early evening.

She even spoke to Aaron for a while who, unlike every other man at the party, was drinking some kind of fizzy juice instead of something alcoholic because he was on call until seven the next morning. He introduced her to the woman she'd seen him with when she'd first arrived, who turned out to be Gazza's sister, Maddie.

It was great to catch up on his progress, and Chelsea was relieved to find out that the leg hadn't suffered any detrimental effects from the tourniquet, and that the doctors in Brisbane were already talking about a discharge date some time in the next few days.

'Dinner's up!' Trent yelled just after six, rallying everyone to the barbecue area to grab something to eat.

Chelsea's stomach growled as the delicious aromas of cooking food saw her join the mass migration to the undercover patio. She hadn't realised she was so hungry until now. While in the queue for her food, she and Siobhan swapped stories of life back home.

'How'd you end up here?' Chelsea asked.

'The same as most people. Came out on a backpacking holiday a decade ago, met Trent at the Crown and been here ever since.'

Laughing at the matter-of-factness of Siobhan's statement, Chelsea said, 'Have you been back to Ireland at all?'

'Couple of times. Introduced Trent to the family. Showed him around the country. But this land…it owns him.' She shrugged. 'And I don't want to be anywhere he's not.'

'How have you found the heat?'

Siobhan laughed. 'Not my favourite part of the Outback,' she admitted. 'But I acclimatised pretty quickly. And frankly I'd prefer it to the bloody flies.'

Having experienced those flies already, Chelsea was beginning to understand the common refrain. She'd not uttered it yet but she was in no doubt that she would.

'Okay, what'll it be?' Trent asked as they reached the start of the queue. 'I have chicken pieces, rib fillet and kangaroo snags.'

Chelsea blinked. 'Really?' Although curious, Chelsea had no desire to try the meat from such an iconic Australian animal. Where she harked from, kangaroos were considered cute—not a culinary delicacy.

He tossed his head back and laughed. 'No.'

'Ignore him.' Siobhan rolled her eyes affectionately. 'They're beef and pork. Although, kangaroo meat is highly nutritious and less than two percent fat.'

'Noted,' Chelsea said to Siobhan before turning back to Trent. 'I'll have some chicken, please.'

After she'd eaten, an impromptu touch football game between the teachers sprang up. There was much laughter and friendly sledging from the sidelines, and when it came to an end Chelsea was roped into a game, despite insisting, as Trent grabbed her hand, that she'd never played before.

'Come on, medical staff,' Trent called. 'Let's go.'

'Hospital versus the OA,' Charmaine suggested as she joined the people forming up in the middle of the back yard.

Trent shook his head. 'Doctors versus nurses.'

'That gives you three local A-grade footy players on your team,' she pointed out. Apparently two of the nurses from the hospital played in the local competition too.

'You have Aaron,' Trent returned.

The man in question dropped his head to either side to stretch his traps as he gripped a foot behind him and stretched out a quad muscle. His shorts, already mid-thigh, rode up, and Chelsea couldn't help but notice it was a *very nice* quad muscle. 'I can take 'em all, don't worry, Charmaine.'

'Plus,' Trent added, 'We have Chelsea, who's never played before and probably doesn't even know the rules. That's like a handicap.'

'Hey,' Chelsea said with a laugh. 'I thought I was the guest of honour.'

'Sorry, Chels,' Trent said, not sounding remotely sorry. 'Guest time's over! This is footy.'

'Yeah, *Chels*,' Aaron teased, a crooked smile hovering on that crooked mouth. 'Footy's serious business around here.'

She wasn't sure she was a fan of having her name shortened but, given it seemed to be a way to express affection out here, a trill of pleasure bubbled up from her middle. Maybe it was a sign that she was becoming one of the gang.

She nodded good-naturedly but stuck her hands on her hips, her feet firmly apart in a Wonder Woman pose as she shot Aaron a *faux* steely look. 'Looks like I better bring my A-game, huh?'

There were a few 'Ooh's from the crowd as Aaron laughed. 'You better bring your A-plus,' he said, matching her stance and tone, 'Because doctors demolish.'

The half-dozen people behind him cheered, *'Doctors demolish!'*, smashing their fists in the air.

Trent laughed. 'Whatever gets you through the night, big guy. Everyone knows nurses annihilate.'

'Oh, Jaysus,' Siobhan said from the makeshift side-line that had been outlined with white plates. 'You two going to play or should I just get out me ruler so you can measure your dicks?'

Everyone laughed and the game got underway. It took all of a minute for Chelsea to be glad she'd put on shorts and not the strappy sundress she'd almost worn, lest it would have ended up over her head from the physicality of the game. It might only be touch football but there were plenty of spills as members of each team smack-talked back and forth.

Aaron had been right—footy was serious business!

'Hey, ref!' Aaron called, pointing at Trent ten minutes into the second half. 'Offside.'

Siobhan had taken on the role of referee. 'Yeah, yeah.' She rolled her eyes at Chelsea who was standing nearby. 'Anybody'd think they were playing for bloody sheep stations.'

Chelsea grinned and used the back of her forearm to dash at some sweat as Siobhan awarded a penalty to the nurses. The play started again and this time, by some kind of miracle, Chelsea managed to intercept the ball for the first time. She stared at it in her hands for a nanosecond before everyone roared, *'Run!'* and she took off for the try line.

The closest member of the opposition team to her was Aaron—in fact he was suddenly very close indeed, his presence big as he loped just behind and to her left.

Chelsea's heartbeat kicked up in a way that didn't have much to do with the exertion and more to do with having Aaron hot on her heels. The anticipation of feeling the tips of his fingers landing in the small of her back, of him *touching* her in front of everyone, no matter how impersonally, caused her to shiver despite how damn hot she was.

She knew there was no way she could outrun him— he was too muscular, too pumped, for that—but she was smaller and nimbler, a fact she proved when he reached for her and said, 'Gotcha, *Chels*.'

Except he hadn't. Her last-second dodge managed to evade his touch. 'Think again, Azza,' she taunted, the cheers of everyone around her filling the night air and her head as she strode for the line which seemed as if it was getting further and further away.

His warm chuckle, so close, followed her and she knew there was no way Aaron would make the same mistake again. So, with the line approaching, she made a dive for it, looking over her shoulder in what felt like slow motion as he too dove, his outstretched fingers coming closer and closer.

She turned back just in time to brace for impact, the ball touching the ground before his hand touched her back. Laughing at her triumph, she performed a quick roll to twist out of Aaron's path but he countered, his reactions quicker than the processing of the information that the ball had already been grounded, his body landing sprawled on top of her, his torso half-pressing her into the grass, one meaty thigh tangling between hers.

Somewhere Siobhan yelled, *'Try!'* and her team mates hollered as they all ran towards her. But Chel-

AMY ANDREWS   99

sea was oblivious. She was only slightly winded by the impact but the effects of Aaron—big and strong, pinning her to the ground with his body—were far more cataclysmic.

They were both laughing, but not for long. Hers died pretty quickly as the thrust of the thigh she had admired earlier pressed between her legs. His followed not long after, as if he too was just realising their position. His gaze zeroed in on her mouth as a hot, dark look passed between them.

They might have agreed to be friends, but Chelsea had no doubt that, had they been alone, they'd be doing more than staring at each other right now, wondering who was going to make the first move. One of them would already have made it.

But they weren't alone and suddenly Trent was there, grabbing Aaron by the shoulder. 'C'mon, get off her, you great big lug, we need to congratulate our girl.'

Whether he was dragged off or rolled off, Chelsea wasn't sure. All she knew was she was suddenly being pulled up and enveloped in the centre of a huge team hug, a lump the size of London lodging in her throat. Grief had seen her withdraw from her social life three years ago. The complicated feelings she'd been experiencing since finding out about Dom hadn't loaned themselves to her being particularly social.

She'd missed it, she realised—just hanging out with colleagues. With…*friends*.

The fact that all these people in this tiny town were now in her friend circle made the moment even more bitter sweet.

'Okay, okay,' Trent said after a bit. 'We still got a few minutes of this half! Let's go kick some more arse.'

The huddle broke up and Chelsea realised Aaron was still lying on the ground on his back. She wondered briefly if he'd been hurt until their gazes locked and the same flare of heat she'd felt when she'd been under him only moments ago burned between them again.

Trent broke the connection by bouncing the football off Aaron's forehead, who swore at him. 'Get up, old man.' Trent grinned. 'We're winning.'

Just then the two beepers Siobhan had been holding—one for Aaron, one for Renee—went off. Everyone around paused as Aaron performed a perfect sit-up, and Siobhan handed both beepers over to their respective owners.

'Car accident.' Aaron read off the screen. 'Two hundred clicks south of town.' Rising from the ground in one smooth move that did funny things to Chelsea's insides, he glanced at Trent. 'Rain check, dude.'

'Any time.' They fist-bumped then Trent clapped his hands. 'Okay, who's going to sub in for hotshot here?'

Someone—a cousin of Trent's whom Chelsea thought was a dentist—stepped forward but she only really had eyes for Aaron as their gazes met and lingered one last time before he said to Renee, 'Meet you at the base in twenty?' and they departed together.

Aaron worked hard the following week to act normally around Chelsea after their crash-tackle incident—no easy feat. He knew he hadn't been alone in that heightened moment and that, had no one been around, it would have had a very different outcome. And every time their gazes had met this week he'd seen that same recognition in her eyes too, no matter how fleeting.

Still, despite the counsel of his wiser angels whispering about the friend zone, his attraction hadn't lessened. Unfortunately, his brain and his body were just not on the same page. The fact that he really *liked* her didn't help. These past couple of weeks, she'd fitted in seamlessly with the team—quick with a laugh, a joke or whip-smart comeback and good-natured about all the teasing over her accent, not to mention efficient, methodical and *kind*.

Everyone—without exception, it seemed—had taken to OA's newest member of staff.

In a lot of ways, liking her was worse than lusting after her, because the latter he could dismiss as bodily urges and that kept him vigilant about maintaining distance. The former made him want to draw closer. To really get to know her and deepen the friendship he'd insisted they have. But he was hyper-aware that the line between the two states was razor-thin and deepening one would inevitably ramp up the other.

And it had only been a couple of weeks!

Thankfully, albeit coincidentally, they hadn't worked together this week, which helped. Not on any of the clinic runs or the three emergency retrievals. They hadn't even been on call together. It wouldn't always be that way, he knew, but perhaps until he was used to being around her, used to this crazy kind of tug he felt whenever she was near, just exchanging a few brief words here and there as they passed by was enough.

Except the universe, it seemed, was determined to keep pushing them together. He took a phone call from

Meg on Friday, the first day of his rostered three days off, asking him if he could pick up and deliver a book case to Chelsea's. Dan, her partner, had been tasked with doing it but had been called out of town for work for the day.

'I'm sure it could wait till tomorrow,' Meg said, 'But I know you have the day off, and Chels was so excited last night about finally getting her books unpacked.'

Yes, *Chels* had stuck.

Ordinarily, Aaron would have been keen to help out in this kind of situation, particularly for a new member of their team. He had the vehicle and the brawn, after all, and had already previously offered. But she'd gone to Dan for assistance with the bookshelf—not him— which told Aaron all he needed to know about how much she wanted to avoid being alone with him.

Something he utterly endorsed.

But now Meg had asked him to do it and it would seem odd for him to refuse when she not only knew he was free, but that Aaron would have done it for any other staff member without thinking twice. Sure, he was going to Curran Downs today, but hadn't planned to leave until after lunch, which Meg also knew.

And then there was the way Chelsea's voice had softened when she'd spoken about her books, as if they were her friends...

So, here he was, knocking on her door at nine in the morning after picking the flat-packed boxes up from a house in the older part of town. Chelsea had obviously taken his advice about the thriving local buy-sell-swap site and found two brand-new bookcases, still in their boxes.

He propped the first box against the bricks beside the door and didn't wait for an answer before turning back for the remaining box. The door opened just as he was lifting it out of the tray of the ute.

'Oh. You're…not Dan,' Chelsea said, sounding discombobulated by his presence.

She could join the club, because that short dress brushing her legs at mid-thigh and her bare feet were utterly discombobulating him. Her was hair was piled up in that messy up-do again, several silken strands falling around her nape.

'He got called out of town for work this morning,' Aaron explained as he carried the box towards her. 'Meg rang and asked me to do it.'

'Okay, well…thank you.' She smiled. 'I appreciate it.'

'It's what we do around here,' he said dismissively. 'Help each other out.'

Which was the truth, but he realised he probably sounded curt rather than neighbourly, and he ground his teeth at his ineptitude. *What the hell, dude?*

He leaned the second box on top of the first, the sun on his shoulders already carrying a real bite. But that wasn't what was making him feel hot as he stood two feet from Chelsea—far closer than was good for him. It was the silky slide of her hair, that hint of cleavage at the V of her neckline and her bright-purple toenails that matched the tiny purple flowers of her dress. He had no idea why *toes* were turning him on.

It wasn't as though he had a foot fetish. Or he hadn't had, anyway.

'Could I squeeze past?' he asked. Not that he wanted to *squeeze* at all. He'd prefer she give him a very wide berth.

'Oh, right yes…here. I'll hold the door.'

As if the universe had heard his preference for distance, Chelsea pushed on the screen door, stepping outside to hold it open, giving him plenty of room to pick up both boxes and transport them inside to the blissful oasis of cool. Propping them against the inside wall, he took the first one in to the living room as Chelsea shut the screen and wooden door behind her.

They passed each other as he headed back to get the second box and she looked fresh as a freaking daisy with those flowers swinging around her thighs. She shot him a small smile and Aaron's fingers itched to slide up her arms to her neck, push into her hair and tilt her chin so he could kiss the hell out of her mouth.

Instead, he said, 'You know your electricity bill is going to be a shocker?' Because apparently he was determined to be Stick Up His Butt Guy today.

Either oblivious to his mood, or choosing to ignore it, Chelsea laughed as she crossed to where he'd put the first flat-pack on the floor near the boxes of books. 'Yeah. I do.' She crouched to inspect the pictures on the front. 'It makes me cringe thinking about my footprint every time I flick it on but…*ugh*…hopefully I'll be more acclimatised for next summer.'

Aaron's step faltered at her talk of next year, as though she might actually still be around, but he refused to give it, or the flare of hope it caused, any oxygen. A year was a long time in the dust, the heat and the flies for someone not used to any of it.

'Everyone acclimatises at a different rate,' he said noncommittally as he placed the second flat-pack on top of the first.

Some never did at all.

Even twenty years after leaving, his mother still re-called the heat of the Outback with a visible shudder.

Despite the sweat drying rapidly in the cool, a trickle ran from his hair down his temple and he wiped at it with the back of his forearm. 'Oh, God,' Chelsea said as she glanced up, catching the action. 'Sorry, you've been carrying heavy loads for me and it's roasting out there.'

'It's fine.'

'Nuh-uh.' She stood. 'Let me get you a cold drink.' Her arm lightly brushed his as she passed and he swore he heard her breath hitch before she continued on her way to the kitchen. 'I have water. Cold or tap. I also have juice if you'd prefer.'

Every instinct Aaron possessed told him to decline the drink and leave. *Just leave, dude.* But it didn't feel right, going without offering to put the flat pack to-gether, and in the end ingrained good manners won out.

'Cold water, please.' Because he *was* thirsty. And, if nothing else, it'd occupy his hands.

'Coming right up.' She turned to the cupboards on the wall opposite to the island bench.

Aaron tried—and failed—*not* to notice the swing of her skirt and the way the hem rose as she reached up and grabbed two glasses. Deliberately turning his at-tention to the flat packs, he crouched beside them, pull-ing out the box-cutter he'd stashed in the back pocket of his shorts. Just in case.

'Have you got an Allen key?' He had a bunch in the tool box in the back of his ute along with sundry other items that would probably be handy.

'Yeah, I bought a set of eight yesterday from the

hardware shop, because the seller said she'd lost the key that came with it.' He heard some clinking as her voice drew nearer. 'But it's okay, I'll be fine. You don't have to stay.' She nudged his shoulder. 'Here.'

Looking round, he took the frosty glass from her fingers, a vision of little purple flowers brushing against pale shapely thighs searing into his brain. 'Thanks,' he muttered before turning back immediately to the flat packs.

Aaron's heart bumped in his chest as he gulped down the water in several quick swallows, the icy cold an antidote to the heat licking through his veins and singeing his lungs.

'Thank you for delivering these,' Chelsea continued, clearly oblivious to his inner turmoil as she plonked herself cross-legged on the floor on the other side of the boxes, almost directly in front of him. 'But you're off home today, aren't you?'

Chelsea had come into the staff room yesterday when Aaron had been discussing heading to Curran Downs for his three days off. He didn't think she'd been listening as he and Brett had discussed the pros and cons of dogs versus drones in mustering.

'I can take it from here.' She held up her ring of Allen keys. 'Have tools, will construct.'

She spoke a good game but she was looking at them as though she wasn't sure which end she was supposed to use and Aaron couldn't suppress his chuckle, the tension in his gut and his neck easing a touch. 'I don't mean to call your furniture construction abilities into question but…do you know *how* to put together a flat pack?'

'No, but that's only because I've never tried. It can't

be any harder than setting up for ECMO in the ICU, or having to resuscitate a patient who's coded mid-flight, surely?'

Aaron couldn't fault her logic—those were complex and highly specialised medical procedures. 'Not harder, no, just a different kind of skill. Also.' He shrugged. 'Less life and death, so there's that.'

She barked out a laugh, her eyes crinkling and her lips parting, her head falling back a little, the fine escaped tendrils of her hair bushing the bare flesh between her shoulder blades. Aaron's heart went *thunk*. Then he joined her because, really, it *was* just a bloody book case, *not* life and death.

'I'm sure I'll be fine. Plus, I've seen this kind of thing being done loads on DIY shows.'

'You're right,' he conceded. 'It's not that hard once you know what you're doing.'

'There you go then. Plus, I have all day to figure it out. I'll just read the instructions thoroughly and take it one step at a time.'

'Ah, yeah…about that.' Aaron pressed his lips together so he wouldn't smile at her 'what now?' expression. 'The woman who lost the Allen key also couldn't find what she'd done with the instructions.'

She huffed out a sigh, her shoulders slumping as a V formed between her brows. 'No wonder it was so cheap.' But her defeat was only fleeting as she straightened her shoulders. 'Okay, well… I'll just… YouTube it.'

'*Or*, I can do it for you and you can be putting your books into your new bookshelf in an hour.'

Aaron wasn't sure why he was being so damned insistent. He told himself he was just being neighbourly, that he'd do the same for anyone. But he didn't think that was the truth. He just…didn't want to leave. Not yet.

'An hour, huh?'

'*About*. Might take me longer.' He shrugged. 'Might take me shorter.'

'Okay.' Chelsea nodded, looking at him assessingly. 'On one condition.'

'Oh, yeah.' He laughed. 'What's that?'

'I don't want you to do it for me. I want you to show me how to do it for myself.'

Aaron tried not to read between the lines of that statement, but he did wonder if Chelsea was so gung-ho to do it herself as a way to prove her independence. Maybe, he—*Dom*—had been the kind of guy who had done everything for Chelsea. Although, she'd mentioned he'd been deployed *a lot*, so that didn't sound practical. Nor did it sound like the highly competent woman he'd got to know these past couple of weeks.

But maybe carving out her independence was the first step in…*moving on*. Like up-sticking and coming to live on the other side of the planet had been. Because Aaron didn't believe that whole 'adventure' bullshit.

His idiotic heart leapt at the idea before his brain squashed the errant thought harder and faster than a bug on a windscreen. She might be inconveniently attracted to him—something that was entirely mutual—but she *was* holding back and, whether that was because she was still in love with her husband or too afraid to risk her heart again, it didn't end well for him.

It was stupid to feel so envious of a dead man, but Aaron realised he did. Not because he and Chelsea had

had a life together but because Dom had known her back before the terrible blow she'd been dealt.

When she hadn't needed to run away.

'If you really want to try and figure this out for yourself, I'm happy to get on my way.' He held up his hands in surrender.

Maybe this stupid book-case assembly *was* just what she needed.

'What?' She cocked a disbelieving eyebrow at him but a smile played on her mouth. 'Are you welching on your offer, Azza? You talked me into it and now you're backing out on the deal? You're sorry now you said an hour, aren't you? Afraid you talked yourself up a bit too much?'

Aaron grinned, assailed by an overwhelming urge to lean across and kiss that smile right off her mouth. He resisted, but only barely.

He laughed. 'Time me, *Chels*.'

CHAPTER SIX

'How do you know what goes where?'

Aaron glanced at Chelsea's perplexed face as they stood side by side, looking at all the pieces he'd laid out on the floor so he could see what was what. 'This isn't my first rodeo, you know.'

'It doesn't look enough. Is it enough?'

'Sure.'

'How do you know? All I see are a bunch of differing lengths of plank and a gazillion screws. With no instructions.'

He shrugged. 'I've grown up tinkering with things. All kinds of engines, running repairs on sheds and fences and water troughs and windmills and tanks and dams. It's just…what you do when you're in the middle of nowhere, with not a lot available and not a lot of money for new things or to hire someone to come and fix stuff. You learn to do things for yourself. To improvise and be resourceful—use what you have at hand.'

She nodded, her head turned slightly to look at him. 'So, you're a…jack of all trades?'

Aaron laughed, glancing at her. 'Something like that.'

She smiled at him then and he smiled back, and

Aaron was aware, once again, how close they were. For a second, he even let himself imagine he was free to lift one of those strands of hair off her neck and drop a kiss in its place. Then he gave himself a mental slap upside the head.

'Okay. Let's get this show on the road.'

It took an hour and fifteen minutes to assemble the two three-metre *faux* walnut bookshelves. Chelsea had been a keen apprentice who'd picked up the ropes quickly, even if those purple flowers had been distracting with a capital D. They stood back to admire their handiwork, which took up almost the entire back wall space.

'*That* is freaking awesome.' Chelsea nodded at it, clearly satisfied. 'How's that for team work?'

She held her hand up to him, clearly after a high five, and Aaron slapped his palm against hers. It felt buddy-like and platonic. Something two friends who'd just worked on a project together *would* do on its completion.

But it only made Aaron aware of how far he had to go until it felt *natural*.

'Not bad at all,' he confirmed.

She laughed. 'See? Shearing sheds and flatpacks—I'm totally kicking adventure arse.'

'Lady…' Aaron shook his head. 'Your definition of adventure su—'

'Needs work,' she cut in, folding her arms as she sent him a mock-stern look.

'Okay, sure.' It was Aaron's turn to laugh. 'Let's go with that.'

'Plus,' she said, bugging her eyes at him. 'I'm not a lady.'

True. Chelsea's plummy English accent reeked of class but she was no wilting flower. 'You only sound like one,' he said with a tone that sounded distinctly like banter.

'You think I should throw in a "crikey" or two and say things like—' she cleared her throat '—that's not a knife, this is a knife?'

Aaron really laughed then. 'Absolutely not.' She sounded as if she were Afrikaans, Kiwi and *drunk* all rolled into one.

'Laugh all you want, buddy boy,' she said with a grin. 'That's exactly how you sound.'

He shuddered. 'I bloody hope not.'

Her brown eyes shimmered with mirth. 'You *bloody do*,' she said, flattening her vowels and deepening her voice, clearly attempting to mimic him now.

Aaron groaned but then he laughed, and she joined him, and they did that for several long moments, just staring at each other and laughing, and Aaron couldn't remember when he'd last enjoyed himself this much with a woman.

Which was why he should leave.

'Well, anyway,' he said as their laughter settled and their eyes didn't seem to be able to unlock. 'I'll…get this rubbish out of your way and you can start loading up your books.'

'Thanks.' She dragged her eyes off him. 'That'd be great.'

Aaron gathered up all the detritus from the assembly and took it out to his ute before heading back inside to say goodbye, because it would be weird just to leave, even if it might be wiser not to put himself in the path of temptation again.

'Um…' Chelsea held up something as he entered the living room, frowning at him. 'Should this be left over?'

She was sitting on the floor surrounded by little piles of books, one of the six boxes open beside her. They were spread out on top of the bookcase, stacked around her on the floor and placed haphazardly here and there on the different shelves.

Aaron plucked the object out of her fingers. It was a screw. 'There's always some random screw left over.'

She quirked an eyebrow. 'If there'd been instructions would there be one left over?'

He grinned as he handed it back, deciding not to tell her that he probably wouldn't have paid more than cursory attention to the directions anyway. 'Of course. It's like the law of flatpacks.'

'The law, huh?'

'Sure. The unwritten kind.'

'Okay.' She laughed. 'As long as the bookcases aren't going to collapse like a house of cards one day, because there's going to be quite a lot of weight in them when I'm done.'

'So I see.' Aaron eyes moved over the multiple towers of books five or six high. And she'd only opened one box. 'I can't believe you have this many.'

'These aren't all.' She made a dismissive gesture with her hand. 'I have about twenty more back in Hackney.'

Aaron refused to read too much into the fact she hadn't brought all the books she professed to love so much and tried to wrap his head around just how many books Chelsea *did* own. 'Twenty?'

'Uh huh,' she said, as if it was the most natural thing in the world to own what must be *hundreds* of books.

'How'd these books make the cut to join you on your *adventures*?'

She smiled at his deliberate use of the word, and he had to look away unless he smiled too and then they'd be smiling at each other. *Again.* He picked up the nearest one off the top of its pile, one by Georgette Heyer. In fact, the whole stack was Heyer books.

Beside that stack was another consisting of classics in their iconic orange cover, and surrounding her on the floor were several piles of what appeared to romance novels, if the covers were anything to go by.

'These ones are my absolute favourites. They made the cut when I moved into Dom's parents' not long after he died. The other twenty are still in storage at a lock-up with all my other stuff.'

There was a lot in that sentence to unpack. Not least of which was, her life was still in boxes in the UK. Which was why he shouldn't be here, trying to be friends when he was just beginning to realise that might not be enough. Also…she'd moved in with her parents-in-law? 'You moved in with your…?'

'Mother-in-law.' She laughed. 'And my father-in-law. Yes.'

'That's…' He cast around for a word that wouldn't cause offence. After all, what did he know? He'd never had in-laws.

'Nutso?'

Aaron barked out a laugh at her candour. 'Well, no, but…it's not something you see a lot of, right?'

'No. And a lot of people thought it wasn't a good

idea. But…' Chelsea shrugged. 'I love his parents, we were all grieving and it made sense to be a comfort to each other.'

Her voice had taken on a plaintive quality as her gaze fixed on a point just over his shoulder. He wanted to ask about her parents—had they comforted her? But it felt too personal and she seemed too far away right now.

'It just…' Her gaze focused back on him. 'Worked.'

Which led to the next question. Maybe that was too personal as well, but she had at least opened this door. 'Did it stop working? Is that why you ended up here?'

Shaking her head slowly, she contemplated him for long moments, her eyes suddenly unbearably sad. 'No.' Her lips pressed together for a beat. 'It was…time.'

Caught up in the raw emotion in her gaze, Aaron nodded. 'When you know, you know, right?' Like his mother, who had drawn her line in the sand.

'Yeah.'

As if she realised she'd exposed too much of herself, Chelsea dropped her gaze to the book in her hand and Aaron, determined not to pry any further, reach for another too. He glanced at the well-loved illustrated cover of a girl, a pig and a spider weaving a web around the title.

'Charlotte's Web?' He opened the book. 'This yours?' A name had been written in faded pencil on the inside cover—*Deborah Tanner*.

Looking up at him again, Chelsea nodded with a wistful expression. 'It belonged to my mother, yeah.'

'This is her?' Aaron's thumb brushed over the pencil. 'Deborah?'

'Debbie.' Her gaze shifted to the book, to the way his thumb caressed the page. 'Her name was Debbie.'

Was. Aaron knew that look. He knew that tone. The weight of it, the bleakness of it. 'She died?'

'When I was four. Car accident.'

'I'm sorry.'

She roused herself, shaking her head. 'I don't really remember her. But I do remember her reading me this book.' She reached for it and Aaron passed it to her, watching as she opened it in her lap and absently flicked through the pages. 'I re-read it usually once a year. Cry every damn time,' she said, with a tiny self-deprecating laugh.

'It looks well-thumbed.'

'Yeah.' She nodded. 'It was well thumbed when she was reading it to me.'

'She was a reader as well?' Aaron was aware he was prying again and he wasn't sure if she wanted him to or if she was seconds away from shutting him down.

'Oh, yes.' Chelsea nodded but didn't look up from her lap. 'I think that's where I got it from.'

'Did your dad take over? After?'

She stared at the book for a long time before shaking her head. 'No. Dad...' She glanced up at him. 'My father...checked out for a lot of years after she died.'

Aaron tried to read between the lines of her carefully chosen words. 'He...gave you up?'

'No.' The loose tendrils of her hair swished against her neck as she shook her head. 'I mean, he provided for me. He went to work, earned a living. I had all the things I needed for school and hobbies and university. I wasn't...neglected.'

'Physically.' But *emotionally*...?

'Yeah.' She nodded as if in acknowledgement of what he *hadn't* said. 'That was all he was capable of, really. His grief was...all-consuming. It was enough for him to just put one foot in front of the other most days, you know?'

Aaron nodded. 'Yeah. I know.' His mother hadn't died but they had lost her nonetheless, and his father had certainly grieved in the only way men of his generation from land knew how to do—stoically. Ironically, he and his sister had the drought to thank for holding their father back from a much darker state, with the station and the sheep demanding every last skerrick of his attention.

It could have been very different.

'Having me there probably kept him back from the abyss but I was also an...intrusion in a lot of ways. Which was why reading was so good. I could do it quietly and not be too much of a bother.'

God... Aaron's heart broke for her. She'd been a kid who'd lost her mother. *And* her father, by the sound of it. But she had still felt the need to make herself small— to not be a *bother*. He crouched then without giving the action or how much closer it brought him any thought.

'I'm so sorry,' he said, their eyes meeting now they were on the same level.

She shrugged. 'It is was a long time ago.'

'Did he...is he...?'

Brightening, she closed the book. 'He remarried, when I was in uni. They live in Spain now. I've visited a few times. I'm happy for them. She makes him smile and he deserves to find love again.'

'But?' Aaron definitely detected a *but*.

'Our relationship is…stilted.'

Aaron wasn't surprised, with all that emotional distance her father had laid down. His dad had grieved the break-up of his marriage deeply, and it had toughened him even more, but he hadn't shut his children out. In his own way, he'd pulled them closer. 'I imagine it would be,' he murmured, because he didn't know what else to say.

Trite platitudes about it taking time weren't his style or what she needed.

She shot him a sad, grateful smile, her eyes shimmering with emotion that lurked in the still, brown depths, and Aaron wished he could draw her into his arms and just sit with her in that weird solidarity that came when two people understood intimately what it was to experience loss.

'Anyway.' She gave herself a shake, dropping her gaze to her lap. 'Sorry, I'm prattling on.' Lifting her eyes again, it was as if a veil had come down on the simmer of emotions. 'You have to get going.'

Aaron contemplated telling her she didn't have to pretend she was okay with him, but that felt really personal when she'd been here for two and a half weeks and her life was in boxes back in the UK.

So he stood instead. 'Yeah. My sister's probably already smack-talking about me to the jackaroos. Last time I was late, she told them I was getting a pedicure.'

Her laughter broke the strange tension that had sprung between them. 'Thanks,' she said, looking up at him again. 'For everything.'

Aaron nodded, knowing it wasn't just about the bookcases. 'See you next week.'

Before Chelsea knew it, they were in the last days of November and she'd been part of the OA team for a month. And she *loved* it! Something she announced to Aaron as the plane taxied to a halt back at the base at four o'clock on Thursday afternoon after they'd finished up at a remote health clinic a couple of hundred kilometres west of Balanora.

Unlike the first couple of weeks, they'd worked together a lot this past fortnight—about seventy-five percent of the time—and familiarity had bred *content* as their rapport had developed. She'd been worried about how they would go, given her pulse still did a crazy tap dance every time she saw him, but it seemed that enforced proximity had helped to dull her reaction.

Or at least normalise it. Allow her to put it in perspective. She found him attractive. He found her attractive. It didn't mean *anything* unless they acted upon it. Which meant *they* had the power.

'Love, huh?'

'Yes.' She nodded enthusiastically as she hung up her earphones on the hook and unbuckled. 'The remote clinics remind me why I wanted to be a nurse in the first place.'

He laughed, his hands sliding absently to each end of the stethoscope he had looped around his neck. 'Even with the heat and the flies?'

'Yes.' She hadn't uttered *bloody flies* yet but it had almost slipped out many times. 'What we do out here feels so much more important than what I was doing back home. Let's face it, if you're anywhere near a city or even a town, help—good professional, medical help—is usually not that far away. But out here? We're it. And that means something. I actually feel like I make a difference out here, a real difference.'

'You know you're preaching to the choir, darlin',' Hattie said from behind.

'Amen,' Aaron agreed, his eyes twinkling.

'Yeah, yeah.' Chelsea laughed at herself but the glow of satisfaction inside her chest was too big to suppress. 'It was just a really good day out there, wasn't it?'

There'd been nothing particularly complicated medically—immunisations, wound management, suture removal, baby checks and diabetes management—run of the mill stuff. Their bread and butter. But the fact the forty people at the clinic didn't have to drive over three hours into town and three hours back on dirt roads for basic care, and the *appreciation* that had been evident, had given her a real high.

'It was.' He nodded in acknowledgment. 'It was a good day.'

Then they were smiling at each other, which felt good too. The hitch in her pulse be damned.

Chelsea was still buoyed an hour later as she restocked the plane. Being in the cool haven of the store room helped, so did her run of three days off stretching ahead. She—*and* Aaron—were on call tonight but that ended at eight a.m. and her days off officially started. Best of all, in the afternoon, Aaron was going to pick her up and take her out to Curran Downs so she could watch the shearing that had started yesterday.

And she was *really* excited about that.

When she entered the front office after the restocking was done, Charmaine and Aaron were debating something at the comms desk. He gestured her over.

'We can't wait for Ju-Ju,' he said to Charmaine as Chelsea approached. 'They're too far out. I'll be fine.'

She shook her head. 'You know them.'

'I know eighty-five percent of the people we see out here, Charmaine.'

'It's Kath. And Dammo. He's one of your oldest friends. They're not just *people*.' Charmaine turned to Chelsea. 'Kath's membranes ruptured and she's gone into premature labour. It's her third pregnancy, a girl. She's twenty-six weeks.'

Bloody hell. Chelsea had hoped she'd get to deliver an Outback baby but not like this.

'She's had an unremarkable antenatal history,' Charmaine continued, 'And both previous children were born at term.'

Chelsea nodded, her midwifery brain rattling through myriad possibilities of how things could go wrong in the middle of nowhere with a very premature baby. On the other hand, the baby could be delivered with no complications at all, or not be born for hours yet, allowing Kath to be safely ensconced in a primary care hospital.

'Her two previous labours were fast,' Aaron added. 'First was two hours. Second was less than an hour on the side of the highway about ten kilometres from town.'

Okay, so maybe time wasn't on their side. 'How far out are they?' she asked.

'Another hundred kilometres west of where we were today,' Aaron supplied.

'It'll take about half an hour in the jet,' Charmaine added.

'Okay.' The jet was fully equipped with a special-ised neonatal transport cot that was practically a mini NICU with multiple monitoring devices, pumps and a transport ventilator set up for every eventuality.

'The neonatal team is being dispatched from Bris-bane but they're two hours away.'

'Right.' Chelsea threw her bag under the table. 'So we need to go and get Kath.'

'Yes.' Aaron nodded emphatically. 'ASAP. We can get there quicker than Ju-Ju, and the jet is here, ready to go.'

'I know, Aaron. But…are you prepared for a situa-tion where the baby might die out there? A twenty-six-weeker could go either way, you know that. What if she's born not breathing and needs resus and dies any-way, while Dammo is yelling and begging and pleading with you to do something, *anything*, to save her? Are you ready for that? Can you deal with it?'

Chelsea watched the slight bob of Aaron's throat, the angle of his jaw blanching white. Premature labour was always high stakes but, if the couple involved were good friends, everything became personal. He nodded, a grim kind of determination emphasising the battered plains of his face.

'If the worst happens, Dammo's going to need me more than ever. Even if it's someone to yell at.'

Charmaine glanced at Chelsea. She was obviously torn between looking out for her team and knowing that time was of the essence. She seemed to be asking Chelsea if she was capable not just of dealing with baby delivery but any raw emotional fallout on an airstrip in the middle of nowhere. Chelsea was no stranger to high emotion in critical situations and, despite having known Aaron for only a month, their connection—acknowledged or not—was such that she felt she could give a slight nod.

'Okay.' Charmaine sighed. 'Fine. But keep me up to date.'

Aaron didn't need to be told twice as he turned to Chelsea. 'Let's go.'

'I can see the vehicle headlights,' Aaron said, his nose plastered to the window. He'd been staring out since the plane had taken off, as if he could will it to their destination faster.

Dammo and Kath had been racing to the airstrip while the plane had been en route and had arrived ten minutes ago. The message from the ground via comms was that Kath's contractions were coming very fast now, which probably meant the baby's arrival was imminent.

While Aaron's leg jiggled and his fingers tapped on his knee, Chelsea went over and over the potential scenarios. They'd set everything up before take-off—the warmer was on in the transport cot and all the appropriate medication had been drawn up and labelled—but preparing mentally for all contingencies was just as important.

'Touchdown in two minutes,' Hattie's calm voice announced in her ears.

The plane banked left and a hit of adrenaline surged

into Chelsea's system. She changed channels on her headphone and gestured for Aaron to follow suit. 'You going to be okay?'

'Yes.' His response was curt, his expression intense.

'We have everything ready… We're prepared.'

'Yep.' He nodded but he was less curt this time. 'How many prems have you delivered?'

Chelsea smiled. 'More than I can count on my fingers and toes. And I've assisted in heaps more prem intubations.'

'Good.' He let out a slow breath. 'Don't really get many out here, so it's been a while for me.'

'Don't worry,' she said, a light tease in her voice. 'It's just like a riding a bicycle.'

He gave her a grudging smile as the plane made a bumpy touchdown.

They taxied to the siding and within five minutes Chelsea and Aaron were striding into the heat of an Outback afternoon, nothing but scraggly bush, occasional trees and red dirt beyond the strip for miles and miles. The sound of a woman crying out broke the almost eerie hush, followed by a frantic male voice coming from the vehicle, urging them over.

'Hurry, Aaron. *Hurry!*'

Aaron made it to the back seat of the vehicle where all the action was happening, just ahead of Chelsea. 'Jesus, Kath,' she heard him say. 'You always did like to be the centre of attention.'

Chelsea heard a huffed out laugh but she also heard pain and panic. 'It's too soon,' Kath said, her voice wobbling.

'It's fine,' Aaron assured her. 'We have all the bells

and whistles and we're going to get you back to Balanora in a jiffy.'

The calm authority in his voice was just what the
situation needed as Chelsea manoeuvred in front of
Aaron. 'Hi, Kath, I'm Chelsea.' The labouring woman
was half-reclined on the bench seat, supported from
behind by a man Chelsea assumed was Dammo. He'd
obviously come straight from the paddock, his clothes
streaked with dirt and all kinds of stains, and he looked
as frantic and helpless as he had sounded.

'Chelsea's a midwife, Kath. And she worked in the
NICU for years, so you're in very good hands.'

Slipping into a pair of gloves, Chelsea smiled into
the anxious eyes of the panting, sweaty-faced woman.
Even with every door open, it was stifling inside the car.
'Do you mind if I have a look and see where you're at?'

Too tired to talk, Kath just nodded. Luckily, she was
wearing a skirt and top, which made easing her underwear off much easier, but it was immediately apparent
that Chelsea wouldn't need to do an internal examination or use the small hand-held Doppler unit she had
stashed in her pocket for listening to the heartbeat. The
head was on its way and it wouldn't be long before it
crowned.

Whatever state the baby was in, it was coming very,
very soon.

'Right.' She patted Kath on the leg. 'Baby's almost
here. We need to get you in the plane.'

Just then a contraction cramped through Kath's body
and she screwed her face up, clutching at the edge of
the seat and groaning, forcing herself to exhale against
her body's natural urge to bear down.

Aaron looked at his mate when it passed. 'Pick her up, bring her to the jet and I'll take her at the door.'

Once Kath was settled on the stretcher in the plane, it was action stations. Dammo was at her head and Chelsea at the business end. Aaron checked the suction one more time and put a fine catheter next to Chelsea's hand to use as soon as the baby was born, to clear the airway.

'Kath,' Aaron said. 'I'm going to pop in an IV while you do your thing, okay?'

The woman nodded as he inspected her closest hand, a cannular at the ready. He had it in within seconds and, by the time it was secured, the baby was crowning and then it was born. She was tiny—but bigger than Chelsea had expected—and a bit floppy, but perfect.

'Is she okay?' Kath asked as she pushed herself up onto her elbows to inspect what was happening between her legs. 'Is she breathing?'

'One sec.'

Chelsea could vaguely hear Kath starting to sob and Dammo asking Aaron what was going on, but her entire focus was on the tiny new-born as she sucked the airway, clearing mucous from the baby's nose and mouth.

She was about to ask for a towel as Aaron said, 'Here,' passing one of the several that had been warming in the transport cot.

Taking it, Chelsea rubbed the baby vigorously—her face and her back—to stimulate breathing. She knew it might not happen, and that she didn't have long before she'd have to hand the baby to Aaron for more potentially drastic measures, but she'd done this often enough to know to start with the basics.

'*C'mon, baby,*' she whispered as she rubbed. '*C'mon.*'

When the baby took her first gurgling gasp a few seconds later, blinking up at Chelsea, it was the best damned noise she'd ever heard.

'Was that her?' Kath asked, hopefulness rising like a tide in her voice.

'Sure was.' Aaron grinned.

'She's breathing,' Dammo said, his voice tremulous.

'Like a champ,' Aaron confirmed as he handed another warm towel to Chelsea and a tiny pink knitted hat, which she promptly put on, feeling the fontanelles as she did so.

'Bloody hell, mate.' Dammo huffed out a strangled laugh. 'That was the longest thirty seconds of my life.'

Chelsea knew exactly how he felt—time always slowed the longer it took to hear that first new-born wail.

'Hello there, baby girl,' Chelsea crooned at the tiny baby, face screwed up and fully yelling her displeasure now at her rude early delivery. 'Happy birthday. Let's get you some skin-on-skin with your mummy, hey?'

The practice was routine nowadays, but even more vital for premature babies for warmth, protection against infection and to decrease stress levels on a system thrust into the outside world well before it was ready. It obviously wasn't possible for premature babies requiring immediate invasive therapy but, for this bawling little madam, most definitely.

Ordinarily Chelsea would have asked the father if he wanted to cut the cord, but the space was cramped enough, so she quickly clamped and cut before glancing at Aaron. 'Can you do the honours while I finish here?'

Manoeuvring from behind Chelsea, Aaron gently

scooped the baby up into hands that were slightly bigger than she was. Inching along the side of the stretcher, he said, 'Kath, I've never seen your boobs before, but I have seen you in a bikini, so let's just pretend we're at the river, okay?'

Kath gave a half-laugh. 'Considering you've seen worse than my boobs today, let's just make a pact that what happens in the plane stays in the plane.'

'Deal.' Aaron grimed. 'Dammo, you want to help lift her shirt so I can slide this little one up under?'

Levering up onto her elbows again, Kath made space for Dammo to pull her T-shirt up at the back as she gathered it up at the front with her non-cannular hand. Aaron gently laid the still squalling infant high up on Kath's chest, her tiny, naked front pressed to her mother's décolletage as he pulled the T-shirt down so the baby's body was fully covered, leaving just her head to stick out through the neck hole of the shirt.

Chelsea, waiting for the birth of the placenta, was only vaguely aware of Aaron adding a couple of warm blankets over the top of the shirt and the sudden, rapid *blip-blip-blip* of the monitor as he connected the saturation probe. Subliminally, she registered that the heart rate was where it should be.

By the time the placenta was delivered, the baby had quietened and Aaron was satisfied with all the vitals—Kath's included. Considering the number of ways it *could* have gone wrong out here in the extreme Outback, the outcome had been spectacular.

The baby—Yolanda—would still need to be transported to Brisbane for a whole battery of health checks and observations, and would probably stay until she

had reached a good weight, but the signs were looking encouraging. Sometimes, of course, premature babies that did well initially could deteriorate and require
varying levels of support in the hours and days that followed, which was another good reason to get her to a
tertiary hospital.

Within half an hour of Yolanda's birth, they were
taking off again, the newest addition to the Balanora
district still snuggled skin-to-skin with her mother, her
heart beat pinging reassuringly over the background
hum of the cabin. Dammo was in the seat behind the
stretcher, leaning forward, his chin tucked in next to
Kath's temple as they admired their baby girl.

Chelsea was at the foot of the stretcher facing Kath
and the monitor and Aaron was in his usual seat, diagonally opposite and directly across the narrow aisle
from his mate. But he wasn't looking out of the window
any more, he was looking at Chelsea, grinning at her,
clearly thrilled with their accomplishment.

As was she, feeling the solidarity of the moment
acutely.

Feeling it, and *other* things, in the hitch of her breath,
the loop of her stomach, the kick in her pulse. Feeling it
in the ache of her face as she grinned right back.

CHAPTER SEVEN

CHELSEA WAS STILL feeling the high from last night when Aaron picked her up the next day after lunch for their trip to Currans Downs. She definitely felt it when she climbed in the cab of his blessedly cool ute and he said, 'Hey.'

His hair was all tousled around his head, as if he'd just shoved his fingers through it this morning and called it done, and his face creased into a smile of welcome. He was all relaxed and loose, and looked perfectly at home in the ute, his Akubra—almost as battered as his face—stashed on the dashboard.

It wasn't that he didn't look relaxed and loose at work, but it was different, and she wasn't sure she'd get used to the contrast between the laidback flight doctor with the stethoscope slung around his neck and the weekend sheep farmer in work shorts, sturdy boots and a flannel shirt rolled up to his elbows. They were both a sight to behold, but the guy in the ute had an ease about him that was overwhelmingly masculine.

And that connection from last night fizzed anew.

'Hi.'

'You ready for a day of roustabouting?'

Chelsea laughed. She had no clue what it was but she was in. 'Bring it on, buddy.' If only calling him *buddy* would make those acute feelings of connection disappear.

'Dammo rang this morning,' he said as they headed on the highway out of town.

'Yeah?' She'd been wondering how things had gone after they'd transferred all three occupants to the Brisbane jet that had been waiting on the tarmac for them when they'd got to base. She glanced at his profile. 'How's Yolanda doing? And Kath?'

'They're doing well.' He kept his eyes on the road. 'Going like a trooper, apparently. Her condition has remained stable. They inserted a nasogastric tube, because she's not strong enough yet to suck adequately or for very long periods of time, but hopefully she'll stack on some weight quickly and be able to feed properly before too much longer.'

Chelsea nodded. The benefits of breastfeeding increased exponentially with premature babies. 'Did they say what her weight was?'

'Nine hundred and fifty-two grams.'

'Wow.' She laughed out loud. 'Nearly a kilo. I thought she looked a decent size for a twenty-six-weeker. No wonder she coped well with her early outing.'

'Yep, it certainly helped.'

'They were lucky, though.' Chelsea returned her gaze to the windscreen and the haze of heat rising up ahead. The long, arrow-straight road seemed to disappear into the shimmering distance. 'If she'd been smaller, if there'd been something inherently wrong causing the premature labour, if she'd needed reviving, it could have been really hairy.'

'God, I know. I gave myself nightmares thinking of all the possibilities last night.'

Chelsea smiled as the pocket in the back of her knee-length denim shorts buzzed and she remembered she'd stashed her phone there as she'd left the house. Leaning forward, she reached behind to grab it, conscious suddenly that Aaron's gazed skimmed the dip of her back and the rise of her buttocks before returning his attention to the road.

Her nipples prickled against the fabric of her bra and, befuddled, she had to tap in her code twice. A text alert sat on the bottom of the screen. From Francesca. She almost didn't answer it until Aaron said, 'That was lucky. Won't be long before the signal runs out.'

And then Chelsea *had* to look, just in case it was something important. Francesca's texting had settled after those first few days and she didn't like to let them go unanswered for too long.

Chelsea opened the text and immediately wished she hadn't as a picture of Alfie appeared on the screen. So like Dom. Dom's dark eyes, fringed with Dom's long, dark eyelashes, smiling Dom's irreverent smile into the camera. It kicked her in the chest as per usual.

Alfie says hi.

She couldn't do anything for long moments, just stare at the picture. It had been so good this past month, not having a constant reminder of Alfie around. After the high of last night, it brought her back to earth with a thud.

Aaron's, 'Cute kid,' broke her out of her funk. 'That a nephew? Or a friend's child?'

Chelsea stared so hard at the picture, her eyes almost watered. 'No.' She shook her head. 'It's Dom's son.'

'Oh. I…didn't know he had a child.'

Chelsea could hear the frown in his voice as well as the hesitancy as she looked up from the phone screen and met his soft gaze. 'I didn't either until a year ago.'

Glancing back at the road, he didn't say anything for a beat or two. 'How old is he?'

'Almost four.'

More silence but, studying his profile as she was, Chelsea could practically see his mental arithmetic. A man who'd been dead for three years had a four-year-old son his widow didn't know about. 'Okay, that…'

He halted, as if thinking better of what he was going to say, his lips pressing together. But Chelsea wanted to know. 'What?'

'It's fine.' He shook his head. 'It's not my business. You don't have to talk about it.'

Chelsea had no idea why she'd told him. But Francesca killing her buzz had stirred up feelings that had receded since she'd arrived and she realised she *did* want to talk—finally.

She hadn't talked to anyone about the impact of Alfie, because she knew no one who hadn't also known Dom and hadn't been touched by his death. So she'd just locked it all down. But suddenly it felt too big to ignore.

And Aaron, it seemed, was her confessional. She'd already told him stuff about her mum and dad that she'd never told another living soul. What was one more steaming chunk of emotional baggage from Chelsea's past?

Maybe it was because of how removed Aaron was. Maybe it was because she knew he understood what it was like to not feel *enough*. Maybe there was another reason she didn't want to examine too closely. All Chelsea knew was she *wanted* to tell him.

'I'm okay to talk about it.'

He flicked a glance at her, as if to check she actually meant it. Their eyes met briefly and she saw the nanosecond he understood she *was* okay. Looking back at the road, he said, 'So Dom…'

His voice drifted off and Chelsea could tell he was trying to find a word that was palatable. 'Cheated on me?' Chelsea raised both her eyebrows. 'Yes.'

His knuckles tightened around the steering wheel. 'With Alfie's mother.'

'Amongst others, yes.'

Shooting her a quick alarmed look, he said, *'Others?'*

'Yeah.' She turned her gaze back to the endless road in front of them and the even more endless paddocks of stubbly grass and occasional flocks of scraggly sheep. 'He'd been dead for eight months when I learned about Shari. She was the first one. Via email.'

Aaron winced. 'Bloody hell.'

Yep. 'She'd been going through the AA steps and had got to the making amends part. She decided that she'd wronged me by sleeping with my husband while he was in Afghanistan and she had to confess to move on.'

'That was *nice* of her.'

Chelsea gave a half-laugh at the sarcasm in his voice.

'I confronted Vinnie about it. That's Dom's brother. They served in the same unit so they always deployed together. He denied that Dom had ever been unfaithful. He said that Shari, who worked for the British embassy in Kabul, was known for her dalliances with anything in a uniform, and that Dom had rebuffed her several times, which had left her bitter. He begged me not to tell Francesca, their mother.'

'You believed him?'

'Yes.' She nodded slowly. 'Ninety-five percent. But it niggled, you know?'

'Uh-huh.'

'Then, a year ago, Krystal turned up on our doorstep in Hackney with Alfie. She'd been a nanny for a British official in Kandahar. Dom apparently didn't know she'd had his child.'

'So why did she suddenly decide to turn up out of the blue like that?'

'Her life circumstances had changed and she'd fallen on hard times, and was at her wits' end with nowhere else to go. Vinnie was angry, denying Alfie could be Dom's kid, and Francesca was equally adamant, and they insisted on a DNA test but… I didn't need one.'

'You knew?' He glanced across at her.

'No. Well…' Chelsea huffed out a laugh. 'Yes, I guess I did. That five percent of me did. But Alfie is the *spitting image* of Dom. I don't know how his family could look at that little boy and possibly deny it. So there was *zero* doubt in my mind.'

'What happened then?'

'The DNA test came back positive—of course— and I confronted Vinnie again, said it was time to stop protecting Dom and that I needed to know the truth. About all his women. Because part of me knew there'd be more. I don't know why I wanted to know. I mean, what good could it possibly do? I'm pretty sure Vinnie felt the same but I *needed* to know.'

'I get that.'

'He blustered around a bit at first. I don't blame him for trying to protect his brother. He was there when Dom died and I know he suffers from terrible survivor guilt. But I was in such a fury at that point that I threatened to tell Francesca about the email from two years ago and he came clean.'

'And there *were* others.'

'Yes. Apparently, the man I loved, and worried about dying over there every single, waking second of the day, was a bit of a man whore when he was deployed.'

'Oh God, Chelsea.' He looked away from the road for a beat or two. 'I am so sorry.'

His gaze was brief before switching back to the road again but it was intense, radiating empathy. The look she'd seen many times these past weeks as Aaron had interacted with patients.

'Vinnie tried to explain the mentality of being deployed in a war zone. How having to confront your own mortality day after day often led to fatalistic behaviour. Living each day like it was your last. Dom loved me, he said, and his liaisons weren't about love, they were about sex.'

'Did it help?'

Chelsea gave a harsh laugh. 'Not really.'

'You must be pretty angry with him.'

She was about to say she was furious but, actually,

she wasn't sure she was any more. Not like she had been. She was just…sad. 'I was.'

'I guess it's hard to mourn someone, to love someone, when they hurt you so deeply.'

'I don't love him.'

Chelsea blinked. It was the first time she'd said it out loud. Her instinct to take it back was strong but she pressed her lips together tight. She glanced across at Aaron, who didn't appear to be horrified by her disloyalty to her dead husband, or annoyed that she'd let him think otherwise that day in the store room when she'd not refuted it.

'I mean… I'm not *in* love with him any more. There's part of me that will always love him. Dom was a massive part of my life for many years but…however he justified it to himself, however much I understand how Vinnie justifies it… Dom betrayed me and our vows and the things I held most sacred. And that just…killed off any deep feelings I had for him. Snuffed them right out.'

A slight rise in the road levelled out to reveal three large red kangaroos up ahead, sitting in the middle of the road. They were far enough away for Aaron to slow, which he did, but the sight never failed to thrill Chelsea. If ever she temporarily forgot she was in a vastly different land, the appearance of kangaroos always brought her back to reality. She'd seen a lot out here, both hopping through paddocks as planes landed or stinking everything up as road kill, but she didn't think she'd ever get used to the sight of the strange, quirky creatures.

They hopped away before the ute even got close and Aaron accelerated away again. He hadn't said anything about her declaration and she wondered if she'd shocked him. Sighing, she rolled her head to one side to study his profile.

'I suppose that makes me a terrible person,' she murmured, not wanting to leave their conversation dangling.

'No longer being in love with the man who repeatedly cheated on you?' Aaron shook his head as he glanced across at her. 'I'd say it makes you human.'

If there could possibly have been a right answer to her question, Aaron had nailed it, and the niggling sense of guilt Chelsea too often felt over her conflicted feelings eased back.

'Who sent it to you? The picture. Are you…in contact with Alfie's mother?'

'No.' Chelsea sighed again. 'Francesca sent it.'

'Your *mother-in-law* sent you a picture of the child your *husband* had with *another* woman?'

Chelsea almost laughed at the streak of disbelief in Aaron's voice. It did sound kind of unbelievable when spoken out loud. 'Alfie and Krystal lived with us for four months until she got back on her feet.'

'*What?*'

She did laugh this time. 'Yeah. I know. It seems bizarre, but Francesca and Roberto had their first grandchild from their dead son, and they weren't about to turn her or him away.'

'Wasn't that hard?'

'Oh, yes.' Chelsea nodded, fixing her gaze on the ever-present heat shimmer ahead. 'Very much so. Dom and I… We had two miscarriages after we'd been married for a few years. The first pregnancy was an accident but the second was planned. When we lost that one too, we decided to give it a rest. Dom was about to be deployed again and we talked about leaving it until after he got out of the military.'

It was hard to keep the emotion of those years out of her voice so Chelsea didn't even try. It had been a long time, but sometimes the searing loss of that period returned with a roaring vengeance.

'So, yeah…' She came out of her reverie, turning her head to focus on Aaron. 'Having to look at a kid that was a replica of Dom, a child that *I* couldn't give him, was hard. Living with the woman who had slept with my husband was hard. Thankfully Krystal got back on her feet and moved out but Francesca and Roberto look after Alfie in the afternoons so she can work, and he usually stays over one night on the weekend.'

'Bloody hell. Do they understand how hard that must be for you?'

'No. They don't see Dom's infidelity when they look at Alfie. They just see… Dom. And they think that I'll love Alfie too because I love Dom—*loved* Dom—and he's Dom's, therefore…' Chelsea shook her head at the convoluted but understandable logic. 'And I do love him. He's a sweet, *sweet* boy, who wormed his way into all our hearts, and none of this is his fault. But…well, let's just say, it's been nice to get away from all that.'

'I bet.' Aaron shook his head. 'Why don't you ask her to stop sending you pictures?'

'Because she's trying to keep me connected and because he's her grandson and she adores him. And she doesn't know that it hurts because I've never told her. She doesn't know the extent of Dom's liaisons. She thinks that Krystal was a one-off. And that I've forgiven him because he's dead. And I'm not going to be the one to tell her that it wasn't, and I haven't, because it'll break her heart and it's already been broken enough.'

Chelsea knew how it felt to lose two babies at a point where neither were much more than a collection of cells. She couldn't begin to image the pain of losing a child who had been a part of your life for over three decades.

'So you just…suck it up. Even though it hurts?'

God, he made her sound like some kind of martyr. It didn't sit comfortably, but it was what it was. 'Yeah.'

Aaron glanced at her incredulously. 'Why?'

'Because sometimes we lie to people we love to protect them, even if it makes us feel bad.'

'Yeah but…' He turned his attention back to the road. 'Isn't it okay to put yourself first at some point?'

'Sure.' And she'd done that. 'It's why I moved here.'

'So…' He slid her another look. 'You *are* running away.'

Chelsea smiled. 'I prefer to think of it as starting over.' She quirked an eyebrow. 'Surely that can be added to your list of reasons people come out here?'

He nodded slowly. 'Yeah. Okay. Consider the list updated.'

She laughed then, and the heaviness that had descended in the cabin lifted. Up ahead, a sign announced a road off to the left, and Aaron slowed the ute and indicated.

'Hold on to your hat,' he said as the car slowed. 'The road gets kinda bumpy from here in out.'

After several hours in the heat of the sheering shed, the stifling air thick with the earthy aromas of lanolin, sheep droppings and sweat, Chelsea's admiration for

Aaron and anyone trying to make a living off the land out here grew exponentially. The fact that he was busily striding around in those boots, those shorts, that hat and just a navy singlet now, after discarding his flannel shirt, didn't hurt.

Rock music pumped through rusty old speakers mounted in the corners of the shed as he cajoled sheep and whistled at dogs and flapped away the ever-present flies and lifted fleece, spreading it out on the wool table to class it then toss it in the presser. He was everywhere and Chelsea could barely keep up as he explained and demonstrated and encouraged her to get dirty.

If she hadn't been heavily in lust with him already, she was now.

Although, it was more than just those sun-kissed muscles straining and bending and stretching and contracting and *sweating*. It was the way he laughed and joked with the shearers, as though they'd known him all his life, and the way he teased his sister, who was also bustling around, yet clearly deferred to her, and the respect he showed his father, while bantering with him about getting old and retiring.

He was clearly as at home here, a broom in his hand, as he was in the belly of a King Air, a stethoscope around his neck, and Chelsea's heart skipped so many beats over the course of the afternoon she started to worry she was developing a condition.

Just before knock-off time, the four-shearer team members—who had already sheared over two hundred sheep each—plus Aaron and his sister had a friendly race to see who could shear the fastest. Mostyn Vincent, sporting the same lived-in kind of face as his son, pulled a stopwatch out of his back pocket as if it was a common occurrence during shearing time and, with all six of them hunched over a sheep, called, *'Go!'*

Chelsea watched as the electrical hum of shears and the hands and legs and instruments all worked in tandem to methodically strip off the fleece in one piece. All four of the pros finished within a few seconds of each other. Aaron and Tracey brought up the rear several minutes later, with Tracey just pipping her brother to the post.

'Now who's the old man?' Mostyn crowed.

Aaron laughed as he finished off the sheep and came up for a high-five from his sister.

'It's those soft hands,' Ed, the team boss, said which earned more laughs all round.

'You want a go?' Aaron asked, his eyes meeting hers.

Chelsea blinked. 'Me?'

'Sure.' He grinned at her as he swiped a muscular forearm over his sweaty brow. 'I'll teach you.'

She glanced at the faces around her to see if this was some kind of set-up. 'Um…'

Before she could get any more out, Ed made *bok-bok-bok* noises and she rolled her eyes at him, which earned her a hoot of laughter. 'What if I…cut the sheep?'

'You won't. I'll be right beside you,' Aaron assured her. 'Where's your sense of adventure?'

Chelsea narrowed her eyes at him but he grinned and she said, 'Okay, fine.'

Before she could blink, she was being ushered to a shearing station as Ed went and got her a sheep. 'Here you are, English, got you a nice docile one.'

The guys on the team had been teasing her all afternoon about her accent and Chelsea laughed as the sheep was positioned between her legs. It felt hot and heavy against her thighs, but there was little time to register that as Aaron turned on the shears and started talking her through the steps.

The shears felt weighty and foreign in her hands and they vibrated like crazy as Chelsea hunched over the sheep and made her first pass on the finer belly fleece as instructed. A little black fly buzzed around the sweat forming on her upper lip and she blew at it, but it was still less distracting then Aaron, who was also hunched over, his body close to hers, his mouth close to her ear so she could hear his pointers.

Even though they were being watched by six other people, it felt as if it were just the two of them. The deep husk of his voice, the warmth of his breath fluffing the flyaway wisps of hair plastered to her neck, the way he occasionally leaned closer, helping her manoeuvre the sheep or showing her how to angle the shears, felt strangely intimate.

Concentrating hard on what she was doing so she didn't nick the poor sheep, she wasn't even aware that she'd muttered, 'Bloody flies,' as she blew another one—or maybe it was the same one—away.

Aaron's warm chuckle drifted down her neck. 'I heard that, *English*, but don't worry, your secret is safe with me.'

Chelsea actually shivered, despite the heat, her concentration officially shot. Standing, she clicked off the shears and stretched out her back. It had been a physically demanding afternoon and she could already feel a niggle in her lumbar area from just a few minutes hunched over.

'Okay, I'm calling it,' she said. 'This is not for the faint of heart.'

Ed grinned. 'Step aside, English, let me show you how it's done.'

Chelsea and Aaron moved over to where Tracey and Mostyn stood and left Ed to it. 'You okay?' he asked.

'Yep.' She nodded. 'I have a feeling I'm going to be sore tomorrow, though.'

'Oh, trust me,' Tracey said. 'You're going to have aches and pains in places you never knew you had muscles.'

'Hey,' Aaron mock-protested. 'Way to kill the adventure buzz.'

Tracey grinned. 'You want to come up to the homestead and take a bath?' she asked Chelsea. 'Get out of those sweaty clothes before dinner?'

'Or,' Aaron suggested, 'She could have an open-air shower at the shearers' digs.'

Chelsea glanced at Tracey who almost imperceptibly shook her head before saying, 'Yeah, tough choice. A long, deep soak for aching bones and muscles with a luxury bath bomb and divine-smelling soap and shampoo… Or a cold shower in a hessian-wrapped cubicle from a bag hanging off a tree branch, a bunch of rowdy blokes nearby belly-aching at you to finish up, and the birdlife dive-bombing you.'

Aaron laughed. 'That only happened to you once.'

What? She might be all about the adventure but bird attack whilst showering did not appeal. Chelsea glanced at Tracey. 'Thanks. A bath sounds lovely.'

'You don't know what you're missing out,' Aaron said.

Chelsea shrugged. 'Maybe next time.'

As soon as it was out she wanted to withdraw it, but Aaron smiled at her reply as if he hoped there *would* be a next time, and she couldn't help but hope the same.

CHAPTER EIGHT

THREE HOURS LATER, Aaron pulled the ute up in the middle of a paddock and killed the headlights, immediately engulfing them in darkness.

'Here?' Chelsea asked after a beat or two, as she peered out of the windscreen and then her window into the inky black of the night.

'Yep.'

She looked around again, as if she'd been expecting stadium seating. 'The best place is near the river, but it's a bit further away, and all we need is to be far enough from the lights of the homestead.'

Unclicking his seat belt, Aaron opened the door, because the temptation to reach for her after their amazing day together was too great. Between how she enthusiastically and uncomplainingly pitched in at the shearing shed, to the way she'd got on with his family, to her easy conversation and witty banter throughout dinner, she'd been building like a drum beat in his blood.

This very English woman just seemed to fit in to this very Aussie setting.

The air was still warm but the sting of the day had dissipated as he strode round to the tray of the ute and grabbed the blanket. Ordinarily, for star-gazing he'd have thrown a mattress in the back, but he didn't want Chelsea to think he'd lured her out here under false pretences.

After today, he was starting to understand his feelings went deeper than how sexy she looked in the strappy dress she was now wearing, or how tempting it was to pull out the band in her hair and let it all fall loose.

Chelsea had been through a lot, and if she really was here not because she was running away but to start over—to *stay*—then they had time to explore whatever *this* was. Because he was sure he wasn't alone in these feelings and he didn't want to screw anything up by going too hard too fast.

She was still sitting in the cab of the car as he came round her side and he smiled to himself as he opened the door. 'Scared of the dark?'

Peering out at him, she blinked. 'I'm not sure I've *been* anywhere this dark.'

He laughed and held out his hand. 'Yeah, moon won't be up for a few more hours. Great? Isn't it?'

The unclicking of her seatbelt sounded loud in the cacophony of silence around them, then her hand slid into his. 'Are we lying on the ground?' she asked as he guided her to the front of the vehicle.

'No.' Aaron threw the blanket on the bonnet of the car. 'We're sitting up here. Best seats in the house.' He shoved his booted foot onto the lower rung of the bull bar and hauled himself up, before turning and offering his hand once again. 'You coming?'

A minute later they were sitting side by side—not

touching but still close—their legs stretched out in front of them, the blanket beneath protecting them from the heat of the engine, reclining against the windscreen he'd washed thoroughly when Chelsea had been in the bath.

'Wow,' she whispered as she craned her neck to take in the sky from horizon to horizon.

Aaron smiled at the awe in that one hushed word. 'Yeah.'

Above him a wonderland glimmered and dazzled. Planets and suns and constellations. Far-away galaxies. All blending together to form the rich tapestry of lights making up the great southern night sky.

'Do you know what any of these stars are called?'

'Some.'

He pointed them out then and they whiled away half an hour talking about all things celestial, Chelsea mostly listening, Aaron mostly talking. But Aaron was hyper-aware of *her*. Every breath, every move. Every brush of her arm against his. Every turn of her head as she glanced at his profile. Every adjustment of that one errant strap that kept sliding down her arm. Every shake of her shoulders as she laughed at something he said.

His entire body thrummed with awareness. With the slow, thick beat of his blood and the hot, heavy flow of his breath.

And then she said, 'You know, the first date Dom ever took me on was to the Planetarium at the Royal Observatory.'

It was kind of a mood killer.

Aaron had believed her today when she'd said she wasn't in love with her husband any more. And it had been like a weight off his chest—one he didn't even know he'd been carrying. So the very last name he wanted to hear on her lips tonight was *Dom*.

But it made sense that lying here under the stars would trigger the memory, particularly given how recently they'd spoken about him. And he didn't want to be that guy—a douche about the men in a woman's past.

'How'd you meet?'

She stared into the night sky. 'I was at uni in London and he and the lads from his unit used to drink at a pub me and my girlfriends used to frequent.'

Keeping his eyes firmly overhead, he said, 'And was it love at first sight?'

She gave a little laugh. 'Good lord, no. He was quite the lothario which, in retrospect, should have been a heads-up.' She laughed again, a shallow echo of the first. 'Sure, I found him attractive, and he kept asking me out, but he was always there with a different girl. He just seemed like a player to me and I wasn't interested in being a notch on anyone's bedpost.'

'But?' There obviously *was* a but—they'd married, after all.

'He was persistent. Not creepily so. Charmingly. And I was so used to being a…ghost at home. Being seen, being wanted, being *pursued*…that was a revelation. Dom gave affection so easily and freely without me having to silently beg for it. I wasn't used to that from a man, so it was hard to trust initially, but when I did, well…it was heady stuff.'

Aaron shut his eyes. Jesus. Poor Chelsea, starved for attention. No wonder she'd fallen for Dom. 'And now?' He glanced across at her, his eyes well and truly adjusted to the night, his gaze following the line of her profile. 'Did Dom's infidelity make you distrustful of men again?'

Surely it had to have had some impact?

She shook her head as she turned her head to look at him. 'It made me mistrust *myself*. But mostly it made me feel…'

The silence grew between them. 'Feel…?' he prompted.

Glancing away, she huffed out a breath. 'It doesn't matter.'

'You can say it, you know,' he murmured, his gaze trained on her profile. 'It's just you and me and the stars.'

Aaron saw the bob of her throat, heard her swallow, heard the rough exhale, and waited. 'It reinforced how I've always felt. Like… I wasn't enough. Not enough for my dad to love me. Not enough for my husband to be faithful to me. Just…' Her voice roughened and her throat bobbed again. 'Not enough.'

The utter dejection in her voice cut Aaron to his core. 'Hey,' he said, rolling onto his side, sliding his hand onto her cheek and into her hair. 'I'm sorry. I'm *so* sorry that happened to you, Chelsea. And that people you loved and trusted made you feel that way.'

Turning on her side, she shot him a sad smile. 'It's okay, you don't have to—'

'Yes,' he interrupted. 'I do.' Someone had to. It was a tragedy that she felt so unworthy, and his chest ached with the unfairness of it because, while his mother leaving had left him feeling similarly, he'd had other people around him—people who loved him—telling him, *showing* him, otherwise.

His hand held firmer in her hair. 'You are enough,

Chelsea Tanner. You are *more* than enough. You've been with the OA for a month and there's not one person on the team that wouldn't say the same thing. And any guy who was lucky enough to be in a position to tell you that, and didn't spend every single second of his life doing so, has a lot to answer for. I'm sorry you weren't loved the way you deserve to be loved.'

The way he wanted to love her. Because he *was* falling in love with her—he knew it as surely as he knew the sun would rise over this ancient landscape tomorrow.

Even though she was everything he'd avoided all his life.

She stared at him then as if she didn't know what to say. Aaron didn't know what to say either so he leaned in and kissed her instead.

She tasted sweet, like the golden syrup she'd smothered all over the warm damper they'd had for dessert, and she smelled like whatever the hell had been in that fancy bath bomb Tracey had supplied. Vanilla or orange or passion fruit. Something edible which had driven him crazy throughout dinner. Her lips were soft and pliant, and the small moan that came from somewhere at the back of her throat unleashed a tsunami of lust that Aaron's better angels had been keeping under wraps for what felt like for ever.

His pulse pumped through his chest, his belly and his groin, and he was only vaguely aware of the loud rasp of his breath as he opened his mouth and deepened the kiss, groaning when she did the same.

Then, somehow, she was closer. Or maybe he was. Had she moved, or had he? Had they both moved?

Aaron wasn't sure. All he knew was the tips of her breasts were rubbing his chest, her knees were brushing his lower thighs and his hand was dropping from her hair, running down her spine to the dip at the small of her back and palming her butt, urging her closer.

Urging her in all the way.

Until her breasts were flattened and their thighs were smooshed and their hips were aligned and there was no way she could not feel the *full* effect of what kissing her was doing to his body.

It wasn't anything like the two kisses they'd already shared. They'd been rash and brief, halted abruptly out of surprise and a sense of transgression. A sense of being wrong.

This didn't feel wrong. It felt like the culmination of what this day had been leading to. What this past month had been leading to.

Hell, out here under the stars, it felt like their freaking destiny.

But, as her kiss plunged deeper and her knee slid between his legs, her thigh pressing against the almost agonising thickness of his erection, Aaron knew if he didn't stop now it was going to be a lot more than just some first-base action on the bonnet of his ute.

It was going to be a home run.

And that would be the very definition of going too hard, too fast. He was a thirty-five-year-old man, not a horny teenager, and he'd waited for this—for *her*—all his damned life. He didn't want to mess up because he let his libido have the con.

Libidos weren't generally known for their detailed decision-making process. Gathering every skerrick of his willpower, Aaron pulled out of the kiss. He didn't go far, just pressing his forehead against hers, their rough pants mingling together.

'*Aaron?*' she asked, her voice small. 'Everything okay?'

God…she sounded as befuddled as he felt. 'Everything is perfect,' he assured her, nuzzling her temple now.

'You…don't want this?'

He shut his eyes. 'Oh, I want it.' He chugged out a laughed as he tipped his head back a little to look at her. 'I'm just trying to be…' God…what? Restrained? Gentlemanly? Respectful? 'I don't want you to think I brought you out here for this.'

She didn't say anything for a moment, then she moved the leg she had jammed between them, causing his breath to hitch and a mini-eruption in his groin. Sliding it over the top of his thigh, she rolled herself up, pressing on his upper shoulder as she went, displacing him onto his back.

By the time she was settled, she was straddling him, the centre of her pressing into the bulge behind his fly. His hands had come to rest on her legs mid-thigh, his palms on warm, bare skin, his fingers on the hem of her dress. Her strap had slipped again but she didn't bother fixing it this time.

'I don't think that.'

'Good.' Aaron was mollified to hear she didn't doubt his motives. His libido, however, didn't care about his motives, it only cared about how good it felt to have her atop him and how easy it would be to push his hands under the fabric of her dress…

'But I'm okay to be going there anyway.'

If she'd applied a cattle prod to his erection, it couldn't have bucked harder than it did and, by the way she shifted, he was pretty sure she'd felt it too. He swallowed. 'Okay.'

She stared down at him for long moments. 'No one had ever said that to me, before…the sorry thing. *Sorry that happened to you, Chelsea.* Not my father. Not Francesca or Vinnie. It means a lot.'

Aaron's pulse thudded thick through his head as an uneasy feeling took up residence in the pit of the stomach. 'So this is a…thank you?'

'What?' She frowned and shook her head. 'No.'

A very distracting piece of hair slid from her up-do to kiss her nape. Aaron's fingers itched to play with it and he dug them into her thighs to suppress the impulse.

'This is… I didn't know I could feel like this. And…' She paused, as if she was searching for the right words. 'I'm so lucky to have shared this day with you. And… I'm attracted to you, and have been since the room mix up at the hotel, and all this…' She looked up and then back at him. 'Makes me want to do something wild and free, and I haven't wanted to do that with *anyone* for a very long time, but I want to do it with you.'

A well of emotion stormed his chest, each word sliding inside his heart, and Aaron knew that whatever happened with them he'd never forget this night underneath the stars, falling in love with Chelsea.

'Well… I can't fault your logic,' he said with a grin, because this wasn't the moment for such a grand declaration.

She grinned too, momentarily, before reaching for

the hem of her dress and pulling it up and off her head, leaving her in nothing but a white pair of panties.

'Holy mother of...' Aaron whispered, his pulse spiking, his gaze fixed on the lush curves of her bare breasts and the pebbled nipples at each centre.

Then she reached up and pulled at the band in her hair and it cascaded down in fine wisps. Christ...she was magnificent. Incandescent against the backdrop of the Milky Way, crowned in a garland of stars.

His hands moved then, sliding up her thighs, glancing over her belly and her ribs to each capture a breast, thumbs stroking across the engorged nipples in unison. Damn if his hands didn't look *good* on her. Big and tanned and a little rough against the pale creaminess of her skin, but *good*.

She moaned and arched her back, and Aaron vaulted up, his mouth landing on her throat as he kneaded the soft flesh, and she rocked against him.

'God,' she gasped as she tugged at his shirt. 'Please tell me you have a condom.'

It took a moment for Aaron to think through the heavy haze buzzing through his system as Chelsea yanked his shirt free of his head and tossed it. 'Wallet. Back pocket.'

But for damned sure they were going to need more than one.

It had been such a long time since a man had held her in his arms like this and Chelsea realised how much she'd missed it as she groped for the wallet. She hadn't for the longest time. Dom's betrayal had torpedoed the intimacy they'd shared and knocked her libido flat. But, in this small dot on an Outback map, it had suddenly roared to form and life and had a name.

'Aaron,' she whispered as his lips drifted south, and his heat, his earthiness, his closeness overwhelmed her.

He made a low humming noise, his hot, wet mouth replacing the fingers toying with a nipple, and Chelsea cried out, her hand fumbling with the square piece of leather she'd somehow managed to wrangle from his pocket. Her head fell back, the action thrusting her breasts out, and Aaron took ruthless advantage, ravaging them with such skill, Chelsea was lost to everything but the flick of his tongue and the pull of his mouth.

At some point, he lifted his head and panted, 'Condom,' before going right back to his deliberations.

With monumental effort Chelsea got back on task, lifting her head to riffle through his wallet, thanking God for her night vision as her ability to coordinate dissolved under the play of Aaron's tongue and the fine rub of his whiskers that prickled *everywhere*.

Locating the condom, Chelsea almost brandished it up high and called out *Huzzah!* But she chose to conserve her energy for what was to come. Sliding her hands onto the smooth acreage of his shoulders, she pressed more urgently against the bulge in his shorts and started to rub. Sensation flared between her hips and she let out a strangled kind of moan at the same time as Aaron's guttural grunt.

His mouth slipped from her nipple as his hand clamped down hard on the small of her back. 'Chelsea…' He puffed out a strangled kind of laugh into the hollow at the base of her throat. 'That'll end messily if you keep doing that.'

The fact that Aaron seemed to be as out of control, as close to the edge, as she did, quashed any thoughts hovering in the back of her mind about her lack of *practice*. Sliding a hand into the rich layers of his hair, she tilted his head back until they were staring into each other's eyes. It might have been dark but his gaze was utterly transparent. She saw desire—*lust*—but also emotion, something that went beyond this crazy, desperate need thrumming between them.

Something deeper.

Chelsea supposed she should feel exposed, embarrassed even, about sharing her deepest, darkest hurts with this man. But sitting next to him in this deepest, darkest night, knowing he too knew something about loss and inadequacy, felt…right.

She kissed him then, her lips opening over his, her hand sliding to his jaw, the rasp of his whiskers against her palm hardening her nipples. Her belly looped then tightened as her pulse fluttered at her temples, wrists and between her legs. His tongue brushed hers and Chelsea moaned as she returned the favour, tangling with him in a delicious dance. Her head filled with the taste of him, the smell of him. Eucalyptus and leather and petrichor.

Panting, she pulled out of the kiss. Part of her wanted to do nothing but keep her lips locked with his all night, but parts *lower* were demanding more. A fever burned thought her blood and only Aaron—hard and good and deep inside her—could break it.

Chelsea shifted slightly as she handed him the condom. 'Open this,' she requested as she reached for his fly.

The sound of husky breathing, the tearing of foil and the rip of a zipper all seemed amplified in the absolute silence of the landscape. Unlike Aaron's, 'Oh, Jesus,' which hovered rough and low around them as Chelsea finally liberated his erection from his underwear.

He felt good in her hand. Long and thick and solid as Chelsea closed her fingers around him, stroking up and down, familiarising herself with his contours, revelling in the shudder rippling through his body. He groaned again, his forehead pressing into the crook of her neck, his breath hot as he pushed her hand aside, muttering, 'Mercy, woman,' as he rolled the sheath down his length.

Chelsea's pulse accelerated as she pressed closer to Aaron once more, reaching for his hardness with one hand, pushing the gusset of her underwear out the way with the other. Lifting her hips slightly, she looked into his upturned face. The thick, blunt prod of him nudged her entrance as his hands slid to the small of her back. Their slight roughness caused her nipples to bead and Chelsea's entire body pulsed in anticipation.

'When you say you haven't done this for a very long time,' he said, his voice husky, his expression earnest. 'You mean…?'

'Not since Dom,' she confirmed.

He nodded slowly. 'Do you need me to…?'

Chelsea wasn't sure what he was going to say, but she didn't give him a chance to finish. She just sank down—not fast, but not slow either—in a measured, deliberate move that filled her all the way to the hilt, stealing the breath from her lungs and causing Aaron to gasp.

She clutched him to her chest, her arms wrapping around his head and shoulders, his arms wrapping around her waist as she breathed steadily through the thick intrusion stretching her so damned good.

'You okay?' he asked after a beat or two.

'Yeah, just...' Her arms tightened around him as she adjusted to his girth and depth. 'Give me a second.'

A wave of emotion rolled from the pit of her stomach all the way to her throat. She'd felt so broken for so long and in a handful of weeks this man, in a place on the other side of the planet, had put her back together. Or at least, shown her that it was possible to be whole again.

He chuckled. 'Take as long as you want. We could just stay like this all night and I'd be totally down with that.'

Chelsea gave a husky laugh. 'I think you mean...' She undulated internal muscles. 'Up.'

He sucked in a breath, his arms tightening around her waist. 'Christ, yes.'

'Well, I...' She undulated again, exaggerating the move, feeling a delicious tug below her belly button as the raw emotion receded and the thrum of her pulse took its place. 'Would not.' Loosening her arms, she glanced down, searching his gaze. 'I'm going to need to apologise in advance because I don't think this is going to take very long.'

'Are you kidding? If you think I'm going to last more than a second or two longer than you do, then you are seriously underestimating what you do to me.'

Chelsea's heart skipped. Aaron Vincent was *seriously* pushing all her buttons.

She dropped her head then and kissed him, slow at

first, then faster and hungrier as his mouth demanded it, his tongue flicking against hers. The fever of her desperation flamed anew and she felt an answering flare in him, *heard* it echoed in the heavy rasp of his breathing. Two large hands slid to her buttocks and squeezed and Chelsea rocked then, setting up a rhythm.

'God...*yes*.' Aaron groaned against her lips as he squeezed harder.

She rocked more but it wasn't enough. Chelsea pushed at Aaron's chest, breaking their kiss. 'Lie back,' she commanded huskily.

Aaron eased back against the windscreen, his hands sliding to her hips, and Chelsea took a moment to admire his big shoulders and his smooth chest and the solid abs that clearly stayed honed from hefting around sheep. She rocked again, her movements freer this time, getting off on the hiss of his breath and the way those abdominals pulled taut.

'God, Chelsea...' He shook his head as his eyes roamed from her face to her breasts to the flare of her hips and to where they were joined, before drifting up again. 'I've never seen anything as beautiful as you with diamonds in your hair riding me into the night.'

Chelsea's heart squeezed hard at the hushed compliment. The awe in his voice humbled her with its intensity and she realised she could fall in love with this man.

And it didn't scare the living daylights out of her.

Sliding a hand onto his stomach, Chelsea felt the ripple of his muscles beneath. Felt every ripple as the other hand joined in and they smoothed their way up to his pecs and then on to his shoulders, her palms grabbing onto their solid roundness. She leaned forward into her extended arms, the position changing the angle of their joining. His hand clutched convulsively at her hip and she shivered as it hit just the right spot.

Staring at each other, he withdrew a little then thrust, and Chelsea moaned and shut her eyes as it felt *so* good. He did it again and it rocked her breasts and her head, and her sex clenched around him. When he went again, she rose to meet his withdrawal and fell to heighten his thrust. He grunted and she gasped, her eyes flying open, their gazes connecting.

They moved together then, just like that, eyes locked, Chelsea leaning into her palms as she rose and fell, Aaron's fingers biting into her hips as he thrust in and out, blood surging and pounding through her belly and buttocks and thighs, every nerve stretching taut, every muscle tightening, ripples of pleasure starting deep inside her sex.

'Oh, God… *Aaron.*'

'I know,' he panted, his eyes boring into hers as he went deeper and deeper with each thrust. 'I know, I know.'

The ripples got bigger and harder and faster until they exploded into an all-consuming deluge. Chelsea cried out, panting and gasping, her eyes wide as a tide of sensation swept her away. 'Oh, God.' Her nails dug into his shoulders as her body trembled with the first pulses of her orgasm. 'Yes, yes, yes.'

As promised, Aaron joined her in the torrent two beats later, shouting his release into the night. *'Chelsea!'*

He vaulted up then, taking her with him, his hands sliding around high on her back, his fingers anchoring from behind on the balls of her shoulders, holding her close as he kissed her, locking her in their starry, starry night together. Stealing her breath and giving her his own, he kissed up the tumult, bucking and shuddering, his climax sustaining hers until the last tremor rocked her core.

Chelsea's mouth left his, her chin coming to rest on top of his head, his lips buzzing her throat as she caught her breath.

'That was…' he said, his breathing still unsteady.

Chelsea waited for him to continue and, when he didn't, she laughed. He sounded satisfied and mystified all at once, as if he couldn't come up with an adequate enough word, and hell if that didn't set up a warm glow in her heart. 'Yeah. I know.'

Chuckling, he eased back, taking her with him, cradling her against his chest, making her excruciatingly aware of how intimately they were still joined. The steady bang of his heart echoed under her ear as his fingers trekked idly up and down the furrow of her spine, and they lay there for several minutes, just breathing in the aftermath.

'You okay?' he asked eventually.

'Mmm,' she said. 'I haven't felt this okay in a long time.'

His arms squeezed around her, and Chelsea snuggled for a beat or two more, but with the night still warm she was conscious of the sweat slicking between them. She roused and pushed up, making to move off him, only to have his hand clamp on her arse.

'Not yet,' he murmured, his gaze settling on hers.

'I'm too heavy,' she protested.

He gave a snort-laugh. 'Half the sheep I moved today

weighed more than you.' But he lifted his hand and Chelsea eased away. She shivered and a low kind of hum came from the back of his throat as he slid from her body.

She settled against the windscreen, her knees bent as Aaron sat and ditched the condom before zipping up. Chelsea supposed she should try and find her dress, but then he was beside her again, his hand slipping into hers, and the thought floated away.

Neither of them spoke for a long time. Somehow, the stars seemed even brighter now, and it was lovely lying here with Aaron under that sky with the memory of their joining lingering in the still night air.

'I hear you can see the aurora down here.'

'Aurora Australis. Yes. But not out here... Gotta go further south. You can see them in Victoria sometimes on a good night, but Tassie's the best place.'

'Have you been to Tasmania?'

'When I was a kid.'

'I'd like to see the southern lights in Tasmania some time,' she murmured, her eyes roaming the sky.

'I would, too. Maybe...' He turned his head. 'We could go together?'

Conscious of his gaze on her profile, Chelsea also turned her head. 'I'd like that.'

When he smiled, she smiled back before she returned her gaze to the sky in time to catch a shooting star flaring across the sequined black dome above. She gasped and pointed at it, her finger following its trajectory.

'You get to make a wish now,' he said.

'Nope.' Her lips curved into a smile. 'I think I've been lucky enough for one night.'

'Amen to that,' he murmured.

Chelsea laughed at his deadpan delivery and rolled up onto her elbow, looking down into his smiling face. The starlight fell gently on the crinkles around his eyes, the crooked smile and the slight asymmetry of his eyes.

'How'd you do this?' she asked, her finger tracing the uneven line of his nose.

'Footy,' he said. 'Two broken noses.'

'And this?' Her finger brushed over the asymmetrical bow of his top lip.

'Fractured zygoma. Also footy.' He laughed, as if everyone who played the game ended up with broken noses and cheekbones. 'Didn't quite heal in perfect symmetry so my face has always looked a bit crooked.'

Chelsea drifted her finger over the cheekbone in question before drifting it back to his top lip. 'I like your crooked face,' she murmured.

She liked it a lot.

He smiled and his hand came up to capture hers, their gazes locking as he kissed her fingertips, and Chelsea's lungs felt too big for her chest. How could she have all these feelings for him so soon? It had taken her months to fall in love with Dom.

Before she blurted anything else out, she snuggled down beside him—as much as one could snuggle against glass—her head on his shoulder, her arm across his chest, her fingers absently caressing a nicely pillowed pectoral muscle.

It was so damned quiet out here. Had she been alone, she might have found all this vast black emptiness eerie, but with Aaron it felt…intimate.

'You know,' he said after a while, his fingers drift-

ing up and down her arm, 'I still have my bedroom at
the homestead.'

Chelsea's fingers stopped their caress. Stay the night
at the homestead? Did he mean sneak in and sneak out
again before morning? Or just go on back and not care
who saw them?

It was tempting, but part of her shied away from that
kind of public declaration. This *thing* was some*thing*.
And that was big—for both of them. Except it had just
happened, and she couldn't help but feel it would be
easier to figure out without the speculation, scrutiny
and expectation of family and friends.

'Too soon?'

Chelsea let out a shaky breath. 'Yeah.' Pushing up
onto her elbow again, her gaze found his. 'Is that okay?'

'Of course.' Levering himself up, Aaron kissed her
lightly, briefly. 'Come on. I'll drop you back to your
place.'

'Drop me?' Her index finger traced the crooked line
of his top lip. 'I was hoping you might stay.'

He raised an eyebrow, his mouth lifting beneath the
pad of her finger into an answering smile. 'I thought
it was too early.'

God…this man was just too damned sweet and con-
siderate, but Chelsea didn't want this night to end. 'For
your place, sure. Not for mine.'

She grinned at him and he grinned back.

CHAPTER NINE

THREE WEEKS LATER, Chelsea was with Travis and Aaron at a large community health clinic set up under the shade of some towering gums a few hundred kilometres north of Balanora. The morning was hot, as per usual, but there was some cloud cover and a light breeze helping to keep things bearable.

It had been the most blissful three weeks of her life. Bliss hadn't been a state she'd thought she'd ever occupy again, but laughing and talking over takeaway and Netflix, followed by long, steamy nights in bed—thank God for air-conditioning—and sexy lie-ins on shared days off was pretty damn close to nirvana.

The fact they were keeping it to themselves gave it a little extra spice.

Some might call it sneaking around but Chelsea preferred the term 'discretion'. And Aaron was fully on board with keeping things quiet for a while so she just relaxed and enjoyed it. She had thought it might make working together awkward but, compared to their original awkwardness over that hotel barge-in and her snatched kiss, this was nothing and they soon learned to cultivate their at-work personas.

And Chelsea was pretty sure they'd pulled it off. Until today.

Blowing away her third sticky fly in a minute, she administered a vaccine to her patient in one arm while Travis took her blood pressure on the other. Sadie was a well-known indigenous elder and artist in the region, and spritely for her seventy-eight years, given her arthritic knees and partial blindness in her left eye.

'Gotta hand it to you, Chels,' Travis said, his Santa hat sitting rakishly on his head. With Christmas less than a week away, they were all wearing one. Even Hattie, who was currently kicking a ball around with some kids. 'It's been almost seven weeks and you've managed to avoid saying *bloody flies*. Didn't think you had it in you.'

Chelsea slid a glance at Aaron, who was bent over Jasmine, Sadie's great-granddaughter, stethoscope hanging down from his neck as he performed her six-week postnatal check. A smile touched his mouth but he didn't look up from the baby.

Sadie glanced at her, then at Aaron, then at Travis as he ripped off the blood pressure cuff. She cocked her eyebrow at him. 'They're doing it, right?'

Chelsea glanced at Sadie, alarmed, as Travis nodded. 'We're pretty sure. We're taking bets back at the base on when they'll make it official.'

Bets? Her cheeks grew hot as she stuck a plaster over the vaccination site. Sadie hooted out a laugh and slapped her thigh, her snowy-white hair flicking around her face as Chelsea snuck another look at Aaron. He was clearly biting his cheek to stop from smiling.

'They're playing things close to their chest,' Travis said. 'But Siobhan saw Aaron skulking—'

'I don't skulk,' he interrupted, not looking up as he gently pushed on the infant's adducted hips to check for dysplasia.

'Skulking,' Travis continued, 'down Chelsea's front path at quarter to eight at night two weeks ago with a bag of Chinese takeaway from the Happy Sun in his hand. And when I asked them both at work the next day what they had for dinner, he said beef and black bean and she said...' he paused for dramatic effect '...a cheese toasty.'

Chelsea remembered that incident. As soon as Aaron had said Chinese, she'd known she couldn't say that too in case it roused suspicion. So, she'd panicked and said the other.

'What?' Sadie shook her head dismissively. 'No one has a toasted sanger when you can have Happy Sun.'

Travis leaned in conspiratorially. 'I know, right?'

'Yep.' She glanced at Chelsea then at Aaron. 'They're doing it.'

That was their evidence? 'We're right here, you know!' Chelsea said as she tossed the empty syringe into the nearby sharps container.

'Reckon it'll last?' Sadie continued, ignoring Chelsea's statement.

'We hope so.' Travis grinned at Chelsea. 'We like her.'

Pursing her lips, Sadie inspected them both again, before returning her attention to Travis. 'Yeah. Reckon it will.'

'From your lips to God's ears, Aunty.'

Sadie narrowed her eyes at Aaron. 'About time, boy.' Clearly, Sadie and Aaron had known each other for a long time.

'No comment,' he said, unperturbed.

Chelsea shut her eyes. No comment meant yes—everyone knew that. Another hoot of laughter escaped the old woman's lips. '*Definitely* doing it.'

They were back in the plane three hours later, having done over fifty different vaccinations, a dozen infant health checks, some post-hospital admission follow-up and seen to miscellaneous other things, from a festered splinter to a mild burn to a case of shingles. Chelsea was buckled into her usual seat, diagonally opposite and facing Aaron. They were waiting for Travis.

'No comment?' she murmured into the mouthpiece as she switched over to a private channel.

He just shrugged and smiled. 'It was bound to get out sooner or later. Is that a problem?'

Chelsea expected to feel hesitancy. Doubt. Uncertainty. But there was none forthcoming. She realised she'd been worried about what people—both in Balanora and back in London—would say about how quick it had been. But, maybe that wasn't *her* problem.

Slowly, she shook her head. 'No, actually.'

He smiled his crooked smile and the slight tension she didn't know had been there seemed to melt from around his shoulders before her eyes. 'Why don't we talk about it tonight?' he suggested.

'Yeah,' she said, and smiled too. They'd been avoiding having a conversation about the future. Or maybe *she* had. But her feelings for Aaron weren't going away, and what was she afraid of exactly? That Aaron would turn out to be like Dom? That he'd cheat?

She'd known him for less than two months and already she could tell he was nothing like Dom. Hell, she'd been able to tell that the second she'd rashly kissed him in her house and he'd stepped away. *He'd* called a halt.

Just then Travis made his way down the aisle, adjusting his headphones. Chelsea feigned interest in looking out of the window as she flicked the channel back to a shared one. So did Aaron.

Travis shook his head. 'You two are so damn cute,' he muttered in their ears. 'Don't keep us in suspense for too much longer.'

Hattie's voice said, 'Amen.'

Aaron's mood was buoyant when they landed just before one in the afternoon. He and Chelsea were going to talk and they'd had a great day out at the clinic. He absolutely loved getting to the outer reaches of the district. He might be the doctor but people didn't treat him any differently than they had when he'd been a boy.

Sadie was a classic example. He'd played in the same footy team as a lot of Sadie's grandkids and assorted other relatives, and she'd always been on the side lines, no matter where they'd played, a staunch supporter of the team. She'd always been the first one to clap and say, 'Good tackle,' or 'Great try,' but also the first to tell him to pull his head in if he gave the ref any lip or if she felt he was getting too big for his footy boots.

'Don't need no prima donnas out here, boy,' she'd say.

It didn't surprise him that she'd twigged to what was

going on between Chelsea and him. He swore the old people—the women in particular—knew what he was thinking even before he did. It felt a lot like having a mother, and perhaps that was what the women out in these small communities, proudly living on their country were—his mothers. Closing ranks after his mum had split, filling that gap, poking and prodding him to do better, be better.

The fact Sadie seemed to approve of the situation with Chelsea said a lot about the type of woman Chelsea was. Inherently suspicious of newcomers, ingrained into generations of old people who had seen too much sadness and grief in their lives, Sadie didn't just take to anyone. But she'd been joking and teasing, and if that wasn't a stamp of approval then he didn't know what was.

Having Chelsea seem pretty zen about being outed had been the icing on the cake.

So, despite himself, Aaron started to hope. He'd told her in the beginning that he didn't get involved with out-of-towners, and how much more out-of-town could a woman from *London* be? But back then he'd thought she was still in love with Dom, and they hadn't spent weeks together laughing and eating and sharing.

And *talking*. About going to Tasmania, and other places he'd suggested they could go to together. Talking about her being in Balanora next year and the year after.

Aaron knew how he felt. He was in love with her. It was that simple. And that complex. But, these past few weeks, he'd started to think that she felt the same way, or that she might be starting to, anyway. Maybe he was just a giant fool, but her willingness to talk about their relationship—there, *he* was labelling it—only filled him with more hope.

As they were the last two to disembark the plane, Chelsea leered at him cheekily on her way out. Glancing at the swish of her ponytail and the perky little stab of her pen, Aaron made a quick grab for her hand, pulling her back and toppling her onto his lap. She gave a little squeak as she landed.

'Aaron!' she protested on a whisper, laughing as she tried to squirm out of his grasp. 'Trent could come back.'

'I don't care,' he muttered.

It was clear everyone pretty much knew anyway, and that not only made him happy but exceptionally turned on. Keeping his hands to himself around her was difficult at the best of times, but suddenly the possibility of a *them* loomed large, and the urge to kiss the hell out of her beat like a mantra through his blood.

She melted against him the second his mouth touched hers, kissing him back with equal abandon. 'Ever heard of the mile-high club?' he murmured a minute later, coming up for some air.

Laughing, she said, 'We're on the ground.'

A loud knock on the fuselage followed by Trent's stern, 'Don't make me bring a blue light in there,' had them both laughing.

Aaron rubbed his nose against Chelsea's. 'Tonight,' he whispered, and her contented sigh was better than any quickie in an aeroplane loo.

'Can't wait.'

But those plans were dashed about thirty seconds

after they deplaned. 'Sorry, Chels,' Charmaine said as she met them at the entrance to the hangar, 'but we've had several phone calls from a Roberto Rossi asking for you.'

She frowned. 'Roberto?'

'He said he'd left you several messages, but I explained that you were in an area with no mobile coverage. He wouldn't say what he wanted but he asked that you ring him urgently and that you knew the number.'

A prickle flared at Aaron's nape as Chelsea delved in her pocket, retrieving her phone and switching it on. Nobody ever had their mobiles on when they went out. They couldn't have it on in the plane, and there was rarely any mobile coverage in the places they went anyway.

Aaron could see what looked like at least a dozen missed-call notifications on her screen as she tapped the first one and put the phone to her ear. He wasn't sure if he should go and give her some privacy, but she hadn't asked him or Charmaine to leave, nor had she walked away, and he didn't want to dessert her in case it was bad news and she needed someone to lean on.

Him, hopefully.

Her brow furrowed further as she listened to what he assumed was one of the messages before she pulled the phone away from her ear and tapped to end the call.

'Is everything okay?' Charmaine asked, getting in before Aaron, who was trying to read her body language, could say a word.

She shook her head as she glanced at Aaron. 'It's Alfie.'

Charmaine frowned this time. 'Is that a niece or a nephew?'

'Yeah.' Chelsea nodded. 'Something like that.'

'What happened?' Aaron asked, moving closer, not touching her but wanting to. Wanting to slip his hand onto her neck or an arm around her waist and hating that he couldn't.

'I don't know, it was pretty garbled. He's in Intensive Care.' She turned to Charmaine. 'Do you mind if I use the phone in your office to ring Roberto back?'

'Of course not.'

Charmaine squeezed her arm and Aaron wished he could do the same. But suddenly he felt very uncertain about where they stood. Her dead husband's child, a child who had *wormed his way into her heart*, was in Intensive Care.

Would she go back? To London. To *home*. The place she knew, where people loved her and most of her stuff was still stored.

And would she return to Balanora?

He felt like all kinds of bastard to be worried about himself in a moment like this, but everything he'd felt less than a minute ago was disintegrating around him, and he wasn't at all sure he'd get it back.

Chelsea placed her hand over top of Charmaine's and returned her squeeze. 'Thanks,' she said before dropping her hand and hurrying across the hangar.

They watched her as she disappeared through the door to the offices. 'You okay?' Charmaine asked, turning to face him.

Aaron gave a snort as he looked at her. 'Am I that transparent?'

Her mouth curved into a gentle smile. 'I've known you a long time.'

'I…love her.'

'That was…' Charmaine paused, as if searching for the right word. 'Fast.'

'Seems like it runs in my family.'

'No.' She shook her head. 'Your mother was a city girl who came here pregnant and always had one eye on the highway.'

'She lives in London, Char.'

'No, Aaron. She lives *here*. She's inordinately qualified. She could have got a job in any of the big capital cities, but she *chose* here. And she's made more effort in the short time she's been here to be part of this community then your mum did in fifteen years. She came to a bloody CWA meeting with me three days ago.'

The Country Women's Association was a service organisation that formed the backbone of any Outback community. His mother had referred to them as the 'blue rinse set'.

'She's going to want to go back.' Aaron wished he didn't know that already, but the sinking feeling in the pit of his stomach said otherwise. Because, as much as Chelsea had wanted out of the situation back home, she was deeply compassionate. He doubted she could turn away from people who had been—*were*—a huge part of her life in their hour of need.

'Okay.' Charmaine nodded. 'We'll work it out.'

'And if she doesn't return?'

She raised her eyebrow. 'Are you that unlovable?'

No, it wasn't that. 'It's new.'

Charmaine gave his arm the same squeeze she'd given to Chelsea. 'Have some faith.' Dropping her hand, she said, 'C'mon, let's go see what she needs.'

By the time they were back in the office, Chelsea was hanging up the phone at Charmaine's desk. Aaron knocked quietly on the door, pushing it gently open. She looked pale and he knew the news wasn't good.

'What happened?'

'He ran out on the road to get his ball. A car knocked him over. He has a fractured skull and a bleed on the brain. It sounds like it's small enough to manage conservatively because they're not talking surgery. Roberto's in shock, so he didn't know a lot of other information. He had a seizure at the scene so he's on a vent and he also has a broken tib-fib.'

'Bloody hell.' That was some major trauma. Aaron moved closer, halting on the other side of the desk. He wanted to hug her but he was conscious of their lack of privacy. 'Is he stable?'

'I think. For now.' She shrugged. 'Roberto was very upset. Francesca was looking after him. She's apparently inconsolable. I…' She paused, placing a hand on her stomach as if she was quelling nausea. 'I have to go.'

Aaron ignored the giant fist ramming straight into his gut and the slick edge of his own nausea as he accepted that this was probably the end of the road for them.

Damn it, *why* had he left himself hope?

'Of course.' He nodded. 'The afternoon flight leaves at four. You could be on that.'

It cost him to slip into organisational mode but the last thing she needed right now was him being whiny about what Alfie's potentially life-threatening condition meant for them. For *him*. She needed him to be a god damned man and step up.

Her shoulders sagged a little. 'There's usually a few flights to London around nine out of Brisbane.'

Charmaine entered and joined him at the desk. 'Why don't you go home, have a shower, grab what you need and I'll get Meg to book the flights? She has all your passport and preference details.'

'Oh, no.' Chelsea shook her head. 'I can do all that.'

'Nonsense. Meg organises flights all the time—it's a huge part of her job. And she's a bloody whizz at it. She'll find the best value last-minute, most direct flight she can.'

'But I'll need to pay...'

Charmaine waved her hand dismissively. 'We'll worry about that later. You just go to your family.'

'But...' Chelsea glanced at Aaron then back to Charmaine. 'I'm leaving you in the lurch.'

'It's fine.' Another dismissive wave. 'There are nurses at the hospital who can and do cover for us when we have a shortfall.'

Chelsea blinked. 'Thank you.'

Aaron moved to the door. 'I'll drive you home.'

'No.' She shook her head firmly. 'I'm fine. I don't need—' She stopped abruptly and shook her head before dropping her gaze. 'I'm fine.'

He stiffened. He could fill in the blanks just fine. She didn't need him. 'Of course.' He took a steadying breath. 'Safe travels.'

She nodded then glanced at Charmaine. 'Thank you.' And then she was pushing away from the desk, slowing as she neared where Aaron was standing in the doorway. 'I'll be back,' she said, looking at him now.

Aaron nodded, his throat as dry as the red Outback dirt. 'Yep,' he murmured, keeping his voice even and friendly.

Her hand slid over his and squeezed, her brown gaze locking on his. 'I *will* be back.'

And then she was gone leaving Aaron about as wretched as he'd ever felt, clinging to her words but not hopeful, despite the utter certainty of her tone. The thing he'd feared the most had come true—Chelsea was leaving—and there was a giant hole in his chest. He'd let his guard down, broken his own rule and fallen head-over-heels in love, like some damned sappy teenager, and now it was all going to hell.

And that was on him. Not her. Because he'd known better.

Chelsea walked aimlessly around the shops in the fore-court of Brisbane international airport, waiting for check-in to open. She'd arrived at the international ter-minal from the domestic one not long after she'd got off her flight from Balanora. She was a few hours early, but there was no point leaving the terminal complex when the flight left at nine-thirty.

She had managed to get through to Great Ormond Street hospital and talk to the neurosurgeon in charge of Alfie's care, whom she'd worked with several years ago at another hospital. The news had improved, it seemed. Alfie's vitals were stable, he had woken and recognised his mother and they'd removed the ventilation. He was sleepy but there hadn't been any more seizures.

All encouraging signs.

The surgeon had stressed that the bleed was tiny and the skull fracture only hairline, and had been cautiously optimistic. She knew, of course, things could turn on a dime, but it had settled the knot of nerves sitting like an oily lump in her stomach and freed up some head-space to think about Aaron.

About his neutral expression and the forced friend-liness in his voice and the way his walls had come up before her eyes. The ones that had been there when he'd stepped back from her clumsy kiss at her house that first night, and in the store room when he'd said they were just going to be friends.

Before that magical night at Curran Downs. And all the ones since.

She'd tried to assure him she was coming back, but she could tell he hadn't believed her, and she hated that maybe she'd made him feel *not enough* by leaving. It wasn't a nice way to feel. But she hadn't been able to face him coming home with her, either. She didn't want him there with those walls in his eyes, watching her pack, taking her to the airport, wishing her a stiff goodbye.

Not to mention she wouldn't *want* to go. They'd have closed her door behind them, shut the world out and she'd have broken down and clung to him. She'd have cried at the unfairness of life and how this pocket of joy she'd found here in Balanora was being ripped out from under her…and what kind of a person did that make her when Alfie was in ICU?

Selfish. Callous. Heartless.

No, she had to do this by herself. Francesca and Ro-berto, who had already been through so much, needed her. And she'd figure out the rest as the next few days unfolded.

With thirty minutes to go until check-in opened,

Chelsea found a quiet corner in a café and ordered a coffee. It had just arrived when her mobile rang—Roberto.

Answering it immediately, she said, '*Ciao*, Roberto.'

'No, Chelsea, it's me,' Francesca said. 'I'm using Roberto's phone.'

'Francesca, how are you?'

She broke down in tears and Chelsea spent the next five minutes soothing and calming her, assuring her she hadn't done anything wrong, that accidents happened, and encouraging her to see the positives in Alfie's condition.

'Thank you so much for coming, Chelsea. Dom would want you to be with us.'

Chelsea gritted her teeth. Not that long ago the mention of Dom's name would have tugged on all her emotional strings, served up with a hefty dose of guilt because she couldn't keep loving him the way his parents clearly wanted her to.

Not so any more.

She wanted to say, *You didn't know Dom. I didn't know Dom.* But Francesca was distressed enough, so Chelsea cut her some slack.

'This is what I was afraid of. Something bad happening after you left, and it's come true.'

Grinding her teeth now, Chelsea took a steadying breath. Francesca was stressed and feeling guilty about Alfie's accident. She *would* cut her slack, damn it. 'It's just coincidence,' Chelsea soothed, well used to this role with her mother-in-law who, despite being born and raised in a third-generation English household, could lean heavily into her Italian *mamma* roots.

'At least you'll be home for Christmas. That's good.'

Christmas. Chelsea's stomach sank.

'Roberto tells me you changed your name back to Tanner but…why, Chelsea? How could you do that to us?' she chided. 'To Dom. Reject his name. Betray him like that just three years after he was put in the ground.'

Chelsea blinked. Okay. *No.* A red mist blurred her vision. She was officially out of slack. Francesca had to be freaking kidding.

'Betray *him*?' Chelsea didn't even recognise her own voice as she gripped the phone.

'Chelsea. Come on now.'

'Betray *him*?' she repeated.

'We don't speak ill of the dead.'

She didn't have to be there to know that Francesca was probably crossing herself. 'He betrayed *me*, Francesca.' Her hand shook and she wrapped it around her coffee cup. 'He *betrayed* me. He slept with another woman and got her pregnant.'

It was on the tip of Chelsea's tongue to unload about the other women too, but she couldn't let the rage storming through her system destroy everything in its path. She would only regret it later.

'Chelsea, *bella*, women always threw themselves at him. You know that. He was such a good-looking boy.'

Chelsea barely bit back her gasp. 'Francesca!' Several people nearby turned to look at her as her voice whipped from her throat. 'Your son *cheated* on me.' She lowered her voice but there was no mistaking the edge of fury. 'He took our vow of fidelity and he stomped all over it and there is no excuse for that. *None*. He can hide from the responsibility of that in death, but I won't let you hide from the truth of it or pretend he was some kind of saint any more. I had to spend the last year in Hackney seeing the woman he betrayed me with and their child almost every day. Do you understand how much that *hurt*? Do you have *any* idea?'

She drew a shaky breath. Every part of her trembled. She'd never spoken to her mother-in-law like this but this was her line in the sand.

No more Saint Dom.

'Dom was my husband and, yes, I loved him. But he *hurt* me and that changed everything. Sure, he was human and he was flawed, and neither of us can go back and change what he did. But *I* can change how *I* feel. And I don't love him any more, Francesca.'

She loved Aaron. Yes—*she loved Aaron.*

A rush of emotion swamped Chelsea's chest as quiet sobbing sounded in her ear, and she sat with the truth of her feelings, growing and glowing, giving her courage not to take back every word in the face of Francesca's tears. It felt as if a yoke had been ripped from her neck and Chelsea wouldn't pick it up and put it back on again.

Dom was her past. Aaron was her future.

'I'm sorry, Chelsea,' Francesca said eventually as her weeping subsided. 'I didn't understand. You were always so good and kind about it, I underestimated how much having Krystal and Alfie around hurt you. How much *Dom* hurt you. I'm so, so sorry.'

Breathing out slowly, Chelsea's chest filled with a different kind of emotion. For the first time since Alfie had arrived on the scene, she actually felt as though Francesca *really* understood how difficult the last year had been for her, and the shackles that had kept them joined together in a cycle of grief and guilt fell away. Which made her next decision even easier.

'I'm not coming, Francesca.'

'Chelsea…please, *bella*.'

She was so used to being the one that Francesca and Roberto relied on since Dom's death, it was strange to realise that they'd be okay without her. They had plenty of family—they'd always had plenty of family. And now it was time to lean on them.

She was drawing a line in the sand.

Charmaine had told her to go to her family, and for a long time Hackney and the Rossis had been her family. More so than the house she'd grown up in. But things happened, feelings altered, directions changed. And, even though she'd been in Balanora for such a short period of time, when she thought of family she thought of that hangar baking under the Outback sun in the middle of nowhere.

She thought of Charmaine and Hattie and Travis. She thought of *Aaron*.

'It's time, Francesca. Krystal and Alfie need you, and Roberto and the rest of the family. They don't need me.' Francesca had been trying hard to hang on with both hands but it was time to let go. 'You've got to let me live my life now.'

There were more quiet tears, but when Francesca next spoke she said, 'You will keep in touch, won't you?'

'Of course. I'm not cutting you out of my life, and I want to keep across Alfie's progress. We're just…turning a new page.'

'You like it there?'

Chelsea smiled. 'I *love* it here.'

Five minutes later, with her carry-on bag rolling behind her—her only piece of luggage—Chelsea strode out into the Brisbane sunshine.

The next morning, just after eleven, and almost seven weeks to the day she'd first landed in Balanora, Chelsea was back. It was still scorching hot as she walked off the plane and onto the Tarmac but she barely noticed. She only had one thing on her mind as she got into the nearest taxi—go to Aaron.

He had a couple of days off now and she knew he'd planned to go to Curran Downs because she'd been going with him. A quick phone call to the house phone confirmed that he'd arrived there last night and had gone straight to the river to camp for a couple of days.

So, the river it was.

Chelsea was home for five minutes—just long enough to divest herself of her suitcase and get into that green strappy dress he liked so much. Then she was in her car and heading to Curran Downs. She'd been there three times now, so she knew the way, but the trip felt ten times longer, her anxiety growing more acute as her car ate up the miles.

What if she'd blown it? What if she'd permanently damaged things between them by her abrupt departure?

When she reached the homestead, Tracey was waiting for her with a four-wheel-drive vehicle. Even though Aaron had taken her to the river last time she'd been to Curran Downs, it was a slightly more complicated path, and Tracey had suggested on the phone that she drop Chelsea there and she and Aaron could come back in Aaron's vehicle when they were ready.

'Is everything okay with Alfie?' Tracey asked as she gave Chelsea a quick hug.

'Yep. Off life-support. Talking. Not quite his usual chatty self but apparently doing well.' She'd checked in with Great Ormond Street and Francesca this morning before her flight to Balanora.

'A good outcome.'

Chelsea nodded. 'Yes.'

'Get in,' Tracey said in her typical no-nonsense way, which suited Chelsea just fine.

She had no desire to swap pleasantries—she just needed to find Aaron. They needed to talk. And she needed to feel his arms around her.

Any other time, Chelsea would have enjoyed the drive. The vast canvas of the Outback topped off by a bright-blue sky was magnificent in that grand sweeping way of all landscape vistas. But today she was too preoccupied to be appreciative of the scenery.

'Is Aaron okay?' she asked, staring out of the window at nothing, conscious only of her own heartbeat as they jostled along through the scrub.

'He's fine.'

She turned sharply. 'Really?'

Tracey glanced over. 'Aaron's not much of a talker,' she clarified as she returned her attention to the bush track.

'I screwed up.' Unfortunately, admitting it out loud didn't help any.

'But you're here to fix it, right?'

'Yes.' A thousand times yes.

'Well, then…'

'What if it's too late?'

Tracey laughed. It wasn't cruel or unkind, merely amused. 'You've been gone one day.'

'That's long enough for regret to set in.'

'Nah.' Tracey shook his head. 'Aaron's not built like that. Our mother leaving taught him to guard his heart, sure. But, unlike me, it also taught him how to forgive, and how to understand that this place isn't for everyone, and that's actually not some horrible kind of flaw.'

Tracey's mouth tilted upwards and Chelsea smiled at his sister's self-deprecation, despite the niggle of anxiety pecking at her brain. 'It's for me,' Chelsea said.

This vast expanse of red dirt and blue sky, so different from where she had come from, had worked its way under her skin. Just as Aaron had.

'Good.' She nodded. 'Tell him that.'

Twenty minutes later, Aaron's ute came into view, parked under the shade of some river gums. Chelsea spotted him sitting on the back tray, a frosty bottle in his hand, the same time he heard the engine, craning his neck in its direction. She could see his brows knit together as he tried to figure out why his sister was here, and who was in the passenger seat, and she clocked the second he realised it was her, his expression briefly surprised before turning guarded.

He leapt off the back of the ute as Tracey pulled her vehicle up alongside his. She put the window down but kept the engine running. 'Brought you a visitor,' she said with a smile.

Chelsea swallowed as Aaron looked at her as if she was some kind of mirage. His eyes ate her up as hers did him. It had been less than twenty-four hours but she'd *missed* him. Missed his crooked face and his carelessly messy hair swooping across his forehead. Missed the way he filled out a T-shirt and shorts.

Missed the way he looked at her as though she was special. As though she was *enough*.

A trill of anticipation caused her hand to tremble as she placed it on the door handle and pushed. Chelsea's pulse fluttered at her temple and she wondered if she'd ever stop feeling as though she'd been plugged into an electrical socket when he was near.

She hoped not.

'Thanks, Tracey,' she said as she slid out of the four-wheel drive, the heat hitting hard after the frigid air-con in the cab.

'No worries,' Tracey replied cheerfully, then winked at her brother as Chelsea shut the door and stood clear. 'You kiddies behave now, you hear.'

She drove off then, but neither of them really noticed as they stood staring at each other for long moments. 'Chelsea?' There was so much hope in his voice as he took a step forward, then his brow furrowed and he halted. 'Is Alfie…? Did he…? He didn't…?'

'No.' She shook her head. 'He's fine, doing well. Off the vent, stable GCS, in a stepdown ward. The fracture was hairline and the bleed quite small. They're confident it should resolve reasonably quickly and he should make a full recovery in time.'

He breathed on a rush. 'That's so good. Everyone must be very relieved.'

'Yeah. They'll feel better when he's home but they're counting their blessings.'

'So, you…' He eyed her speculatively and she swore she saw hope in his eyes. 'Didn't get on the plane?'

She smiled as she shook her head slowly. 'I did not.'

'Because Alfie's condition had improved?'

'Not because of that, no.'

'Okay.' He looked as though he wanted to come closer but shoved his hands on his hips instead. 'Because?'

Chelsea took a step towards him instead. 'I had an epiphany at the airport.'

'Oh.' He swallowed. 'You did, huh?'

'I did.'

'Care to share?'

Taking another step, Chelsea halted about three metres from him, aware suddenly of the volume of silence all around them. 'I realised that I wasn't responsible for Dom's family. And that it wasn't fair of them to expect me to keep playing the part of grieving widow. That I needed to move on. That we all needed to move on.'

A beat or two passed between them then Aaron took a tentative step in her direction. 'That sounds…healthy.'

Chelsea nodded. The husky edge to his voice sounded strained. 'I also realised that I'd fallen in love with you.'

He blinked. 'You…did?'

'I know it's crazy, Aaron.' Her pulse was jumping all over the place as she inched closer to him. She was pretty sure he felt the same but he didn't seem to be leaping for joy at her admission. 'I know it's not been very long but…'

Within two strides he was grabbing her up and hauling her close, her breasts flattened against his chest, his hands cradling either side of her face as he kissed her—hard. Her pulse thrummed madly, the scent of the bush and the taste of beer filling her senses, making her dizzy.

'God,' he muttered, breaking away to kiss her eyes and her nose and nuzzle her temple, his fast, raspy breath ruffling her hair. 'I didn't think you'd come back.'

Chelsea's breathing was equally as erratic. 'I'm sorry, I'm so sorry I left so quickly, I just panicked and reacted without thinking things through properly.' She shut her eyes as his lips caused all kinds of havoc. 'But I always planned on coming back. Always.'

'I thought the pull of home would be too much when you got there.' His lips trekked down the side of her face. 'With everything familiar that you knew and loved at your fingertips again. And I've been sitting here, kicking myself one moment for being such an idiot to fall for you, and planning on moving to the UK the next.'

Chelsea blinked. '*What?* Moving to the UK?'

'Of course. If it means being with you? Absolutely.'

She drew back, needing to make eye contact. Needing him to know. 'There's no need for that. *This* is my home now.' Her gaze captured his and locked. 'Balanora. And you. *You're* my home. I love you, Aaron, and I swear I'll never leave you like that again. *Never.* I think we've both spent a lot of our lives feeling like we weren't enough for people, but now we get to be each other's enough, and that's all I want. Just you and me for ever.'

'That's what I want too.' He kissed her again quickly, as if to assure her. 'I love you, Chelsea Tanner...and

I know I've said this before, but you are *more* than enough. You are my everything. I am yours, and *only* yours, for ever and always.'

And that was all she needed. This man loving her in the same way she loved him—as big and as vast and as fathomless as the landscape around them.

For ever and always.

EPILOGUE

One year later, Christmas morning

CHELSEA STARED OUT of the window of the King Air as it made its descent to the graded red earth of the community airstrip below. Just beyond the strip, behind a low, tinsel-emblazoned partition, stood a gaggle of cheering kids, their eyes squinting expectantly at the approaching plane.

She was excited to be part of the annual Christmas Express run by the OA, which involved hopping from community to community on Christmas day, distributing gifts to kids in isolated areas and giving every child a chance to have a photo with Santa. It was one of the highlights of the OA calendar and Chelsea had been looking forward to it. Last year she'd been on call, and therefore unable to take part, but not this year!

She glanced across at Aaron as Hattie landed the plane with her usual light touch. He was dressed in a red Santa suit, complete with snowy beard and a pillow for his belly, and Chelsea laughed as the plane taxied. 'Have I told you how hot you look in that suit?' she said into the headphone mic.

Santa might not usually be considered a sex symbol but it sure worked on Aaron.

'You look pretty hot too, elf girl.'

Chelsea blew him a kiss. She'd bought the elf suit online a few months ago when Charmaine had asked her what she wanted to dress up as for the Express. Seeing Aaron's face in the office this morning when she'd changed into it just prior to boarding, she was very pleased she had. The skirt was shortish and flirty, and the top, with the addition of a push-up bra, showed off a hint of cleavage.

It wasn't overtly sexy but he'd obviously liked what he saw and had whispered to her, 'You better wear that to bed tonight,' as he'd passed her by.

Thinking about it now, her heart overflowed anew with the depth of her feelings for this man who had filled her life this past year with so much love and joy. She couldn't remember ever being this happy. Their relationship had gone from strength to strength, and they'd moved in together six months ago. Three months ago, they'd spent two fantastic weeks in Tasmania, including one glorious night witnessing the spectacle and majesty of the aurora.

And now this. Christmas day playing Santa in the Outback. Pinch her!

Alfie, who had made a full recovery, had been impressed when she'd told him she was flying with Santa today, and she'd promised him a picture of her with the man himself.

The plane came to a halt and Chelsea removed her headphones, unbuckling and springing up from her seat, eager to get outside, the bell on the end of her jaunty elf hat tinkling as she scooped up the Polaroid camera.

It was Aaron's turn to laugh. 'Having fun?' he teased as he pulled his headphones off and reached for the sack in front of him, neatly labelled by Meg as being for this stop.

She grinned, her heart full of love and Christmas spirit. 'Santa baby, this is the best time I've ever had.'

He shook his head slowly, his gaze capturing hers. '*You're* the best time I've ever had, Chelsea Tanner.'

Chelsea's insides melted to goo. The man said the sweetest damned things. *All the time.* 'Merry Christmas,' she murmured.

'Merry Christmas,' he replied. 'Here's to many more.'

Then, from a pocket, he produced some plastic mistletoe, held it up high with one hand and snagged her closer with the other, kissing her in a very un-Santa-like way.

Yes, Chelsea thought on a sigh. *Here's to many, many more.*

* * * * *

ONE WEEKEND
IN PRAGUE

ALISON ROBERTS

MILLS & BOON

CHAPTER ONE

Oh... How amazing was this?

It was late enough to be dark on a summer's night and Hanna Peterson was somewhere she'd never been before in her life. Somewhere so magical, the views from the taxi windows seemed like glimpses of a fantasy city as the driver negotiated busy roads and narrow streets to take them into the ancient centre of Prague.

'I can't believe this,' she said, turning her head to where her best friend, Jo, was sitting in the back seat of the taxi. 'I feel like I've stepped into a fairy tale.'

Everywhere Hanna looked, there was something astonishing. Lights gilded the spires of Prague's famous castle on the hill and all the statues that guarded the length of the bridge leading over to that side of the river. There were cobbled streets and squares and every building looked unique. Dramatic in their extravagant architecture, mysterious in their antiquity and, oh, so romantic with their myriad rooflines of steep slopes and domes and spires stretching into the night sky.

'Mmm...' But Jo wasn't looking out of the windows right now. She was resting her head on the shoulder of the man sitting beside her, gazing up adoringly at her new husband, Cade. 'Me, too…'

Hanna shook her head. 'I also can't believe I've crashed your honeymoon. I feel like the biggest gooseberry ever.'

Jo sat up. Slowly. In the last trimester of her pregnancy, the long international flight had been more uncomfortable than usual. 'Don't be silly,' she said. 'You're not on our *whole* honeymoon. We just happen to be all going to the same conference for the weekend. Then Cade and I will go to the nearest beach where I'll lie there like the beached whale I am for another day or two and you'll go off on one of your adventures.' She put her head back on Cade's shoulder. 'Anyway, this could be seen as a babymoon instead of a honeymoon.'

Cade laughed. 'Wouldn't you have a babymoon *after* the baby arrives, like a honeymoon is after the wedding?'

'Are you kidding?' Hanna grinned. 'Nobody gets a holiday after a baby arrives. You'll be dreaming of having one. For years and years and years…'

It was easy to tap into the jokes. The ones that emphasised that Hanna had never wanted kids. Or a husband, for that matter, because they tended to want the ankle-biters that stopped you going on holidays.

Mind you, she'd never seen Jo look this happy. She'd been the bridesmaid and witness at the private wedding ceremony, just a few days ago, on a beach near Dunedin in the South Island of New Zealand and, despite the incredibly long journey to get to this part of Europe and how tired Jo had to be, she was still glowing with the joy of it all.

Hanna turned back to stare out of the window again,

partly because she didn't want to miss anything but it was also to distract herself from that twinge of something she didn't like.

Envy? Surely not. But there was something niggling deep down that was disturbing and it had started when she'd been standing on that beach, watching Jo and Cade exchange vows. It seemed to get slightly sharper edges every time she caught the way they looked at each other, too, so maybe it was best to keep looking at the enticing view outside. She'd be able to appreciate it even more tomorrow when she went on that walking tour she'd booked online as soon as she'd known she was coming here.

The tour was the only thing Hanna had booked for the next three weeks, apart from her flights. She'd always loved to follow her nose and make impetuous decisions when it came to travel because the very best discoveries and adventures could be found that way. And, if they turned out to be disappointing, she could just change her plans instantly and try something else. She hadn't been on an overseas trip for more than a year and Hanna could feel the tendrils of a familiar and very welcome excitement flickering with enough strength to make that niggle disappear.

Maybe this trip to Prague and whatever awaited her after the intensive two days at the conference was a timely reminder that being single and childfree was the ticket to the most amazing, memorable adventures. It always had been, after all.

Hamish MacMillan had unpacked his toilet bag but he took a moment to make sure he hadn't forgotten anything.

His toothbrush was in the glass the hotel had provided on the shelf above the basin, wearing its plastic cap to keep clean, accompanied by toothpaste and floss. His hairbrush and comb were beside the glass. With a satisfied nod, Mac noted that his shaving kit was ready for use first thing tomorrow morning and walked back into the lavish bedroom in a rather wonderful hotel in the Old Town Square in Prague.

His shirts hung neatly in the wardrobe already, along with a smart, pinstriped suit and a small selection of ties. The more casual clothing, which he could wear when he wasn't being a keynote speaker at a prestigious international medical conference, could stay in his suitcase for now. Mac had a laptop bag with other things he needed to check before he could finally get to bed.

Important things, like the USB stick that had the transcript and images that went with the presentation he would be giving to open this two-day conference on Emergency Medicine. It also had a folder containing all his arrangements for the holiday he had planned to fill in the week between this speaking engagement and the next one, which was in Paris. The prospect of a few days of some early summer warmth in Europe had been so much more appealing than flying back to his home in Scotland that had been closed up for over a year and would, no doubt, be about as inviting as walking into an oversized refrigerator.

It had been a pleasure to find a luxury bus tour where every detail of accommodation, transport and meals was prearranged. Mac would be able not only to enjoy exploring places he either loved or had never visited but also genuinely relax knowing that he could rely on the organisation skills of others to make sure everything would run smoothly.

Registration instructions for the conference were also in the folder but the main desk wouldn't open until tomorrow afternoon. That left an entire morning and Mac intended to make the most of it. He was on his first visit to a city with a fascinating history and he wanted to learn as much as possible but where would be the best place to start?

Probably right here in front of his hotel, he decided, and the thought prompted him to abandon the plan to fire up his laptop and scroll through the conference programme to see what he might like to listen to. Instead, he went to the doors set inside the arched window of his room and stepped out onto the balcony. It was completely dark now but the square was humming with life. There were people walking, sitting on the steps of a huge, central monument and crowding outdoor restaurants and bars. The spires of ornate churches and facades of other buildings were bathed in spotlights and there were vehicles pulling up to hotel entrances.

A taxi had just stopped in front of this hotel and Mac's gaze caught briefly as he watched a man holding out his hand to help a woman from the back seat of the car. A rather heavily pregnant woman. A third passenger was already out of the car. Another woman, but this one was tall and slim and had a long braid of hair hanging down the line of her spine. There was something about her that caught his attention. Perhaps it was the way she seemed oblivious to her companions or the luggage the taxi driver was hauling from the boot. She was staring at something, utterly entranced. The churches?

No…maybe it was that building almost directly opposite the hotel. The one with the chunky tower that had
a crowd of people gathered in front of it.

Mac didn't need to hear the chiming of a clock to
know what was happening. And a glance at his watch
told him why people had gathered. He'd learned about
the famous astronomical clock when he was no more
than ten years old and he'd fallen totally in love with
it. That clock had probably been the main incentive to
accept the invitation to speak at this particular conference but it had been pushed firmly to the back of his
mind as he'd dealt with the logistics of finding his hotel
and unpacking.

A curious sensation was growing in Mac's gut as he
took in the chimes fading and heard the faint sound of
clapping and cheers from across the large square, but it
took a moment to recognise that it might be excitement.
A kind of excitement that made him a little nervous, to
be honest, because memories of feeling like this told
him that this feeling could morph into fear in a heartbeat. That the feeling that something amazing might be
about to happen wasn't to be trusted.

The woman with the braid turned away from the
view and looked up at the hotel. Mac knew she couldn't
see him but he could see her quite clearly. Clearly
enough to see the expression on her face that told him
she totally trusted that feeling. That she had absolute
confidence that something amazing was already happening and that she was going to enjoy every moment
of it.

Mac found himself smiling as he went back into his
room. He opened up his laptop but, instead of finding

the conference programme to study, or the contact details of people he needed to liaise with for his own commitments to that programme, he typed a query into the subject line of the search bar.

Tours that include the astronomical clock in Prague

He clicked on one that promised to cover the main attractions of Prague in a two-hour period and chose the earliest time for tomorrow morning. It was a walking tour that started right in front of the clock, which sounded like a perfect way to start his day. Eight-forty a.m. seemed an unusually precise time to start a tour but that only made it more attractive and, with a satisfied nod, Mac booked himself in.

Hanna had to run across the square to make it in time because the lace on her most comfortable sneakers had broken. Fortunately, Jo was going to rest this morning, so she'd pulled a lace from one of her trainers and lent it to Hanna. Also fortunately, it was obvious who the guide was, because he was holding up a red flag with a white 'W' on it. Hanna arrived just in time to hear the middle-aged man explaining that the letter was not only because this was a walking tour but that his name was William.

'Welcome to Prague, ladies and gentlemen. It will be my pleasure to introduce you all to the beautiful capital of the Czech Republic, also known as the City of a Hundred Spires. Prague is my home and my native language is Czech and, while this tour is in English, I'm also fluent in French and German. How many of you have English as your first language?'

Hanna cast a quick glance around the group of about a dozen people, noting that only half of them were raising their hands along with her. A man at the front, who was very tall and had a commendably good posture, turned as if he was wondering the same thing and, weirdly, when he saw Hanna his eyes widened as if he recognised her.

He must be mistaking her for someone else, she thought, because if she'd met *him* before she'd certainly remember it. It wasn't simply his height or posture that would make him stand out in a crowd, he was immaculately dressed in a short-sleeved, open-necked white shirt and well-fitting khaki chinos and his face was... distinctive. A bit craggy, with deep lines from his nose to the corners of his mouth and eyes that—even at this distance and for only the space of a heartbeat—gave her the impression that he was examining whatever he could see with great care.

Hurriedly, Hanna tuned back into what William was saying. 'We are standing in the Old Town Square and, as I'm sure you're all aware, we're standing in front of one of the most popular tourist attractions in Prague—our medieval astronomical clock or the Prague Orloj.' He checked his watch. 'In fifteen minutes it will provide its animated hourly show of the apostles' march and that gives me just enough time to tell you a few things about it. Let's get a little closer so that we'll have the best view.'

William smiled at Hanna and she got the impression he'd seen her running across the cobbled square to get here in time. She smiled back as she moved with the group to stand as close as possible to both the clock and their guide. Hanna ended up at the front of the group on the opposite side to the tall man in chinos and she found her gaze drifting sideways shortly after William started talking again.

'The clock was installed early in the fifteenth century,' he told them. 'Legend has it that, when it was completed, the clock maker was blinded by the city councillors to prevent him making a better clock for any other city. In return, it is said that he ended his life by throwing himself into the workings of the clock to damage it and he put a curse on anyone who tried to repair it. They say it didn't work for a hundred years after that.'

The grim story had certainly caught everyone's attention but Hanna was still watching the man as he gave a slow nod, as if he thought that was fair enough, and Hanna found herself suppressing a smile. He was staring up at the large, ornate dials on the tower wall, clearly fascinated by what was obviously a mechanical and mathematical triumph, but Hanna wasn't concentrating on what William was telling them about how the positions of the sun and moon were shown or which medallions represented months of the year. She was simply taking in the moment and letting that bubble of excitement in her belly grow, knowing that this was the first step of her new adventure.

Which was probably why it took a moment longer than it might have to realise that something wasn't quite right.

'The four figures you can see at each side of the

clock are representations of things that were the most despised.' William was rubbing his forehead, his expression suggesting he was in pain. 'The man on the left is…is admiring himself in a mirror. This is…' William paused as if he'd forgotten what he was about to say and, when he did say something, it made no sense whatsoever.

The prickle of awareness Hanna could feel was something that could only be developed from years of experience in dealing with medical emergencies. Something physical was interfering with William's ability to think. It could be something like a very low blood sugar in a person with diabetes but the worst-case scenario would be that he was having a stroke where a blocked or burst blood vessel could be starting to cause catastrophic damage. That would explain him looking as if he'd had a sudden onset headache.

Poised to move to his side, for some reason, Hanna took a heartbeat to look across at the tall man and his head turned at exactly the same moment. There was recognition there. They were both on high alert. They both knew that something was about to happen.

And happen it did. Even as they both moved forward in the same instant, their guide crumpled, his head striking the cobbled ground with a sickening crunch. A few seconds later and his body began convulsing in a full tonic-clonic seizure.

Hanna's first action was to scan the immediate surroundings for any object that needed to be moved. William had already injured his head—she could see it was bleeding—and they needed to prevent any further injuries. She picked up the metal pole with the red flag on the top and handed it to someone behind her.

'Please move back,' she requested. 'We need some space.'

A glance sideways showed her that the tall man had his phone out but he wasn't speaking to call an ambulance and Hanna knew that he was most likely activating the stopwatch function to record both the time of onset of the seizure and how long it lasted.

It was certainly not showing any signs of stopping yet. Above them, the clock was now in motion with a tinny, repetitive chiming sound that had the effect of ramping up the tension of this situation. So did the press of people around them, staring in horror at the sight of William's head still bumping against the ground. Hanna looked around. She needed to put something between William's skull and the unforgiving cobbles. Preferably an article of clothing that was thicker than the soft, peasant-style blouse she was wearing over a camisole, although she was starting to pull it off already.

'Here, use this.' The man had a pullover draped over his shoulders. 'It should provide enough protection.'

He had a Scottish accent but Hanna was more impressed with his manner of speaking and the effortless way he was taking charge of this situation. He folded the soft woollen garment and eased it under William's head. There was nothing more they could do now, other than to protect the man from any further injuries as they waited for the seizure to finish. That wasn't the opinion of others in the small crowd around them, however, which was understandable because it was distressing to hear the sound of abnormal breathing from their tour guide and see skin colour changes from the lack of circulating oxygen.

'We need something to put in his mouth.' The man shouting loudly had an American accent. 'Someone got a spoon? Or a pen? A toothbrush, even? He's going to swallow his tongue and die if we don't do something.'

Hanna's companion raised his voice to be heard above the chiming of more church bells in the square but his tone was perfectly calm. 'It's not possible for someone to swallow their tongue,' he said. 'And we know what we're doing. I'm a doctor.' He glanced at Hanna.

'ED nurse,' she told him.

He gave a single, approving nod, his glance shifting to his phone. 'We need to call an ambulance,' he said. 'He's injured himself and I can't see any medic alert bracelet, can you?'

'No.' William's wrists were bare but Hanna checked inside the top of his shirt for a necklace. 'A lot of people who have epilepsy choose not to wear one, though.'

'It could also be a first seizure.'

It was Hanna's turn to nod. If it was a first seizure, it could be a symptom of something seriously wrong in William's brain, like a tumour.

'Could someone call an ambulance, please?' he called. 'And move back a little more, please. Let's give this man a bit of privacy.'

Nobody had taken any notice of Hanna asking them to move back but this man's calm request had everybody shifting and she got the distinct impression that he could probably take command of any situation without being ignored or challenged. Some people on the edge of the group even turned to walk away and she could hear the call going out for an ambulance.

'How do you say "ambulance" in…?' The man who'd asked for a spoon was still louder than anyone else. 'What is it they speak here?'

'Czech,' someone else said.

'Záchranka,' someone else called. 'I've got a translation app.'

'It's on the way, already.' A local policeman was pushing through the onlookers. 'Can I be of assistance?'

The jerking of William's limbs had stopped. He was breathing normally again but was still unconscious. Hanna helped the doctor to put him into a recovery position, crossing one arm over his body and using his shoulder and hip to turn him. She automatically bent his leg to provide more stability, shifted the arm trapped underneath his body and then tilted his head back to ensure his airway was open.

The sound of a siren was already close and an airhorn was being used to clear pedestrians as the vehicle approached. The policemen helped translate information about the event and the length of time the seizure had lasted. The paramedic team were efficient, and William was conscious but confused, with his head bandaged, as they made him comfortable on a stretcher and then loaded him into the ambulance. Spectators dispersed quickly after that with the loud tourist expressing his disappointment.

'Well, so much for that walking tour,' he said. 'I wonder if we can get a refund?'

Others shook their heads and the group rapidly dispersed, leaving Hanna and the doctor alone. He was stooping to pick up his jumper from the cobbles.

'Don't do that,' she said.

'Sorry?' His eyebrows rose sharply at her command.

'It's got blood on it.'

'Yes, I know. But I can hardly leave it here, can I?'

'I've got a bag.' Hanna fished in her shoulder bag to take out a small ball. Releasing the string, she unfolded the reusable shopping bag made of parachute fabric. 'It'll keep you safer.'

'Thanks. I can get it back to you later.' He folded the jumper inwards so that he didn't touch any bloodstains. 'We're staying in the same hotel.'

Hanna blinked. How on earth did he know that?

Her astonishment was clearly visible. 'I saw you arrive last night,' he added. 'Given that you're an ED nurse, I'm guessing you're attending the conference?'

'Yes.' Hanna couldn't hide her smile. 'I'm really looking forward to it.'

Maybe, a small part of that pleasure was due to the thought that not only had this man taken notice of her arrival last night but he'd remembered her today. That explained why he'd given the impression that he knew who she was when she'd arrived at the tour group's meeting spot.

Her smile faded. 'This morning was my best chance to learn something about Prague, though. I was looking forward to this tour, as well.'

'Me, too.' He was giving her that look again, his eyes very slightly narrowed as if to focus on something important. 'Perhaps we could complete it ourselves? I printed out the itinerary and a map. I'm sure the newsagent stall over there would be able to provide a guide-book that would give us some information about each of the destinations.'

'That's a great idea.' Hanna was smiling again. 'So much better than trying to do it by yourself. My name's Hanna, by the way. Hanna Peterson.'

'I'm Hamish MacMillan,' he told her. 'But I've been called Mac all my adult life.'

The nickname suited him. It was unmistakeably Scottish as a name but it also suited how tidy this man looked. Buttoned up?

'You're not related to the raincoat people, are you?'

It was his turn to blink as he processed what she meant but then he smiled. 'It's a Mackintosh raincoat, not a MacMillan,' he said. 'There are many names in Scotland that start with a Mc or a Mac.'

It was the first time Hanna had seen this man smile and, for just a heartbeat, she forgot about everything else. It wasn't just that she could *see* his smile. She could *feel* it—filling her head and then sneaking down to curl itself around her heart. And it didn't stop there. It kept going down, to pool somewhere deep in her abdomen where, by some mysterious alchemy, it started to generate heat. She had to drag her gaze away from his smile but she only managed to lift it to where she found a pair of very dark eyes locked onto hers.

Oh, *my*…

Hanna might have to tap into her experience of deal-ing with potential emergencies again if she was going to be able to speak without revealing any effects of feel-ing completely blindsided by an attraction that was far more than anything she'd ever experienced in her life.

Oddly, it felt like Mac knew what was going on. Perhaps, by some miracle, this feeling was mutual but, if it was, he was an expert in hiding how he felt.

'Destination One,' he said, waving his hand at the clock above them. 'Prague's famous astronomical clock. Something I've always wanted to see but, somehow—' his tone was deadpan '—I could never find the time...'

Hanna gave a huff of laughter. 'I see what you did there.'

So he had a sense of humour on top of being the most gorgeous man she'd ever seen? Her level of anticipation for what this latest adventure in her life could possibly deliver had just gone through the roof.

'We've got time now,' she said. 'Let's not waste a minute of it.'

CHAPTER TWO

WALKING BACK FROM the newsagent's kiosk, a guidebook
in his hand, Mac came to the conclusion that whatever
it had been that had captured his attention about this
woman last night was even more intense at close range.

He couldn't quite put his finger on what it was, but he
suspected it had something to do with her sheer vital-
ity. The energy that she was radiating. She was a hundred per cent involved in what she was experiencing,
and he got the impression that Hanna Peterson wanted
total immersion in whatever was going on around her.
To combine using all her senses but also to learn whatever she could. The curious mind of an intelligent person could be more attractive than a physical feature.
Not that Hanna was lacking in physical attractiveness,
mind you. Quite the opposite.

Her curious mind had had enough of the clock, however. When he'd stopped in front of it again, opening
his guidebook to find any information other than what
William had been able to tell them, she had given him
a look that made him laugh out loud.

'You remind me of a dog I saw in Central Park recently,' he told her.

'Well, thanks very much.' Hanna was doing her best to look, and sound, highly offended.

'Not in a bad way,' Mac assured her. 'The dog was trying so hard to sit still but he was desperate to be let off his lead to run.'

Her lips twitched. She wanted to laugh. She was trying hard not to.

'It was a beautiful dog,' Mac added. 'It had a lovely, shiny coat.'

That did it. Her mouth curved into the most delightful grin and there was a sparkle in her eyes that made that hazel green colour come alive within a very distinctive dark rim. With the sun reaching past the spires of the Old Town now, the light made her skin look as delicate as porcelain and the smattering of freckles across her nose and cheekbones was as captivating as the fiery tones of her hair.

Yes, she was undoubtedly physically beautiful. And very smart. But Mac knew there was something else about her that was pulling him in like some kind of magnetic force.

Something irresistible.

'Woof,' Hanna said. 'And you're right. Can you throw the ball, please and take me to destination number two?'

Mac consulted the map and then nodded. 'Follow me.'

It was only a few minutes' walk from the Old Town Square to the Charles Bridge, which had been the next destination on the walking tour. He could understand that Hanna had already ticked the astronomical clock off the list of city highlights. He knew that very few people would have the same fascination for it that he had. He couldn't help throwing a last glance over his shoulder as they headed out of the square.

'You really do have a thing for that clock,' Hanna observed.

'I do,' Mac confessed. 'I blame it on the documentary I saw on telly when I was about nine years old. I was absolutely riveted.'

Hanna's glance was curious. Impressed, even. 'I'm pretty sure I was still watching cartoons when I was that age,' she told him. 'Were you a child genius?'

'Hardly. I just got mesmerised by its complexity, I guess.'

He could remember how enthralled he'd been at the precision of so many working parts, never missing a beat, as they did exactly what they were supposed to do. They were so controlled. Predictable. Dependable. It had been a glimpse into a concept that was alien in an unpredictable life that had the potential to veer across a spectrum with utter neglect at one end and terrifying violence at the other.

Not that he was about to tell a stranger anything about that. It was so far in his past that he didn't need to think about it himself but that wouldn't stop him coming back to have a private moment with that clock before he left this city. A quiet celebration of having achieved some of that predictability and control in his own life?

He was channelling some of that control now, as he cleared his throat and put on his best 'tour guide' voice.

'So, here we have one of Prague's most loved attractions, the Charles Bridge. Completed in 1402, it links the Old Town with the Lesser Town across the Vltava

River. You can see the fortifications of the towers at each end.'

'I can…' Hanna was gazing up at the tall, intricately decorated stone construction with its impossibly steep roof and small spires that was the entrance to the bridge at this end.

'The book says it's one of the most beautiful gothic gateways in the world.'

'I love it.'

Mac could see that she loved it. Her face was glowing with the kind of wonder you might see when a small child was almost overwhelmed with something that amazed them. The way he'd felt when he'd seen that documentary about the clock. When was the last time Mac had felt like that? Too many years to count, that was how many. Because, when you felt like that, you could get pulled in an unexpected direction and well… he wasn't even going to think about what had happened the last time he'd allowed that to happen.

'Would you like to climb the one hundred and thirty-eight steps to the viewing platform?'

'I'd love to.' But the way Hanna then screwed up her nose contradicted her enthusiasm. It also made Mac think of a rabbit sniffing the air to identify an unseen threat and it was…seriously cute. 'But we haven't got that much time and it looks like there's already quite a queue.'

Mac nodded his approval. They had a plan and they needed to stick to a timetable. 'Let's walk across the bridge. I can see the castle already and that's destination number three.'

Hanna's smile had all the anticipation of that small

child again, this time waiting to open a Christmas gift, perhaps. It was impossible not to take pleasure in seeing the joy this exploration was giving her. Like the parent of that child, he was able to see something with a perspective that was both poignant and refreshing.

'There are thirty statues of saints,' he told her, scanning the text in the book as they walked. 'And the most famous of all is the first one that was installed. St John of Nepomuk. Apparently, if you touch the statue, it will bring you good luck.'

'Cool.' Hanna tossed him another one of those smiles that lit up her face. 'We should all collect as much good luck as possible. You never know what's just around the next corner, do you?'

'No…that's very true.' Mac was smiling back at her. This time yesterday, he certainly hadn't known that he was going to meet one of the most intriguing women ever. Definitely one of the most attractive. How inappropriate was it, having only met Hanna a matter of minutes ago, that part of his brain was wondering whether kissing her might also be a one-of-a-kind experience?

'I mean, poor William.' Hanna paused for a moment, between the statues and the trestle tables of vendors selling all sorts of tourist friendly items. 'I do hope he's not about to find out something nasty, like that seizure is the first sign of a brain tumour.'

Mac had to wonder if Hanna had any idea how much of what she was feeling was showing on her face and in the tone of her voice. He'd worked with enough people in situations that were sometimes devastating and his instincts were telling him that Hanna was a very genuine person. Compassionate to the point where she possibly became too involved with the patients she treated? Oddly, he felt a note of concern for her—as if her mental wellbeing was important to him.

He shook off the strange sensation by changing the subject after no more than a murmur of agreement.

'I'm still trying to place your accent,' he said. 'You're not Canadian, are you?'

'Nope.' Hanna was looking down at the river below them.

'Australian?'

'Getting warmer. Hot, even…' The glance he caught was teasing. 'You must have heard of my hometown. It's supposed to be the most Scottish city outside of Scotland.'

'You're from New Zealand,' Mac said, his steps slowing. 'I don't believe it…'

Hanna's eyebrows rose. 'Why is that so surprising? We're known as a nation of travellers. I suspect you'd be able to find a Kiwi in almost any corner of the globe.'

'I know. It's just…a coincidence, I guess.'

'Why?'

'My sister grew up there.' The words were out of Mac's mouth before he remembered that he never told anybody such personal information. 'My twin…'

It was Hanna's turn to look astonished. And Mac could see something else in her gaze, as she processed what hadn't been said, that looked like…what, concern? He got the impression that she was more than willing to listen and that she was ready to offer support and he found he had to curb an urge to tell her more. The notion of having someone like Hanna on his side was oddly compelling but Mac knew better than to let his guard down.

'I didn't know her,' he said. 'We were separated as infants. I didn't even know she existed until I was old enough to be allowed to make enquiries about who my biological parents were.'

'They separated twins? That's awful…'

Mac's breath came out in a soft huff. 'I think my adoptive parents were only interested in a boy. Someone to carry on the family name.'

'Did you manage to find your sister?'

Mac shook his head. 'No. She'd died several years before I found out about her, of a brain tumour.'

'Oh, no…' The sympathy in Hanna's tone was like a physical touch. 'That's so sad.'

'Not really.' Mac shrugged. 'As I said, I never knew her. We didn't even share a surname. Her name was Jenny Dalgliesh.'

'It still sounds Scottish.'

'Her parents were Scottish. They emigrated just after they adopted her. It did make me curious about how different our lives must have been. I thought that, maybe one day, I'd like to go and see what it was like in New Zealand.'

'You should,' Hanna told him, turning to walk on. 'You'd love it.' She threw him a sideways glance as he caught up with her. 'You know what's even more of a coincidence than me coming from where your sister grew up?'

'What's that?'

'I almost got adopted.'

'Almost?'

'My father had a passion for flying and both my parents were killed when his plane went down when I was young. My grandmother had no real interest in doing the child-raising thing again but, in the end, she decided she couldn't send me away.'

Mac looked at this confident, vivacious woman beside him, imagined how enchanting she might have been as a young girl and found himself smiling. 'It seems like it worked out pretty well.'

'Gran did her best,' Hanna agreed. 'But there were so many rules. And I wasn't that good at following them all.'

Mac laughed. He could imagine that, as well.

'The problem was that we didn't understand each other,' Hanna said. 'Like, I wanted to learn to dance but I got sent to ballet lessons. And then ballroom lessons. Not at all what I wanted.'

Mac shuddered. 'I had to do ballroom dancing lessons at boarding school.'

'Lots of rules. Not so much fun.'

'Is dancing ever *fun*?'

The flash in her eyes made them light up. 'Have you ever seen the movie *Dirty Dancing*?'

Mac shook his head, not because he had no idea what she was talking about but because his imagination was threatening to run away with him this time. He cleared his throat, needing to change the subject before his thoughts became entirely inappropriate considering he'd only just met this woman.

'This statue we're coming to is the one I was telling you about. The most famous on the Charles Bridge,' he told her. 'See those shiny parts of the brass plaques on the base of the statue? They've been polished by the thousands of hands that had touched it for luck.'

'Oh…' Hanna was well distracted. Or perhaps she was responding to his unspoken warning that their conversation had been getting too personal. 'You can never have too much luck, can you?' She joined a small queue, waiting to take her turn to touch the statue.

Mac stayed where he was, needing a moment to himself because he could feel a ripple of something that threatened to disturb the pleasure of Hanna's company and a new city to explore. He hadn't thought about how he'd felt to discover he'd had a sister in too many years to count but he could remember that pull that could have taken him to the other side of the world, just to see what it was like. He'd been well trained not to respond to the temptation of doing something when the consequences hadn't been considered enough, however. He'd known that responding to that kind of pull could lead to the kind of trouble that could make life a lot less bearable.

But here he was, with someone who had links to more than one aspect of his life—his work that he was so passionate about and to a buried part of his past that had shaped who he actually was to such a large extent. Someone who was becoming so increasingly captivating that Mac was actually tempted to let himself get pulled—a little way, at least—in whatever direction Hanna Peterson wanted to take him.

Good grief… Mac followed Hanna and stepped towards the statue of John of Nepomuk. He might have zero belief in unscientific concepts like superstition, but it might be prudent to touch this particular statue. Just

to be on the safe side. Because it seemed like he could
do with a bit of luck himself…

Hanna had been on plenty of guided tours in her years
of travelling the globe but she'd never been on one quite
like this.

Because this was Prague and it was an enchanted
city.

Because her attraction to her guide had been there
right from the start and it was steadily increasing as
she noticed more and more about him. Like the way
his eyes creased a little and made his gaze quite piercing as he focused on anything. It could have made him
look suspicious, but his lips seemed to have a resting
position of a faint smile so, instead, he looked as if
he might be enjoying a private joke. His grooming—
including his haircut—was immaculate. Hanna could
imagine Mac wearing a tuxedo and looking as if he'd
stepped straight out of a Bond movie from the leading
role. His accent made her toes curl with delight to the
extent that she was probably missing a lot of the information he was reading aloud from the guidebook, but
it didn't matter.

Hanna was thoroughly enjoying herself.

They spent an hour exploring Prague Castle and
it felt like they barely scratched the surface of the
UNESCO monument.

'This is the largest continuous castle complex in the
world,' Mac told her. 'It covers almost seventy thousand
square metres.'

Hanna nodded solemnly. 'I think my feet are somehow already aware of this fact. They may be planning to stage a protest.'

'Do you want to stop?'

'*No...*' Her denial came out with slightly more emphasis than Hanna had intended but that was because the possibility had just occurred to her that when they stopped and parted ways, she might never see Mac again. And that prospect was...well, it was just something Hanna would prefer to put off for as long as she could.

'This is the best bit yet,' she added hastily, in case Mac could guess the main reason why she didn't want to stop. 'Look at that ceiling.'

She tilted her head back, relieved to escape catching Mac's gaze so she couldn't reveal *why* she didn't want to stop but she could feel his gaze resting on her face. Weirdly, it was making the skin on the rest of her body tingle. There was no doubt at all that there was some serious chemistry floating in the air between them. Hanna had to catch her breath as she found herself wondering what it might feel like if her skin was in contact with his. Or her lips...

'We could have a coffee soon,' Mac said. 'Or an early lunch? We passed some very nice-looking restaurants as we came off the Charles Bridge.'

They had. Restaurants with outdoor seating areas shaded by trees and umbrellas. Hanna had the feeling that Mac would choose one that also had linen tablecloths and polished silver cutlery and a wine list that he could peruse because he probably knew all about fine wines...

That summed him up completely, didn't it? He was

a gentleman. Or the Scottish equivalent of high social ranking—a laird, perhaps? Whatever... A traditional class system was an alien concept to most New Zealanders and Hanna was beginning to wonder what it would be like to see Dr Hamish MacMillan unbuttoned a little.

She had a feeling she would like what was revealed very much indeed.

Oh, help... Hanna made herself focus on what she was staring at, high above them on the ceiling of this huge hall they were in. 'They've made the beams look like flowers,' she said. 'How gorgeous is that?'

'It's ribbed vaulting,' Mac said, consulting his book. 'Late Gothic style. Work started on Vladislav Hall in 1486 under the orders of the King of Bohemia and the hall was completed in 1502.'

'Bohemia,' Hanna murmured. 'No wonder I feel like this place is touching my soul.'

'You're boho?' Mac was grinning. 'Of course you are. I should have guessed from that floaty sort of top you're wearing. The strings with the tassels are a dead giveaway come to think of it.'

'There are way more important aspects than clothing to having any traits that might be seen as bohemian,' Hanna chided.

'Such as?'

'Being a wanderer. I've always loved to travel. To just arrive somewhere and follow my nose.'

'Really? You don't book tours? Or hotels?'

'Nope. It's not so much of an adventure if you know what's coming, is it?'

'I wouldn't know.' Mac was shaking his head. 'I've never tried it. What else?'

'Well, I'm a bit unconventional,' Hanna said obligingly. 'And I tend to like other people who don't slot into what might be considered "normal" boxes.'

'I'm super normal,' Mac said.

'No.' Hanna shook her head. 'I don't think so.'

Mac's eyebrows rose. 'What makes you say that?'

'I meet normal people every day. I've met countless thousands of them in my lifetime but...'

'But...?' He was giving her that piercing look again.

Hanna caught her lip between her teeth. Would it be a death knell to say the words that were on the tip of her tongue out loud? She gave herself a mental shove with the vague encouragement of fortune favouring the brave.

'But I've never met anyone quite like you,' she added softly.

He held her gaze for the longest time. Long enough for Hanna's heart rate to pick up and even skip a beat. For that tingling sensation to sink well beneath skin level and take up residence deep in her belly where it found and instantly merged with the excitement that a new adventure always bestowed.

For a moment, she forgot the real reason she'd come to this beautiful European city. The conference where she hoped to learn so much and reconnect with the passion she had for her work seemed almost irrelevant—a mere background that was providing the opportunity of a meeting that felt significant enough to be potentially life-changing.

Which was ridiculous. For heaven's sake, she knew virtually nothing about this man, other than that he was a doctor who was going to be attending the same conference as herself and that he had a sister he'd never known who happened to live in Hanna's homeland. He could be the laird of a Scottish estate, for all she knew. He could well be married with half a dozen children. But it really did feel as if she was on the brink of something so big, it was almost scary. Okay, they clearly had very different personalities. He was so buttoned up and Hanna was open to almost anything but…well, everybody knew that opposites could attract.

And that made it easy to shrug off any significance. That was all this was. An attraction. The kind that was best suited to a brief period of time where it could erupt into flames instantly and burn itself out rapidly enough to not create anything more than a pleasant memory. Hanna Peterson didn't do significant. She really did have the soul of a wanderer and they always tended to be lone wolves, didn't they?

She had, however, had the pleasant experience of indulging in a holiday fling before now and, even if playing with the chemistry between them was as far as this went, it was still rather delicious.

'You know what?' she said to Mac.

'What?'

'I'm starving. Let's go and find some lunch.'

Perhaps he shouldn't have given Hanna the choice of where to eat but he'd expected that she'd choose one of those pleasant looking restaurants with their charming terraces, not a truck selling street food.

The glance she'd given him had made it clear that this was some kind of test, however. She knew that he'd prefer to sit at a table and order something from a menu, didn't she? Was she pushing a boundary to see if she could put a label on what box to slot him into? If so, even though Mac wasn't sure why this was so important, she was going to be disappointed because he intended to pass this test with flying colours. He didn't want to be normal enough to be labelled.

He wanted Hanna to like him.

So he carried cardboard boxes of what was apparently a local specialty while Hanna searched for an acceptable place to stop and eat. He couldn't fault her choice, which was a low stone wall, under a tree, not far from a boat ramp advertising river cruises.

The food had an unpronounceable name and consisted of deep-fried cheese balls that came with salad, a bread roll and a small wooden fork. It was surprisingly delicious but alarmingly messy. When Mac bit through the crunchy, crumbed exterior of the ball, warm, gooey cheese dripped onto his fingers and would have ended up on his clothing if he hadn't immediately shifted it to arm's length.

Hanna laughed. 'You look like it's a bomb that's about to explode.'

'It's already trying to.'

'Try what I'm doing.' Hanna had torn open a section of her bread roll. She added salad and squashed a melty cheese ball into the middle.

Sure enough, it worked a treat, and it wasn't lost on Mac that if he'd been alone he might have discarded the food rather than end up with it all over his clothes and, if he had, he would have missed out on what ended up being the perfect lunch.

'This is heaven,' Hanna declared, happily, as she

ate her last mouthful and wiped her fingers on a servi-
ette. 'I'm officially in love with Prague.' She watched
a river boat pulling up to moor at the jetty. 'Oh, look...
I'm not the only one in love. There's a wedding party.'

They both watched as the group of people took their
time disembarking as the bride and groom posed for
photographs. Hanna was still smiling.

'I'll tell you a secret,' she said.

'What's that?'

'I'm here on honeymoon.'

Mac blinked. Surely that sensation suddenly filling
his chest wasn't disappointment? *Envy*, even? Marriage
was the last thing he'd ever want for himself, after all.
He'd learned that lesson a very long time ago.

But there was a mischievous twinkle in Hanna's expression. 'Not my honeymoon,' she added. 'My friends'.
And they did invite me along. Given that it's the closest I'll ever get to having one, I thought I'd try it out.'

That strange, unpleasant sensation escaped with his
next breath.

'You're never going to have a honeymoon of your
own?'

'I did say I was unconventional, didn't I? Marriage.
Kids. Not for me.' Hanna was still watching the bride
so Mac couldn't detect anything that might have under-
mined how genuine her statement was.

'We're on the same page there,' he said.

Hanna's sideways glance was curious. 'How old are
you?'

'Forty-four.'

'And you've never been married?'

'Nope. I was engaged once,' Mac admitted. 'That was once too often.'

He could still see questions in her eyes, so he looked away to let her know it wasn't a subject he wanted to continue.

'Same,' he heard her say quietly. 'Guess we both dodged the marriage bullet.' She let her breath out in a sigh as she turned to watch the bride gathering her skirts to walk away. 'Pretty dress, though...'

Mac didn't say anything, distracted by a connection he could feel with Hanna that was so much deeper than their similar career choices. And spending time with her had also just become a lot safer than it might have otherwise felt.

'Fancy a cruise?' he asked. 'That wedding party is finished and it only takes forty-five minutes according to that sign.'

It didn't really matter if he didn't go through the conference registration process as soon as it opened, the way he normally would, did it? The desk would be open until this evening, after all, and there would be plenty of time to talk to his international colleagues over the next couple of days.

He'd thrown caution to the winds eating a meal he would never have chosen for himself, after all, and he'd thoroughly enjoyed it so who knew what he might be missing if he walked away from what was, in fact, the type of well-rehearsed tourist attraction he preferred? As a bonus, he would get a little more of Hanna's company before he had to focus on the professional reasons that had actually brought him to Prague.

A short time later, they were looping through the

archways under the Charles Bridge and sailing slowly along the 'Devil's Channel', a canal with buildings crowding either side that was reminiscent of Venice. They listened to a commentary as they floated past historic buildings and got a wonderful view of the castle from a distance. Wearing the earplugs for the recorded information meant they weren't talking to each other but the way they kept sharing glances made it feel as if they were still communicating and that made it feel so very different from any other tourist tour that Mac had ever taken. If he was honest, he wasn't listening nearly as intently as he would have if he'd been alone and he probably completely missed all sorts of interesting facts about Prague's history.

And he didn't give a damn…

Hanna's feet were reminding her how far they'd walked by the time they were heading back to their hotel. Over the bridge again, through streets that were starting to look familiar and into the square where a new crowd was gathering in front of the famous clock, waiting for it to chime the hour.

'We never did get to see the apostles appear, did we?'

'We didn't,' Mac agreed. 'I seem to remember we were a bit preoccupied.'

'We've got time…' Hanna could see that Mac instantly recognised what had the potential to become a private joke. His eyes were doing that crinkly, focused thing again.

Hanna wasn't about to admit it, a couple of minutes later, but the windows sliding open and the brief parade of small figures appearing was a little underwhelming.

She wouldn't have missed it, though, because it gave her an extra few minutes with Mac.

A complete stranger she'd just shared half a day with.

A man who, on surface appearances, could be her total opposite, and yet it felt like she could possibly be more than half in love with him already.

But it was time to say goodbye. She saw his glance shift to their hotel across the square and then drop to his watch. She could almost feel his withdrawal from being a carefree tourist who was happy to soak in the ambience of a fascinating new city to a professional who was here to attend an academic event.

There were hundreds of people attending this prestigious conference and it was quite likely that Hanna wasn't going to get another chance to talk to Mac, let alone spend any one-on-one time with him.

'It's been the best tour ever,' she told him. 'I really enjoyed it.'

'Me, too. I'm delighted to have met you, Hanna Peterson from Dunedin.'

'Thank you. I feel the same way, Hamish MacMillan, from not the raincoat clan in Scotland.'

They grinned at each other, and on impulse Hanna stood on tiptoes, put her arms around Mac's neck and kissed him.

Just a brief press of her lips against his but the effect was startling. Taken by surprise, Mac hadn't moved a muscle but it felt as if he'd just kissed her senseless because Hanna could feel her bones trying to melt.

Oops…

She caught his gaze for no more than a heartbeat, offering a quick smile to let him know it was no big deal. She kissed people goodbye all the time.

Then she turned to leave the clock in the same way she had arrived this morning.

At a run.

CHAPTER THREE

IT WAS LATE that evening that Hanna remembered the shoelace.

Not that Jo had mentioned it, when they'd met up late this afternoon to register for the conference and then find a quiet table at one of the outdoor restaurants in the Old Town Square to have dinner together, but what if Jo wanted to go for a walk tomorrow when she needed a break from the conference programme and couldn't wear her comfortable shoes because Hanna still had her shoelace?

She'd be asleep by now and Hanna had no intention of disturbing the newlyweds but she put the lace into an envelope and walked quietly along the hotel corridor, hoping no one would see her. She'd been getting ready for bed herself when she'd remembered the borrowed item and was wearing only leggings and a sweatshirt over her camisole. Her face was scrubbed free of makeup, her feet were bare and her hair hung in a rough braid down her back.

It was easy enough to slip the envelope under Cade and Jo's door and Hanna headed back to her own room. She ignored the doors to one of the lifts sliding open as she went past until she heard what sounded like her own name. And then she froze. She knew that voice.

That accent…

Oh, help… Hanna knew, even before she turned, that Mac would still be more than acceptably dressed for appearing in public and that his hair would look as if it had been combed very recently. If she'd wanted to accentuate how different they were from each other or confirm his opinion that any leanings towards being Bohemian meant dressing like a misplaced hippie, she couldn't have done a better job, could she? Good grief, her sweatshirt featured a peace sign made up of colourful flowers and, for heaven's sake, she had a tiny, braided silver toe ring on.

Mac had already noticed that toe ring, dammit. Or was he caught by the fact that Hanna was wandering the hotel corridors barefoot and braless? There was certainly something she hadn't seen before simmering in those dark, dark eyes.

'You're still up?'

The question was rhetorical but Hanna nodded as if it required an answer. Then she smiled. 'So are you.'

'I had an invitation to a cocktail party that went on rather a long time.' Mac held up a bottle he was holding as if it was part of his explanation. 'I tasted a champagne that was so good, I bought a bottle.' One of his eyebrows quirked. 'Maybe you'd like to try it?'

He was giving her that scrunchy eyed intense gaze again and Hanna could feel it all the way to that toe ring. She could feel herself swallow rather carefully because she knew exactly where this was heading. This was pretty much a textbook beginning to a holiday fling and this was the moment that Hanna had a choice.

Except it didn't feel like she did have a choice because the attraction that had been there between them since early this morning had flames licking its edges and it would only take a breath of oxygen in the right place to have it explode into an inferno. But it would be all the better for having that breath held for as long as possible.

So Hanna simply tilted her head as if she was giving the invitation careful thought.

'I do like champagne,' she said.

What on earth did he think he was doing?

There was only one reason that you invited a woman into your hotel room at this time of night. It wasn't the first time Mac had gone down this track but it was most definitely the first time with someone he'd only met a matter of hours ago.

Maybe that toe ring had tipped the balance and made him lose any common sense. Or maybe it was that Hanna Peterson was simply becoming increasingly intriguing.

Or perhaps it was as simple as knowing that he wanted this woman. A desire as old as time for a single male instinctively searching for a mate that had hit him like a brick earlier today when Hanna had brushed her lips against his in farewell. Or was it just a human need for a connection he hadn't had for too long?

Whatever... He wasn't about to make a move on Hanna. Not this soon. He just couldn't resist the chance to be near her again. To let this feeling of desire fizz through his veins and make him feel more alive than he had in a very long time.

They drank the champagne, sitting out on his balcony, listening to the chimes in the square strike eleven o'clock.

'Did you ask for this room specially so you could sit out here and see your clock?'

'No. It was an unexpected bonus.' Mac raised his glass. 'Like meeting you.'

'I had the best time on our tour,' Hanna agreed.

'Me, too.' Mac couldn't look away from her. He loved the way those tiny curls of hair were escaping that long braid to frame her face and the way her skin looked almost pearlescent in the soft light from a streetlamp below. His mouth tilted on one side. 'Time seems to be a bit of a theme for us, doesn't it?'

'Everybody needs reminding sometimes that time can be short,' Hanna said. 'And that it's important to make the most of it. Especially when you're only going to be somewhere for a day or two.'

Oh…man… Was Hanna taking the first step to making this happen? Was she offering him a night he could be quite sure he was never going to forget? He'd always been quite sure he was immune to being seduced. That he could always stay completely in control at all times. It seemed that that assumption might be incorrect.

And, in this moment, Mac couldn't have cared less.

But he could see a flash of what looked like vulnerability in those amazing eyes. Because Hanna was offering an invitation that might be rejected?

As if…

He could take at least an element of control back,

couldn't he? And let her rest assured that her invitation was more than welcome. Mac got to his feet. He only needed to hold out his hands for Hanna to take them and it took only the tiniest tug for her to be on her feet and then in his arms. It didn't really matter who initiated that kiss because it seemed they both wanted it just as much as each other. As Hanna's lips parted beneath his and he felt the exquisite touch of her tongue against his, Mac gave up overthinking any of this.

There were no rules.

Time was indeed short and they should both absolutely make the most of it.

Walking into the hotel dining room the next morning, Hanna quickly spotted the table where Jo and Cade were sitting near a window. By the time she joined them, with a cup of strong coffee in her hands, the chimes in the square had finished announcing that it was eight o'clock. In an hour, the conference would be opened by a welcome speech in the main hall before the attendees would splinter into groups for the first of many presentations and workshops spread over the entire conference facilities.

'Morning.' Hanna took the empty seat beside Jo. She looked at the breakfast Cade had chosen of muesli with yoghurt and fruit and then at the plate in front of Jo that had a pastry stuffed full of what looked like custard. 'Mmm…healthy,' she murmured. 'What is that? A cronut?'

'I'm not sure.' Jo grinned. 'But it's delicious. And the pregnant lady gets to eat whatever she wants for breakfast.' She was about to take another bite but took another glance at Hanna instead.

'You look…different,' she said.

'Oh…?' Hanna closed her eyes, taking a sip of her excellent coffee. She needed it. She suspected she might look different because she'd had almost no sleep last night.

Thanks to Hamish MacMillan.

Or maybe it was thanks to the Gods of Holiday Flings. Or the sheer luck of bumping into Mac when she'd left her room, late last evening, on her way back from returning the forgotten shoelace.

'Maybe it's your hair.' Jo was still staring at Hanna when she opened her eyes again. 'You don't usually braid it like that, do you?'

'No.' Hanna had put braids along the side of her head as well as in the length of her hair. 'It needed taming.'

Because it had been such a mission to get all the knots out this morning that it had made her long hair extra wildly wavy. The pain of combing out every tangle had been worth it, though. Hanna had to push away the memories of Mac pulling the tie from the bottom of her loose braid and raking it loose with his fingers so that its length tickled her naked back as he held her head and kissed her until her bones really did melt. Or had she been kissing him? There was no getting away from the fact that she'd been the one to blow on those flames in the first place and create the wildfire.

'Hmm…' Jo took a bite of her pastry and her words were muffled. 'Suits you.'

'Is that a spare seat by any chance?'

The voice with its lilt of a Scottish accent came from

right behind Hanna. Luckily, she'd already put her coffee cup back onto its saucer so nothing got spilt. She sent out a silent plea to the universe that nobody would be able to guess the effect that Mac's voice was having on her body. That ripple felt like an aftershock of the most amazing sex she'd ever experienced in her life.

'Yes. Please…join us.' Cade pushed his chair back.

'Don't get up.' Mac set a plate of scrambled eggs and bacon onto the table. 'Good morning, Hanna. How are you?'

Hanna wasn't sure she was quite brave enough to make eye contact with Mac. A mere glance at the rest of his body was doing odd things to her heart rate. He was wearing an immaculate pinstriped suit that included a waistcoat. So very formal. He was buttoned up again, but Hanna knew the astonishing flipside of that coin now, didn't she? Could she even bring herself to say anything to him or was a sudden embarrassment stealing her voice? Had she been testing herself or Mac last night, being more adventurous than she'd ever been in bed before?

Wild. That was the only word for the sex they'd shared. And how amazing was it that Mac had gone along with every move? Not that they'd swung from the chandeliers, exactly, but…oh, *my*…

It was Jo who spoke quickly enough for any hesitation from Hanna to be disguised.

'You two know each other?' Her sideways glance was eloquent. Hanna hadn't said anything about how attractive her companion had been.

'We met yesterday.' Mac nodded. He was unwrapping his cutlery. As cool as a cucumber. Nobody would ever, ever guess just how well they now knew each other.

'Really?' Cade also sounded surprised.

'I told you during dinner last night.' To her relief, Hanna's voice sounded perfectly normal. 'I had the pleasure of Mac's company to explore Prague, after my walking tour didn't happen.'

'Ah, I remember...' Cade mirrored Mac's nod. 'The tour guide who gave you such an appropriate introduction to the conference by providing an emergency situation on our doorstep.'

'This is Hamish MacMillan,' Hanna said. 'Mac, these are my friends, Cade and Jo. Jo's an emergency medicine specialist from the hospital I work in and Cade is a critical care paramedic.'

Mac smiled across the table at Jo and shook hands with Cade. 'You've all come a long way to attend this conference.' He turned to Jo. 'The trip can't have been easy for you.'

'My feet are a bit puffy still,' Jo admitted. 'But I had to come. Cade's presenting a paper about the pre-hospital use of CPAP.' Her pride in her husband was obvious. 'And it's our honeymoon.'

'Oh...congratulations.' Mac shot a glance at Hanna and she grinned back at him.

Hanna knew that he was remembering their conversation yesterday when she'd told him she was sharing her friends' honeymoon, but she could see beneath that layer as well, to where he was also thinking about what had happened in his room last night. It wasn't so easy for him to appear in such control of his facial features, after all, was it?

'Hanna was our bridesmaid when we got married last week,' Jo told him. She grinned. 'It seemed a bit rude not to invite her to join our honeymoon.'

'We are having some time to ourselves after the conference,' Cade added. 'Just a couple of days for me and Jo, sadly, but we need to get home well before the new addition to our family thinks it might be a good idea to make an entrance. Hanna's the lucky one—she gets to float around Europe for another couple of weeks at least.'

'Where are you based, Mac?' Jo asked. 'I think Hanna said something about New York?'

'You mentioned you were in Central Park recently,' Hanna said. To her relief, it was not as hard as she expected to keep sounding completely casual. 'I might have made an assumption.'

'Not an entirely incorrect one,' Mac admitted, around mouthfuls of his breakfast. 'I have been living in New York for the last eighteen months. I had a fellowship at a research institute attached to a hospital with an excellent emergency department while I was working on a PhD.'

'And that's completed? Congratulations.' Jo's tone was impressed. 'I know how much work that is.'

'I completed it a little faster than expected,' Mac said. 'Which is why I'm currently unemployed.'

Hanna's eyes widened. Partly because of Mac's surprising comment, but also because his foot was touching hers under the table. Even if it wasn't deliberate, it was sending another one of those aftershocks rippling through her body. She wasn't avoiding eye contact this time, however. She was waiting for him to look up so she could see if he might be as aware of that touch as she was.

But Mac seemed to be trying to fit exactly the right combination of eggs and bacon onto a very small square of toast, so Hanna was left to remember not only the way he'd licked drippy cheese off his fingers yesterday but the touch of his tongue on parts of her body that had been the most extraordinary sensual experience ever.

'I took two years' leave from my position at an Edinburgh hospital,' Mac continued. 'Which means I might need to find an adventure or two to keep me out of mischief for a while.'

His foot moved against Hanna's. Deliberately. Her breath left her body in a long sigh. A quiet sigh, but Mac had heard it, judging by the flick of a glance that grazed her own. The way the lines around his mouth deepened made her wonder if he was suppressing a smile.

'Well...' Cade was grinning at Mac. 'If you get desperate, I know of a locum position in New Zealand that's going begging. Jo needs cover for the maternity leave that I hope she's going to start very soon.'

Mac's huff of laughter sounded no more than a polite acknowledgement that he'd heard the suggestion. He shifted his foot away from Hanna's, ate the last mouthful of his breakfast and got to his feet. 'If you'll excuse me,' he said, 'I have a bit of preparation to do before the programme starts. It's been a pleasure to meet you. I hope we get the chance to talk more later.' His gaze rested a moment on Hanna and, while he didn't say anything aloud, she got the distinct impression that he intended to do more than simply talk to *her* later.

She could feel her toes curling inside her shoes.

She was rather hoping that might happen herself.

'Nice guy,' Cade said, watching Mac stride across the dining room. 'Shame he isn't keen on the idea of a locum in New Zealand.'

Hanna couldn't see Mac sitting anywhere amongst the crowd gathering for the opening address of this conference but that was hardly surprising. There were hundreds of attendees packed into this auditorium. Jo's obviously advanced pregnancy had people scrambling to find them the best seats, however, and they settled in as a conference organiser welcomed them and attended to administrative information such as fire exits, bathroom facilities and where to access details on the scientific programme available. Then he turned to introducing the speaker who was going to open this conference.

'This man will be no stranger to a great many people here, with his more than three hundred published papers and numerous engagements to speak at international conferences. As a recipient of awards that recognise and celebrate innovative and extraordinary work by healthcare individuals and teams in the field of emergency medicine and having just come from a limited tenure as a director of a research collaboration in the United States, it's my pleasure to welcome Dr Hamish MacMillan.'

Hanna's jaw dropped. She barely felt the nudge from Jo's elbow or heard her soft exclamation because she was watching Mac walk across the stage to stop in front of the lectern. He was silent for a moment, looking out at his audience, and even from a distance, Hanna knew it was that focused look that deepened the tiny lines at the corners of his eyes. She was still so stunned by the fact that she had spent most of yesterday playing with possibly the most eminent conference attendee here that she barely listened to him congratulating the conference organisers on the wide-ranging topics being presented over the next two days. She wasn't watching the images appearing on the screen behind Mac, either. She was simply watching him, so aware of how intimately she now knew this man. It was a real effort to tune into what he was saying.

'Adversity, like necessity, can inspire invention or advances that can accelerate changes likely to benefit us all. The challenges we've all faced in recent times, dealing with a global pandemic, has given us a new perspective on the big picture areas like the management systems and surge capacities of our hospitals and emergency departments. Advances in technology are becoming a beneficial part of the "new normal" but cyber-attacks are a very real threat. Like all of you, I'm looking forward to hearing about the latest advances and innovations but I'd like to finish my welcome by a reminder that—like the pixels in a digital image—the big picture is made up of a great many small pictures. And I'd like to leave you, this morning, with the example of one of those small pictures.'

The screen went dark behind Mac. The lights in the auditorium seemed to soften and there was a long pause before Mac started speaking in a very different tone. His voice was quieter. Compelling. Hanna could feel a tingle that had nothing to do with what she and Mac had been doing in the hours before dawn. She suspected that everyone in this vast room was as captivated as she was by what Mac was about to say. He had his entire audience in the palm of his hand as he began to talk about a four-year-old boy who was sitting in a cubicle in an emergency department. Mac was as much in control of what was happening in this auditorium as he had been yesterday, directing a crowd and taking over the management of a medical situation in a public square.

'So his mother says that the wee lad got a new bike for his birthday and he's taken a tumble while learning to use it without his trainer wheels. You hear the unspoken message that this is a family that cares enough about their child to give him a brand-new bike. The mother's not trying to comfort the boy but she's tough. Working class. Old school. It's not as if this hasn't happened before. The child is clearly accident prone, isn't he? And maybe the lad's not saying anything, but an ED is a scary place for any child, isn't it?'

Hanna wasn't missing anything Mac was saying now. She could see that little boy, sitting on a bed behind the curtain of a cubicle. Maybe his mother was sitting on the chair beside the bed. As nervous as her son?

'You're busy,' Mac continued. 'Your department is stretched to almost breaking point. There's a major trauma in Resus One and multiple victims from a pile-up on the motorway are on their way in with an ETA of less than five minutes. Have you currently got the resources to cope? Could you be on the brink of a Code Black where you're beyond capacity enough to affect patient care? Okay, so this kid has bruises in places you might not expect to find them. Like on his ears and the angle of that small jaw. But look at how happy he is to get picked up by the nurse and carried off to get an X-ray on that probable arm fracture. You're happy, too. You can get back to the big picture of keeping your department functioning within acceptable parameters.'

Hanna was holding her breath. She knew what wasn't being said here because she'd had training in recognising non-accidental injuries in children who were the victims of abuse. She'd seen cases herself that would haunt her for ever and she could actually feel the prickle of tears behind her eyes.

Another tone-change in Mac's voice as he continued speaking sent a shiver down Hanna's spine. He was passionate about this. She felt like she was getting a glimpse into the soul of a dedicated and compassionate physician. A person she could have the utmost respect for.

'Think about this,' Mac said softly. 'What if that wee lad—that tiny pixel in the grand image—might be happy to go with that nurse because your emergency department is becoming his safe space? Perhaps it's the only space where it feels like someone cares about him. It might not be as dramatic or have the instant results of cracking a chest in Resus but it's quite possible that paying more attention to that tiny picture can also save a life.'

Hanna only let out that breath she was holding as Mac finished his speech by more words of welcome and his prediction that the next two days would be inspirational, motivational and a very real pleasure for everybody lucky enough to be here.

He'd hit that nail on the head, she decided. Hanna was feeling incredibly lucky to be here. Lucky to have spent time with the most astonishing man she'd ever met. And it was lucky she hadn't known exactly who he was when she had met him. It was unthinkable that she'd told an international rock star of emergency medicine that he wasn't at all normal and it was almost appalling in retrospect that she'd practically offered to jump into bed with him without waiting for an invitation.

But there it was. It had happened and, judging by that look on Mac's face as he'd left their breakfast table, it might well happen again.

Yeah…she was very, very lucky…

CHAPTER FOUR

THE FIRST FULL day of the conference programme passed in something of a blur for Mac, who was in high demand to participate in discussion panels and sought after for conversations regarding his research work or for networking amongst a large group of people who were passionate about their careers.

He managed to slip into a spare seat at the back of a small lecture theatre where Hanna's friend Cade was presenting his seminar on CPAP—Continuous Positive Airway Pressure—a ventilation technique that was well proven to be beneficial in a wide variety of clinical situations ranging from acute heart failure and respiratory failure from viral causes to the inhalation of toxic fumes or simply a complication from morbid obesity. From the viewpoint of prehospital medical care, he was on a mission for the single-use, disposable devices to be adopted as standard operating procedures in every emergency medical service because anything less had become a failure in duty of care.

Cade was undoubtedly preaching to the converted here, but he was an engaging, confident presenter and had clear and effective diagrams and graphs to back up his position and statistics. Like Mac had done himself this morning in his welcoming speech, Cade used a case history that gave a personal touch to what could be merely clinical data. The paper deserved to be published and could make a difference by reaching a much greater audience that way. Mac knew he had to move on swiftly to his next highlighted slots on the programme, so he got to his feet, ready to leave the room, as soon as the applause for Cade's presentation began. Someone else also jumped up in the front row of seating. Someone who was holding her hands a little higher and clapping a little louder than other people. She was also beaming with pride and Mac found himself smiling as he left the room. It wasn't any surprise that Hanna's congratulations for her friend were as enthusiastic as the way she approached many things in her life.

Including sex…

Good grief… Mac had never experienced a night quite like last night in his entire life. The way Hanna could simply be in the moment and both give and receive a physical pleasure with what seemed like no limits had been more than the most satisfying sexual experience Mac had ever had. There had been a joy to be found in even something as fleeting as an unexpected few hours in bed with someone you might never see again in your life. A memory that Mac suspected would be able to bestow an echo of that joy whenever he chose to let it surface in the future.

For now, however, it needed to be tucked away where it belonged. Maybe it would be a good thing if he didn't see Hanna again because he might need to find a very secure mental space to ensure he didn't get completely distracted from the job he was here to do.

His next commitment was to join a discussion on emerging vulnerabilities in emergency care, like high consequence infectious diseases that, as they had all learned only too well recently, carried the risk of crippling even the most highly regarded health care systems. He could relax a little after that, perhaps, with what should be an enjoyable extended session as he facilitated a disaster management workshop for a limited number of attendees, but he would still need to be focused. Mac had never let anything personal interfere with how he did his job and he wasn't about to start now.

'I'm so excited about this workshop.'

'Me, too.' Cade was leading the way to the last session of the day that Hanna was also registered for. 'It'll be great to do something hands-on after listening to so many presentations today.'

'Are you enjoying the programme?'

'Absolutely. I just went to a panel discussion on advances in PPE, which was very useful. You?'

'The best one so far was a presentation on closing wounds on old, fragile skin. That's something I do all the time and sometimes you end up making things worse but there's these new dermal clips that are not only fast and effective but virtually painless.' Hanna beamed at Cade. 'I'm inspired. When I get home, I'm going to make it my mission to have them available.' Hanna stopped at the door of a seminar room. 'How's this going to work? I can't see anything set up for a disaster management scenario.'

'I heard someone say that there's a bus. Sounds like we get taken somewhere else after the introduction.'

'Oh…wow… I can't wait.'

Hanna followed him into the room that already had its lights dimmed in preparation for a multimedia presentation. Maybe that was why she didn't notice who one of the people standing behind the lectern was. Until he started speaking, anyway.

Until that irresistible accent was making her skin tingle and she could barely focus on what was being said about the content of this session and how it would run. Who knew that the famous Dr Hamish MacMillan was also an expert in an emergency medical response to a multi-casualty disaster?

She'd managed, by and large, to not let him intrude on her thoughts as she'd navigated back-to-back, attention-grabbing presentations but even the excitement of feeling inspired by something new, like those dermal clips, was only a distant hum as she tuned in to what Mac was actually saying instead of being totally distracted by a visceral reaction to his presence.

'A disaster is any event that overwhelms the available resources. It can be natural, accidental or intentional. We're talking earthquakes, tsunamis, hurricanes. A fire in a multi-storey apartment block, perhaps. A plane crash or train derailment. Or a mass shooting or detonation of an explosive device in a crowded space. Unfortunately, we see far too many examples of these kinds of disasters and no country or community is immune.'

There were images appearing behind Mac, as a backdrop. The kind of images that they had all seen on international news broadcasts—a silent portrayal of the human suffering in the immediate aftermath of a cat-astrophic event. People covered in dust streaked with blood, stumbling to safety amidst collapsed buildings or other carnage or trying to help those who were un-able to move. By the time the screen changed to outline the response they were going to practise today, every-one in the room was intently focused on what Mac was outlining. It didn't matter how many times they might have heard it before, this felt different, and Hanna had no doubt that it was because of the charisma of the man who was speaking.

A charisma that had drawn her in far enough during their first meeting to make her realise how easy it would be to fall for him. And that was before she'd listened to his opening address this morning and she'd heard some-one who was internationally respected in his field, ca-pable of running an entire emergency department, focus his attention on a single child who might get lost in the system. The idea that he could zoom in on the kaleido-scope of his professional arena and care about a small boy who might be a victim of abuse had pulled Hanna even further down that track and that was entirely sepa-rate from knowing how skilled he was as a lover.

Oh, my…

Hamish MacMillan might well be the perfect man. He was probably setting a bar far too high for anyone else to ever compete with but why would that matter when Hanna had pretty much given up on finding a life partner anyway?

'You're going to be taken to an abandoned ware-house complex, which isn't far away. Our colleagues here in Prague have staged a simulation of a bomb blast and we have approximately fifty local volunteers who are acting as patients for us in two separate locations.'

Hanna caught Cade's gaze as her jaw dropped. This was far more than she had been expecting and she was suddenly nervous.

'You will each have a kit with minimal equipment—triage tags, oral airways and tourniquets—and you will have a limited time to individually triage and record your findings and decisions. When that time is up, whether or not you are finished, you will have to stop so the scene will be reset for the next person. One of the session leaders will accompany you to answer your questions in English and provide clinical data when appropriate. They will also discuss your results with you afterwards.'

Any hope that she might have been able to partner with Cade for the exercise vanished. Hanna could only hope she wasn't about to make a complete fool of herself in front of Mac. She wasn't the only person who was listening intently as Mac swiftly covered the basics of the START triage system they would be following.

'Simple Triage and Rapid Transport. I'm sure you're all familiar with the principle, which is to swiftly identify issues that could be fatal within an hour—breathing problems, head injuries and significant bleeding.'

For an intense thirty minutes Mac made the process look simple.

'Clear any minor injuries or green labels from the scene. If people can understand directions and can move to a designated area without assistance, they are unlikely to die soon. Those that are left, unless there are hearing or language issues, are those injured too badly to move, or they are unconscious or dead and these patients are your priorities.'

There were specific instructions to be followed. If a patient wasn't breathing you could reposition them to open their airway, but if they didn't start breathing spontaneously you had to assume they were dead and move on immediately. Red tags to designate critical condition were given to people including those who had a respiration rate greater than thirty a minute or less than ten, no palpable radial pulse or with a lowered level of consciousness.

Hanna's head was spinning as she tried to lock every instruction into her brain. It didn't help that she could feel Mac watching her as she followed the group to where a bus was waiting outside. This was the kind of challenge she'd always loved in her training, but it had never felt quite this important to perform at her absolute best. She wanted Mac to notice her, of course she did—but preferably for reasons she could be proud of.

For some unknown reason, Mac had been quite confident that Hanna would not be at any of the conference sessions he was involved with. Perhaps he had seen his interaction with her as simply part of his personal life and therefore quite separate from anything professional? Had making that distinction made it more acceptable to have told her things he wouldn't have dreamed of saying to a colleague? Had it also made acceptable something he would never have dreamed of doing normally—like taking a woman he'd only just met to his bed?

Having even an imaginary boundary between personal and professional blurred to this extent was disturbing and the only defence mechanism that Mac could come up with on the spot was to focus more fiercely on the professional aspect of this unexpected encounter. Maybe that was why he found himself pushing Hanna harder than any of the other workshop attendees when he found he was the session leader to accompany her run through the scenario.

He'd already seen more than one person completely fazed by the horribly realistic scenario his Czech colleagues had put together. Would Hanna also get caught in the headlights and miss the first—and possibly most important—step of the triage process?

Apparently not.

She stopped for a long moment in the doorway of this space that had groaning bodies lying on the floor, people stumbling around amongst upturned furniture and broken building materials. There was background noise of some machinery and a smoke machine was adding to the atmosphere. Several of the volunteer victims were calling for help and the last workshop attendee to come in for their run had immediately gone towards the loudest of them.

Not Hanna. She took a long, sweeping gaze around this big space.

'Is the scene safe?'

'Yes,' Mac confirmed.

She put the tip of her thumb and forefinger into her mouth and let out a whistle that could have been effective in bringing sheepdogs back from the far corners of a large paddock. It startled everybody—volunteers, helpers and Mac—enough for the noise to diminish instantly.

'Could everybody who can walk please come over

here?' Hanna called, her voice loud and clear. 'Stay in this corner until somebody comes to see you.'

And, just like that, the scene became more manageable as at least ten people removed themselves. Hanna could now start her run, knowing that she wouldn't be wasting time on patients that weren't critical.

Mac followed her. He wasn't about to let her know how impressed he already was, which was just as well as he only became more impressed within the next minutes.

Victim number One was unresponsive and Hanna immediately tilted his head back to open his airway.

'No spontaneous breaths,' Mac told her.

Hanna gave a single nod, put a black label on the victim and moved on only seconds after she'd arrived. Victim number Two was groaning. The moulage to present the look of an injury had been excellent and this person appeared to have his femur protruding through the skin of his thigh. The artists had also been generous with the fake blood.

Hanna felt for a radial pulse.

'No radial pulse,' Mac said instantly.

'Respiration rate?'

'Twenty-eight.'

'Do I see active bleeding from the open fracture?'

'Yes. Active, pulsatile bleeding.'

Hanna opened her kit, pulled out a tourniquet and slipped it around the top of the man's leg. She fed the end of the strap through the buckle but only tightened it a little and didn't twist the rod.

'Bleeding has stopped.' Mac nodded.

'I'll be back as soon as I can.' Hanna smiled at her

patient as she gave him a red, immediate attention required label. 'I promise...'

She was already on her way, actually running to cover the space between this person and the next in the shortest time possible. Mac followed, noting the smile on the face of the volunteer and the thumbs-up signal that Hanna had missed. This might only be pretence, but he had appreciated the reassurance and, if this scenario was real, that could have made all the difference to someone who was in severe pain and terrified.

She dealt with another half a dozen patients just as efficiently. Someone who was sitting, holding their head but apparently too dizzy to walk, received a yellow, priority two label. The person who was loudly calling for help and crying with pain, who had a fracture/dislocation of their elbow, was encouraged to get to their feet and join the other mobile patients in the green category.

Hanna got through the whole scenario in less time than the doctors Mac had previously accompanied, and her triage labelling had been faultless, but he wanted to push her further.

'Why did you re-categorise patient number eight who had no visible injuries from the bomb blast and a good radial pulse?'

'Because he didn't make it to the green category area. He had to sit down due to chest pain and needed to be seen soon so that a heart attack could be ruled out so I changed him from green to yellow.'

'And the woman with the baby who had been able to walk? Why did you change her?'

'Because of the baby. Any child under twelve months

old is automatically a priority one and needs a red label, don't they?'

Mac had another half a dozen questions on the tip of his tongue but found himself shaking his head as he smiled.

'You've done this before, haven't you?'

Hanna also shook her head. 'I've had some training in triage but I've never done a scenario like this.' Her face lit up. 'It was brilliant.'

'*You* were brilliant,' Mac finally had to tell her. 'I'd have you on my response team anytime.' And, just like that, the boundary between professional and personal evaporated.

'I'm in,' Hanna said. 'After this, I'll have far more confidence if I ever have to do it for real. I'm so glad I came.'

So was Mac. He was still holding Hanna's gaze. Until someone called from the other side of the space.

'Reset completed. We're ready to go again.'

'No rest for the wicked.' He smiled. 'Maybe I'll see you again tonight at the conference dinner?'

The volunteers were in place and had started their groaning and calling as Hanna turned to leave. The smoke machine was puffing out another, realistic addition to a post-explosion scenario. And Hanna smiled back.

'See you there.'

The glow of having Dr Hamish MacMillan tell her that she had met the challenge of the disaster response scenario so well—that she was *brilliant*, in fact—was still with Hanna as she arrived for the gala dinner that evening, having paid somewhat more attention to her attire and makeup than usual. When she saw Mac, at the centre of a group across the elegant venue that was part of Prague Castle itself, that glow got ramped up to a heat that had the potential to melt her bones.

'Ooh...' Jo was right beside Hanna. 'That's your personal tour guide over there, isn't it?'

'Mmm...'

She couldn't look away. Mac had been gorgeous in his crisp, white shirt and chinos yesterday, immaculately professional in the suit he'd been wearing this morning but dressed up in a formal, black-tie outfit, he looked more than ever like the hero of a Bond movie.

He also looked as if he was excusing himself from the group of people around him. Hanna watched him make a beeline for one of the waiters balancing flutes of champagne on silver platters, but she only realised he had spotted her entrance when he turned to come in her direction, holding the two glasses he had picked up. People were turning to see who had caught his attention and Hanna felt suddenly, uncharacteristically, shy. Thank goodness she hadn't known how famous Mac was when she'd first met him.

She took a steadying breath as she accepted the glass he offered. 'How did you guess I like champagne?'

'Everybody likes champagne, don't they?'

It looked as if it had taken an effort for Mac to drag his gaze away from hers. To not sink into the reminder of what the offer of champagne had led to last night. He turned towards Jo.

'I'm so sorry. I would have brought you a glass as well but there didn't seem to be a non-alcoholic option.'

'No worries. Cade's gone to find me a sparkling water,' Jo said. She seemed to be fighting an urge to smile as she shifted her gaze to Hanna. 'I might just go and see where he's got to.'

'Did I chase her away?' Mac dipped his head so that he could lower his voice and still be heard. 'I'd say "sorry" but…' His voice was a low growl now. 'But I'm not really sorry. I much prefer to have you all to myself.'

Okay… Hanna was definitely melting now. She struggled to find something coherent to say. 'I had no idea you're so famous,' she confessed. 'I had a bit of a cheek expecting you to become a private tour guide, didn't I?'

'It could become my new hobby,' Mac said. 'Perhaps I should take notes on how the professionals do it this week. I'm booked on a tour across Germany.'

'Oh? Apart from a visit to Berlin a long time ago, I've never spent much time in Germany.'

'Neither have I. I chose this tour because it was an exact fit for the time I have available and it starts right here in Prague. I can miss the first day tomorrow but join the group in the evening. On Monday, we head to Lauf, in Bavaria and then it's Würzburg, Frankfurt and numerous other highlights before the trip ends in Amsterdam. From there I can fly straight to a conference in Paris where I'm presenting some of my research results.'

With a national reputation for less than flexible organisation, Germany was still not on Hanna's radar as a preferred destination. She could imagine Mac enjoying it, however.

'I'm heading off tomorrow as well,' she told him.

'Where to?'

'I have no idea. I'll get onto one of those "last min-ute" or "grab-a-seat" websites and see what's available. Or I might just head for the train station or the airport and see what fate has in store for me.'

Mac nodded. 'I remember you saying that you liked to follow your nose rather than booking things.'

'Because you find the best adventures that way,' Hanna agreed.

'That sounds like a more exciting hobby than being a tour guide.'

'This trip is certainly proving memorable so far.' Hanna took a rather large gulp of her drink. 'Perhaps I should consider making holiday flings *my* new hobby?'

Mac blinked. The commendable speed with which he caught up on her train of thought was unsurprising in someone of his intelligence, but his next words took Hanna completely by surprise.

'It might be possible to combine our new hobbies,' he said. 'In order to test whether they are worth pursuing?'

Hanna's gaze was fixed on his, her eyebrows lifting in a silent query.

'I have double rooms booked for my tour across Ger-many and I happen to know that there is an empty seat on the bus beside me. I'm sure I could arrange a ticket for you. Entirely my treat. And, if we're both doing something new, that could also be an adventure, yes?'

'But what would be new for you?' Hanna asked. 'Apart from getting tips on being a tour guide?'

'Having my first "holiday fling",' Mac told her. His slight hesitation was telling. 'Having company…'

Oh…

Was having company an unusual thing for him? Did

Dr Hamish MacMillan, internationally acclaimed emergency specialist and sought-after conference speaker, have a gap in his personal life that meant he was lonely?

The fleeting image of a small boy transfixed in front of a television screen, those dark eyes as big as saucers as he soaked in technical information about an historical clock because he'd fallen in love with its complexity reminded Hanna that this man had already captured a little part of her heart.

The poignant tug on her heartstrings at the idea that he might be lonely, even if it was a personal choice, for whatever reason, to be single had just captured an even larger part of her heart. This might not be wise, but it was definitely irresistible.

Hanna drained her glass of champagne as a waiter went past. She put her empty glass on his tray. She met Mac's gaze over the rim of the full glass she had exchanged it for and it looked as though she was taking a deep breath at the same time.

'Okay,' she said. 'I'm in.'

CHAPTER FIVE

HANNA CAME CLOSE to changing her mind about the bus trip through Germany when she arrived at the meeting place to catch the bus on Monday morning and found a young German tour guide, glaring at her.

'This is most unusual.' According to her name badge, the guide was called Katarina. 'To have one person join a tour a day late is unsettling for everybody else. But… *two* people? One who is not even on my manifest?'

Hanna eyed the queue of people outside this hotel, who were waiting to board the bus. They looked as if they had a lot in common with each other, and having had a day to explore Prague they gave the impression they had clearly bonded as a group intending to have a wonderful holiday together. They were all at least a generation older than herself. Some looked old enough to be her grandparents and she could tell that her jeans with their frayed cuffs and her smocked top were being deemed to be on the scruffy side. She caught the moment they relaxed a little and, to her amusement, found that it was because Mac had arrived. Looking as tidy as ever and totally responsible, he was making it clear that Hanna was here with him.

'She's a good friend, Katarina,' he said, giving the tour guide one of those crinkly-eyed looks, along with that charming smile of his. 'We found, quite by chance, that we were attending the same conference and I bought another ticket for her because…well…' Mac lowered his voice and Hanna knew the effect it was probably having on a woman who was younger than she was. 'You know how it is when you don't want to say goodbye to someone too soon?'

Katarina might have fallen under Mac's spell, but it was only long enough to accept Hanna's presence with a resigned nod.

'Please get on the bus immediately,' she instructed, as she made a note on her clipboard. 'We depart in exactly three minutes. The driver will attend to your luggage.'

Katarina stood at the front of the bus, holding a microphone, as it pulled away exactly three minutes later.

'Our first stop will be at Amberg,' she told the group. 'We will visit the Sanctuary of Maria Hilf, which is a notable cathedral. You will be able to enjoy this attraction at your leisure for forty-five minutes. For the benefit of today's newcomers, I ring a bell when it's time to get back on the bus. Please do *not* be late as it will disrupt our itinerary for the rest of the day.'

Hanna bit her lip, her gaze flicking up to meet Mac's. She didn't have to say a thing and a quirk of his eyebrow told her that he knew perfectly well that her inner rebel had just been triggered. The look also suggested that she should go with the flow and might even find she was enjoying herself.

Like the way he'd looked at her as he'd trapped her

hands late last night, when they'd finally escaped the dinner to get back to his room. She'd been putting her arms around his neck so that she could kiss him sense-less but he'd caught her wrists and held them above her head as he took firm control of this private greet-ing. Hanna had stepped back to find herself against the wall, her hands still above her head as Mac proceeded to kiss *her* senseless and it had been the start of another, astonishing physical encounter. Hanna could feel her-self melting inside just thinking about it and she knew that her gaze was softening. Giving in. Agreeing that 'going with the flow' might be a good thing in this new adventure.

'A delicious morning tea will be provided in a nearby restaurant,' Katarina continued. 'After that, we will travel to Lauf an der Pegnitz for a tour of the pictur-esque capital of the Nürnberger district, in Bavaria. Lunch will be provided there, and I will tell you about the afternoon's activities at that point. Please sit back and enjoy the ride. I have many interesting things to tell you about along the way.'

Mac had insisted that Hanna take the window seat so there were many interesting things for her to see along the way. She didn't turn her head again, but she moved her hand to where Mac's was resting on his thigh. She slid her hand beneath his and curled her fingers over his. She could feel both his initial surprise and then, a softening on his part as well. Perhaps he was giving in to the experience of having company.

Someone to share an adventure with. This might be only going to be a brief, holiday relationship but Hanna wanted it to be something special for both of them. And she was going to make sure that Mac never felt lonely.

Nobody had ever, ever held Hamish MacMillan's hand.

Not when he was a child and certainly not as an adult.

He almost pulled it free but something stopped him, and within a very short period of time he was very glad he hadn't. To outward appearances, Mac was looking through the window and enjoying the same scenery that Hanna was. In actual fact, he was barely aware of the countryside they were travelling through because the warmth of that human touch that had nothing to do with anything sexual was stealing through his entire body, stirring up an emotional response that was initially so difficult to define that he gave up trying and decided to simply enjoy another new experience.

It wasn't until Hanna withdrew that apparently casual link between them, as they climbed off the bus at their first stop, that he realised how deep that response had actually been.

Because he could feel the absence of it even more than its presence?

Because it made him feel lost? Abandoned, even? Was it possible he had memories he'd never known he had, from being rejected as an infant and given away to be raised by people with whom he had no biological link? When he'd been separated from the sister he'd been able to touch since he was aware of being alive? Perhaps he'd held hands with his twin sister when they'd been in their mother's womb, like he'd seen photographs of unborn twin siblings doing.

And, perhaps, that was what made holding hands with Hanna feel like he'd found his way home…

Mac shook off the notion as being no more than an overreaction to a different physical experience as he followed the group to gather in front of the church. Katarina was holding up a large, artificial sunflower.

'You will be able to see this—my favourite flower—at all times,' she said, looking directly at Mac and Hanna. 'The rest of the group had practice yesterday, but this is new for you both. Please stay close, so you will be able to hear all the information I have to share.'

Hanna tilted her head to speak in a whisper to Mac even though the group was already climbing the stone steps to the entrance. 'What about the forty-five point seven minutes for us to enjoy this notable attraction at our own leisure?' She looked as though she was trying not to laugh aloud. 'Before the bell rings to make us get back on the bus.'

'Or possibly salivate?' Mac whispered back.

That did make Hanna laugh. The sound made Katarina turn and even from this distance they could see that they were the subject of a disapproving look. Churches were clearly not the place to be laughing aloud but the reprimand made Mac feel defensive on Hanna's behalf. Why would anyone want to stifle the sheer *joie de vivre* with which Hanna approached life—the kind of positive energy that made her such a delightful companion?

He found himself hanging back, reluctant to follow the group inside and contribute to stifling anything and it seemed that the universe agreed as a raised voice nearby caught both Mac's and Hanna's attention.

'Lucy…stop that right now. Do *not* push your

brother.' A mother had two small children who were fighting over something. The girl was obviously not taking any notice of the instruction and, moments later, the younger boy was taking a tumble down the long flight of stone steps. He landed with a bump and, after a beat of shocked silence, let out a piercing shriek.

Hanna was already halfway down the steps, reaching the child at the same time as his mother. Lucy was now crying as well.

'Oh, my God… Thomas…are you all right?'

Mac joined them. 'Making this much noise is usually a good sign,' he told her.

Hanna was watching as Thomas threw himself into his mother's arms. 'His movement's not restricted in any way. And I couldn't see any bumps on his head.'

Both children were still wailing. Hanna held out her hand to Lucy. 'It's okay, sweetheart,' she said. 'I know it was an accident. Do you need a cuddle, too?'

She did. Hanna sat on the step beside the mother with Lucy in her arms. Thomas calmed down enough for Mac to give him a quick check.

'Can you wiggle all your fingers for me? Like this? Does anything else hurt?'

Thomas wiggled his fingers and shook his head.

'Let me see if I can feel any bumps on your head.'

Hanna could actually feel how gentle his touch was as he examined Thomas for any sign of a head injury. Not that she needed any confirmation of the kind of skills he had as a doctor, but it was heart-warming to see how good he was with small children.

Thomas wasn't crying any longer but he was clinging to his mother like a small monkey. 'I think I need an ice cream, Mummy.' There was still enough of a wobble in his voice to persuade his mother.

'Thank you so much for your help,' she said, as she prepared to leave with both her children. 'I knew that sightseeing in a church probably wasn't the best idea with these two. We'll go ice cream hunting instead.'

Mac sat down beside Hanna on the step. 'Would you prefer an ice cream, too?'

Her smile made him an accomplice in her reprieve from the tour group. He liked that. Rather a lot, in fact.

'Can we go for a walk instead? Over there?'

'You're good with kids,' Mac said, as they walked towards a patch of forest on the far side of the car park.

'So are you.'

'But you really like them, don't you? If you were Thomas and Lucy's mother, you'd probably be giving them a holiday adventure in this forest, not dragging them into an ancient church.'

Hanna laughed. 'Yep. That would be much more fun for me, too.'

The patch of forest was cool and green and deserted. After the busy flow of tourists and the noise of crying children, the peace and quiet of being amongst the trees was more than welcome. It also had the invitation of a private, almost intimate, space. It was peaceful. Safe. Mac remembered the moment when he'd begun to feel this safe in Hanna's company—when she'd told him that she wasn't interested in marriage or kids. There was a note of sadness in the thought that she'd never be that amazing mother providing adventures for small people, though.

'Have you never wanted any kids of your own?'

'Can't have them.' Hanna's tone was dismissive. 'I had an emergency hysterectomy when I was sixteen so that I didn't bleed to death.'

'Good grief…what happened?' Mac was taken aback by what must have been a traumatic, life-changing injury. It also seemed somehow disappointing that such a vibrant, warm person was never intending to create a family of her own.

'It was an ectopic pregnancy,' Hanna said quietly. 'My gran might have been right to think that only ballet or ballroom dancing was okay. I got pregnant to someone I met in a salsa class.'

'That's a terrible thing to have happened… I'm so sorry.'

'Don't be.' Hanna offered him a smile. 'It happened a very long time ago and, on the plus side, I spent so long in hospital I discovered that I really, really wanted to become a nurse. I also discovered that I didn't actually want to have kids at all. The whole idea of parenthood was so scary it was a relief to know I'd never have to go there. It felt like a "get out of jail free" card.'

'Of course it was scary. You were no more than a kid yourself.'

'But I haven't changed my mind since then. Even when it turned out to be a dealbreaker for the guy I thought I was going to spend the rest of my life with and I tried to change my mind, I couldn't. We talked about surrogacy and adoption and all the different ways it's possible to create families these days.'

'You can't change how you feel about something that big because someone else wants you to.' Mac blew out a breath. 'And if you have to change that much to try and make a relationship work, it's doomed anyway. It might not have felt like it but it would have been far less painful to find that out, make a clean break and move on.'

'Wow...' Hanna's glance was curious. 'Sounds like you're speaking from experience.'

'You could say that.' Mac drew in a long, slow breath. 'Coincidentally, it was an accidental pregnancy that made me realise I didn't want kids, either.'

Hanna blinked at him. 'No way... How old were *you*?'

'Nineteen. In my first year of med school.' Like telling Hanna about his unknown sister, this was something else Mac had never shared with anyone but this was a connection that was on a very different level. How many people could understand how confronting it was to be faced with parenthood when you were barely out of childhood yourself?

'There was no choice about accepting it,' he told her. 'Not for me. Not when it was my first serious relationship. I was in love. I thought we could make it work but my girlfriend had other ideas. She wasn't going to give up her career or her life for a baby she wasn't ready to have. She only told me she'd gone and had an abortion on the day she broke off our engagement. That was when I made my real choice.'

'That you didn't want to have kids?'

'That I was the only person who was going to make any decisions that might change my own life. And the only way to be sure of that is to do it by yourself.'

Any relationship was dangerous. Because if you loved someone and you wanted to be loved, you were handing control of a significant part of your life over to them. If they didn't feel the same way, they could destroy too much.

Hanna was nodding slowly. Of course she got it. She wasn't chasing any dream of marriage and kids. She was living her life exactly how she wanted to, wasn't she? Independently. Adventurously.

And maybe it was the opposite side of the coin to the way he'd chosen to keep his life meticulously organised and predictable but, on a fundamental level, it felt like they were kindred spirits. How lucky were they to have this unexpected time to enjoy being with the company of someone who could understand and accept them for who they were?

'This works, though, doesn't it?' Mac said softly. 'I think I approve of holiday flings.'

Sunlight was filtering through the canopy of the trees in visible, misty rays that caught Hanna's eyes. It lit up the sunburst of colour around her pupils, before her iris became a mix of gold and brown and green that collided with that dark rim.

Extraordinary eyes.

Eyes that were as unique as Hanna Peterson.

He remembered her looking up at him like this last night, when they'd finally reached his room. When he'd caught her wrists and held her captive, like some sort of caveman, pushing her up against the wall and giving in to the desire to kiss her until a lack of oxygen forced him to stop long enough to take a breath, only to start again and, this time, to hold her wrists with one hand so that he could use his other hand to find her most intimate point of pleasure...

What was it about this woman that made him totally

unaware of the kind of inhibitions he'd always had when it came to sex because giving in to desire like this was its own form of losing control? Good grief…he was thinking of doing it again, right now. Backing her up against the trunk of a tree in broad daylight when they could be discovered by anyone at any moment.

Just a kiss would be okay, though. Wouldn't it?

Hanna seemed to think so. And it wasn't until they could hear the blaring of a loud horn that they finally remembered where they were.

'Is that the bus?'

'I think so.' Mac could see the way Hanna was trying to blink off the drugging effect of their kissing. 'We'd better run. I didn't hear the bell, did you?'

'No. Oh, dear… Katarina is not going to be happy.'

Katarina was, in fact, furious. 'It is entirely unacceptable to disrupt the timetable of everyone else on a tour they have paid for,' she told them. 'And I will not allow the reputation of my company to be tarnished. If this happens again, the bus will not be waiting for you.'

Katarina wasn't the only person who was less than happy. Mac and Hanna had to get past the highly annoyed glares of everybody already well settled in their seats as they made their way to the back of the bus.

It should have been highly embarrassing.

It really shouldn't have made Mac feel as if he was finally tapping into a teenaged rebellion he'd completely missed out on experiencing.

Would it have been this much fun back then?

As he slid into his seat and caught Hanna's gaze, he decided that the answer to that was a resounding 'yes'— it would have been, if she'd been his partner in crime.

A little while later, when they were on their way to the next stop on their tour and Hanna's hand once again crept over to take hold of his, Mac squeezed back without hesitation.

Yes…this felt like coming home. To something familiar and beloved.

And then it hit him.

Was he breaking what had become an ironclad barrier and falling in love with someone again? Was it because Hanna didn't seem to have emotional barriers of her own that it hadn't occurred to him to ensure that his own were firmly in place?

And, if he *was* in danger of falling in love with Hanna Peterson or it had happened already, was it really something to be worried about when he was enjoying himself *this* much? It was only for a few days, after all.

A mere blink in his lifetime.

'I'm really sorry, Mac.'

They had both known the bus would have long since left without them but staring at Mac's suitcase and Hanna's backpack, abandoned by a stone wall in a corner of the parking area and under the amused gaze of other tourist bus drivers, made it all too clear that Mac's holiday was in ruins.

'This is my fault,' Hanna added. She bit her lip as she sat down on the top of the wall. 'We should have stayed with the rest of the group and Katarina and gone shopping in the marketplace.'

'To buy souvenir lederhosen or cuckoo clocks?' Mac's snort was dismissive. 'I doubt that we would have been welcome at the restaurant they were all having lunch at, either. We weren't the most popular people on board, were we? We were the disruptive latecomers.'

Was it her imagination or was there a note of pride in Mac's voice? Hanna couldn't imagine that being punished for unacceptable behaviour was something that he was familiar with. That glimpse into his childhood of being so captivated by the meticulous workings of a clock suggested that he had been a very intelligent and probably extremely tidy and well-behaved youngster. Was he looking at this as part of his new experience of travelling with company?

An adventure?

Thank goodness he didn't seem to be furious with her. Or was he skilled at hiding how he really felt?

'Will you be able to get your money back?'

'I doubt it.' Mac shrugged. 'It doesn't matter.'

'It is my fault,' she said. 'It was me who suggested that a balloon ride would be fun.'

'And my choice to make it happen.' Mac met her gaze and…yes…there was definitely a hint of amusement making his eyes sparkle. 'We're equally at fault, here.'

That was true. Hanna would never have spent so much money on a short ride in a hot air balloon to see the sights of this city, like the castle and other historic buildings lining the riverbanks, from above. She should have protested more but, to be honest, she'd loved that look in Mac's eyes that told her he wanted to pay for it—that it would be a pleasure to give her something she would enjoy. It also looked as though it was meant to happen, because there was a balloon that seemed to be getting ready to take off and…well, why not see if they had the space to take another couple of passengers?

By skipping the group lunch, they would still be back in plenty of time to catch their bus, so they bought their tickets and climbed into the basket, clutching each other's hands as flames roared and ropes were dropped and they rose slowly into the air. It was certainly the best way they could have seen the sights and, really, it was no one's fault that wind conditions unexpectedly changed and blew them off course so that they ended up in a farmer's field some distance away and had to wait for the balloon company's van to come and collect them.

'What do you think we should do?' Hanna asked.

Mac laughed. 'I was hoping you'd tell me,' he said. 'I've never been expelled from a bus tour before. Didn't you tell me how much you liked to arrive somewhere and follow your nose?'

'Mmm...' Hanna took out her phone and opened a browser. 'Nuremberg airport is only about fifteen kilometres from here,' she told him. 'That seems like a good place to start. I can call a taxi to get us there.'

'Where do you want to fly to?'

Hanna caught his gaze. 'Where would *you* like to fly to?'

'I'm something of a beginner in nose-following.' Mac was showing nothing on his face, but his gaze was holding hers with that intensity Hanna was starting to love. 'Surprise me.'

Did that mean Mac was not only happy to let her take the lead but that he was still happy to spend the next few days in her company? She needed to make her choice a good one, then. Hopefully, an experience Mac would remember for the rest of his life and one that would erase any of her own guilt about her part in ruining his bus tour. She clicked to open another window and began scrolling.

'There are direct flights from Nuremberg to quite a few destinations,' she told him. 'It'll be up to chance what seats are available but today, it looks like we could potentially end up in Cyprus, Athens, Istanbul or Barcelona.'

'And we just go? Without even a hotel booking?'

'Nose-following.' Hanna nodded, her tone serious. 'I've never ended up sleeping on the streets,' she added. 'But there's always a risk that adventures might not turn out to be quite what you expect. Are you up to taking that chance? Living a little dangerously for a few days?'

He was holding her gaze again, so intently it felt as if he was searching her soul, as he was deciding whether to take that risk. It was obvious that behaving so impulsively was totally out of character for Mac but she knew that already about him. And she knew why he'd learned that he needed to have as much control as he possibly could over his life. He might not have been ready to be a husband or father when he was only a teenager but it must have been an absolute betrayal to have the future he'd chosen to accept torn away from him. She could understand why he had never trusted another woman that much again but…but she wanted him to trust her. Just for a little while, at least. For the few days they had planned to have together before they both returned to their real lives and never saw each other again.

Hanna couldn't make any promises about how things might turn out by taking him on an unplanned adventure but she could hold her own breath and hope that he would choose to come with her. Choose to trust her…

Maybe that hope was showing in her eyes because Mac's gaze softened as his lips curved.

'What is it about you?' he murmured. 'That makes it impossible to say "no"?'

CHAPTER SIX

THIS WAS A new planet for Mac.

A world away from a well-run emergency department or even the kind of rules that kept his personal life organised and efficient. This was a world where responsibilities could be abdicated, and rules ignored. You could eat whatever you liked without considering its nutritional value, take a few days away from reality and not feel guilty about ignoring almost every email and dismissing increasing tension from any approaching commitments and deadlines. You could even give someone else the control of where you might go and what you might do when you got to the mystery destination.

The destination chosen at Nuremberg airport had ended up being Barcelona and they'd arrived so late that evening there was only time to find a hotel, but it became clear the next morning that there were going to be small adventures they were going to find each day and more rules that could be broken.

Okay…there did seem to be one rule that was unbreakable and that was that time—like life—was short and it had to be made the most of. A large part of that process appeared to involve living in the moment and

Mac was learning that he'd never quite known how to do that before meeting Hanna Peterson.

Perhaps it had been something he'd learned *not* to do when he was too young to understand what a protective mechanism was and how to use it. And then it became something to juggle in his work life when he had to be aware of every single thing happening in each moment of a medical emergency but he also needed see a bigger picture of what could have happened to lead up to this situation and how to manipulate what was going to happen next in order to provide an acceptable outcome.

He'd never learned to simply *be* in the moment and savour it. To feel things on an emotional level and find joy that made that moment something to treasure. Like the taste of his chocolate and mint ice cream that he'd almost finished by the time Hanna finally found the perfect patch of sand to sit on and dropped the sandals she'd been carrying in her hand.

'How good is this?' She beamed. 'I had no idea that train was going to bring us to the beach.'

'We might have ended up in France,' Mac agreed. He'd been carrying his shoes, with the socks stuffed into their toes, to follow her example of walking barefoot on the sand and, along with that taste of chocolate and mint, he'd been aware of the movement of soft sand trickling between his toes.

He watched Hanna chase a drip of ice cream and capture it with her tongue and felt a different kind of lick happen in his gut. Good grief…it was a revelation that desire could actually increase when you kept having sex with the same person. Or was that because the person was Hanna? Because he was visiting Planet

Hanna where so much of life was about the senses and emotions. Bohemian stuff that he'd stayed well clear of in his life so far.

She was nodding in response to his comment. 'That's actually not a bad idea,' she said. 'We could go there next. Have you ever been to Corsica? Isn't that where the French Foreign Legion hangs out? There might be a ferry we could catch.' Her glance was mischievous. 'If I'd lived in those days, I might have disguised myself as a boy and joined the Legion to go and have adventures.'

'That doesn't surprise me in the least,' Mac said. 'I imagine you get bored with real life.'

'Not at all.' Hanna brushed a stray curl of her hair out of the way of her ice cream. 'I love my job. I wouldn't want to work anywhere other than in the emergency department, though—where you can never know what might be coming through the door next. Don't you love that adrenaline rush?'

'I've almost forgotten what it's like,' Mac admitted. 'And I'm missing it. I've spent too much time being no more than a guest in someone else's ED while working on my latest thesis.'

'What was the subject of your research?'

'In a word, bruises.'

He could see the moment and the impressive speed with which Hanna joined the dots.

'Paediatric injuries? Non-accidental?'

Mac gave a single nod. 'I'm working on guidelines for an updated screening tool that will hopefully mean that it's easier to identify at-risk children. There's a lot of technical stuff comparing methods of imaging as well. Conventional and cross-polarised, infrared and ultraviolet.'

'Ultraviolet like they use in crime scenes to show up blood or other body fluids?'

'It can also be used to identify trauma that may have happened months ago. And infrared imaging can give us additional information about injuries below the surface of the skin. It can cancel out the effect of a higher level of melanin in the epidermal layer, too, which makes it particular useful on bruises that can be invisible on darker skin.'

'I did a postgraduate course on triage in the ED a while back,' Hanna told him. 'Part of that was a set of tools to help us differentiate between accidental and intentional bruising. The TEN 4 guidelines?'

Mac nodded. 'Bruises on the trunk, ears or neck on a child under four years old.'

'And any bruise at all on a baby under four months old.'

'If they can't cruise, they can't bruise.'

It was Hanna who broke the rather subdued silence that fell between them.

'That speech you gave to open the conference—I was so close to tears with your story.' She seemed unaware that melted ice cream was starting to drip onto her fingers. 'I've seen that little boy myself, more than once, and…it's heartbreaking.'

Yes… Mac could see that heartbreak in her eyes and that, in itself, was a revelation about this woman. She could live in the moment even when it was distressing, and she could embrace that emotion as much as she captured and celebrated something positive like joy. Life was a roller-coaster for Hanna but she wasn't about to miss any of the ride.

'I'm still haunted by the first case I saw,' Hanna continued. 'I'd just started in the ED and the mother of this toddler was so upset because she'd only taken her eyes off him for a minute, she said, and he'd managed to climb onto the table and then fallen off. He'd hit his head and had a seizure. I was trying to comfort her. I was telling her it wasn't her fault.'

Mac let his breath out slowly. He knew what was coming.

'One of the doctors noticed there was something odd about the shape of his elbow. And one of his legs was swollen. When they did a scan they found half a dozen fractures. Social Services got called and then the police. The mother blamed her boyfriend but it turned out to be both of them. I couldn't believe it. I couldn't understand how anyone could deliberately hurt any child, let alone a baby. I've never forgotten it. I always have it at the back of my head with every paediatric patient I get.'

'Me, too,' Mac said quietly. 'When that kind of trust in people is broken, it never comes back, does it?' He cleared his throat. 'But that's a good thing. It means that you're more likely to pick up cases of non-accidental injuries and get a child out of an abusive situation.'

'Mmm…' Hanna still sounded subdued. 'Was he a real case that you were involved with, that little boy in your story?'

'Yeah…' Mac closed his eyes for a heartbeat. He couldn't tell her how real, though. He knew better as an adult, of course, but there was a level of shame that never quite vanished. That feeling that it was somehow his fault that it happened.

That he'd never been good enough. Or really wanted. That the people who were supposed to love him couldn't be trusted.

'I hope he got all the help he needed,' Hanna said.

'I believe so. Eventually.'

'I bet he grows up to become a doctor,' Hanna said. 'Because he felt like someone cared about him in the ED?'

Mac shrugged.

'I wish I could have looked after him,' Hanna said softly. 'I wish I could have given him a cuddle and made him believe, even for a little while, that he was special.'

Oh...*man*...

With the kind of control that Hamish MacMillan had over his life—and his emotions—it would be unthinkable to cry in private, let alone in a public place or in front of someone, but he had a lump in his throat that felt like a bit of broken glass. He remembered the initial shock of Hanna holding his hand on that bus ride—of a physical touch that had nothing to do with sex. Of feeling that he wasn't alone. That someone cared about him. It had been disturbingly powerful as an adult. To have felt anything like that as a small, frightened child must have been completely life-changing.

Hanna had finally noticed the remains of her melted ice cream and dug a hole in the sand to bury it. Then she got to her feet, a thick layer of sand covering her hands.

'I need to go and find a wave to wash my hands in. I might even have a paddle if it's not too cold. Coming?'

Of course he was. Moving would be the best way to

clear that jagged lump he could still feel in his throat. Besides, Hanna had just wound another thread around his heart and it felt like he needed to stay close so they didn't break just yet. She might have no idea of the chord she'd struck by her compassion for that little boy in his story but Mac had the odd sensation that he was being truly seen for the first time for who he truly was. That this bond he'd found with Hanna was more real than anything in his life before this.

A reality that was, ironically, completely separated from his real life. Mac knew his time in Hanna's world was short but that was a bonus in itself, because it gave him the freedom to make the most of every moment.

Hanna had reached the wash of waves on the sand and just walked in, not caring that the hems of her jeans were getting soaked. She swished her hands in the water and looked up to smile at Mac.

'It's not cold at all,' she told him. 'Not in comparison to the liquid ice we get in Dunedin even in the middle of summer. Do you reckon we could get away with swimming in our undies?'

And, just like that, the moment changed from one that had echoes of the sadness associated with such a grim topic of conversation, and a somewhat disturbingly intense feeling of connection to another person, to one of pleasure in the feeling of sunshine warming your skin and the fizz of seawater rushing over your feet. To the grounding and a reset of mood that being in the moment could provide.

Mac dropped his shoes and strode towards Hanna and he was laughing as he scooped her up into his arms. She wound her arms around his neck and they were lost in their kiss as the next wave and then another rolled in around his feet.

The past evaporated and the future was invisible and whether or not this was what being in love was all about didn't matter. Mac just wanted to bottle this moment and keep it for ever so that, when he needed to in future, he could take the cork out and live in this moment again, even if it was just for a heartbeat.

Because *this*...

This was what most people considered to be the holy grail of being alive, wasn't it?

Finding out what happiness felt like.

Mac had always been of the opinion that the pursuit of personal happiness was not only futile because it was usually so fleeting, it was also supremely selfish.

Now, he was beginning to wonder if he'd got it all wrong...

Barcelona was a magic city.

Or, perhaps, the magic came from a combination of the company Hanna was lucky enough to have, the gorgeous summer weather and the unexpected delights that surprised them around every corner.

They lost count of how many times they walked up and down La Rambla and explored the fascinating alleyways that led off from Barcelona's famous tree-lined central street. They wandered hand in hand through the bustling marketplace with its astonishing array of meat, vegetables, cheese and flowers and sampled every different, delicious variety of tapas they could find in the cafés and restaurants. They were excited by a wonderful Salvador Dali exhibition they came across quite by accident and they marvelled at still unfinished Sagrada Familia, the iconic work of Spain's most celebrated architect, Gaudi. What Hanna loved most of all, however, was another of Gaudi's creations—the Park Güell. From the fairy tale, gingerbread houses with their white icing roofs at the entrance, past the stunning mosaics and up the hill into the soft, green spaces of grass and trees, it was a wonderland.

The surprise of finding a busker, sitting beneath a tree at the side of a gravelled path, playing one of her favourite songs on a twelve-stringed guitar as he sang, was a moment of pure joy for Hanna. She stopped and stared for a moment and then dropped her shoulder bag, unable to resist the urge to dance. The ruffled layers of her summer dress swirled around her legs as she twirled, her arms in the air, but it was the look on Mac's face as she saw him watching her that took this space and time to a completely different level.

If she'd stopped to think, Hanna might have remembered that Mac had told her how much he'd hated dancing lessons at his boarding school but she was acting on impulse when she caught his hands and perhaps the surprise was enough to suck him into this bonus moment of magic. Whatever the reason, she knew instantly that he had either paid attention to those lessons or he was a natural dancer. And that he'd forgotten that he'd believed dancing could never be enjoyable.

He held her in his arms and they danced in the dappled shade, lost in the music and the lyrics. Hanna's arms were bare and the touch of Mac's hands skimming her skin as he sent her away from his body and then twirled her and gathered her close again added to her total immersion in this unforgettable moment. Maybe they weren't dancing in the dark, or barefoot on the grass like the lyrics they could hear, but it still felt as if they were an integral part of this romantic song—as if it had been written for them—and Hanna found herself closing her eyes as their dancing slowed until they were merely swaying together.

Was it Mac who dipped his head to touch her lips with his own, or did Hanna go up on tiptoes as she lifted her face to his?

Whatever...

It was just fortunate that Hanna still had her eyes closed. That Mac wouldn't be able to see any reflection in her eyes of what was in her mind right then. In her heart. In every damned cell of her body, in fact.

She knew this feeling and had been prepared for it to surface. She'd known at the end of her first day with this stranger who was practically her polar opposite that she was probably halfway to falling in love with him and she'd also known that her heart had been even more firmly captured by every new thing she learned about Mac. Experience had taught her that holiday flings could accelerate emotional involvement or create a depth that would never have been there if they'd met in real life but, even knowing all of that, Hanna had not expected anything like this. She'd never felt it take hold of her quite like this, with a power that was almost frightening, and Hanna knew why.

Because she and Mac had a connection that could change everything. Hanna couldn't have children. Mac didn't want any. For the first time since Hanna had had her heart well and truly broken long ago, it seemed as if it might be safe to fall in love. To dream of a future?

Except that she knew that the kind of future she was thinking of was the last thing that Mac wanted in his life. He was travelling alone. By choice. And she could understand why when the first time he'd been shaping a new future as a husband and father, it had been shattered by someone he'd loved. It was no wonder he felt the need to be in control—to keep himself so buttoned up. A few days of a perfect holiday was hardly likely to change his mind about the way he lived his entire life. Was it…?

Maybe Mac felt the ripples of what Hanna was feeling even if he couldn't see her eyes. Perhaps even the musician was aware of what was hanging in the air surrounding them because the music suddenly faltered and the spell was broken. Or it could be that Hanna's imagination was running away with her and she was the only person with an emotional overload. She was the only one who'd tripped up and fallen in love.

Mac found money to drop into the busker's open guitar case, Hanna collected her bag from where she'd dropped it and they simply carried on with their walk as if nothing momentous had just happened.

But something *had* happened.

Something had changed.

In the same way Hanna had sensed that the attraction between herself and Mac was the kind best suited to a holiday fling because it was going to erupt into fierce flames, she could feel the moment that it began to burn itself out.

On Mac's part, anyway.

'What will you do next?' he asked as they walked on, the music behind them fading. 'You've still got two weeks before you fly home, yes?'

'I do.'

Two weeks of travelling.

Alone. With the freedom to go anywhere she chose and experience whatever new adventures each day could present. But, for the first time ever, there was no excitement to be found in the prospect and that was more disturbing than the realisation of how hard she had fallen for Hamish MacMillan. Hanna needed to ground herself again, urgently, before she lost any of the pleasure that anticipating this trip had given her. She took a deep breath and found her brightest smile.

'I shouldn't admit this because it's not really in the spirit of nose-following, but I think I do have a bit of a plan.'

'Which is?'

'I liked my idea of catching a ferry to Corsica. There should be another ferry that goes to the south of France on the other side of the island and then I could drift down into Italy. Or I could jump from Corsica to Sardinia and skip France.' She threw Mac a glance but kept her tone casual. 'Want to see if we could find a ferry later? You could have at least a day in Corsica.'

The tiny hesitation on Mac's part made Hanna's heart sink. 'I think it might be a flight I need to find. I've been reminded that there's a satellite symposium happening in Amsterdam the day before my next conference. I had an email from a colleague who's hoping to meet me there.' Mac's steps were slowing. 'I didn't say anything because...' He stopped and faced Hanna. 'I wanted more time with you. But it can't last for ever, can it? Isn't that the definition of a holiday fling?'

Hanna managed to smile even though she could feel her heart already beginning to break.

'I'll never forget this,' Mac said softly. 'I'll never forget *you*, Hanna Peterson.'

'You'd better not.' Hanna made her tone stern as she started walking again. 'You've learned how to follow your nose now.'

Her inward breath caught somewhere in her chest. She wasn't about to forget any of this, either—including how buttoned up Mac had been when she'd met him in front of that clock. She'd never have imagined him walking into waves on a beach and getting his tidy trousers stained with seawater or dancing in a public park and kissing her so passionately in broad daylight. There was something sad in the thought that he might go back to his real life and this time together would be no more than a memory for him.

'You need to let yourself be impulsive more often, Mac. Take a risk or two.' She caught his gaze over her shoulder because this was important and she needed to know that he was listening. 'Remember that clock that you love so much and use it to remind you to find the time to do something new. Or to do something that you've thought of doing but you've never got around to it.' She offered him another smile. 'You'll never know what you might be missing out on otherwise.'

Mac watched Hanna walking a little ahead of him, heading downhill, which would lead them to the way out of this astonishing park.

He wanted to catch her hand and pull her to a stop again but he couldn't. What if it made him feel like he had moments ago when she was dancing with him to that guitar music? When it felt like another moment of the kind of happiness he'd experienced on the day they ate ice creams on the beach? What if he ended up risking too much by saying what he was really thinking?

Mac might tell her that these few days had changed everything. That he felt like he might be falling in love with her and he couldn't bear the thought of never seeing her again. But…she hadn't disagreed with him when he'd said that it couldn't last for ever. That this was no more than a fling. She already had plans for the rest of her holiday and it wouldn't surprise Mac at all if she met someone else along the way. Someone who was more like herself and could embrace the kind of freedom and openness and ability to live life to the absolute limit that was such a part of Hanna's soul.

He wasn't about to spoil anything for her by making their parting difficult in any way and he wasn't about to make a fool of himself by suggesting that this was anything more than Hanna believed it was so it was just as well he was a master at hiding his feelings. He'd been telling the truth when he'd said he'd never forget her but he had his doubts about following her advice to take more risks in his life. Risk was the opposite of control, after all, and he'd spent his life keeping as much control as he could to avoid exactly that.

Control kept you safe from the kind of emotions that, right now, were threatening to become unpleasantly overwhelming so the sooner he got on with restoring familiar levels of normality the better. Mac pulled his phone from his pocket, opening a browser as he continued walking.

Because it wouldn't hurt to check if there were any flights from Barcelona to Amsterdam later today. If nothing else, it would be a good first step in the right direction. Back to the ordered reality of his own planet, which might lack the same levels of personal indulgence and pleasure but at least it was safe.

And being safe was almost the same thing as being happy.

Wasn't it…?

CHAPTER SEVEN

'HANNA... THANK GOODNESS you're back. I've missed having you around.'

'I've missed being around.' Hanna hugged Jo back—as best she could over a now impressively pregnant belly—and found herself very unexpectedly blinking back tears, which, of course, her best friend noticed instantly.

'You okay? Did something happen on your holiday?'

Oh...where would she start? Yes. Something had indeed happened on her holiday. Something huge. An emotional roller-coaster like no other and the plunging dip that had started when she'd said goodbye to Mac was apparently still going despite her homecoming yesterday. The ride had been bumped up at times on her continued travels but, despite Hanna's determination to make the most of a trip she'd been looking forward to so much, those temporary lifts had only seemed to speed up the next dip into a very unfamiliar, *lonely* space. At some point in the near future, she might have to stock up on wine and chocolate and have an evening with Jo to tell her everything.

Outside the internal double doors that led to Dune-

din's Princess Margaret Hospital's emergency department, when they were about to start a morning shift
was certainly not the time to even hint at such personal woes.

'It's just jetlag.' Hanna smiled as she hung her stethoscope around her neck. 'And, on top of that, I got home
to find my flatmates had a big party last weekend. They
hadn't noticed that someone had crashed in my bedroom
so I had to change my sheets and do a full load of laun-
dry before I could even start unpacking.'

'Ew…' Jo made a disgusted face. 'I don't know how
you can still cope with flatting.'

'I'm beginning to wonder myself.'

'My wee house has got a temporary tenant, but it'll
be available to rent again sometime soon if that's an
option. I might even sell it before the end of the year.'

Hanna loved Jo's quirky cottage but…living alone?
When she was currently trying to get used to a loneli-
ness like nothing she'd ever experienced before? She
needed to change the subject.

'Are you and Cade still loving your new house on
the peninsula?'

'Oh, yeah…you'll have to come and see it. Maybe
we can have a last barbecue before winter sets in properly. I need to show you our holiday photos, too. I'm
still on a high from that idyllic beach. It was perfect…'

'I'm so glad.' Hanna was looking through the glass
panels of the doors. 'Looks busy in there. I'd better get
to work.' She pushed one of the doors open and gestured for Jo to go ahead of her but Jo shook her head.

'I've got to duck up to Admin. There's some final
paperwork for my maternity leave to sign off. Offi-

cially starts today, actually—I'm just here to tie off some loose ends.'

'Any luck with the locum?'

'Mmm…' Jo was already turning away but there was an odd gleam in her eyes as she threw a glance over her shoulder. 'I wanted to let you know who it was before you got back but Cade thought it might be a nice surprise. They're rostered on today for second shift so you'll find out soon enough.'

'It's someone I know?'

But Jo was already on her way to where she needed to be and only raised a hand in farewell. Hanna stepped through the doors into ED and immediately forgot about it. As the charge nurse for the upcoming shift, she needed a detailed handover so that she was on form to supervise the department's nursing staff and use any opportunity to teach the less experienced nurses. She would also have to field any patient complaints, liaise with specialists for consultations, keep an eye on medical supplies and be available at all times for a trauma code. On the plus side, not only would she have no time to think about her own emotional state, her jetlag would be well and truly dealt with by the time Hanna had coped with the next nine hours. She could then go home and crash and, with a bit of luck, life would seem far more back to normal by tomorrow.

Shifts were arranged to overlap so there wasn't a complete changeover that could disrupt the continuity of patient care so Hanna had been working for a couple of hours before the second shift started. The department was busy enough for her to feel she was totally back in the swing of things so she was unprepared for the blow that came completely out of the blue. Feeling pleased that she'd found time to give one of the new nurses a tutorial in placing leads to take a twelve lead ECG on a cardiac admission, she felt it like a body blow to glance across the department and see the back of someone reading the electronic census board, which was the access point for any operational and patient-related information.

Someone tall, with dark hair, who was standing with commendably good posture, which made them look an awful lot like Hamish MacMillan.

Hanna had every reason to go and check the board herself and make sure that the requested consult with the cardiology department was now recorded for the patient she'd just seen but she found her steps slowing as she approached. Because this was more than simply seeing someone that reminded her of Mac. The weird tingling sensation that was getting stronger with every passing second was surreal. The realisation that Mac was, in actual fact, standing right in front of her—giving her that crinkly-eyed intense look and *smiling* at her—was overwhelming.

'Hey, Hanna…'

She couldn't say anything. For that first, long moment of suspended time, all Hanna was aware of was a joy like no other. A feeling that the huge, empty space she'd been living with for the past two weeks had suddenly vanished. Filled by the physical presence of the man she felt so strongly about. Her words came out in no more than a whisper.

'Mac…what on earth are *you* doing here?'

As she spoke, Hanna could feel the wash of something that felt like…anger?

How on earth was she supposed to get over how she felt about Mac if she had to go back to square one again?

'I followed my nose,' Mac said. His voice was low enough for nobody else to hear. 'And I put my hand up to be Jo's locum.' He hadn't broken their eye contact. 'At least for a while. You did tell me I should do something new.'

'Yes…but…' Hanna was lost for words. He hadn't needed to come to the other side of the world to do something new. Had he come this far because *she* was here? With another twist, a flash of hope cut through her tumbling emotions. Perhaps Mac had been following his heart and not his nose?

'Hanna?'

The tone of the person calling her from the central desk made Hanna turn her head swiftly. She could feel that kaleidoscope of her own feelings evaporating instantly.

'Ambulance notification.' A senior nurse was putting down the dedicated phone. 'Penetrating mechanism chest injury. Systolic BP less than ninety. Heart rate greater than one twenty. Shall I initiate a trauma Code Red?'

Hanna was there in no more than a few steps. 'Yes. What's the ETA?'

'Four minutes.'

There wasn't much time and it was Hanna's job to get everything organised. Alerts had to go out to members of the team. In addition to the most senior emergency consultant available in the department, they needed an anaesthetist, radiologist, a surgical consult on standby and all the usual staff for a resuscitation area. The blood bank needed to be contacted and have blood products and thawed plasma available. Hanna wanted to ensure that a rapid infuser was primed and ready for use in Resus and that an ultrasound machine was at the bedside. A check that tranexamic acid—to reduce or stop traumatic haemorrhage—was amongst the available drugs was also high on her list.

'Who's on as trauma team leader today?'

'Jo. No, wait…it's her locum.' The nurse must have noticed something in Hanna's expression. 'Don't worry. Word is that he's the best.'

It was Mac's first trauma call on his first day of this locum position in a small—by international standards—hospital at the bottom of the globe. With his level of expertise and experience, it shouldn't be anything out of the ordinary but Mac was aware of a heightened alertness that made this somehow more significant.

Because this was the first time he would be, officially at least, working with Hanna Peterson and…he wanted this to be successful. Impressive, even? Or to erase what had looked disturbingly like a flash of something like fear in her eyes when she was struggling with unexpectedly seeing him again?

Whatever. There was no time to spare even another thought about Hanna as Mac donned his PPE and tried to familiarise himself with this new resuscitation space as rapidly as possible.

Finding that the paramedic bringing this critical trauma case into the department was one of the only three people Mac had ever met from this city helped ground him. And Cade's handover was giving him vital information about this case.

'This is Sean Watson. Forty-one years old. Forestry worker who got caught by the canopy of a falling tree. A branch penetrated the left side of his chest, third intercostal space, leaving a puncture wound but no visible impaled object. BP is currently one hundred over sixty-five, up from eighty-five over sixty on arrival. Suspected tension pneumothorax but fluid seen on ultrasound did not suggest a cardiac tamponade. He's had bilateral decompression but he's having increasing difficulty breathing. GCS thirteen on arrival but probably twelve now.'

'Oxygen saturation?'

'Variable. Between eighty-six and ninety-four.'

'Sean…can you hear me?'

The patient groaned beneath his oxygen mask. He opened his eyes but his agitation made his speech hard to understand. His skin was grey and he was clearly terrified.

'You're in hospital now,' Mac told him. 'We've got you, okay?' He glanced at the team around him, including Hanna, who seemed to still be assigning roles. A scribe was ready to record everything, a nurse was stationed beside the drugs trolley and an orderly was standing by, probably to deliver bloods samples to the laboratory and bring back the products that might be needed from the blood bank.

'Let's get him onto the bed,' Mac directed. 'I'd like to do another ultrasound.'

His FAST examination—the Focused Assessment

with Sonography in Trauma—confirmed Cade's impression that there was no blood to be seen in the area around the heart, which was consistent with other signs like the patient's neck veins not being distended. That they were dealing with a life-or-death situation became more apparent in the short time it took to use the bedside ultrasound, however. It was Hanna who called out the warning that Sean's blood pressure was falling rapidly and it was only seconds later that their patient lost consciousness.

It was Hanna who assisted the airway doctor when Mac made the call to sedate and intubate Sean and he could see her in his peripheral vision, efficiently checking and then administering the drugs needed and then providing the assistance like pressure on the cricoid cartilage to aid the passing of the endotracheal tube. At the same time, she was clearly supervising the setup of the O negative red blood cells and the thawed plasma and Mac was relieved to have them available when he made an incision in the chest wall to try and get to the blood that was accumulating internally.

Even in a space full of people who were accustomed to dealing with major trauma, there was a collective gasp as an estimated blood loss of more than two litres happened the moment Mac opened the anterolateral incision he'd made. The resus area immediately took on the appearance of a war zone but the glance he caught from Hanna as she positioned herself beside him to assist was calm and the silent message perfectly clear.

I'm here. What do you need?

'No pulse,' the airway doctor warned.

With the direct vision Mac had of the heart, he could

see that it had stopped beating. He placed one hand behind the heart and the other in front and began a rapid squeezing motion from the apex upwards. The movement was easy to continue automatically, as Mac controlled the chaos around him. Blood products were being rapidly infused, the patient was being ventilated. Drugs were being drawn up and blood samples sent for analysis including rapid measurements of oxygen levels. Vital signs measurements were called out for the scribe to record. Pauses in the cardiac massage initially revealed the potentially fatal rhythm of ventricular tachycardia but, at one point, after drugs were administered, it reverted to a normal sinus rhythm, which gave everybody the hope that this dramatic emergency department intervention might be one of the few that could succeed.

Except that Sean was still losing blood. Eight units of blood and fluids had now been infused but the blood loss was ongoing and it was impossible to see where it was coming from.

'I can see it pooling on the front wall of the ventricle.' Mac pressed the swab Hanna passed him against the outer wall of the heart to try again. 'But I can't see the puncture wound.' He caught Hanna's gaze. 'I'm going to have to open the sternum.'

A single nod and Hanna opened a new sterile roll onto the trolley to hand Mac a scalpel, then a bone saw and then retractors. This was a desperate last attempt to save this patient's life and Mac wasn't about to think about how unlikely it was to be successful. Especially when he could now see the two-centimetre hole in the right ventricular wall.

'Suture, please, Hanna,' Mac said quietly. 'And we'll

need a Teflon patch if we've got one. I want to get this as secure as possible before we shift to Theatre.'

Against all odds, that was what they managed to achieve only a short time later, as Sean's blood pressure finally started to rise to an acceptable level as the injury was closed and his heart was able to start beating normally to restore his circulation.

Mac went with his patient to Theatre but, as the senior consultant on duty in the department, he couldn't stay to watch the surgery. He did have to take the time to completely change his scrubs, though. Even the best PPE hadn't been enough to prevent the bloodstains. The resus area would be out of action for a while as well—there was a team still cleaning up as Mac arrived back in the ED.

Hanna was the first person he saw as he walked through the doors and, this time, there was none of the shock he'd seen on her face earlier this morning. He could see the hope in her eyes first of all and he nodded.

'It was still looking good when we got him into Theatre. Sinus rhythm, systolic BP just over a hundred.'

The consultant who'd been in charge of Sean's airway and ventilation came past and stopped to offer Mac a handshake.

'First time I've seen that happen successfully,' he told Mac. 'That's some way to introduce yourself, mate.'

'Yes. Welcome to Dunedin, Mac.' Hanna was smiling. 'We're lucky to have you here.'

He could see admiration in her gaze, but Mac shrugged off the praise. 'I'll be waiting to see what the post-surgery ultrasound can tell us about heart function. And whether there are any neurological sequelae. Where am I needed next, Nurse Peterson?'

And there it was…

A flash of something extremely personal and a very long way from being unpleasantly surprised to have him appear in her life again. An acknowledgement of the astonishing physical connection they'd discovered with each other in Europe, if nothing else, which was one of the reasons he'd talked himself into finally visiting this far corner of the globe.

Because he'd started missing Hanna Peterson the moment his plane had taken off from Barcelona.

She was the one to break the eye contact. 'Let's have a look at the board,' she suggested. 'I'm not going to tempt fate by mentioning the "Q" word but it might be possible for you to grab a coffee. Do you know your way to the staffroom?'

'I do. Perhaps you might be due for a break as well?'

The glance he received was speculative. 'Perhaps. I have to say I'm looking forward to finding out what persuaded you to come and be Jo's locum.'

'It was you,' Mac told her, as they stopped in front of the digital board.

The glance he got this time was startled. Disconcertingly, he could see something in her eyes that reminded him of her silent query for an update on their dramatic chest-cracking case—a question that was steeped in hope… Had he said too much? The wrong thing? Was she taking it to mean something too personal, which would be unwelcome given that she had spelled out her feelings about marriage and, presumably, any committed relationships? He tried a wry smile to defuse any tension.

'You told me to do things I'd thought of doing but never got around to, remember?' Mac kept his tone off-hand. 'Well, visiting New Zealand was definitely one of those things and when I remembered Cade mentioning the locum position to cover Jo's maternity leave, it seemed like fate, as well as you, were giving me a bit of a nudge.'

'Ah...okay...' Hanna's smile looked a little forced. 'I guess I can't take all the credit for being responsible for you being here to save a life in such dramatic fashion on your first shift, then.' Her gaze shifted as she looked over her shoulder. 'I'd better go and check on the clean up in Resus One and order any new surgical supplies to restock. You should go and have a coffee while you can.'

In the flash of time between Hanna turning towards the resuscitation area and when she actually began to move, Mac's thoughts tumbled one on top of another at the speed of light.

He knew he'd definitely said the wrong thing that time. He could feel the protective barrier that Hanna had suddenly activated around herself.

He'd been trying not to alarm Hanna with the idea that he'd come all this way because the pull to see her again had been so powerful but it had been a stupid thing to say, anyway, because Mac didn't believe in fate. It was coincidence, rather than fate that he'd met Hanna and her friends and discovered that there was a locum position in a country he'd thought of visiting long ago. A position that just happened to fit with an unexpected gap in his professional life.

Like risk, the idea that fate could determine what

happened in your life was in the category of being the opposite of being in control and he'd left Barcelona with every intention of re-establishing exactly that kind of control.

It had been a conscious, controlled decision to come to New Zealand.

Or had it?

If Mac was really honest with himself, his decision had been very much influenced by things he was struggling to control—namely the way being with Hanna had made him feel. How much he had missed being with her and how badly he wanted to see her again. It was more than simply 'wanting', however. Mac could feel a *need* to be that close to the only person he'd ever met who made him feel connected to another human on such a significant level. Someone who could see him for who he truly was. Maybe a part of what had driven his impulsive decision was wondering whether the way Hanna made him feel was simply a part of a fantasy that came from being on holiday with the total freedom of seeking nothing but pleasure in their surroundings and each other's company.

If it was something that evaporated in real life it would make it so much easier to move on and not be haunted by…what…the feeling of having thrown away something truly significant? More important than anything else in his life so far?

He had stepped into Hanna's real life and, so far, that feeling hadn't changed at all. If anything, working with her had made it feel even more as if they were kindred spirits. Two halves of the same whole?

'Hey…' His soft call made Hanna pause. Just for a

heartbeat but it was long enough. 'There was another reason, as well.'

She didn't say anything but she lifted her gaze to meet his with a question filling her eyes.

Mac kept his voice low enough that it was no more than a whisper. Only Hanna could hear him.

'I couldn't stop thinking about you,' he said.

CHAPTER EIGHT

MAC *HAD* COME all the way across the world because she was here, hadn't he?

He might have convinced himself that it was a combination of other things that had led to him deciding to come to this small country at the bottom of the world, but Hanna wasn't fooled. Okay, maybe he did have an unexpected gap in his professional life that was providing a kind of sabbatical leave and time to do things he might not have otherwise considered. There was also his newfound appreciation of following his nose instead of planning everything he did in his life, including travel, to the nth degree, and, of course, an unexplored curiosity about where his twin sister had been raised. And maybe he'd needed to fool himself in order to feel safe making his choice, but it had been a simple combination of words that had made Hanna's heart sing.

I couldn't stop thinking about you...

The way she hadn't been able to stop thinking about him? Snatches of memories that had coloured so many moments of every day since she had last seen him? And every single night?

Memories of conversations. Of laughter. Of emotions

that could steal her breath without any warning. Feelings that could make everything look so much brighter, like the joy of being in Mac's arms when he'd whirled her around in the waves of that Spanish beach or the tenderness as he'd held her so close when they'd danced under that tree in the park. The sheer enormity of the love that filled her heart with every memory was both a blessing and a curse.

Hanna had spent the rest of her holiday in Europe trying to find a way to stop those feelings morphing into the pain of heartbreak.

And now, she had to find a way to stop reading too much into what she'd seen in Mac's eyes when he'd told her he hadn't been able to stop thinking about her. Or into what was happening so unexpectedly by his arrival in her normal life. She needed to be careful not to say too much, too. Even when, late that evening, she found herself holding her breath as she waited for Mac to open the front door of the little terraced Victorian house that Jo had made available for him to rent.

Hanna knew it well. She loved the high ceilings with their decorative plaster work, the beautiful, tiled fireplaces with solid, wooden surrounds, the polished floorboards and the narrow staircase that led to the cosy bedrooms upstairs. Not that she was thinking of any of the features of this small house as the door closed behind her. Hanna wasn't even aware of where she was, in fact.

This could have been a hotel room in Prague for all it mattered the moment that Mac's gaze captured hers and the rest of the world was shut out. It could have been a private patch of forest in Germany or a beach in Barcelona. Place was irrelevant because there was something else that Hanna knew so well it felt like it was imprinted on her soul.

This...*desire*. The magnetic pull that was so strong it felt like surrendering to it was the only way to ever feel whole. All she needed to do was to stand on tiptoes so she could brush his lips with her own. Except that she didn't need to stand on tiptoes, did she? Because Mac was waiting for it and then, suddenly, he wasn't waiting. He was the one who was moving. Dipping his head and covering her mouth with a kiss that tasted like...

Oh...what *did* it taste like, exactly? She had all the time in the world to decide, as one kiss melted into another with no more than a heartbeat of a gap between them that provided the gasp of a new breath or a blazingly intense beat of eye contact. The knot of sensation deep in her gut grew until it was too big to be in one place. It unfurled and spread until it seemed to touch every cell in her body and then it threatened to scramble the ones in her brain, but not before she realised that she knew the answer to the question she'd asked herself.

These kisses tasted—and felt—like Hamish MacMillan.

It was that simple.

And that complicated.

Because it wasn't just that she'd seen—and *felt*—that connection in his eyes when he'd told her he hadn't been able to stop thinking about her. She'd seen the shadows as well and it had broken her heart. She'd sensed the fear of being vulnerable and giving someone else the opportunity to hurt him.

To reject him, even?

Maybe it went even further back than his broken first love. Maybe it was something a lot deeper. Had he always lived with a feeling of having been rejected because his mother hadn't kept him?

To have come here at all was a huge step for Mac to have taken and she knew it had a tentative shape to it. Good grief, he'd been enough out of his comfort zone to take the risk of their impulsive travel to Barcelona. A wrong word from her carried the risk of planting or nurturing any seeds of doubt he might well already have and the last thing Hanna wanted was for Mac to do a U-turn and vanish from her life again.

Falling into his arms again like this might be a risk but Hanna could no more prevent herself from taking it than from taking her next breath. That Mac already trusted her enough to have crossed the world to see her only made Hanna love him even more. She was not about to do anything to break that trust.

She knew that Mac needed to hang on to all those other reasons he'd used to persuade himself to come this close again. He wasn't ready to think any further ahead than the weeks, or months, of this locum position he'd chosen to take. And she was happy to give him that time. And yes, there was hope to be found— of course there was—and a glow of happiness that had already obliterated the downside of jetlag and any trace of heartbreak.

This extra time together felt like a gift for them both. An appropriate one, even, considering they'd met in front of one of the world's most famous clocks. And, like she'd said, when they'd had the time to explore Prague together, she didn't want to waste a minute of it.

* * *

Mac had learned long ago to avoid impulsive decisions of any kind and that included how he might feel about any given situation. It wasn't that he didn't have the ability to make split second decisions and then act on them because that was a part of his job and he was confident that those rapid decisions could be justified because his experience meant he could gather facts and figures and predict what the outcome might be.

That confidence was purely associated with professional decisions, however. Personal ones, especially to do with anything emotional, were a very different story but Mac had perfected a method of making those decisions as well. He kept a safe distance behind well-constructed barriers until he could control any emotional reaction and then he could make well-considered choices that were both practical and unlikely to cause problems in the future. It had always worked particularly well when it came to his relationships with women and there were a few ironclad rules.

He'd never had a liaison of any kind with someone he worked with on a regular basis. Spending time in their company was always a well-planned, often formal, occasion such as a show or dinner. And a sexual encounter was never in his own bed because, that way, he was always in control of when he chose to leave.

He'd given himself permission to ignore all those rules when it came to Hanna Peterson because it was only going to be a temporary lapse of good judgement, but it could be argued that that could also apply to being here in New Zealand. Like a holiday fling, a locum position had a definite endpoint that was clearly on the table and that meant that working with Hanna was an exception to that rule.

Sharing his own bed with her was another exception because it appeared to be the only option for whatever private time together they were able to find.

'You don't want to come to my place,' Hanna had told him. 'Apart from it being horrendously untidy a lot of the time, one of my flatmates—Amanda—is a Theatre nurse here and you know what hospital grapevines can be like with a bit of new gossip.'

Mac liked the fact that Hanna didn't want people talking about them. A lot. It not only made it feel like they had something special that was purely their own, but it felt as if Hanna respected his need to be in control of his own life.

His first couple of weeks in Dunedin were so busy they passed in a flash. He needed to get up to speed with different protocols for patient treatments, how the department was run and to get to know his new colleagues. Out of work hours were also busy as Mac learned his way around a new city and dealt with life admin like sorting a vehicle and shopping for essentials. Having been invited to cover Jo's position as a HEMS doctor if needed, he had training sessions with the local emergency helicopter service to sign him off on their operational requirements.

It became apparent that Hanna wasn't even talking to her closest friend Jo about what was going on because Cade clearly had no idea that Mac had anything more than a professional relationship with Hanna. Cade was looking apologetic, in fact, as he pushed an empty stretcher past where Mac was signing a patient's discharge summary that Hanna was waiting for.

'I'm so sorry we haven't had you out to dinner yet,' Cade told Mac. 'I've been working too many shifts and Jo's pretty tired what with getting the house set up for the baby. I hate to think you might not feel as welcome as you are.'

'It's not a problem,' Mac assured him. 'I'm still settling in.' He smiled at Hanna as he handed back the paperwork. 'And I'm being very well looked after.'

'That's good to hear.' Cade also smiled at Hanna. 'Jo said to invite you to dinner as well. It's been ages and we haven't even seen your holiday photos yet. Did I hear you went to Barcelona? And Corsica?'

'Mmm…' Hanna was already turning away. 'Tell Jo I'll call her soon. We've got lots to catch up on.'

Cade began moving away, too, but then turned back. 'I was telling our station manager about that disaster response triage workshop you ran in Prague and he got excited by the idea of running one here. Any chance you'd be up for sharing your expertise?'

'Count me in,' Mac said. 'There might be ED staff that would be interested as well. And what about the fire service here or the police? It can be very useful to combine a training exercise that involves extrication and possibly police exercises. I've still got a template for a scenario based on a terror attack that we used in Scotland. It brought all the emergency services together, with the police clearing the area first, then the fire service managing extrication from collapsed buildings and ambulance coming in to do the triage at the end. A fair bit of work to set up but I remember we got great feed-back from that one.'

'Sounds perfect.' Cade reached for his pager that was beeping loudly. 'I'll organise a barbecue in the next few days and we'll talk more.' He glanced at the message on his pager. 'Gotta run,' he said. 'MVA on the motor-way. Car versus motorbike.'

It wasn't just a new hospital in a new country that Mac was experiencing. With the boundaries of his rules blurring he was in a strange space that straddled pro-fessional and personal elements. It had aspects of the unfamiliar, like a holiday, but it was most definitely the real, everyday life he'd been working in ever since he graduated and there was nothing quite like having to deal with all the good, the bad and the ugly that an emergency department could provide in the way of caseloads and challenges.

Working, sometimes very closely, with someone he knew intimately and was coming to trust on many lev-els was also a completely new space to be in and…

And it was a revelation.

Working with someone whose brain worked as quickly as his own and was on the same wavelength enough to sense and communicate urgency without say-ing a word. When that person could anticipate what he needed and provide the kind of support required with-out instructions, obstacles that could slow down his in-terpretation of the overall picture and what needed to happen next were removed. It almost felt like he had an extra pair of hands that were as trustworthy as his own and, when an emergency began unfolding, that could tip the balance firmly in favour of saving a life.

Like it did only a day or two later when Mac sensed Hanna's concern about a patient she was with when he happened to be walking past the cubicle she was in with a young, female patient. When he caught her glance, it reminded him of when they had met for the very first time—when they had exchanged that glance that was a mutual acknowledgement that something significant was happening to their tour guide, William, and it was about to get more serious.

On first glance, Hanna's patient did not seem to be particularly unwell.

'This is Alisha,' Hanna told him. 'She's twenty-nine and her friend brought her in to Emergency because she was getting some chest pain and she's a bit short of breath. Alisha, this is Dr MacMillan.'

Mac unhooked his stethoscope from around his neck. 'Can I have a quick listen to your chest?' he asked.

'Sure.'

'Lean forward a little for me?'

'Heart rate's one ten and regular,' Hanna told him as he positioned the disc of his stethoscope on Alisha's back. 'Respiration rate is twenty-four, SPO2 is ninety-four per cent on room air and her blood pressure is one-oh-five on seventy. I was about to do a twelve-lead ECG.'

Mac nodded. 'Good idea.' Age was no guarantee that chest pain might not be cardiac.

He lifted his stethoscope as Alisha coughed and then coughed again. When he saw the tissue she pressed to her mouth, Mac could feel the hairs on the back on his neck prickle slightly. A rapid upward glance revealed that Hanna hadn't missed the bright smear of blood on the tissue.

'Have you had any trauma recently?' Mac asked. 'Like a broken leg or a bad bruise?'

'No.'

'Any surgery?'

'No.'

'Long haul flights?'

Alisha shook her head. 'I should be so lucky,' she said. 'I haven't had a holiday in a long time.'

'Any chance that you could be pregnant?'

She shook her head. 'I'm on the pill.'

Hanna knew exactly what Mac was thinking—that Alisha might have a pulmonary embolus and/or a deep vein thrombosis. She had ripped open a plastic bag and was plugging the end of the attached tubing to the plug on the wall that was an outlet for the main oxygen supply.

'I'm going to give you a bit of oxygen,' she explained to Alisha. 'It should help your breathing. We might get you out of your jeans, as well. Have you got any pain in your legs?'

Alisha nodded. 'My left leg was sore when I got up this morning.'

Her leg was swollen and red as well as tender.

'It's possible that you've got a blood clot that's formed in one of the veins in your leg,' Mac told her. 'If bits of it are breaking off, it would explain what's happening in your lungs.'

'A clot?' Alisha's eyes widened in fear. 'That's really bad, isn't it?'

'You're in exactly the right place to get it sorted,' Mac said. 'I'm going to do an ultrasound on your leg, which will tell us if something's happening. We'll do an X-ray of your chest, too.' He turned to Hanna. 'We'll need an arterial blood gas measurement soon but I'd like to get an IV in first.'

It didn't surprise him that Hanna already had the IV trolley in the cubicle. With deft movements, she opened drawers and gathered everything he would need. A tourniquet, alcohol wipes, a cannula and sticky patch to cover it, a syringe and an ampoule of saline to flush the line. She was moving rapidly enough for Mac to see that she was sharing his sense of urgency, even though her manner was completely calm.

'This is nothing to worry about,' she told Alisha. 'We're going to need some blood samples to help us figure out what's going on with you and if we have a line in, it means we don't have to poke you again if we need to give you some medication.'

Alisha was coughing again as Mac slid the cannula into place. Hanna began taking another set of vital signs as she finally flopped back against her pillows.

'I feel kind of dizzy,' she told them.

'Systolic blood pressure's dropped,' Hanna informed Mac. 'It's less than ninety.'

Alisha had her eyes closed now. They could see from the movements of her chest wall that her respiration rate had increased noticeably since the coughing.

Mac stepped towards the end of the bed and lowered his voice. 'We've got a PERT available, haven't we? A Pulmonary Embolus Response Team?'

'Yes. It's a collaboration between specialities that's activated from here. It's your call.'

Mac gave a single nod. 'Let's do it. I'm comfortable that a Wells score puts the priority for a PE as high. I'm going to get an ultrasound of her leg and set up a heparin infusion but I'd like the team here asap.'

Bleeding risk needed to be assessed and a decision made about using clot-busting thrombolytics to treat the clot, if it was indeed as big as Mac suspected, or whether surgery or catheter-based techniques would be used before Alisha was admitted to the Intensive Care Unit.

In the end, the young woman was administered catheter-directed drugs to treat the massive clot and then mechanical removal to clear her vein. If any residual areas were narrow enough to potentially cause a recurrence, she might need further treatment with angioplasty and stenting.

'They've placed a filter in the inferior vena cava to prevent any further PEs.'

Hanna seemed fascinated by the images Mac was able to show her that evening when they were discussing the case. And this was another huge bonus of a relationship that went beyond being colleagues. Mac loved a good debrief.

'It's only temporary. Once things are stable, she should be able to take blood thinners.'

'How did you know that the clot was so massive? I can't believe it went all the way from her calf to her groin.'

'I didn't. And I probably should have taken the time to properly rule out all the differential diagnoses, too.'

'Such as?'

'Aortic dissection. Tension pneumothorax. Triple A.' Mac was counting them off on his fingers. 'Ectopic pregnancy.'

'You sounded like you knew.'

'I was trusting my instinct. Also, I've never forgotten a case I was involved with treating when I was a med student. The guy was being thrombolysed and I was monitoring him when he had a syncopal episode that started just like when Alisha began feeling dizzy.'

'What happened?'

'His heart rate and breathing rates went up and he was going blue with hypoxia. A minute or two later and he was unresponsive and pulseless. You can imagine how panicked I was.'

'Did he survive?'

Mac shook his head. 'Which is why I've always remembered him. Huge PE on both sides and a massive clot that disabled the right side of his heart. Did you know that seventy per cent of patients who have a fatal PE die within the first hour of the onset of symptoms?'

'I do now.' Hanna blew out a breath. 'And I won't forget it, either.' She smiled at Mac. 'There you go... for the rest of my working life, whenever I see someone who might have a DVT, I'll be thinking of you.'

Oh... Mac liked that idea. The whole benefit of any debrief was that lessons were learned and perhaps a different case in the future would benefit.

He liked the way Hanna was looking at him right now, too. It was obvious she'd had enough of talking about work and it was time for the kind of wind down from a busy day that could take them both to a place that had nothing to do with anyone but each other. The expression on her face reminded him of…what was it? Oh, yeah…that time when they were in front of the clock in Prague and he'd told her that she looked like a dog who couldn't wait to be allowed off leash.

He also told her, in a somewhat roundabout fashion, that he thought she was beautiful. And he realised that being here, in this space between holiday fantasy and real life, wasn't, in any way, changing what he thought about this astonishing woman. She was just as enchanting. Just as captivating as the first moment he'd noticed her outside that hotel in Prague.

'Do you know,' he said softly. 'I suspect I'll be thinking of you for the rest of my life whenever I see a clock.'

'That's way more romantic than a DVT.' The smile curving the corners of Hanna's mouth was reaching her eyes and making them distinctly misty. 'Okay… I'll think of you whenever I hear someone talking about Barcelona.' Her gaze dropped to his lips. She was thinking about kissing him, wasn't she? 'Or see people dancing, perhaps,' she added softly.

'It was the best holiday,' Mac said. 'The best fling.' He was looking at *her* mouth, now, savouring the moment before that imminent kiss. 'We should do that nose-following thing again.'

'Mmm… When?'

'Next summer?'

'Northern hemisphere summer or southern hemisphere summer?'

Mac lifted his gaze. 'Why not both?'

Hanna laughed as she leaned closer. 'I like the way you're thinking.'

Her lips brushed his, a soft butterfly kiss that was teasing him into making the first move and Mac needed no more encouragement. In the heartbeat before he began what was becoming a familiar but no less delicious prelude to their love making, he was realising something else.

That Hanna was the perfect woman for him. They shared a passion for the same career in emergency medicine and would always, always have interesting things to discuss. They both loved travel. The sex, that had been the best ever from that first night, wasn't losing any of its attraction and, perhaps the biggest connection of all, they both felt the same way about marriages and families of their own.

Like the locum position Mac was currently in being a blurred area between real life and a holiday, the idea of going away with Hanna twice a year was like a soft-edged space between a relationship and a holiday fling.

It could be safe.

Perfect, even…?

CHAPTER NINE

'Is THERE SOMETHING going on that I should know about?'

Hanna tried a surprised expression on Jo but she should have known that her best friend would see straight through it.

'Oh, my goodness…there *is* something going on, isn't there?' Jo's smile was growing. 'You can thank me later for helping choose him for covering my maternity leave.'

Hanna cast a glance over her shoulder from where she and Jo were sitting on a couch in front of the bay window with the amazing view out to Dunedin's picturesque harbour, but Mac was still busy in the kitchen of Jo and Cade's house, opening the bottle of wine they'd stopped to buy on their way here.

'To be honest,' she said, 'it started in Prague.'

'*No…* You didn't say anything.'

Hanna bit her lip. 'Maybe I didn't want to admit I'd jumped into bed with someone the first day I'd met them.'

Jo laughed. 'Hey…no judgement here. It was the first date for me and Cade. There's no getting away from that kind of chemistry.' Her glance in Mac's direction was thoughtful. 'It's that good, huh?'

'Gets better every day,' Hanna murmured.

Not just in gradual increments, either. After that evening last week, when Mac had suggested they had two summer holidays together every year, there was a new, stronger thread that was binding their connection even more tightly.

Because it suggested permanence.

Not in the normal sense of a couple choosing to spend the rest of their lives together but Mac was never going to ask Hanna to marry him, was he? Or suggest that they lived together. So this…the idea that they would meet up, to have a wonderful adventure somewhere, was probably the closest he was ever going to come to committing himself to a significant relationship.

And it was enough for Hanna.

Enough to fill her heart with the kind of joy that could only come from being in love. From knowing, deep down, that Mac was feeling the same way. Even if he wasn't admitting it, even to himself. She could feel it in the way he touched her when they made love and now, because he was thinking of ways they could be together in the future.

Perhaps Mac could sense that he was under observation. He looked up from where he was pouring red wine into two glasses.

'What can I find for you, Jo?'

'There's some orange juice in the fridge. I'd like that diluted with some soda water, please. Half in half.'

'No worries.'

Jo grinned at Hanna. 'He's starting to sound like a Kiwi.' She lifted an eyebrow. 'He might decide to stay?'

Hanna shook her head. 'I don't think so.'

But the idea of Mac leaving as soon as his locum finished wasn't scaring her. After all, it was only a short time ago that she thought all she would ever have with Mac were the memories they had already made. His idea of all those holidays to come was giving her a whole future of opportunities to keep making memories and, when they weren't together, they could be staying in touch and planning for the next time and that would be enough to keep this joy alive.

Wouldn't it?

Jo was distracted by the vibration of her phone on the coffee table. 'I hope that's Cade,' she exclaimed. 'He should have been home half an hour ago. He's the one who's supposed to be doing the barbecue.'

She read the message and groaned.

'What's up?' Hanna asked.

'He's been stuck. The patient he was called out to see was deceased by the time he got there and he had to wait for the police to arrive. He's only just heading back to the station.'

'Oh, no...' Mac had heard Jo as he came in with the drinks. 'That sounds like it could take a while?'

'We won't wait for him. I'm sure you'll be able to drive the barbecue, Mac.' Jo put her glass down on the table. 'I can get it going to warm it up.' She started to get up from the sofa but fell back with an even louder groan than reading the message had elicited.

Mac frowned. 'Are you okay?'

Jo nodded, but her eyes were closed. 'It's getting

harder every time,' she said. 'I've had trouble staying on my feet today because it makes my back ache and then, when I sit down, it's too hard to get up.'

'Don't move,' Mac instructed. 'I'll sort the barbecue.'

'And I can do the food,' Hanna said.

'There's not much to do.' Jo still hadn't opened her eyes. 'There are some salads in the fridge, fresh bread that just needs slicing and a potato bake that's already in the oven. The sausages will take longest so they need to go on the grill first. There's steak and bacon as well.'

'Sounds delicious,' Hanna said. 'But let's wait a bit before we start cooking in case Cade gets away soon. Or are you starving?'

'I'm not even hungry,' Jo confessed. 'I don't think there's any room in my belly for food now.' Her smile was wry. 'Remind me why I thought it was a good idea to get pregnant at my advanced age?'

'Advanced age?' Mac raised his eyebrows. 'What… I thought mid-thirties was the usual age these days.'

'Mid-thirties?' Jo laughed as she threw Hanna a meaningful glance. 'I can see why you fell for this guy.'

There was a beat of something in the air that Hanna had not expected. It felt like Mac was startled—as if it hadn't occurred to him that Hanna might have fallen in love with him? She didn't dare meet his gaze but, from the corner of her eye, she could see that he hadn't moved a muscle. He was still focused on Jo.

Jo shook her head at Mac. 'I'm forty-six,' she told him. 'So this is my one and only shot at motherhood. You're not likely to see a primigravida more elderly than me.'

Mac blinked and that odd frisson that Hanna had been aware of evaporated.

'Okay... I'm impressed,' he said. 'Even more so that you travelled all the way to Europe when you were *how* many months pregnant?'

'Close enough to six. But I wouldn't have gone if there'd been any complications. The trip home was the hardest. I got such a backache on the plane that Cade was scared I was going into labour.'

'When's your due date?' Mac asked.

'Not soon enough,' Jo sighed. 'I've probably got at least another four weeks of this.' She used the arm of the couch to haul herself properly upright as her phone began to ring, leaning forward to grab it from the coffee table.

'Cade?' She listened for a moment. 'Okay... No speeding.' She was smiling as she ended the call. 'He's on his way,' she told her guests. 'And he loves a run on the peninsula road on that bike of his. He won't be...'

Jo's smile was being overridden by a grimace that suggested severe pain. Mac did look up to catch Hanna's gaze this time, but he wasn't thinking about anything Jo had said. This was the kind of glance that was becoming familiar. The one that signalled a level of alertness when an internal alarm had sounded. The sort they'd exchanged within minutes of meeting before their tour guide had collapsed. Just like the more recent occasion when Mac had realised that their patient with the pulmonary embolus might be critically unwell.

But this was about Hanna's best friend and there was no reason to think that she was in trouble, was there?

'Do you need something for that back pain?' she asked. 'Have you got a heat pack or a hottie somewhere?'

'I'm fine.' Jo was getting to her feet. 'I just really need to go to the loo. An empty bladder will help.'

She had a hand pressed to her back as she tried to straighten up but she didn't lift her head and Hanna was aware of another strange beat—as if the universe was holding its breath. The feeling intensified as Jo spoke slowly.

'Uh-oh…'

She was still looking down and Hanna shifted her gaze to see what Jo must have felt happening. There was fluid soaking her leggings.

'Did I just wet myself or is it what I think it might be?' Jo was sounding perfectly calm as she lowered herself back onto the couch. 'Han…would you mind getting a towel or two out of the linen cupboard? It's in the hall, beside the bathroom.'

Hanna could hear Mac sounding just as calm as Jo as she rushed out of the room.

'Tell me about this back pain of yours, Jo. When did it start? Give it a score out of ten…'

The soft, clean towels Hanna grabbed were a pale, oatmeal colour. In the time it took to put them between Jo and the couch, the faint bloodstains were obvious.

'I think we should call an ambulance,' Mac said.

'No…' Jo shook her head. 'Cade will be home any minute. It's quite normal for there to be a bit of blood in amniotic fluid and it's also normal for contractions to not even start for twenty-four hours after waters break. There's no need to panic.'

Except that in the silence that followed her words, there was an odd expression appearing on Jo's face.

'I can feel something weird,' she said quietly.

Hanna felt her heart sink. 'What sort of weird?'

'Pulsatile weird,' Jo whispered.

'Okay…' Mac was rolling up the sleeves of his shirt. 'Let's get you lying down, Jo, and find out what's going on.'

It was Hanna who helped remove Jo's lower clothing so she was the first to see the loop of umbilical cord. They all knew the implications of a cord prolapse. The oxygen supply to the baby was in danger of being cut off by pressure from the baby's head and it could be catastrophic. Severe oxygen deprivation could lead to brain damage or death. They all knew the recommended management, which was to keep the pressure off the cord until the mother could be rushed into Theatre for an emergency Caesarean section. And they all knew that being this far away from hospital was a significant addition to the risk factors. It was Hanna who helped Jo turn onto her knees, putting her head down to let gravity help with easing the pressure on the cord. As she moved away to call for an ambulance without alarming Jo, she was grateful to hear the reassurance in Mac's voice.

'I'd say you're very close to being fully dilated. I can feel baby's head.' He still sounded calm as Hanna returned within a few moments. 'Okay…you're going to feel me pushing a bit now that the head's far enough down to elevate. It's a good thing you've got a full bladder. That's going to help take pressure off as well.' He looked up at Hanna. 'What's the ETA for the ambulance?'

'Ten to twelve minutes,' she said quietly.

Jo groaned. 'I knew there had to be a downside to living in a place where you got a panoramic view of the city in the distance.'

'It's okay,' Mac said. 'Guidelines for the diagnosis to delivery time for a cord prolapse is less than thirty minutes. The team will be waiting and we can get you straight into Theatre.'

Cade had clearly got through any traffic with ease, thanks to his motorbike. He came through the door of his home only minutes later and his training and experience as a critical care paramedic gave him the ability to take in both exactly what was happening in his living room and the potential implications. Jo was his absolute priority, however. He knelt beside her on the floor to support her physically and, more importantly, emotionally.

'We've got this,' he told his wife. '*You've* got this…'

'Oh, God…' Jo cried out a minute later. 'I need to push…'

'Hang on.' Mac's voice was too calm now. His features were set in lines that Hanna hadn't seen before. Grim lines. This wasn't part of any recommended protocol. Even if Jo was fully dilated, an assisted delivery with forceps was needed to make it as fast as possible. In order to deliver the baby, the measures being used to protect the blood and oxygen supply through the umbilical cord, with the position Jo was in and the pressure Mac was keeping on the baby's head, would have to be abandoned and, as soon as that happened, the countdown would be on.

The potential need for a neonatal resuscitation was

another factor they needed to consider because the only resources they had available were the combined skills of the people here. People who would have to cope without the benefit of the kind of specialist medical equipment that might well be needed to save a tiny life. People who were all too aware of the stakes involved.

None were more aware than the parents of this longed-for baby that was trying to arrive in a very less than desirable way.

Jo cried out again and this time, there was a note of agony in the sound. 'I *really* need to push...'

'We've got two options,' Mac said. 'We try and slow the delivery until we can get to hospital or we try and speed it up.'

Hanna watched as Cade and Jo locked gazes on each other. She knew how huge this decision was. How precious this baby was to both of them. Having been so closely involved in the wedding and even the honeymoon of her best friend, Hanna had learned a lot about a love story that was so powerful it was easy to believe it was meant to be. She knew that this pregnancy was quite likely to be Jo's only chance to become a mother and that Cade had already had the devastating loss of an almost full-term baby, long ago. There was such intensity in the way they seemed to be communicating silently. There was also so much love it was palpable enough to bring the sting of tears to the back of Hanna's eyes.

And the decision was made. It was going to take too long to wait for the ambulance, try and keep stalling delivery for the return trip to the hospital and then to get to Theatre. Whether delivering the baby here, as fast as possible, carried less risk was a terrifying choice to make but it was one the parents made together.

With the first signs of the next contraction, Jo was turned onto her back, half sitting, cradled in Cade's arms as he knelt behind her. Hanna had seen Mac glance at his watch the moment he'd moved his hand and she knew that he was silently recording how long this was going to take.

It already seemed to be too long.

'You can do this.' Cade's mouth was right beside Jo's ear. 'I've got you. Take a deep breath and squeeze my hands. And...*push*...'

Jo pushed. And pushed again. She gasped for air and cried out in pain.

'It's coming,' Mac told her. 'You're doing so well, Jo. One more push...'

But Jo was shaking her head and the sound she made was a strangled sob. '... I...*can't*...'

'Yes, you *can*,' Hanna told her fiercely. 'You can do this, Jo. *Push*...'

'I'm here.' Cade's voice was remarkably steady. 'Hold on. Just one more push, baby. *One* more...'

Jo's head was tipped back so that she could see Cade's face and he wasn't breaking the eye contact. Hanna could actually feel the strength that Cade was giving and it was no wonder that she was hanging onto him as if her life depended on it. They were in a world of their own right now and all they could possibly need was each other and Hanna found the tears that had threatened moments ago were now rolling down her cheeks.

And then she realised she'd been wrong. As Mac lifted the baby and Jo and Cade got their first glimpse of their daughter, she knew that they needed this just as much as each other.

Their baby.

Their *family*...

The relief that the baby had been delivered so quickly couldn't be savoured yet. Mac was now completely focused on the physical condition of this infant. Getting her dry was the first priority and he took the soft, clean towel from Hanna to start gently rubbing the pale skin on this tiny body and limbs. He had to ensure the baby didn't lose any body heat and providing stimulation could kick start the signs of life he was desperately looking for.

Was the baby breathing yet? Was her heart rate slow enough to mean she needed CPR? The first APGAR score was needed so that Mac could fill in the paperwork accurately later but, oddly, the criteria and scoring system were a blur in the back of his head as he watched the baby open her eyes and stretch her arms. And then her mouth opened and Mac watched her take her very first breath, pulling the air into her tiny lungs and then scrunching her face into a scowl before letting it out in a scratchy, hiccuping cry that was the best sound Mac had ever heard.

'We should wait at least three minutes to cut the cord,' he said. 'Let's get this little girl skin-to-skin with her mum.'

Cade hadn't moved. He still had Jo in the circle of his arms, his head pressed against hers as Hanna helped shift Jo's remaining clothing and they nestled the baby against her breasts. Mac checked his watch. They'd need to do a five-minute APGAR score at about the same time as cutting the cord. He needed to keep an eye on both the mother and baby until the ambulance arrived but he also needed to find a quiet spot and use his phone to dictate everything he could remember about this birth for the medical records. Lists of what he needed to monitor and warning signs to keep a watch for, like any post-partum bleeding from Jo, were crystal clear in his head now, thank goodness. He could tick them off and stay on top of this situation without being ambushed or distracted by the kind of emotions he could feel swirling around him.

Even Hanna being a complete puddle wasn't surprising. Jo was her best friend and Mac hadn't realised quite how high risk this pregnancy had been. Or that it had been a bit of a miracle in the first place. Hanna would be feeling the wash of that relief Mac wasn't allowing himself to indulge in just yet but her expression, as she watched Cade and Jo, oblivious to being observed herself, gave an even more intense impression.

It didn't look like something he would expect to see on the face of someone who'd never wanted to have a baby of her own.

It looked like a longing that was so bone-deep it had been there for ever.

Mac knew what that kind of longing felt like and he wasn't going to step anywhere near that space. It was a decision he'd made a very long time ago and he wasn't about to question the wisdom of something that had served him very well ever since. The sinking sensation of realising that Hanna wanted a very different—incompatible—future from his own, even if she

didn't realise it, was something that it would be irre-
sponsible to ignore.

He got to his feet. Both Jo and the baby were in great
hands being monitored by Cade and Hanna.

'I think I can hear a siren,' Mac said. 'I'll go out to
the road and flag them down.'

CHAPTER TEN

IT CAME IN WAVES.

Hanna could feel them, taking turns, washing her in one direction and then the completely opposite direction, over the next few days. Like a tide going in and out with no prospect of it stopping anytime soon.

At one end of what was becoming an unwelcome emotional spectrum were the beliefs that had underpinned her choices ever since she'd become an adult. She wasn't going to let the fact that she couldn't have children detract from living life to the full. It could be seen as a blessing, in fact, because it gave her no distraction from giving everything she had to a career she loved, the freedom to travel anywhere she desired, and the independence to live where and how she wanted.

Not that she wanted to continue her current living situation, she told Jo, when she was having a hands-free chat on her phone as she drove to work to start a night shift in the emergency department.

'I actually got up this morning to find a strange, *naked* man standing in the kitchen.'

'No way...' But Jo sounded amused. 'What was he doing?'

'Making coffee.'

'Mmm…coffee. I need some. Stat.'

'Not enough sleep again last night?'

'Almost none. Our daughter might be small but she's mighty. Mighty hungry, anyway.'

'Have you decided on her name?'

'Yes. Olioli. It means joy in Samoan. We'll just call her Oli, though.'

'Oh, nice… I love it.' Hanna was smiling as she turned into Princess Margaret's staff car park. 'It's perfect.'

She could feel flashes of the joy that had come from the dramatic but fortunately safe arrival of this special baby amidst the chaos of the first few days of her friends becoming parents a little earlier than expected.

She could also feel the shock of realising that she might have been totally wrong for her entire adult life. That her conviction that she was never going to miss being able to have children herself had just been exposed as the biggest lie ever. Had she really brushed off Jo's determination to have a baby before it was too late by emphatically saying 'rather you than me'? She completely understood that longing to be a mother now. Because it was eating a hole in her heart at the other end of that emotional spectrum. Maybe it was more like a pendulum than a tide, Hanna thought. She was swinging from one side to the other and it was making her feel a little sick.

Jo's voice broke into her thoughts. 'We've made another decision too.'

'What's that?'

'I'm not going to go back to work full time after

my maternity leave. These early years with Oli are too important.'

Hanna could understand that, too. How hard would it be to balance a full-on career with how much you wanted to be the one to care for your precious baby?

'So I'm going to resign,' Jo added. 'Hey... You should tell Mac. Maybe he'd like to apply for the permanent position?'

Hanna laughed. 'I doubt it. He's an international figure. Why would he want to move to a tiny city at the bottom of the world?'

'Um...because you're here? I saw the way he was looking at you the other night when you had Oli in your arms.'

Oh, help... Had Mac guessed any of what had been going on in her head in that moment? With their opposing shifts, it had been easy to excuse the lack of contact since then but was it possible he was avoiding her? She shook off the thought. It had simply been a very emotional moment for everybody concerned.

'I wouldn't trust your opinion,' Hanna said lightly. 'You kind of had a lot of other stuff going on at that point.'

'I guess so. Who was he, anyway?'

'Who was who?'

'Um...the naked man in your kitchen?'

'Oh...' Hanna gratefully returned to the start of their conversation. 'A "friend" of Amanda's.' She let her breath out in a disparaging huff. 'That's the second new "friend" she's brought home this week. I'm totally over having flatmates.'

'I'm not at all surprised. You need a place of your own.'

'I'm thinking I might like to buy yours.'

'You could move in with Mac for a while and give it a trial run?'

'What—the house, or Mac?'

Jo laughed. 'Why not both?'

'Now, there's a thought.' Hanna had parked her car but didn't end her call by cutting the engine and the Bluetooth connection. Because this was the middle point of that emotional spectrum and perhaps she wanted to enjoy being there for a moment or two longer.

It was the only point she was consistently sure about. Her love for Mac. Her desire to be with him above all else.

She was never going to change her mind about how she felt about him but he might very well change his mind if he thought she hadn't been entirely honest when she'd told him that marriage and children were not for her.

And there was another wave. Washing Hanna towards the space where she was filled with that astonishingly powerful longing and seeds of doubts that could potentially grow like weeds if she didn't pull them out and get rid of them.

That she could hear baby Oli's cry on the other end of the line wasn't helping. The plaintive sound reminded her that she hadn't actually seen anything of Mac in the last few days because he'd started covering some night shifts before Hanna was rostered for any. Today was the first time their work hours—and by default their hours off—would match since the day that Oli had arrived. Since that pendulum had started swinging.

'Sounds like you're needed,' she told Jo, reaching for the button to end the call. 'And it's time I got to work.'

Hanna Peterson was the first person Mac saw in the department when he arrived to do his last rostered night shift. He only saw her back as she pushed a trolley into an examination room but there was no mistaking that long braid hanging down the centre of her back. Hair the colour of flames and as soft as silk. As unique as Hanna's hazel green eyes that had caught his attention so emphatically that first day in Prague. Eyes that should have come with a warning that they belonged to the most captivating woman he was ever going to meet.

The woman who was perfect for him in every way except for one thing that he hadn't seen coming. He'd wondered, later that night, if he simply imagined what he'd seen in Hanna's face when she was holding that newborn baby, but he'd had too much time, in the last few long night shifts and the days where sleep had been hard to catch, to unpick everything that he'd seen and, more importantly, felt that night.

And, because their shift hours meant they hadn't been able to share more than a text conversation or two, he hadn't been completely distracted by being physically close to Hanna, either. He hadn't been able to smell the fragrance of that gorgeous hair. Or feel the silk of her skin. He hadn't been ambushed by the overwhelming desire to sink into the astonishing intimacy they always seemed to find so effortlessly, which automatically seemed to disarm any warning signals and stifle any doubts.

In some ways it would be preferable to ignore what

he'd seen. To keep enjoying his time with Hanna here in New Zealand. To let himself dream that they could come up with a plan that would mean it didn't actually have to end at all…

But his new knowledge, that had come straight out of left field, was too big to ignore. Too important, because it changed everything. Ironically, they'd actually discussed it that day in the forest.

You can't change how you feel about something that big because someone else wants you to…

He'd tried to argue with himself about that. He'd wondered if he could change *his* mind about wanting children himself, but he could hear the echoes of his own voice.

If you have to change that much to try and make a relationship work, it's doomed anyway.

It didn't matter how often he went over and over it all in his head, approaching it from every direction. There was no getting away from the clincher.

It might not have felt like it, but it would have been far less painful to find that out, make a clean break and move on…

It might be the right thing to do but Mac hadn't come up with an acceptable plan for quite *how* he was going to do it. Somehow, he had to end things without hurting Hanna any more than was inevitable but convincingly enough that she would move on and find someone who could give her so much more than he ever could.

The family she might not even realise how much she actually wanted.

He was still watching the woman he was going to have to walk away from, even though it was the last thing he *wanted* to do. The last thing a big part of him wanted to do, anyway. There was another part that was going to be relieved, of course. The part that embraced control and made careful plans and checklists. The part that kept him on track and maintained those careful boundaries in his personal life that he'd strayed too far past recently.

The part of Mac that had kept him safe for so long now. After that disastrous slip up in his youth where he'd been prepared to discard his life plan for the woman he'd loved and the baby that would give him another chance of having a family, only to have it all ripped away from him, he'd never let his control slip.

Was what he knew now perhaps his version of a 'get out of jail free' card?

Hanna had vanished into the examination room and that was a reminder that it was time to push any personal issues completely out of sight while he did his job. It helped that the part of his brain that kept those lists and that control in his personal life also provided the distance that enabled him to keep sight of a bigger picture when it came to diagnosing and treating patients within the framework of keeping an entire emergency department running smoothly.

It did run smoothly, in both a personal and professional sense, until the early morning hours of that night shift, when he saw Hanna coming through a cubicle curtain, with a baby in her arms, a concerned frown on her face. An older woman, behind her, had red eyes as if she'd been crying and a handful of tissues pressed to her face as she blew her nose.

Mac could feel his control slip a notch. Because this

was Hanna. Because she was holding a baby, which tapped into everything he'd been thinking about so much. Because seeing her look so concerned made him want to step in instantly and help. But this wasn't about Hanna. Or himself. It was about a very vulnerable small person who'd been brought into the emergency department.

Instantly using the assessment tool of the paediatric triangle was as automatic as taking his next breath. Within taking a couple of steps closer, Mac was not alarmed by the general appearance of this baby and couldn't see any obvious signs of poor circulation like mottled hands or a blueish tinge to the face. He could, however, hear the sounds of a baby who was in respiratory distress with overly rapid breathing and audible wheezing. And he would never forget the golden rule that adequate evaluation was impossible if a child was fully clothed.

'Follow me,' he directed. 'Resus One's free. What's going on?'

'His grandma's just brought him in because he wasn't feeding properly and wouldn't settle. He's not running a temperature and hasn't got a runny nose, but she noticed a sudden onset of wheezing and his breathing's got noticeably worse in the few minutes I've been with them.'

Mac let Hanna go ahead as he spoke to the woman following her. 'Any chance that baby's inhaled or choked on anything?'

'I don't think so.' The woman shook her head. 'Except he did seem to be having trouble swallowing his milk an hour or so ago. That was when he started coughing and I thought his breathing didn't sound quite right.'

'Has he been unwell in any other way before this?'

'No… A bit unsettled, maybe, but he has been, right from the start. And he's never been a good sleeper. That's why I told my daughter and son-in-law I'd take him for the night—so they could get a decent sleep themselves.'

'How old is he?'

'Four months. His name's Taika.'

Hanna was gently putting the baby down on the bed in the middle of the room. She began unbuttoning the stretchy sleep suit he was wearing, distracting and soothing him with a constant singsong explanation of what she was doing.

Mac was fitting his stethoscope to his ears.

'Any family history of allergies or asthma?'

'I'm not sure.'

Mac froze, blinking slowly. 'Sorry?'

'Taika's adopted,' she said. 'Sorry, I should have told you this before, shouldn't I? I do actually forget sometimes. He's such a wanted baby and he couldn't be loved any more—by any of us. Oh, my…' She was reaching for her tissues again. 'I didn't want to wake them up before I had to but I should ring them now, shouldn't I?'

Baby Taika began crying as Mac approached with his stethoscope, which wasn't a bad thing when assessing a baby's appearance or reactions but it made it impossible to auscultate a chest effectively. Hanna picked him up and held him against her shoulder with one hand cradling his head and he settled enough for Mac to listen to some worrying lung sounds, with the possible causes and more questions that needed answering lining up in his head.

Was this a case of a viral illness like bronchiolitis or RSV even though he wasn't yet showing other symptoms of a respiratory infection? Was it an allergic reaction that might lead to his condition deteriorating rapidly? Or was it an aspiration pneumonia from milk or a foreign object? The wheeze that was getting louder suggested obstructive pathology and a chest X-ray was high on the list for investigations to rule out something caught in tiny airways.

There was another reason to take an X-ray that became apparent as Hanna put the baby down again so that he could look for other indications of respiratory distress like the retraction of the muscles between ribs.

Bruises.

Just faint marks on his ribs but Mac's focus narrowed sharply as another automatic thought process was triggered by a solidly embedded alarm system.

If they can't cruise, they can't bruise...

He couldn't let that alarm bell sound so loudly it drowned anything else out, however. Tunnel vision, thanks to one sign or symptom standing out enough to disguise others, was a trap for the unwary. Mac always had mental checklists available to cover possibilities for a differential diagnosis and he wasn't about to jump to any conclusions.

But Hanna had noticed the bruises as well. She only caught his gaze for a heartbeat but he couldn't miss the sudden change in the atmosphere in this room as Mac felt a nasty knot forming in his gut. Was she thinking the same thing he was—that Taika's grandmother had potentially given them cause to be on alert by saying that his parents were suffering from sleep deprivation? That this baby was not their biological child?

When the X-ray images were available a short time later, that knot in Mac's gut expanded so fast he actually felt sick.

'There,' he said quietly, his finger on the screen as Hanna looked over his shoulder. 'And there…'

'Oh, my God,' Hanna breathed. 'Those marks are all *fractures*?'

'Very recent ones,' Mac said grimly. 'On both the clavicle and these ribs. It could well be the reason his breathing is affected.'

'But his grandmother's so involved with his care and she obviously loves Taika. She says her daughter, Gemma, is finding things tough but she adores her son. She's apparently worried sick. She's on her way here now.' Hanna was biting her lip. 'Do we need to bring Social Services in?'

'Not just yet.' Mac took a slow breath in. There were steps to this process. A case of child abuse couldn't be allowed to slip through but, on the other hand, a mistaken accusation was also unacceptable. 'I'd like to do a much more thorough physical assessment. But we'll get some more images done. Of his long bones and spine.'

'To look for other fractures?'

Mac nodded. 'But also to look for any evidence of underlying bone disease. I can't see any beading on the ribs in these images, but it's quite possible to have a mild form of osteogenesis imperfecta that won't be that easy to diagnose. It's a shame we can't find out if there's any family history of scoliosis or fractures or dislocations, but we might see thinning of the long

bones if there is inherited disease. There are other investigations that can be done like skin and bone biopsies.
We'll keep Taika in, and I'll get a specialist orthopaedic consult booked as early as possible in the morning.
I need to talk to his parents, too.' His heart was sinking
even further at the thought of a conversation that could
be distressing for everybody involved. 'It's going to be
a long night, I think.'

The case of baby Taika cast a pall over the rest of the
night shift, especially after his parents arrived and were
so clearly shocked to be faced with what had already
been discovered about their son's condition. Hanna
spent much of her time with the family and watched
their care of the baby as he was treated with pain relief
for his fractures and oxygen along with an inhaler for
his breathing. She became more and more convinced
that this wasn't a case of a child who was being abused.

She completely understood why Mac was being so
thorough, however. This was beyond important to him.
Hanna only had to remember that opening address he'd
given at the Prague conference to be reminded of that
little boy who thought an emergency department was
his 'safe' space. She'd told him how heartbreaking the
story had been and how much she had wanted to cuddle that little boy herself but there was nothing about
Taika that struck the same kind of chord. Her instincts
told her that he was a longed-for and much-loved baby.

'They're beside themselves with worry,' she said to
Mac as their shift was finally ending. 'How long will
it be until they get some answers?'

'I've spoken to the paediatric orthopaedic guy who

will be reviewing the initial X-rays. He's going to meet the family at nine o'clock and he'll call in anyone else he deems necessary.' Mac glanced at his watch. 'I might hang around and see what he has to say.'

'That's two hours away.' Hanna looked at the deep creases around Mac's eyes. She knew how tired he had to be, but she could also sense how tightly strung he was. 'I don't suppose you're going to try and catch some sleep first?'

Mac simply shook his head. 'I'll go and find some coffee. Take a walk, maybe. It should be getting light outside soon.'

'Want some company?'

Another shake of his head was accompanied by a smile this time. 'You need to sleep.'

'Not going to happen,' Hanna said quietly. 'Not when I'm worried about you.'

The beat of silence that fell between them made it feel as if she'd just told Mac exactly how she felt about him and, in a way, she had. She'd let him know that his wellbeing was just as important, if not more so, than her own.

The hesitation before he caught her gaze was telling. A hollow feeling inside Hanna's chest was expanding to the point where it was difficult to take a breath and it only got worse when Mac spoke.

'Okay…come for a walk with me,' he said. 'It's been a while since we've had a chance to talk properly.'

His gaze slid away from Hanna's as he spoke and she was aware of a heaviness—as though there was too much air inside that hollow space. People usually only said they wanted to 'talk' when they had something to say that the other person was not going to like. Chillingly, this took her back to that moment in the park in Barcelona, after that amazing dance under the tree, when she had sensed that the heat of the passion they'd discovered was burning itself out and Mac was either pulling away or putting some kind of barrier in place.

That, for whatever reason—probably because there was too much emotion involved—he needed to escape into his safe, buttoned-up space where everything was under control.

Hanna swallowed hard. Something had changed for Mac as well, hadn't it? But when? Had it been the birth of Oli, as it had been for her, or was it the case of baby Taika tonight that had got under his skin so much? Whatever it was, Hanna knew that it was going to affect her as well.

'Where would you like to go for a walk?'

Mac shrugged. 'Doesn't matter. You choose.'

Hanna could feel the chill of the frosty dawn approaching as they walked outside. It did matter, she thought. This might be one of the most significant decisions she'd made in a long time.

'Where are we?'

'A special place,' Hanna told him. 'Tunnel Beach.'

The idea of bringing Mac here had occurred to Hanna the moment she'd turned out of the hospital car park, knowing they had a couple of hours up their sleeves. This was where she had come to take part in a very significant event not so long ago when she'd been the bridesmaid for her best friend. Given the even more significant event of the birth of their child that both she and Mac had been a part of, it seemed exactly the place they needed to be.

'I can't see the beach.' Mac turned his head as he looked through the windscreen. 'But it looks like the apocalypse is about to happen.'

Dramatic blood red and tangerine orange streaks outlined their uninterrupted view of the horizon above a still inky black ocean.

Hanna grinned. 'I was hoping it was going to be a stunning sunrise. They often are with a frosty start to the day. And it's kind of a secret beach,' she added. 'It's where Jo and Cade got married. Where they had their first date, in fact. You have to climb down steps through a tunnel, which probably isn't the best idea while it's still dark, but we can watch the sunrise and then have a walk if you don't mind getting cold.'

'It would certainly keep me awake.'

'I don't think you need anything more to keep you awake, do you?'

It wasn't just the deep crinkles around Mac's eyes, or the dark shadows beneath him. Hanna could feel how tense he was and the need to offer him comfort or support or whatever it was that he needed was a glow as strong as the sunrise unfolding in front of them. She reached to touch his face softly with her fingertips and, when he turned and smiled at her, she felt a little piece of her heart crack.

'What is it?' she whispered. 'Is this about Taika? About his injuries? Or is it because he's adopted that makes you feel so involved?'

Mac looked away. He let his eyes drift shut. 'Both,' he admitted quietly.

Hanna stared at him. She couldn't say anything. She could feel the silence in the car folding in on her as she realised what had been there in front of her all along. Hidden in plain sight.

'Oh, my God.' Her voice shook. 'That little boy in your story...who only felt cared for when he was being taken care of in hospital... It was *you*, wasn't it?'

Mac didn't say anything. He didn't need to. Or maybe he guessed that Hanna was shocked enough to need a moment to process things.

So much was suddenly making sense to her. Like why Mac was so buttoned up. That being so organised and predictable and never putting a foot out of place might have been the only way to try and keep himself safe as a child. That the need to protect his own unborn child must have been overwhelming and to be told that baby no longer existed would have seemed like the ultimate failure when he'd been determined to take responsibility.

No wonder this man had never simply followed his nose to find an adventure. Or let himself get close enough to anyone to contemplate marriage or the responsibilities of bringing children into the world. Why would anyone make themselves vulnerable to yet another instance of being abused? Letting themselves feel unwanted. Rejected.

Unloved...

That crack in her heart was growing into a full-on break. Like the way she'd wanted to cuddle that little boy in his story, all Hanna wanted to do was to gather Mac into her arms and hold him tight.

To let him know how much he was loved.

But that would be the worst thing she could do, wouldn't it?

Deep inside this intelligent, skilled, perceptive and sensitive man, who had a wonderful sense of humour and the ability to be the most generous lover ever, was a small boy. One who'd been hurt often enough to learn not to trust the people who should have loved him. Who might have even *said* that they loved him but acted very, very differently. And there was a young man, about to grasp the freedom of making his own choices and willingly stepping up to make sure his own child didn't feel unwanted or unloved, who'd been hurt again, so badly he'd chosen to travel alone through life.

She'd known she couldn't ask for his trust or a commitment of any kind. He had to be the one to offer it. Right now, it felt like he was moving further away from her rather than closer and it also felt like there was nothing she could do about it. If she went after him, in an emotional sense, she knew he would only run faster. Because that was the only way he could feel safe? If she stayed very still, maybe he would slow down enough to think about things. Perhaps, if he was allowed to choose himself, he might turn around and come back?

Even the spectacular sunrise was fading in front of them now.

It was Mac who broke the silence in the end. 'It's ancient history,' he said. 'But you're the only person I've ever talked to about it.'

Hanna swallowed carefully. 'Thank you,' she said softly. She waited until he turned his head to meet her gaze and then she waited for another heartbeat, just to hold his gaze. To try and tell him what she couldn't say aloud.

'What for?'

It felt like Mac was holding onto her gaze as if he was searching for something. He had that focused, narrow-eyed expression that told Hanna she was the only thing that mattered in that moment.

She loved that.

It felt like love, even if Mac still couldn't let himself admit it.

Hanna smiled at him. 'For trusting me...'

She broke the eye contact, before the moment could get any heavier, by looking out of the window. 'It's light enough to be safe to walk along the top of a cliff,' she said. 'We could even go down the tunnel.'

Mac checked his watch. 'Maybe we should head back. I'd hate to miss that meeting. We could come back another day?'

'We could...'

Hanna was smiling as she started the car again. Because this way, it was easy to do that standing still thing and not push Mac somewhere he wasn't ready to go. And 'another day' suggested he wasn't going to run too far, too soon.

It was a reprieve.

Wrapped up in hope...

CHAPTER ELEVEN

FINDING WHAT FELT like a justifiable reason to avoid doing something difficult or unpleasant—like telling someone that a relationship couldn't continue—made it easier to continue doing it.

It also felt like a much kinder option and there was no one else on earth that Mac would want to be kind to more than Hanna Peterson.

Fate was also lending a helping hand. Jo's decision not to return to work full time after her maternity leave led to an almost instant offer of a permanent position for Mac, apparently due to the glowing reports of the time he had already spent in the Princess Margaret's emergency department.

'I can't take it, of course,' Mac told Hanna that evening, when they found time to be together in Jo's little house, relaxing on the couch in front of the fire. 'I've got far too many commitments, including a job in Edinburgh and research projects I'm involved with in Europe and the States. I've loved being here but it was never going to be for ever.'

'I know...' Hanna snuggled in under his arm to tuck her head against his chest. 'I doubt anyone expected the world-famous Dr MacMillan to emigrate to a wee town at the bottom of the world. We're lucky you decided to come for a busman's holiday.'

That summed it up nicely, didn't it? Doing his real job but in a very different location. That blurred space between a holiday and real life. Like the space between a relationship and a holiday fling that he and Hanna had claimed as their own. Neither could work on a permanent basis, however, despite any plans they might play with to meet up again on holiday. Mac doubted that Hanna expected that to work, either. They would drift apart as their real lives took over. Hanna would meet someone else. Someone who could give her far more than Mac could.

He bent his head, placing a kiss on Hanna's hair.

'Did you know that Jo dropped by to give me a heads-up that the position was going to be advertised so it could well impact the length of my locum? I suspect it was because of her that I got approached directly.'

'You're her favourite person right now. You played a big part in Oli's safe arrival.'

'She had Oli with her. It's a great name, isn't it?'

'The full version is Olioli. It means "joy" in Samoan.'

Mac nodded. 'So Jo told me. The name suits her. She was spreading joy right through the department. Or maybe it was because Jo's looking so extraordinarily happy.' He reached for the glass of wine on the low table beside the couch. 'She also told me that she's planning to sell this house. She's hoping you'll buy it.'

'I'm seriously thinking about it.' Hanna seemed to be watching the flames in the gas fire that was flickering in front of them. 'I'm kind of over having flatmates. I think it's time I grew up and settled down.'

'I can't imagine you settled down,' Mac murmured. 'I'll always see you as a free spirit, following your nose and finding amazing adventures.'

It was only a heartbeat of silence but it felt…odd. As if he wasn't the only one who was avoiding saying something difficult? Mac felt the need to break it.

'I forgot to tell you. The results on Taika's bone biopsy came through today. You were right. There's a reason for his fractures that has nothing to do with abuse.'

Hanna lifted her head. 'It *is* osteogenesis imperfecta?'

'Yes.'

'Oh…his parents must be devastated.'

'It's Type One, which is mild. And there are treatments available now, like cyclic infusions of different drugs that can reduce incidence of fractures and increase bone density. The whole family is completely focused on whatever needs to be done to help.'

'I knew they loved him.' Hanna's eyes had the kind of shimmer that advertised imminent tears. 'His parents had wanted a baby for *so* long…'

'He's a lucky little boy,' Mac agreed.

One of those tears escaped Hanna's eyes as she leaned against him again. 'I hate that you weren't so lucky, Mac,' she whispered.

It was another one of those silences, but Mac couldn't think of anything to say.

'Maybe your sister was one of the lucky ones, too,' Hanna said. 'I know it's tragic that she died so young but maybe she had parents who adored her. A grandma, even, like Taika?'

Mac shrugged. 'Guess I'll never know.' He placed another kiss on the top of Hanna's head. 'It's getting late. Come to bed with me?'

But Hanna ignored the suggestion. 'Where did she grow up?' she asked. 'Didn't you want to know what that was like for her to live in New Zealand?'

'I checked a map before I came. Dunedin's close enough.'

'To where?'

'Oamaru.'

'That's where she lived? Oh…that *is* close,' Hanna exclaimed. 'It would be so easy to go and have a look. It's only a bit over an hour's drive away. I've been through it often enough but I've never stopped to really explore it. And, hey…we've both got a day off tomorrow…'

Mac stood up. He held out his hand, knowing that Hanna would take it and he could pull her to her feet. It would only take another tug and she would be in his arms and he could kiss her lips instead of her hair and they would be upstairs and in bed very, very soon and he wouldn't have to come up with a reason why he didn't want to go and see exactly where his sister had grown up. He didn't need another link to this country that would make it any more difficult to leave.

But he could see a glow in Hanna's eyes that he'd seen before. That excitement that she could find in throwing caution to the winds and following her nose. Or her heart.

'There's so many things I could show you. We could

go the scenic route into Central Otago and up through Danseys Pass. I've heard about a famous old hotel at the top but I've never found the time to go there. It's been a long time since we had an adventure.'

She stood on her tiptoes and kissed Mac on his lips and it reminded him of the way she had said goodbye that first day they'd met before she ran back towards the hotel. They would be saying goodbye again, possibly sooner than he'd expected and Mac knew how much he was going to miss Hanna. He also knew how unlikely it was that he would ever do something truly impulsive again without her encouragement.

And that sparked another memory. Of something Hanna had said in front of that same clock.

We've got time now... Let's not waste a minute of it...

It wasn't that he couldn't say 'no' to her.

He just didn't want to. Perhaps because he wanted to make the most of every minute he still had to spend with Hanna?'

'So...this road is called the Pigroot.' Hanna's sporty little Mini was eating up the miles of the road heading into Central Otago after they'd turned off the coastal road north of Dunedin.

'Hmm...' Mac had his phone out already. 'According to this, we're on State Highway 85.'

'Technically, that would be correct,' Hanna agreed.

'It says that we're going through some of the most historic gold mining territory in New Zealand.'

'Most of Central Otago was gold mining country.'

'It also says that the Maniototo plain has the most

extreme climate in New Zealand. Well below zero in winter and over thirty degrees Celsius in summer.'

'That would explain why my gran used to take me to Naseby to go ice-skating when I was a kid. She was the one who told me it was called the Pigroot. She just didn't tell me why.' Hanna cast a sideways glance at Mac, who was so focused on the information he was taking in that it wouldn't have surprised her if he started taking notes. Or making a list of everything he wanted to see.

She loved that about him. His curiosity and attention to detail. His focus...especially when it was on herself. It was one of the first things she'd noticed about him, in fact—the way his eyes narrowed and the creases appeared as his attention was caught. Not that it stopped him from still being aware of the big picture and was that part of why he was travelling alone in life—that ability to consider consequences of all sorts of possibilities? As always, the thought that Mac had been lonely in the past or could be in the future gave her heart a painful squeeze.

He didn't need to be. She would be happy to be with him for the rest of her life. So happy...

'Okay...there are different stories about how the road got its name.' Mac put his phone away. 'The winner seems to be that the local wild pigs were so friendly that they'd come and rub their noses with any travellers' horses.'

'I like that.' Hanna smiled. 'Friendly locals. We're coming into Naseby now and I'd love to see the lake where I used to go skating but, if you're not too hungry yet, it might be better to wait till we get up the Danseys Pass to get lunch.'

The wild, winding gravel and sand road of the pass cut through the tussock-covered land of high-country farms with snow-dusted mountain views at every turn. The long, low stone building of the hotel blended into the landscape and offered the perfect place to take a break. There was a roaring open fire heating the interior, with a display of antique bottles on the mantelpiece. Bleached deer antlers hung on the wall near the table that Hanna and Mac chose and the beer-battered fish and chips they both ordered for lunch were delicious.

'I used to ice-skate when I was a kid, too,' Mac told her. 'That lake in Naseby reminds me of the one we had on our property.'

'You had a *lake*?' Hanna's jaw dropped.

'Still do. Not that I've skated on it in the last thirty years or more. The estate's a fair way out of Edinburgh so it was easier to get a manager in and live near the hospital.' Mac shook his head. 'I've been putting off deciding what to do with it but I think it's time to sell up. I'll never live there again. It's far too big for one person.'

'Sounds like a castle.'

'More of a manor house but the villagers used to call me the "kid from the castle". It was probably a good thing I got sent to boarding schools from an early age because no one from the village wanted to have anything to do with me.'

Hanna made a small sound of agreement. It would have saved Mac from more than simply being bullied by other children but how lonely had it been?

'I think I will buy Jo's house,' she said quietly. 'It's a perfect size for me.' As a bonus, it would also be filled with memories of being there with Mac. She put down her fork. 'Do you ever worry about getting older?' she asked. 'And still being alone?'

Mac shook his head. 'I'm used to it,' was all he said.

He turned to glance at people settling at a nearby table. A highchair was being found for a baby who looked to be about six months old. A little girl who dropped her toy and began crying as she was put into the chair. Her father retrieved the fluffy rabbit and made it pop up from beneath the tray of the chair and the baby's cry changed to a gurgle of laughter.

Hanna was also watching them, smiling at the sound of the baby's laugh. That would be Jo and Cade in a few months' time, she thought. Out together as a family.

Never alone.

She put down her cutlery moments later, her appetite fading. She'd been used to being alone, too, especially when she'd gone travelling but there was no appeal to be found in doing it again. After being with Mac in Barcelona, she'd felt so alone as she went on to Corsica and then Italy. Things that she would have previously revelled in—like a stunning sunset on the Amalfi Coast—felt so diminished by not having someone to share it with that it might as well have never happened.

Okay…by not having Mac to share it with.

Another peal of laughter from the baby made Hanna smile again but she was suddenly aware of Mac's gaze focused on her. She turned to find an intensity in that gaze that made her catch her breath.

He knew, didn't he? He knew about the longing deep within that had been born at the same time as Oli. Not simply changing her mind about wanting a child but the need for a whole family of her own.

* * *

That smile…

Mac loved that smile.

The joy that Hanna was getting from just observing someone else's child made Mac remember the way she'd looked the night that Jo and Cade's baby was born and she'd held that tiny person in her own arms.

That thought morphed into his body reminding him of what it felt like when *he* was in her arms. And the way he'd felt that day on the bus trip when she'd taken hold of his hand and…and he hadn't felt alone…

Hanna had so much love to give. She was the warmest, bravest, most generous person he'd ever met and he loved that about her.

No…

He loved *her*. Not just her different attributes but the whole of Hanna. He was *in* love with her. He couldn't imagine willingly walking away from her, in fact. How could he go back to his old life and be an entire world away from her?

He could change his life, though, couldn't he?

It was the baby's laughter behind him that sparked the moment that fear stepped in. A reminder of why he couldn't change his life that much. Why he couldn't allow himself to step into the vulnerability of loving anyone like this. Giving them the power to affect every decision you made for the future.

Losing control…

That fear was always there, wasn't it? Buried for so long now but it would never go away completely. Even as a child he'd known that control was the key. If everything was in its place and doing what it was supposed to do—like the intricate workings inside a clock—it was less likely that something bad would happen.

Something that could hurt in ways that cut far deeper than anything purely physical.

Was it his imagination or could he see a reflection of what he was feeling in Hanna's eyes? A flicker of that fear? He broke the eye contact before she could sense any more of what he was thinking.

He managed to find a smile. 'Cute baby.'

'Shall we go?' Hanna's tone held a note of forced brightness. 'We don't want to run out of time.'

Mac paid the bill and followed Hanna outside. 'Would you like me to drive? So you can enjoy the scenery more?'

'Sure.' Hanna handed over the keys. 'You can't go wrong for directions. We just follow this road until we get to the end and turn right to go to the coast.'

She was quiet as they drove further through the pass and Mac could feel a tension between them that had never been there before. A tension that he didn't like one little bit but what could he do to get rid of it? Having to concentrate on his driving wasn't helping. He had to go slowly around bends knowing that there would not be enough room if they met a campervan or a farm vehicle coming the other way and there was an alarming drop to one side into a gorge with a river at the bottom.

When he saw an intersection with another road ahead of them, he slowed to peer at the signpost.

'Island Cliff Road.'

'We need to keep going,' Hanna said. 'We haven't got to Duntroon yet.'

But this road looked as if it went somewhere. It was

sealed, at least at this point, and it was wide enough to have a white line in the middle.

Mac lifted an eyebrow. 'How 'bout we follow our noses instead? I've heard that you find the best adventures that way.'

At last, the tension seemed to be receding. A slow smile curved Hanna's lips and reached as far as her eyes. He held the direct gaze and could actually feel the love that was there, just for him, as if it was a three-dimensional gift. Or maybe a four-dimensional one given that there was no time limit?

Except there kind of was.

Hanna might have said that they didn't want to run out of time but, really, they had no choice, did they? Time was running out on them and maybe that had been the root cause of that tension. They both knew that this was nearly over.

Perhaps that had something to do with the fact that Mac was driving a lot faster on this sealed road that led to who knew where? Maybe the steepness of the hill was contributing as well, along with the curve in the road that was deep enough to conceal the approach of a large milk tanker.

Mac thought he had enough room to get out of the way. What he didn't factor in, as the truck roared past and kept going, were the shingle verges of this rural road and how you could lose all control of your vehicle when the tyres hit the loose material. He did know the moment he lost control of this little car, however. He could feel it sliding.

Spinning.

Bouncing off the road and taking out a post and

wire fence before the passenger side of the car came to a sickening, bone-jolting crunching halt against a massive rock the size of a small hill.

There was only one thing Mac was aware of in the moment the airbags exploded around them.

Fear.

Had he hurt Hanna?

This fear was bigger than anything he'd ever felt before. Darker. It had the potential to be the forerunner of something utterly soul-destroying.

Had he *killed* Hanna?

The fear grew into horror as he turned his head to see her head slumped sideways, her eyes closed, her skin so pale it looked like every freckle had been painted on by hand.

'Oh, my God...' The words were torn out of Mac. *'Hanna...'*

CHAPTER TWELVE

HER EYES OPENED as she heard his voice.

Or maybe it was the touch of his fingers on her cheek. Hardly the best medical practice to check to see if someone was still breathing or had a pulse but the need to make physical contact was driven by emotions, not logic.

Mac had seen these eyes countless times now. He was intimately familiar with that tawny, auburn shade that was an exact match to her hair, around the blackness of her pupils, with its sunburst rays going into the mix of green and gold that became hazel. A unique, wild combination of colours and shapes that were neatly contained by rims as dark as their centres.

He'd seen these eyes glow with the excitement of a new adventure, soften with tenderness and sparkle with tears when she was moved. They were her emotional barometers. The windows to her soul. He'd seen them flicker with fear only recently and he knew she might see far more than that in his own eyes right now.

The fear that he might have lost her for ever. Mac hadn't cried since he'd been a very young child but he could feel the prickle of tears forming behind his eyes now as he watched Hanna open hers. Because for a tiny moment in time, she looked dazed as she stared back at him. Blank. He could see the moment they began to focus but he could *feel* the moment she recognised him and he knew he was lost.

He could never walk away from this woman.

She hadn't simply taken a place in his heart.

She *was* his heart.

It only took a heartbeat. A moment suspended in time that vanished as soon as Hanna blinked.

'Don't move,' he told her. 'Just tell me if anything hurts.'

Hanna blinked again and then gave her head a tiny shake as she lifted it. 'I'm okay...'

'Don't move your neck,' Mac ordered. 'Try and take a deep breath.'

Hanna did draw in a deep breath, but she was ignoring the direction to stay still as she sat up straighter. 'Honestly... I'm fine. Nothing hurts. Are *you* all right?'

'I'm fine. It wasn't my side of the car that hit the rock. But you were knocked out. Can you remember what day it is? Where we are?'

'I have no idea where we are exactly. We were following *your* nose, remember?' Hanna unclipped her safety belt. 'And I didn't get knocked out. I was just a bit dazed by that bump. And the fright of those airbags going off like bombs. I remember everything. That milk tanker. Skidding in the gravel. Going through the fence. I could see the rock.'

Mac could see it now, through the broken window on Hanna's side of the car.

'It was my fault,' he said. 'Oh, God, Hanna. I'm so sorry.'

'Don't be daft,' Hanna said. 'That truck was going far too fast around that bend. His wheels were way over the centre line. You managed to avoid a head-on collision that would have killed us both.'

Amazingly, there was a smile on Hanna's face now. And a softness in her eyes that Mac had seen before but not in broad daylight like this. It made him think of those moments he held her in his arms when they'd finally finished making love. When they were drifting in that space between ecstasy and reality that only existed because they were together. Time that had a dreamlike quality that almost made you believe in magic.

Except…was that sparkle in Hanna's eyes now due to tears?

No. She was still smiling.

'You're my hero,' she said, her voice wobbling. 'I love you, Mac.'

And there it was.

It had been there all along, hadn't it? The words were forming themselves in his head and escaping and it felt like the moment the car's tyres had hit gravel and he'd lost any control of its trajectory.

'I love you, too, Hanna,' he said softly. 'I think I always have. I know I always will.'

Sitting in a crumpled car in a paddock with huge rocks in the middle of nowhere shouldn't have been a romantic setting.

But it was.

It was the most romantic moment in Hanna Peterson's life and it wouldn't have mattered where they were or what was—or had been—happening around them. Because Mac loved her. He was *in* love with her and, most significantly, he knew he was.

He'd said the words aloud. And then he'd kissed her as if nothing else on earth mattered but to hold her face between his hands and touch her lips with his own so tenderly it was heartbreaking enough that Hanna suspected they weren't simply her own tears causing the dampness on her cheeks.

And Mac knew she felt the same way and it wasn't scaring him off despite any fear of letting someone close enough to create a vulnerability he'd spent his life trying to avoid. If anything, any vestige of barriers between them had been completely removed. That focused look of his as he watched her for any signs of being in pain was sharper than ever before, as if his gaze was completely unguarded. Even the touch of his hands, as he helped Hanna climb out of the driver's side of the Mini because the passenger door was crumpled enough to have jammed, felt different.

Protective.

It felt like a promise, even, that it would always be there to support her if she should need it. Something that she could trust. When she put her feet on the grass outside the car and Mac pulled her to her feet and straight into his arms to hold her close to his body it felt like the place she would always be waiting to get back to.

It felt like home.

But this was not the time to sink into the bliss of that feeling. There were things that needed to be done. They couldn't stay standing in some farmer's paddock when any real warmth from winter sunshine would soon be fading as the afternoon wore on.

'Oh, help…' Hanna pulled back from Mac's arms. 'I hope this isn't a sheep paddock. With that hole in the fence, we'll have to try and stop them getting out onto the road.'

'We need help,' Mac decided, looking around. 'I can't see any sheep, but I don't think we'll be driving your car anywhere else today.' He pulled out his phone but then frowned at the screen. 'I don't have any reception.'

Hanna reached into the pocket of her jacket. 'I've got one bar. No…that's gone too. Maybe if we get away from these big rocks the signal might be better?'

'Let's walk along the road. If we can't get a signal, we could flag down someone driving past and they might be able to take us to the nearest garage.'

They walked hand in hand. For whatever reason, the traffic appeared to be non-existent at this particular time but that didn't bother Hanna because this still felt like a special bubble of time that they could never have again and she wasn't ready to share it. They walked across short grass between the clumps of tussock in this vast field without feeling the need to talk just yet. There were many decisions that would need to be made but, for now, it was enough to know that they were in love. That they would be sharing those decisions and what was to come.

The rock they'd crashed into wasn't the only protrusion in the landscape around them. There were enormous rocks all over the place. Weird rocks. Huge but almost soft looking. Smooth and rounded like hunched shoulders. They had to stop and simply stare for a while.

'What is this place?' Mac wondered aloud. 'It's extraordinary.'

Hanna stood on tiptoes and put her arms around Mac's neck. 'It's our place,' she whispered. 'Did I tell you that I love you?'

He bent his head to kiss her. Slowly. So, so tenderly. 'I do believe you did.'

He kissed her again. 'And did I tell you I love *you*?'

'You did.' Hanna smiled up at him.

'I thought I'd killed you.' Mac was holding her gaze. 'The accident was my fault, you know. If we'd gone the way you said we should go we'd never have been on that corner when that truck came around.'

'And if we hadn't been, we wouldn't have had that accident.'

'See? I told you it was my fault.'

Hanna ignored him. 'And if we hadn't had that accident you wouldn't have looked at me like that and I might never have been brave enough to tell you that I love you.'

'Why not?'

'Because I didn't think you'd want to hear it. I thought you'd disappear from my life and I didn't want that to happen.'

'I *was* going to leave,' Mac said slowly.

'I know.' Hanna nodded. 'I know you can't stay here. Your home is Scotland. Your work is on the other side of the world.' And she would be happy anywhere as long as she was with Mac.

'That wasn't the reason.'

Hanna caught her breath. She'd known that, too, hadn't she? She'd sensed Mac had been getting ready to leave more than simply a place.

'I saw the way you looked the night that Oli was born. How important having a family was to you even if you didn't realise it. I couldn't give that to you but I wanted you to have the chance to find whatever it is that would make you happy.'

The breath Hanna pulled in was shaky. 'I did realise that it wasn't true that I didn't ever want to have children,' she said quietly. 'But I also realised that I would rather not have children if it meant losing you.'

'I never want to lose you either,' Mac said. 'I only realised how much it mattered when I thought I *had*. But… I don't want you to miss out on something that would make you happy.'

'*You* make me happy.'

'You make me…a different person.' Mac was smiling. 'Someone who can have adventures.'

'Who can dance in a park.' Hanna nodded. 'And follow his nose.'

'Someone who can take risks,' Mac added softly. 'And trust someone else.' He took her hand. 'But only if it's you.'

By tacit consent, they were walking towards the road again. It was time they sorted out the problem with their transport. Finding the reception had improved, Hanna made a call to her roadside assistance service to organise a tow truck.

'No,' she had to tell them. 'I'm not sure exactly where we are. Hang on…' She turned to Mac. 'Can you remember the name of this road?'

'Island Cliff? Wait… There's a sign on the other side of that gate. That might help.' He opened the gate.

'We're at a place called Elephant Rocks,' Hanna was able to tell the roadside rescue call taker a moment later.

'They know exactly where we are,' she told Mac as she ended the call. 'This place is famous. It's even been used in movies.'

'I'm not surprised.' Mac was still on the other side of the gate, reading the sign. 'Those big rocks are limestone outcrops. Twenty-four to twenty-six million years old.' He was looking impressed. 'Did you know about them?'

'I've never heard of them,' she admitted. 'But you did remind me that following your nose led to the best adventures.'

'We need to go back and have a proper look,' Mac said. 'Apparently you can see remnants of the ancient sea floor in the rocks.' He came back through the gate. 'Do you think we have enough time?'

'The tow truck's coming from Oamaru,' Hanna told him. 'It'll take a while.' Her smile felt misty. 'But you know…we do have the rest of our lives. I reckon that's plenty of time to have adventures, don't you?'

Mac's smile was looking suspiciously misty as well. 'We do. And it is.' He caught her hand. 'But let's not waste a minute of it.'

So, holding hands tightly enough to make it clear that neither of them wanted to let go anytime soon, Hanna and Mac turned back to go and explore Elephant Rocks.

No… Hanna knew it was bigger than that. They were taking the first steps of the best adventure ever. Their future together. She squeezed Mac's hand even tighter.

And he squeezed hers back…

EPILOGUE

Several years later...

THE SMALL WEATHERBOARD house with a riot of colour from the dahlias in the tidy front garden looked exactly the same as it had when they'd parked in front of that picket fence years ago.

'Do you remember that first time?' Hanna asked Mac. 'When we were too scared to get out of the car and go and knock on the front door?'

'How could I forget?' Mac smiled at his wife. 'We had to rent a car to get here to Oamaru because your Mini was still getting repaired. It was never the same after I drove it into that rock, was it?'

'Nothing was ever the same,' Hanna agreed. But she was smiling. 'It was so much better, wasn't it?'

'It was.'

The creases around Mac's eyes deepened. The move he made to lean towards Hanna and the way she met him in the middle to exchange a kiss suggested the ease of something that happened so often it was automatic.

'I did think it might have been a mistake to encourage you to come here, though. We had so much going on already, with planning our wedding and you shifting your whole life to New Zealand. There was no way to know whether raking up the past would turn out to be a blessing or a complete disaster.'

The small whimper from the back seat of the car could have been a sympathetic agreement to that possibility but it made Hanna smile again.

'Someone's waking up.'

'Which means they'll both be awake in about ten seconds flat. Shall we take them in? I think we've been spotted.'

Sure enough, the front door of the little house was opening by the time Hanna and Mac got out of the car and opened the back doors to unbuckle the restraints in the child car seats on either side. A woman with curly, white hair and a huge smile on her face came down the path between the dahlia bushes with a speed that was impressive for someone who was well into her eighties.

'You're here already,' she said.

'We are.' Hanna was reaching into the car to lift a young girl with a riot of red curls from the seat. 'How are you, Maureen?'

'All the better for seeing you.' She opened the gate. 'Oh, my… Haven't you grown, Ella?'

Hanna put the just-awake toddler down and she ran straight towards the older woman, holding her arms up. Maureen ruffled the flame-coloured ringlets and bent down for a kiss.

'How was the drive?' she asked Mac when she straightened, a tiny hand now holding hers and tugging her towards the house.

'In, Granny. *In…*'

'It's always a pleasure,' Mac said. 'I love the countryside between Dunedin and Oamaru. You get those gorgeous sea views and those lovely hills. Let's get inside and I'll show you the photos. Come on, wee man.' He lifted a still-sleepy boy from his seat.

'They've both grown so much,' Maureen said, a short time later. The twins were now wide awake and busy finding all their favourite toys that were in the big basket in the living room.

'Like weeds,' Hanna agreed. She sat down on the couch beside Maureen. 'I'm run ragged. It's good to have a break before we get to the next part of our day.'

Maureen laughed. 'You're clearly thriving on it, love. Does my heart good to see. Now, tell me everything that's been going on.'

Mac hadn't sat down yet. Like the very first time he'd been in this room, he was standing beside the window. Not because he was too nervous to sit down, this time, but because it was a touchstone to look out into the back garden of this home and see the old fruit trees and the swing that his sister, Jenny, had played on so many years ago. He would never forget the relief of how obvious it was that she had been a very much-loved child and that her sadly short life had been a very happy one.

There were dozens of photographs of Jenny at various ages around this room, from a tiny heart-shaped frame of her as a baby on the mantelpiece to a framed image of her just before she became sick, a gorgeous young teenager, with her long dark hair and eyes that were so like Mac's he'd felt a shiver down his spine the first time he'd seen it. No wonder it had been such a shock for Maureen when he'd turned up on her doorstep that first time, even though they'd been in contact and she was expecting him.

'If only we'd known that Jenny was one of twins,' she'd told him that day, with tears streaming down her cheeks. 'We would have taken both of you in a heartbeat. I'm so sad my Jack isn't here to meet you now. He would've been over the moon to have a son. Not that we didn't both adore our Jenny, of course…'

That picture still gave him a frisson of something that couldn't be explained. It wasn't simply that he and Jenny had looked so alike. It was also that that particular photograph had been taken with a background of the Elephant Rocks.

'Her favourite place,' Maureen had told Mac and Hanna. 'We had all our family picnics there for so many years.'

The sound of his children's delight in the toys and the conversation between Maureen and Hanna became a background blur as Mac's gaze shifted to a much more recent photograph that was also framed and hanging on Maureen's wall. It had the same background with the distinctive shapes of those rocks—the herd of elephants gathered in their soft, grassy haven. There were quite a few people in this photo, however. He was in the centre, wearing his best kilt and Hanna was beside him in the most beautiful wedding dress he'd ever seen. Cade and Jo were there, having been the best man and maid of honour for their wedding, and Oli was holding her basket of petals upside down over her head.

Maureen was there too, of course. Tucked into the line-up on Mac's side. She might not have had the opportunity to adopt him as her son from the start, but she wasn't going to let that make any difference to how she felt about her beloved daughter's twin brother. Or to her sheer joy in becoming a grandmother to Liam and Ella, thanks to the wonderful surrogate that had helped create a miracle for Hanna and Mac.

He shifted his gaze again, away from the photos to the real people in this room.

His family.

A mother figure that was filling a bigger gap in his life than she would ever realise.

Two amazing children that he loved so much it could bring a lump to his throat just watching them like this.

And his wife...

Hanna.

The woman who'd changed his entire life, filling it with light and love and...adventures. Every day was an adventure. And, okay...maybe some of them didn't turn out quite how they might have wanted but that didn't matter, did it? If Mac had learned one thing over the last, amazing years with Hanna, it was that he'd been quite wrong to assume that keeping control of your life and being emotionally *safe* was the same thing as being *happy*.

What better way to celebrate their wedding anniversary than to continue what was becoming an annual event—a picnic visit to the place he'd discovered for them by following his own nose for once in his life. When he'd crashed that car and almost literally pushed them into a future he might never have otherwise dreamed of.

Thanks to that adventure going awry but mainly

thanks to Hanna, Mac had learned what real happiness was like.

As if she felt his gaze, Hanna looked up and then held his gaze and Mac could feel that contact like a physical touch. Like the way he'd felt when she'd taken hold of his hand on the bus that day.

As if he'd found the way home even though he hadn't been looking for it.

Even then, he'd known he didn't want to waste a moment of the time he could have with this woman. But, if he'd known he was going to be lucky enough to be with her for the rest of his life, that wouldn't have changed anything.

He was always going to make the most of every moment with her. Including this one.

Hanna was still holding his gaze. It seemed like she was reading his thoughts at the same time because she was getting to her feet. Coming towards him.

'Happy anniversary,' she whispered when she was close. 'I love you.' Her eyes were shining with that love. 'Fancy a family picnic?'

* * * * *

COMING SOON!

We really hope you enjoyed reading this book. If you're looking for more romance, be sure to head to the shops when new books are available on

Thursday 29th September

MILLS & BOON®

Coming next month

A FAMILY MADE IN PARADISE
Tina Beckett

The elevator doors opened, and he was dumped onto the fourth floor. Rounding the corner, he pushed through the glass door to Neves's waiting area. He frowned when he spied Rachel in one of the chairs. He glanced around. No one else was here.

Hell, he hoped this wasn't about what had happened between them last year. In all honesty, he'd been waiting for that to catch up with him. But after a year?

You're being paranoid, Seb.

They'd both been consenting adults who'd agreed to remain mum about the night they'd shared. Not that the hospital really had any rules against colleagues sleeping together, although the unspoken consensus was that it could be a sticky situation. But it evidently worked for some. There was at least one pair of surgeons at Centre Hospitalier who were married. And his and Rachel's encounter had only been one night long.

Rachel didn't even look at him. Dressed in a gauzy white skirt and a blouse that was as blue as the ocean, she looked almost as inviting as the warm currents a short distance away. And when she crossed her legs—that slow slide of calf over calf was reminiscent of… He swallowed. Okay, don't go there.

But at odds with his thoughts were the tense lines in

her face and her refusal to glance his way. It couldn't be a coincidence that she was here. Did she know why they'd been summoned? Was this about the girl at the beach yesterday?

He glanced at Neves's administrative assistant, who must have guessed his thoughts, because she nodded. "He hoped you were in the building so he could meet with you both together."

His eyes went back to Rachel before returning to the desk. "About?"

"Hey, I just work here." Cécile raised her hands, palms out, in a way that said she had no idea why they were here. And he couldn't very well ask Rachel if she knew. Not in front of Neves's assistant.

Cécile picked up her office phone and murmured something into it. Then she looked up. "You can go on in."

When no one moved, she grinned. "Both of you."

Continue reading
A FAMILY MADE IN PARADISE
Tina Beckett

Available next month
www.millsandboon.co.uk

JOIN US ON SOCIAL MEDIA!

Stay up to date with our latest releases, author news and gossip, special offers and discounts, and all the behind-the-scenes action from Mills & Boon...

 @millsandboon

 @millsandboonuk

 facebook.com/millsandboon

 @millsandboonuk

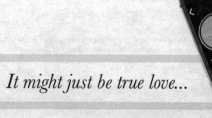

It might just be true love...